THE NIGHT OF THE COMET

BOOKS BY GEORGE BISHOP

The Night of the Comet
Letter to My Daughter

THE NIGHT OF
THE COMET

A NOVEL

GEORGE BISHOP

BALLANTINE BOOKS   NEW YORK

Published in the United States by Ballantine
Books, an imprint of The Random House
Publishing Group, a division of Random House,
Inc., New York.

BALLANTINE and the HOUSE colophon are
registered trademarks of Random House, Inc.

Grateful acknowledgment is made to Alfred
Music Publishing Co., Inc., for permission to
reprint an excerpt from "Woodstock," words and
music by Joni Mitchell, copyright © 1969
(renewed) by Crazy Crow Music. All rights
administered by Sony/ATV Music Publishing,
8 Music Square West, Nashville, TN 37203. All
rights reserved. Used by permission.

Library of Congress Cataloging-in-Publication Data

Bishop, George.
    The night of the comet: a novel / George Bishop.
    pages cm
    ISBN 978-0-345-51600-8
    eBook ISBN 978-0-345-53879-6
1. Adolescence—Fiction. 2. Dysfunctional families—Fiction.
3. Comets—Fiction. 4. Louisiana—Fiction. 5. Domestic
fiction. I. Title.
    PS3602.I7565N54 2013
    813'.6—dc23   2013004334

Printed in the United States of America
on acid-free paper

www.ballantinebooks.com

987654321

First Edition

Book design by Elizabeth A. D. Eno

With deep gratitude to Jane von Mehren

We are stardust, we are golden,
We are billion-year-old carbon,
And we've got to get ourselves back to the garden.

—Joni Mitchell, "Woodstock"

"Hey, look! It's right out there. I tell you, it's one of the
most beautiful creations I've ever seen. It's so graceful."
   "It's yellow and orange, just like a flame."

—astronauts Edward Gibson and Gerald Carr, on spotting
   Comet Kohoutek from *Skylab*, December 1973

HERE in Baton Rouge you can still see the stars at night.

Our backyard abuts the last patch of pastureland in the neighborhood, a piece of the old Pike-Burden farm still hanging on at the edge of the city. On a clear night like tonight, when my wife and boy are busy inside, I like to leave my desk for a few minutes and walk down to the rear of our yard, down to where my quarter acre ends at a low ditch and a barb-wire fence, and take in the night air. Beyond the fence the land stretches out flat as calm water. Stands of pine and oak ring the field. Off in the far corner a cow pond gleams in the moonlight. From the east comes the swish of cars passing on Perkins Road; from the north, the distant rumble of trucks on I-10.

But a person can't stand for long on a night like this without looking up. Call it the lure of the ineffable: your eyes are drawn skyward, and there they are. The stars. The night is filled with them. They cluster, they scatter, they shine, they go on forever. They're beautiful, aren't they? I'm no expert; I can name only the brightest ones, pick out the most obvious constellations: there's Polaris and Vega; Ursa Minor, Aries, and Capricorn . . . But no matter how little I know them, I still love the stars. How could anyone not? Wherever you go, you know they'll always be there, shining. All you have to do is turn your eyes up.

Also up there, I know, somewhere behind the stars, is the comet. You don't hear much about Kohoutek these days—"C/1973 E1" as it's known by its modern designation. You can't see it now; not even the most powerful of telescopes can see it. It's billions of miles away, far beyond the edge of the solar system, a small lump of ice and rock spinning out into the black vacuum of space. In the planetary scale of things, Kohoutek barely registers as a speck of dust; really, it's nothing anyone needs to be afraid of anymore. And yet, lately, when the sky is clear and the neighborhood is quiet, I find myself thinking about it. In fact, more and more, I find I can hardly stop thinking about it.

I suppose it's because I'm turning forty soon, the same age my father was when the comet came crashing through our lives, and I worry that heredity might catch up with me at last—that a genetically preprogrammed crisis is due for a generational reoccurrence right about now and I won't be able to dodge it.

Or perhaps it's because in not so many years my own son will be the age I was then, and I worry for him, worry that he'll finally have to step up to the world, the real world of hope and love and loss, and I don't want him to have to go through all that like I did. I believe if I could, I'd put a blindfold on Ben and pick him up and run with him through all the burning years of his adolescence and not set him down again until he's safe on the other side, when he's thirty or so and I know he'll be all right.

Because it's not true what they say, that you get over it—that with time, whatever happens to you, good or bad, drifts away into the harmless river of the past. You never get over it, not really. The past never leaves you. You carry it around with you for as long as you live, like a pale, stubborn worm lodged there in your gut, keeping you up at night.

My son's in the house behind me now, helping his mother clean up after dinner. The kitchen window's open. I can hear the soft rattle of dishes as they load the washer, their voices as they talk about beautifully inconsequential things. ("If you use too much soap, then what happens?" "I don't know. Maybe the dishwasher will explode." "No, it won't!")

The comet, I know, is long gone, not to return for millions of years. In another sense, though, it never left. It's still there; it'll always be there, hanging like a black star above my head wherever I turn. And on an evening like this, all it takes is the sound of my boy's voice, and the bright stars above, and the cool air wafting around me, to stir the worm of memory. Then the past comes flooding back, and whether I want to go there or not, I'm instantly transported again to that night.

"Dad? Dad, is that you?"

I sat up in bed to listen. The night was quiet; the Moon shone in at my window. I wasn't altogether sure if I was still dreaming or not. I heard a rattling noise outside at the garage shed, and I got up and went to the top of the stairs.

"Dad?"

But his bedroom door was ajar and the house was empty, as I knew it would be. There was the tilting Christmas tree in the corner, the TV set, the couch, the rug, the chairs, all looking abandoned. The broken telescope, what was left of it, sat in pieces on the floor near the back door. I paused just long enough to pick up the phone in the living room and dial a number.

"Something's wrong. Something terrible is happening. . . . Hurry," I said before replacing the receiver.

Outside was cold; I hadn't stopped to put a coat on over my pajamas, and I could see my breath rising in front of my face. A breeze stirred the trees. Up above, stars and a bright slice of moon. A dog began barking from a nearby backyard as I jogged out of our driveway and down the street. Here and there a neighbor's house was still blacked out, with the curtains drawn and the lights off. Some had sheets of newspaper taped up behind their windows, giving them a ruined, desolate air. The streetlights, though, those were back on, and as I ran below them I passed from light to dark and light to dark again. I came out of the neighborhood at the end of the block and turned right toward the square. There were no cars at this hour on Franklin Street; there was no sign of life anywhere, as if the whole town had packed up and fled in the middle of the night.

Up ahead, set back from the road, stood the town water tower—an ugly industrial thing, a hundred feet tall, four spindly legs supporting a round tank that glowed a pale blue-green in the moonlight. I was still some distance from it, half a football field away, when I spotted the wooden ladder from our garage toppled on the ground below it. That was when I looked up and saw my father climbing one of the support legs of the tower.

Yes, my father. I immediately knew it was him. He was wearing his black Sears McGregor over his blue-striped pajamas. His elbows jutted out, his head was twisted to one side, and his glasses hung on the tip of his nose. As he scrambled up the leg of the tower, his shoes clicking on the metal rungs, his coattails flapping below him, he looked almost comical, like a giant, jittery black bug.

I halted in the road to watch, hugging myself as I stepped back and forth from one foot to the other, still not quite believing what I was seeing, although at the same time I knew exactly what was happening.

When my father reached the top of the tower leg, he disappeared under the belly of the tank and then reappeared seconds later standing on the catwalk. He steadied himself with a hand on the railing and began walking carefully to the left. At the hip of the tank, he stopped, turned back, and seemed to look directly at me.

"Hey!" I shouted, and jerked a hand up to signal to him.

But he quickly began moving again, looking back over his shoulder as he circled around to the dark side of the tower.

I stepped to the left, tracking his orbit from the street. When I caught sight of him again he was no longer standing on the catwalk but was hanging on the outside of it. This was so strange and unexpected that I only slowly understood it: my father had somehow crawled under or over the railing, so that now he was balanced with his toes on the edge of the catwalk, gripping the handrail and leaning in awkwardly toward the water tank.

He shifted oddly at the rail, sliding one shoe out and then back along the edge of the catwalk, as though he was feeling for something with his toe. He groped with one hand behind him at the empty air. He paused; he seemed to be thinking about something. Then all at once he threw out his right arm and leg, flipped around, and gripped the rail behind his back so that he was facing the air with his heels hooked on the edge of the catwalk. I gasped; at the same time, my father made a small exclamation, as if he was pleased and a little surprised at having been able to execute this tricky maneuver: "Ha!"

But the abrupt motion had jarred his glasses from his nose. My father and I both watched them dropping through the air. "Oh—" he said. As his glasses fell and turned, I thought of gravity, and of Galileo and the Tower of Pisa, and I knew my father must've been thinking the same thing. There was a faint cracking sound as they landed on the sidewalk below the tower.

When I looked back up, he was gazing out at the night sky. Head tilted back, mouth ajar, he might've been standing at the rail of our back porch instead of dangling from the edge of a water tower a hundred feet up in the air. For a moment we were both perfectly still, my father watching the sky, me watching him.

Following his gaze, I turned my eyes to the stars. The Moon was a waxing gibbous, the left side dark, but the right side so bright that I could see the mountains and craters shadowing its silvery landscape. Off to the east of the Moon I made out Leo. And was that Hydra creeping up over the top of the water tower? My father would've known all the others; he could point out even the near-invisible constellations, the ones with the names that made his students laugh out loud when he said them: *Cassiopeia, Camelopardalis, Sextans* . . .

He moved at the rail, drawing my attention back down. As I watched from the street, an unnatural charge filled the air, an electric premonition that raised the hairs on my arms and told me something terrible was about to happen. It was happening right now. The red light atop the tower blinked on and off. I wanted to cry out a warning, I wanted to do something, but I couldn't move or speak, struck dumb by the awful realization of what I was seeing.

My father leaned out from the railing and lifted his head, like he was trying to touch his face to the sky. He stretched his arms behind him and opened his mouth wide. Then he squatted, preparing to launch himself into space, and as I looked on in horror his black raincoat un-furled behind him so that for one heart-stopping second he appeared not to fall but to fly, up, up from the tower and into the air, where, flashing like a beacon in the sky above him, ever so faint but visible at last, was his beloved comet, its tail pointed away from the Moon as it hurled back along its orbit to its home in the stars. . . .

God help me, I may never forget it. Twenty-six years later, and I still see it all as clearly as if it had happened just yesterday.

THE NIGHT OF THE COMET

CHAPTER ONE

SUMMER 1973
TERREBONNE, LOUISIANA

"WELL?" my mother asked, reaching in to straighten one of the candles.

My father touched her arm. "Shh. Don't rush him. He's thinking."

The blue and yellow flames danced in the draft of the air conditioner. Crêpe paper streamers dangled from the overhead lamp, and colored balloons decorated the corners of the doorways. We leaned in around the table, all of us wearing cardboard hats, as blithe and unsuspecting as partygoers on the *Titanic*.

In my usual chair on the left sat my father, Alan Broussard. His arms were crossed on the table, his hair slicked over to one side, his black-rimmed glasses slipping, always slipping, down the slope of his large nose. My mother, Lydia, sat next to him, dressed up for the occasion in a pink pantsuit with a white belt, her red hair styled in a low bouffant with a curl flattened against either cheek. On my right was sister Megan, an angry seventeen-year-old with an embroidered blouse, contact lenses, and a weight problem: a wannabe hippie trapped in the most unhip household in the world.

And I—I sat in my father's chair, the seat of honor for the evening. Alan Broussard, Jr.: "Junior" to family and friends, a slight boy in a striped polyester shirt, tight blue jeans, and a cardboard Burger King crown.

What did I wish for, staring into the blaze of candles on my cake that summer of my fourteenth birthday? I wished for so many things that it would've been impossible to name just one; I was a swirling fog of dreams and dissatisfactions. I wished that I was somewhere else. I wished I had a different name, a different family. I wished that something, anything, would happen to change the unpromising course of my life.

I had no obvious talents, no great looks, no exceptional humor or intellect or passions. I couldn't sing, I couldn't dance, I couldn't play an instrument or throw a ball or ride a horse. Except for that odd suffix on my signature, the loopy "Jr." that linked me to my father and gave me my nickname, I was as close as anybody could get to indistinguishable.

The only thing I had any affinity for—and I hardly considered this a talent—was reading. I was a reader, a bookworm. My tastes weren't sophisticated; just give me a ripping good yarn (a phrase I'd gotten from a book: "a ripping good yarn") and I could stay up half the night with it. Best, of course, if the story had a swarm of deadly army ants, or a jet plane crashing in a desert, or submarines, or jungles, or a raft lost at sea. But really, I would read almost anything I could lay my hands on. Slumped in my bed or a corner of the couch with a good book, I'd look up and feel nothing but disappointment at my own world, so dull and colorless in comparison. If I could have, I would've gladly spent the rest of my life in books. Stories were my escape, my refuge, my consolation, my love—

My sister razzed a noisemaker at my cheek. "Jesus, hurry up."

"Stop it!" I hissed, and knocked her hand away.

I narrowed my eyes on the candles until my family receded into a blurry background. An image rose up at the front of my mind, like a genie conjured by the flames: a tanned girl in pink standing on a lawn. That was all. It was only a glimpse, barely a notion. I hadn't expected to see her here tonight; this girl in pink was so far outside the realm of possibility that she might have been a fiction herself, an imaginary character from one of my books. But here she was at my birthday, signaling to me through the fog of my desires, and I instantly felt, rather than understood, that she represented everything I could ever wish for. I puckered my lips and blew: *Gabriella.*

My family cheered, and my mother plucked the candles from the cake and began passing pieces around.

"Are you excited about starting high school?" she asked.

"A little, I guess."

"Why would he be excited?" Megan asked.

"Oh, I'd be excited. New classes, new teachers. Meeting new friends. Dances, dating, all that."

"Your first kiss. That's something to look forward to," said my father. "Maybe Meg can give you some pointers. Huh, Meg? What about that? Huh?" He laughed, an abrupt snorting sound.

Megan frowned. "Dad, you're being gross."

"Yes, Alan, that is a little gross," my mother said.

"Anyhoo. I know I'm excited," he said, settling back and digging into his cake. Though it was summer, he wore his teaching outfit: black shoes, dark pants, white short-sleeved shirt, and a narrow tie. He'd just returned from a science-teaching seminar in Baton Rouge that day, where, he told us, he'd picked up some nifty ideas for his class this year—group projects, cross-curricular study activities, interactive demonstrations.

"That's how you make a lesson more fun," he said, gesturing with his fork. "You get the students up and moving around. Science *is* interesting. It's just the teachers that are boring. Of course, it would help if we had a decent lab. We can hardly do anything with that junk we've got now."

He launched into his usual complaint about the lack of support for the sciences in the Louisiana public schools. No respect, he said, none at all. Football and baseball, that was all anyone cared about. While Principal Lee showered money on Coach DuPleiss, his labs meantime were falling to pieces. . . .

Megan rolled her eyes, and my mother gave a little sigh as she began picking at a ridge of frosting with her fork. We had no interest in what my father had to say, but we were his family, after all, the kindest audience he had, and so we ate our cake and let him talk.

Other people—tellers at the bank, cashiers at the IGA—all had a way of grinning when my father began to speak, as if they couldn't take him quite seriously. And certainly, he was peculiar. A tall, angular man, he was always blinking and peering around, like he'd just stumbled into a room and wasn't sure where he was. He rode a rattling Raleigh three-speed bicycle to school, instead of driving a car like any normal person would do, and he carried a brown briefcase that he swung stiffly at his right side with a ridiculous air of importance. More than once I had seen students, high schoolers, even third graders, following my father down the hallway and imitating his jerky walk, swinging invisible briefcases, twitching and snorting and then falling all over themselves with laughter.

That year I would be entering his freshman Earth and Space Science class, and the thought of being his student, sitting in his classroom, filled me with dread.

"God help you. Although not even God can help you there," my sister had warned me. "I have yet to recover."

He pushed back from the table. "I picked up something else in Baton Rouge." He winked. "Special order. Be right back," he said, and disappeared into the bedroom.

"He's really excited. He could hardly wait to give it to you," my mother whispered as she bent in to take my plate. "At least try to pretend you like it, okay? It means a lot to him."

My father reappeared carrying a bulky gift-wrapped box. "Here we are." He rested it carefully on the coffee table and called us into the front room. "Go ahead, open it. It's yours."

My heart sank. I knew what it was. He'd been hinting at it all summer. I sat on the couch and cradled the gift in my lap. Megan settled heavily on the armrest. "What is it?" she asked. My father stood at the edge of the rug, bracing his hands on his hips and twitching all over, like he was holding himself back from diving in and ripping off the paper himself. "You'll see. You'll see."

"It's a telescope," I said when I got the wrapping off. "Wow. Gosh. Look at that." I turned the box around and looked it up and down, trying to show some enthusiasm.

"Huh? Yeah? Huh?" he said.

"Look up. Smile!" my mother called, and took a Polaroid.

My father already had his own telescope, of course, but his was old and not very powerful. What a person really needed, he'd been saying—if you really wanted to get good resolution—was a Celestron C8. It was the Mercedes-Benz of telescopes, the latest thing, made in California. A high-quality telescope like that wasn't cheap, but a good one would last a lifetime. An investment, he called it. Wouldn't I like something like that? We'd be able to track the comet with it, catch it before anyone else saw it, follow it all the way to the Sun and back.

"That's not a toy, you know," he said as I lifted it out of the box. "It's a serious piece of scientific equipment. But I figured that you were old enough now. . . ."

Megan asked practical questions about the telescope: How far could you see with it? How did it work? And why was it so short and stumpy-looking? I knew all the answers; my father had already schooled me on the C8. It was a compound refractor-reflector, which was why it was so short. The light came in at the open end, bounced off a big mirror at the back, bounced off another mirror at the front, and then was focused down to the viewing lens, here—

My father interrupted my explanation. "With the forty millimeter Plössl eyepiece, you'll get a magnification of about fifty power. Although theoretically, with the C8 you could get a maximum magnification of four hundred and eighty power. Cool, huh?"

"Far out," said Megan. Her interest spent, her family obligations fulfilled, she headed upstairs to listen to records. "Happy birthday," she called and closed the door to her bedroom.

My father couldn't hold back any longer. He scooted in and squatted next to me. Soon he had the telescope in his own hands, running his fingers excitedly over the tube, his eyes bright behind his glasses. "How about that? You like it? Huh? You like it?"

While he checked all the parts, my mother, to make the occasion

more festive, put a Pete Fountain record on the hi-fi and made drinks,
a Coke for me, a rum and Coke for her and my father—"For fun," as
she liked to say. If our family had anything like a cheerleader, she was
it. She was the one who staged all our birthdays, planned our holidays,
arranged the group photos, and signed our names to Christmas cards
when she mailed them out. That we had any sense at all of "the Broussards" as a family unit was mostly due to her—although, to be sure,
she rarely got credit for this. If anything, my sister and I wondered why
our mother bothered to make such a fuss over such a lost cause.

She was just returning with the drinks when my father stood up.

"Let's bring it outside," he said, and, carrying the scope in his arms,
he headed for the door.

The air was swampy and warm. To either side were more homes like
ours, small boxy hutches with clapboard siding, screened-in porches,
and muddy yards. A broken line of bald cypresses and tupelos marked
the edge of Bayou Black, a low, sluggish creek that passed behind the
neighborhood. When a north breeze blew, as it did tonight, you could
smell the Gulf. Bullfrogs and crickets kept up their noisy racket, lend-
ing a feeling of wildness to our damp little backyard, and a reminder
that we barely had a foothold here—that given half a chance, the water
and swamp would rush back in and reclaim the land from under us.
"*Terra non firma*," my father liked to call it, stamping his foot on the
ground as though to demonstrate its unsoundness.

I stood by while he set up the telescope. My mother stood back by
the porch, arms crossed lightly over her chest with her drink in one
hand, smiling at her two boys.

"Check the ground surface first to make sure it's level, no rocks or
holes," my father said as he bobbed around the tripod. He still had on
his party hat, a red cone with white polka dots, like what a clown
would wear. "Be sure the legs are locked. You don't want it tipping
over. Now, the first thing we do is polar align it."

I looked over the top of his hat, across the black water to our new
neighbors' house on the opposite bank of the bayou. Spotlights shone

on the walls and up into the fronds of tall, freshly planted palm trees on the back patio. Upstairs and down, lights glowed goldenly behind the windows, suggesting a rich, vibrant interior life. Their house stood out like a jewel in the darkness.

"Man-oh-man. Look at that. Sharp."

My father stepped back and called me over. I bent to the eyepiece, curious in spite of myself. A bright blob wavered into view.

"What is it?"

"It's the Moon, silly. Don't you recognize the Moon?"

"Oh, right."

"You have to hold still. Breathe easy. I trained it on the Sea of Tranquility. They were right there, Mr. Neil Armstrong and Buzz Aldrin, walking around. Pretty amazing, isn't it?"

I blinked and breathed. The image steadied itself in the glass, revealing a silvery, desolate landscape. My father squatted at my side, pointing out some of the more prominent lunar features while reciting their names at my ear: *The Sea of Serenity, the Sea of Fecundity, the rays of Tycho, the rays of Copernicus.* I peered closer, hoping I might see something interesting, an American flag, maybe, or leftover pieces of a landing module, but all I could make out were dusty hills and shadows. I wondered why anyone would ever want to go there, it looked so cold and lonely.

"Come see," he called to my mother.

She tottered down the yard in her high-heeled sandals and, holding her drink aside in one hand, bent to the telescope.

"Careful you don't spill on it," he said.

"I won't!"

She had a slim figure, narrow shoulders, and a straight back. Even though she was my mother, I could see it was true what people said about her, that she was a pretty woman. Even in a cardboard party hat, Lydia Simoneaux Broussard managed to look pretty. It was only lately that I had begun to notice what an unlikely couple my parents made: she petite and stylish and full of spunk, he gawky and birdlike and dull as a stick. I sometimes wondered what they were even doing together in the first place. Did they love each other? What did love even look like between two adults like them? And who in the world were these two strange creatures, Alan and Lydia, who called themselves my parents, anyway?

"Is this the comet?" my mother asked, blinking into the eyepiece.

"No, it's not the comet. It's the Moon! My god, doesn't anyone recognize the Moon when they see it?"

"Wowser. Gosh. Look at that. It looks really close," she said, and then pulled away and headed inside, as little interested in the Celestron as Megan, apparently.

"Let's see what else this baby can do," my father said.

He fiddled some more with the knobs, talking about declination and right ascension and azimuth. After some time studying the Moon, he went for Venus, and then Mercury. Then he began scanning the spaces between stars, "just to see what's out there."

"You'd be surprised," he said. There'd been some remarkable discoveries made by amateurs doing just what we were. A Japanese man, a factory worker, had discovered half a dozen comets on his own using an ordinary old Seiko Polarex. Another man, a British pastor, found a new comet while looking out his living room window one night with a pair of binoculars. All it took was time. Time and perseverance. Tradition held that the comet was named after its discoverer.

"What if we found one, huh? Wouldn't that be neat? Comet Broussard. How about that? Comet Junior."

But I'd soon had enough of the telescope, too. I didn't want to leave all at once, for fear of disappointing my father, so at first I stood a little distance apart on the lawn, and then sat on the back porch steps, and then stood near the door, before finally saying I had to use the bathroom and ducking inside. My father didn't seem to notice. He was gone, lost in his love for worlds millions of miles from our own.

I retreated upstairs to my room. There was my bed, my desk, my bookcase full of books. My junior high school twenty-five-pound junior barbell set rested against one wall, gathering dust. Next door, my sister played "Killing Me Softly with His Song" over and over on her stereo. From the window I could see my father down in the backyard working the telescope beneath the big, deep sky.

I had just turned fourteen and nothing had changed. I could wish all I wanted, but I was still the same lonely, frustrated boy I was when I was thirteen. My parents, too, were the same, my sister the same. My room, our house, our small dull town, the night sky, everything exactly the same. Birthdays, I was beginning to suspect, were a kind of dirty trick, a way to get you all excited about nothing.

CHAPTER TWO

I moved closer to my dormer window. The window was up, the air outside tepid and still. By leaning to the right, I could see between the trees and across the bayou to her house. Its lights fell on the black water, creating a shimmering, inverted double of itself, like a castle floating upside down in a dream. I wondered what she was doing there tonight, at home in her dream castle. Only a twenty-foot-wide canal separated us, but it might as well have been an ocean, and she was on the other side of it, as remote and inaccessible to me as a Roman princess.

Over the past year and a half, my mother and I had watched as the new house went up on the other side of the water: first the sprawling foundation, then the ground floor, then the second floor. A walled-in patio with a pool and a cabana were added, then a fanciful gazebo in the side yard, and then a boardwalk leading down to a boat dock on the water. The house was so marvelous, so grand that it looked almost absurdly out of place there at the edge of our muddy bayou. "Good lord, it's huge," my mother said.

All the neighbors on our side of the canal were curious. People knew that Frank Martello was an oil man from Shreveport—he'd been coming here for years on business and he kept a condo in Thibodaux. But what about the rest of the family? We sometimes caught glimpses of a lady, sometimes two, stepping out of a white Cadillac at the front of the building site. "Wowser," my mother said, straining to make out their clothes and features from our back porch. "Look at them. Like movie stars at a premiere."

When the family finally moved in two weeks ago, I biked across the Franklin Street bridge and watched from the end of the block as freight trucks from New Orleans department stores came and went and men in uniforms unloaded furniture all day. That's when I first spotted her, standing beside the fountain in their yard of newly plugged grass. She was wearing pink shorts and a pink top that showed off her bare arms and legs. Her skin was tanned a golden brown—although it wasn't a tan, exactly, but a hue. Her color came from inside her, as if she held the heat and glow of the Sun inside her. Her hair was thick and black, pulled up in back. Standing in the yard perched on one leg, the other craned up with her foot resting on her inner thigh, she looked like some exotic tropical bird who'd flown off course and landed by mistake in our town. Even then, even in that first view from a block away, I knew she was special. The movers, every one of them, stopped to talk to her—grown men sweating and grunting under heavy pieces of furniture, lingering in the yard just for a chance to speak to her, to admire her lithe teenage body. My mother soon managed to learn their names: Frank's wife was Barbara, and their daughter was Gabriella.

Gabriella: even her name was beautiful, angelic, impossible.

Down in the backyard, I saw my father fold up the telescope and carry it inside. In a minute he appeared at my bedroom door with it, talking excitedly about what an amazing instrument it was and how good it'd be for viewing the comet.

"We ought to take it out of the town some night soon. Get away from the lights and find some elevation. Wouldn't that be fun?" Save my money, he said, and I could buy a more powerful eyepiece. A good twenty-five millimeter wouldn't be that expensive. He could help me out if I wanted.

He carefully stood the telescope in the corner and stepped back, hands on his hips, admiring it, this fine, expensive instrument, the Mercedes-Benz of telescopes. His present, I understood, was meant to be a bond between us, the thing that would hold us together even as my adolescence tried to pry us apart. In his eyes, nothing could have been better than this: a father, a son, their telescope.

"Well. Happy birthday, son."

"Night, Dad."

My father looked at me as if he meant to say something more. He still wore his clown hat—he'd forgotten he had it on, apparently. He blinked and nodded, shoved his glasses up on his nose. Then he inexplicably laughed—one short, goofy snort—turned, and left.

I looked at the Celestron standing in the corner of my room. What kind of a gift was that? What kind of a father was this? I didn't want a telescope for a birthday present. Who would? No doubt he meant well, but my father moved in a universe of his own—"His head in the stars," as my mother put it. I wondered if he could even see me at all, blinking behind the thick lenses of his glasses. As a parent, he was practically useless. Like the telescope—good for nothing. I felt like kicking the damn thing.

But then, staring at his ridiculous present, an idea occurred to me. Yes, of course.

I pushed my desk chair out of the way, pulled the telescope over to the window, and adjusted the legs. The angle was a little awkward, owing to the narrowness of my dormer window, and the brick wall around their patio blocked most of my view of the downstairs. But by panning along the wall, I found the set of tall iron gates giving access to their patio. I adjusted the focus until I could see across the patio to the back of their house, where a room with large windows and a sliding glass door faced the pool.

Inside I found Mr. Martello sitting in a leather recliner, drinking from a bottle of beer, his image jittering in the lens of the scope. I panned a fraction of a degree to the right and discovered the corner of a

TV cabinet, and then a painting of a horse and hound, and a wooden floor lamp, and the edge of a couch. And there, hanging out over the corner of the couch, was a bare, tanned knee. My breath caught in my throat. It was her. It had to be her. I could hardly believe my luck.

She was sitting with her legs crossed Indian style, watching TV with her father while reading a magazine she held in her lap. She turned a page of the magazine, and then she tilted her head into view and lifted her hand to her hair. She twirled her fingers in her hair, curling and uncurling strands of it around her index finger. Her fingernails, I could see, were painted a bright, playful, achingly suggestive pink.

The telescope, with its magical arrangement of lenses and mirrors, had carried me across space and set me down in the room right beside her. I was so close I felt I could reach out and touch her. I could almost hear her breathing; I could read her thoughts in the small changes flickering across her face, the way she pursed her lips and then widened her eyes when she found something she liked in her magazine. I could practically see her whole life story in the dainty way she stroked the corner of the paper with the tip of her middle finger to turn the page. . . . My father was right, the Celestron was an amazing instrument.

My mother laughed. "Clever!"

I spun around. "What?"

"Enjoying your new telescope?"

I sidled away from it. "It's okay."

"You know," she said, stepping into my room, "with the Plössl whatever-whatever eyepiece, I bet you could see into the next neighborhood. You could probably see right inside someone's house."

"Huh? What?"

"What what what?" she mocked. "Don't worry, I won't tell anyone. It'll be our little secret. You've got good taste. She's a cutie."

She asked if I wanted to come downstairs to watch an old movie on TV with her, *Lost Horizon*. Ronald Colman's plane crashes in Shangri-La, where he meets Jane Wyatt, an orphan girl brought up by a Tibetan wise man.

"No, thanks."

"You're sure? It's supposed to be good."

"That's okay."

"Well. Goodnight, then." She kissed me on the side of the head, her breath sweet with rum and Coke. "Let me know if there's anything else you want for your birthday." She paused, frowning thoughtfully at the Celestron.

"He does love you. You know that, don't you? He just has a funny way of showing it sometimes," she said. We both stared at the scope, nodding in agreement, and for an instant I had the feeling she might've been speaking for herself as much as for me.

As soon as she'd left, I grabbed the telescope and aimed it again at the Martello house. There was the television, the lamp, Mr. Martello's chair . . . but the couch was empty. Gabriella had disappeared.

I found a light shining in an upstairs room with two balconies that overlooked the patio. Was it her room? Yellow curtains were closed across the French doors behind the balconies, so I couldn't be sure. I toyed with the telescope some more, adjusting and readjusting the focus, trying different windows and different angles, but an hour later, I still hadn't found Gabriella again.

I had, however, become more adept with the instrument, and before I went to bed, out of a drowsy sense of curiosity, I aimed the Celestron skyward.

From my dormer window I could only see a wedge of the sky, but even in that small view there was an astounding array of astronomical bodies. I saw what I knew to be stars, and what could've been the planet Venus. I saw the incandescent smudge of the Milky Way and a moving speck of light that must've been a satellite.

And somewhere up there, high above it all, was the comet, fiery and silent, hurtling toward us.

CHAPTER THREE

MY father, the teacher.

Sometimes I got the feeling that he hated it. He never said so, but by the end of the week he'd come home from school looking tired and defeated, the dark crescents below his eyes visible even through the lenses of his glasses. He might've been a boxer stumbling out of the ring after losing another round to his students, those bored, gum-smacking teenagers who showed so little love for Earth and Space Science.

Looking up from marking tests at the dinner table on Sunday evening, his hair sticking out on one side of his head, he would say how he could've gone on to graduate school, how, if only he'd stuck with it, he might've had a career in research by now. He talked fondly of his college years at LSU in Baton Rouge: working all night in the Nicholson Hall lab to meet a deadline . . . swapping ideas with the older students at the coffee machine . . . the smell of acetone wafting in the corridors. How he had loved it, the pure, heady joy of intellectual pursuit. His old astronomy professor, Dr. Brewer, always said he showed great promise, told him he had "the mind of a scientist," an ability to get inside a problem and visualize a solution. Not everybody had that, Brewer said; it was the kind of talent they looked for in their graduate students.

"But instead . . . ," my father would say, gesturing wearily at the papers spread on the table, the red scrawl of his pen bleeding all over them.

He didn't have to say it; the gesture said everything. It was short-hand for all the complaints we'd heard him muttering for years: He had sold himself short. He deserved better than this. If only he hadn't got-ten married so young, if only they hadn't had two children and a house and a car that needed to be paid for, then he wouldn't be sitting here at this table, correcting these papers for kids who didn't give a damn, teaching at a poor public high school with a broken-down lab and an indifferent principal. Instead, he'd be working at NASA, or Raytheon, or the Palomar Observatory, where the real scientists went and where people cared about your work. Because he still had it, he said, that feel-ing for science. That wasn't something that went away. It was like a fire that burned inside you, a passion to know more.

"Our mad scientist," my mother would joke.

He wouldn't laugh. He'd glare at her, as though the blame were all hers. Then he'd pick up his red pen and go back to correcting papers, his frustration settling like a black cloud around his shoulders. No one appreciated him, no one cared, no one knew the talent and ambition simmering inside him. *If only, if only, if only . . .*

But still, every Monday morning, as dependable as the Sun, he'd be up and at it again—because, after all, this was his job, and we were his family, and someone had to feed us, didn't they? He shaved, dressed, slicked his hair, and knotted his tie at the mirror above the sink, as carefully as if he were getting ready for church. He gathered his books and papers and repacked them into his worn leather briefcase. He lined up his pens in his breast pocket, three colors, red, blue, and black. He finished his coffee, handed off his cup to our mother, gave her a per-functory kiss on the cheek, and set off on his bicycle.

I'd watch him go, wobbling as he caught his balance on the driveway. The morning would be bright, the air already warm; the yard, forever in need of mowing, and the weeds, sprouting along the drainage ditch out front, were spangled with dew. Turning down the street, he'd wave to me and Megan waiting at the corner for the bus.

"See you at school!" he'd call, and we'd both cringed a little at the sight of him:

My father, that stubborn, half-blind optimist, with his shirtsleeves flapping in the wind and his trousers rolled up above his ankles, pedaling away on the shaky hope that *this* week, *this* semester, *this* year might finally be better than the last.

"Comet Kohoutek."

He wrote it on the board and had us repeat it out loud.

"Ko-hou-tek."

"Ko-hou-tek."

"Anybody ever heard of that? Yes? No? Maybe?"

The first day of class, my father stood at the front of the room gripping a stick of chalk and peering at us through his glasses. I sat as far back in the room as I could, hiding behind my curtain of bangs and praying he wouldn't do anything too embarrassing. An oversized fan on a pole in the corner ruffled the papers of students sitting nearest the front of the class. On the walls were a chart of the periodic table, color posters of the planets, and a large picture of Albert Einstein making a funny face, with the caption "Science is fun!"

When no one answered him, he went on.

"Well then, you're in for a real treat this year. Something really special. I think you're really going to like this."

He sniffed, pushed up his glasses, and launched into an elaborate explanation of the comet.

It came, he told us, from the great crystalline sphere that surrounded our solar system. We couldn't see it—nobody ever had—but it was there: out in the interstellar dark, out beyond the outer planets, was a vast, glittering cloud of stardust. This was the stuff left over from the birth of the solar system, trillions and trillions of pieces of icy rock and gas, some the size of pebbles, some the size of cities, all turning in slow, silent revolution around the Sun.

Waving his arms, he described how the comet must have looked then: a frozen, rocky mountain powdered with snow, twenty-five miles across, twenty-five miles deep, weighing more than a trillion tons—an iceberg floating in a black sea of space. It might have floated forever in its crystal cloud, except that a gravitational perturbation, a passing star perhaps, nudged it loose from its orbit and sent it tumbling toward the Sun. It fell slowly, so slowly you could hardly have called it falling; it fell for millions of years before it finally grazed past Pluto. It sailed through the orbits of Neptune, Uranus, Saturn. By then, warmed by the Sun, its ice had begun to melt; and as it turned end over end, its crater-pocked crust spewed geysers of gas, giving it a gauzy halo.

The comet was first spotted in March as it passed the planet Jupiter, by Dr. Luboš Kohoutek, a Czech astronomer working at the Hamburg Observatory who gave the comet its name. Next in its path was Mars, and then Earth. Kohoutek was due to reach perihelion, its position closest to the Sun, around Christmastime, when it would light up the sky over our town like a giant star, the brightest star we'd ever seen.

This was truly a remarkable discovery, my father said. Historic, even. Comet Kohoutek might very well be the biggest comet ever witnessed by mankind, bigger even than Halley's. Scientists were already calling it the comet of the century.

He stopped and blinked. His shoulders twitched, like a small electric current had shot through his body.

"The comet of the century," he repeated. "Wow! Just think about that for a minute, everyone. Wow."

My classmates, silent, seemed unimpressed. Some listlessly took notes—"the comet of the century." Some stared blankly at him. Others ignored him completely and turned their gazes to the open windows, where outside, water sprinklers tossed rainbows across the new grass on the football field.

My father, undeterred, turned back to the board and drew a sketch of the comet, a circle with three horizontal lines extending from it. He added labels to show the nucleus, coma, and tail. He told us how as the comet came closer, its nucleus would grow hotter, its coma would swell, and its tail would flare out until it was millions of miles long, streaming behind it like an immense, glittering trail of stardust. . . .

And still, girls checked their fingernails, boys shifted in their seats and scribbled in their notebooks. Mark Mingis, a big, athletic fellow, closed his eyes and jigged his leg up and down in the aisle, like a sleeping dog dreaming of running. At the next desk over, my friend Peter Coot looked at me and rolled his eyes up into his head like he was dying.

I slumped lower into my seat, wishing myself into invisibility. It was true, dear god, it was true. Not even fifteen minutes into the first lesson, and already I could see that what my sister had warned me about our father was true: he really was a terrible teacher. Nobody listened to him, nobody cared what he had to say. The problem wasn't his lack of knowledge; he was smart enough, certainly. It wasn't his lack of enthusiasm, either; anybody could see how much he loved science. The problem, so I dimly understood, was that he had no idea how to communicate all his love and knowledge to other people.

He wanted to, I know. He tried so hard, my father—and if dedication and hard work were any guarantees of success, then my father would've been the best teacher in the world. I'd seen him rehearsing this very lesson the night before, pacing and gesturing in the backyard as though he were lecturing the stars. But in the classroom, in his eagerness to share with us everything he knew, he seemed to have forgotten that we, his students, were there. It was as though a thick glass wall stood between him and the class. We could see him on the other side of it, waving his arms and moving his mouth. He obviously had something important he wanted to tell us, but what this was, and why it was so important, we didn't know. We could barely even hear him, and he seemed not to be able to quite see us. And so my classmates, bored and baffled, sighed and closed their eyes. They rubbed their faces and watched the clock, praying for the hour to end so that they could go outside and join their friends and laugh and talk like normal people did.

At the board, he was busy drawing a diagram of the solar system now—"Not to scale," he informed us—with concentric circles showing the orbits of the planets around the Sun. Talking all the while, he traced the path the comet would take as it passed through the solar system, looped around the Sun, and journeyed back to outer space and its home in the crystal cloud. . . .

On and on he went, and soon I, too, felt myself sinking under the spell of his dullness. I couldn't help it: he was so damn boring. My eyelids became heavy, gravity tugged my head down to my desk. The fan hummed in the corner, swallowing his words, until his voice became a sleepy, distant drone: *Oort cloud, highly eccentric elliptical orbit, perihelion, aphelion . . .*

There was a knock on the door, jarring everyone awake. My father stopped short and stared at it. The door creaked open.

"Mr. Broussard?" said Gabriella, peeking in.

I sat up. She introduced herself and apologized for coming late, saying something about going to the wrong classroom. My father sniffed and welcomed her in. "Fine, fine," he said, and put his nose in the roster to check off her name.

Having only ever seen her at a distance, I'd never been fully convinced that she was real. But here she was walking into our classroom, the living, breathing proof of her existence. She wore a sleeveless white blouse that set off her tanned arms and shoulders, and her dark, extravagant hair hung loose down her back. She carried a brown leather purse and an armful of books. She gave a quick smile to the nearest students as she slid into an empty desk at the front of the room. She took a fresh notebook, opened it, and removed a pen from her purse. Then she sat up straight, looped her hair behind her left ear, and put her pen at the ready.

I looked around to see if my classmates were as startled as I was by her arrival. A girl at the rear of the room leaned forward, tapped her friend on the shoulder, and whispered something in her ear. At his desk in the middle of the room, Mark Mingis had his eyes wide open now. His right leg began to bounce more vigorously in the aisle.

At the board, my father had resumed his lecture. Gabriella watched him for a minute, frowning slightly. Then she went to work copying the words and diagrams from the board into her notebook. I was impressed by her diligence. When she filled a page, she turned to a fresh one and continued writing. Her fingernails, I saw, were painted the same tantalizing shade of pink they'd been when I spotted her with my telescope. Around her left wrist she wore a gold watch, and around her neck—I could just make it out through the drape of her hair—a thin gold necklace. When she moved her head, looking up at the board and then down at her notebook, her hair seemed to ripple with life. She was so pretty, so elegant, it made me lonely just to look at her.

My father came back to the center of the floor. Wrapping up his lecture, he explained how in addition to our regular lessons, we'd be paying special attention to our cosmic visitor from outer space. Together with NASA and scientists all over the world, we would track him, we would study him. We would learn all we could about Kohoutek.

"This is a once-in-a-lifetime astronomical event," he said. "Something you'll remember for the rest of your lives. Something you can tell your grandchildren about. You were right there, you can say, in Mr. Broussard's ninth grade Earth and Space Science class when Comet Kohoutek came. Wow. How cool is that?"

Abruptly, my father struck a dramatic pose. He hunched forward and raised his hands in front of him, as if he were getting ready to catch a basketball. Standing crouched like this, his dark hair and tie sprinkled with chalk dust, his glasses reflecting the light, he looked like a weird, giant alien insect.

"Think of this comet as a messenger. A messenger from our past, who, if we listen carefully, may be able to tell us who we are, where we came from, and how we got here. Listen! What do you hear?"

He cocked his head up and froze. For a moment, everyone, Gabriella included, listened with him. We listened, but all we heard were the sounds of the school rustling around us, the fan humming, the clock ticking, and our own restless teenage bodies shifting and growling and straining beneath our clothes as we waited for the bell to ring.

CHAPTER FOUR

"YOUR father's kind of strange, isn't he?"

Peter and I sat on the bleachers after lunch, looking out over the football field. My father stood at the edge of the parking lot with one arm braced across his chest, the other propped up to his face. He rubbed his chin as he gazed skyward. Large white clouds hung high and motionless in a blue-gray sky. Now and then he would point to a cloud and shake his finger at it, as though he were arguing with it.

"What's he doing?" Peter asked.

"Checking the weather."

"What for?"

"Who knows? He likes to check the weather is all."

Peter scratched with a stick at the wood between his feet while I scanned the school grounds, searching for Gabriella. The hot, thick air lent a hazy aspect to everything. Boys were lazily throwing a football back and forth along the sideline of the field, still off-limits on account of the new grass. Groups of girls clustered in the shade of the gym. The

black students hung around the temporary buildings at the far end of
the field, mostly keeping to themselves. No sign of Gabriella, though.

Peter was talking about his visit to his uncle's house in Napoleonville last weekend. He and his cousin Trent had gone hunting in the
woods behind their farm, where he'd shot a rabbit with his uncle's
twenty-two. He had the skin drying back at the house if I wanted to see
it, he said. He was thinking of making a hat with the fur.

"You're what?"

"Making a hat."

"A rabbit hat?"

"Why not? It's a good fur."

"With ears?"

"No, not with ears. Asshole."

Peter and I had been friends since third grade, mainly because we
were the same age and we lived in the same neighborhood. We'd been
Cub Scouts together. He was a runty boy, with crowded teeth, straight
hair, and a high, excited voice. He hated school and was always getting
into trouble with the teachers. He didn't care much for our classmates,
either, and they repaid him by teasing and shunning him. But four
years earlier, I happened to know, his older brother had been killed in
Vietnam when he stepped on a land mine, and soon after that his
mother had left his father; and knowing all this, I couldn't help but see
him in a more sympathetic light than I might have otherwise. Besides,
he was, I was reluctant to admit, my only real friend.

Peter went on to say how his daddy had promised him a twenty-two
for Christmas. While a twenty-two was fine for small game like rabbit
and squirrel, he'd really prefer something more powerful. He knew
plenty of boys our age who already had their own shotguns. His cousin
Trent had a Remington twenty-gauge pump rifle—which was an excellent firearm, there was no denying that; the Remington was your in-
dustry standard. But personally, his ideal gun, what he really wanted,
he said, would be a Winchester thirty-thirty. For deer hunting, that'd
be the best. A Winchester thirty-thirty.

"What would be your ideal gun?" he asked me.

I wasn't listening: I'd caught sight of Gabriella stepping out from under the covered walkway beside the gym. She was accompanied by a group of the prettiest, most popular girls of our class—the cheerleaders, the homeroom presidents, the girls with boyfriends. They began a slow walk along the edge of the football field. As they strolled, Gabriella smiled and turned her hair over her ear, nodding and answering the girls' questions as though she were being interviewed for membership in their club.

"Are you listening? You aren't even listening to me," Peter said. Then he saw who I was watching. "Do you know her?"

"She just moved into that big new house behind us."

"Man. She is hot. She is gorgeous. She may be the most gorgeous girl I've ever seen. If that girl lived behind me, I'd be swimming across the bayou every night and sneaking into her bedroom."

"Sure you would."

"I might."

"Please."

Peter was always talking about what he would do with girls, which struck me as laughable, because if anyone had less of a chance with girls than I did, it was Peter. The only thing he knew about girls was what he'd read in *Playboy*. His father owned the Conoco station in town, where he kept a stack of girlie magazines on a shelf in his office. Peter and I would bike there sometimes after school for free Cokes, and when Mr. Coot wasn't looking, Peter would pull down the magazines to show me. "Oh, man, look at her," he'd say, rubbing his fingers on the greasy photos. He spoke critically about each girl's features, which girls he preferred and which he'd most like to have sex with. "This one. I love her. I'd actually marry her. Miss Amber. *Mm-mm.*"

Gabriella and the girls had rounded the far corner and were strolling along the end zone. I saw that if they continued walking around the field, it would bring them directly in front of the stands, and despite my rational expectation of what might happen—which was nothing— I grew excited to see her coming our way. I tugged my shirt from my chest, wiped the sweat from my forehead, and sat up straighter.

Peter said that the least I should do was to try and kiss Gabriella. That would be a reasonable plan for the ninth grade, he said. Freshman year, kissing and deep French kissing. Then sophomore year, I'd want to be making out with her. By sixteen we should be having oral sex, and by seventeen or eighteen, full frontal sex. Of course, it could go faster than that, but basically, he said, that was the standard progression. Before I finished high school, I should be having full frontal sex with her.

"Full frontal sex. You don't even know what you're talking about."

"More than you do."

"You have no idea what you're talking about."

Gabriella and her group were heading our way down the edge of the field. "Here they come," Peter said, and eagerly rubbed his knees.

I knew I didn't stand a chance with Gabriella Martello, and I told Peter so. Girls like her didn't even notice boys like us. We moved in completely different circles. It was like a law of nature, something that should've been taught in school but wasn't. I tried to explain it to him.

"It's obvious. Look—see? The black kids are over there hanging out with the black kids. The jocks have their territory. Mary Ida and those other sorry girls are standing over there at the water fountain where you know they'll always be. We're sitting here on the bleachers, where boys like us always sit. It's only the first day of school, but we're already stuck where we'll all be for the rest of the year. Who said you had to go there? Nobody. But you did. You went automatically. You had no choice. It's like, I don't know, in your blood cells or something. That's what I mean, a law of nature. The universal law governing the motion of bodies at school."

"The law governing . . . Where the hell'd you get that?"

They were approaching the bleachers now. Gabriella walked in the middle of the group, her head held high; she'd obviously passed the interview, and with flying colors. You could practically see the other girls already trying to model themselves after her, eyeing her walk and gestures, the way she lifted her shoulders and flopped her head back when she laughed.

As they crossed in front of the bleachers, Gabriella turned and lazily scanned the stands. I felt my heart quicken. When her gaze drifted over me she hesitated, as if she'd caught sight of something that she recognized but couldn't quite name. I sat up. I started to wave; my hand got as far as my chest. But then a football tumbled into the girls' legs, and as quickly as that, I disappeared.

The girls skipped out of the way, squealing and complaining, as Mark Mingis came jogging after the ball. The girls shouted insults at him, but you could tell they all secretly adored this tall handsome boy with the blond hair and blue eyes. Mark stopped to talk to them, tossing his head to shake the hair out of his eyes while he bounced the ball from hand to hand. Gabriella was introduced and they spoke for a minute. Then the girls moved on, huddling together excitedly like birds fluttering over crumbs.

"Look at him," Peter said. "God, I hate him. Don't you hate him?"

"Observe. The universal law in action."

I shaped my two fists into a spyglass and aimed it at Gabriella's back. By squeezing my fists closed I could cut out everything else from the picture but her and her long dark hair bouncing back and forth across her shoulders in time to her steps. How could anyone look at her and not be astonished? She was lovely . . . remote . . . untouchable. A million light-years away.

"Watch and dream, Pete. Watch and dream."

The bell rang. Peter cursed, and we climbed down the bleachers to go inside.

In the parking lot my father still stood, pointing and waving his hands at the sky like some magician of the weather. High overhead, ponderous dense clouds drifted slowly across a blue-gray sky.

CHAPTER FIVE

MY mother liked to read her horoscope while she drank her coffee in the morning. It was the first thing she looked at in the newspaper, even before the headlines. The world could wait; more important was what the stars had in store for her that day. She was an Aries, which, she told us, explained why she sometimes forgot to iron our clothes or ruined our dinner. She was impulsive, impatient, adventurous, passionate—"just like Bette Davis." Spreading the paper on the table, she would read her entry aloud to us while we ate our breakfast cereal before school.

Today. Trust your instincts! Your first reaction is your best, so don't hold back. You may end up making a family member uncomfortable, but that's a small price to pay for doing what you know in your heart is right. Things should return to normal soon.

My father would laugh. First of all, he'd say, leaning back against the counter in his shirt and tie, coffee cup in hand, those predictions were fluff, practically meaningless. And second, the whole premise of astrology had no basis whatsoever in reality. Logically, physically, scientifically, it was impossible that the motion of stars or planets could have any influence on human activity. It was only egotism, plain and simple, for people to believe that they were somehow personally connected to bodies in space. The stars didn't care when you were born, or how your day would be, or whether or not you would meet a tall, dark stranger. They were here long before us and would be here long after we were gone. They had no interest in our petty little lives.

"But still, sometimes . . . ," my mother would try to argue, and speak abstractly about the Moon's gravity and ocean tides and the percentage of water in the human body.

"Nonsense," he'd answer, and try to set her straight, talking patiently to her like she was a confused but redeemable student. Astrology was nothing but superstition, he explained—entertaining perhaps, but in the end as silly as trying to predict the future by studying goat entrails. Like any rational person, he put his trust in the evidence of his senses. True knowledge could only begin in a clear-eyed observation of the facts. And then, "Hypothesize, experiment, analyze, repeat. Hypothesize, experiment, analyze, repeat." This, as he liked to say, was one of the greatest gifts that modern science had given mankind: a methodological way of reasoning that helped us to understand the world in which we lived. It was this very understanding that lifted human beings out of the Dark Ages and put us in homes with lights and electricity and running water. Cars. Airplanes. Submarines. Computers. *Skylab*! Where would we be without scientific thought? We'd all still be half apes shivering in holes in the ground, trembling and screeching every time the sky thundered.

" 'The fault, dear Brutus, is not in the stars but in ourselves,' " he'd say, raising a finger and shaking it to finish his lecture.

In this, I had to agree with my father. I didn't put any faith in my mother's horoscopes, either. It seemed unlikely that a planet millions of miles away could determine what happened to us on any given day. People did things for a reason, not because some star in the sky told them to. To be sure, the reasons behind our actions might be murky and difficult to understand at times, but if we only looked closely enough, all our behaviors became as clear and predictable as math: A + B = C.

And yet . . . and yet, when this new comet appeared in our lives, there was no denying that it had an effect on people—and most of all on my father. The comet changed him; anyone who knew him could see that. It was gradual, almost imperceptible at first, but as the summer slipped away and the comet crept closer, his transformation became more and more apparent until it was unmistakable.

A person might argue that it wasn't the comet but my father himself who effected these changes. But didn't the comet come first, and didn't the comet lead to the changes? And what was a cause if not that?

The next week he plowed into the classroom, set his briefcase on his desk, and stepped forward. Twitching lightly in his clothes, he said he had some exciting news to tell us. He'd been talking to the other teachers about the comet, and during their last staff meeting, they agreed to a proposal he'd put forth:

Given that the appearance of Kohoutek was an astronomical event of historic proportions, and given that such an event presented unique educational opportunities for students, 1973 would be designated "The Year of the Comet" for the freshman class at Terrebonne High.

He wrote the phrase on the board, saying each word out loud as he did so, "The—Year—of—the—Comet." Then he drew a big circle around it, just in case any of us missed the point.

Dusting off his hands, he explained how, per their agreement, all ninth grade teachers would include space-related themes in their lessons this semester. So our history teacher might discuss the cosmologies of different civilizations through time, our art teacher might have us draw posters of comets, and so on. Comets, comets everywhere.

"Sound fun?" he asked, and my classmates exchanged doubtful

looks. At the next desk over, Peter turned to me, lifted his hands, and wobbled his head, as if to say, *What's with all the comet crap?*

My father took the lead by tacking up a long chart of the solar system to the side wall of his classroom. He'd made the chart himself from sheets of freezer paper, with a drawing of the Sun at the front of the room and Pluto near the back. He said how we would use this chart to track Kohoutek's approach over the upcoming months. Every Friday he would phone the Astronomy Department at LSU for the coordinates, and every Monday morning, a special comet person would be chosen to position the comet on the chart.

He held up a disk of cardboard, trimmed around the edges with pinking shears and wrapped with aluminum foil. "Here it is. The comet. Ouch. Hot," he said, and snorted a laugh.

This might've been an awfully dumb activity for ninth graders, except that the first comet person he chose, whether by accident or design, was Gabriella.

"Comet person," he said. "Arise! Take the comet."

"Yes, sir." Gabriella came to the front of the class and took the silver comet. She turned it over in her hands, looking at it.

"Distance," he said, checking his notepad, "two point eight four four astronomical units."

"Where's that?"

"Here." He pointed to an X penciled halfway between Mars and Jupiter. Tossing her hair over her shoulder, Gabriella bent in and stuck the comet on the chart. Then she stood back, sliding her heels together and cupping her hands below her waist. She had a marvelously upright bearing, as if she wasn't afraid of standing in front of the class, as if she enjoyed it even. All the girls watched her with envy, and Mark Mingis, slumped in his desk, grinned approvingly.

"How does our current location correspond with the projected location?"

"Looks to be about the same."

"Any estimates on the date of perihelion? Same? Different?"

"Um—the same?"

"Excellent. Thank you."

"Aye-aye, sir," she said, and gave a brisk kind of sailor salute before taking her seat. Good god, I thought. Had there ever been a girl as clever and adorable as Gabriella? And was everyone as in love with her as I was? How could they not have been? After Gabriella, everyone wanted to be the comet person.

Our other teachers gradually picked up on my father's Year of the Comet idea, some more enthusiastically than the rest. In fine arts, we spent a couple of lessons making posters that went up in the hallways. "Comet Kohoutek, Superstar!" they said, and "Depictions of Comets Through History," and "Interpretation of When the Comet Hits the Planet and Everything Is Destroyed, the Dinosaurs Return." In math, we used algebra to try to calculate rate, time, and distance for the comet. And in English class, our teacher set aside a day for us to compose poems about the comet.

Miss Benoit was a nervous young black woman with large round glasses that made her look frightened and sad, like she was always on the verge of crying. She was a great lover of literature, as she often told us herself, and although her lessons were generally dull and confusing, from time to time she would read stories aloud to us in class with a hushed, dramatic voice that made even the most apathetic students lift their heads up from their desks. For her comet lesson, she showed us pictures of stars and planets, and then she pulled down the shades, put on a record of classical music, and told us to close our eyes and "write what you feel," and "don't worry about sense. Sense is for scientists." We spent the better part of an hour working on our poems, and at the end she loved everybody's. But she was especially taken by mine. She asked me to read it aloud for the class. I didn't want to.

"Please?" she pouted. Miss Benoit had already singled me out as one of her favorites because she'd seen me checking out a stack of nonrequired reading in the library. "A like soul," she called me. "A lover of literature. A son of Shakespeare."

"*June-yurrr!*" my classmates jeered when I came to the front of the room.

I lifted my arms from my sides and tugged my shirt from my chest. I could feel the sweat dampening my underarms. Miss Benoit stood to one side with her hands pressed together in front of her, as if she were praying for me. My voice sounded shaky and weak to my ears; I didn't dare look up for fear of exposing myself. " 'I Am the Comet,' " I began.

I Am the Comet

Far, far away
Sailing pale and quiet past the stars
I am the comet
You are the Sun
Beautiful Sun
Unfreeze my heart
And see me shine

Miss Benoit made a small gasp when I finished reading, like someone had poked her in the side. "I cherish your poem," she said. "I wonder who the Sun is? Oh, that lucky Sun!"

I didn't say who the Sun was; I was careful not to even look in her direction. But I thought that it must've been obvious to anyone with eyes to see: there she was in the front row, blazing.

"I wonder who the Sun is?" Peter whispered as I returned to my seat. He slid his hands under his shirt and rubbed his chest obscenely. "Ooh, that lucky, lucky Sun!"

For Coach DuPleiss, who couldn't see any link between comets and phys ed, my father volunteered to write the lessons himself. He planned a module called Space Age Fitness and made ditto copies of handouts on which students were to record their daily caloric intake and expenditure while practicing the same exercises the astronauts in *Skylab* did. He visited my P.E. class on the day we were to begin Space Age Fitness, and while my father spoke about the importance of fitness not only for astronauts but for teenagers as well, Coach DuPleiss, a short, tough man with hairy arms and a mustache, made faces behind his back.

"Thank you, Professor," said the coach, winking and grinning. "I'm sure we can all appreciate that." As soon as my father had gone, the coach stuffed his handouts behind an equipment locker and made us run laps instead.

"You're comets!" he shouted, snapping a towel at us. "Pick it up. Hey Junior, let's go! Run!"

Nothing discouraged my father, though, not mocking coaches, or skeptical students, or a disinterested family. When it came to his comet, he was indefatigable.

Nights, he would take my telescope and head for the back door.

"I thought you said we weren't going to see it for another couple months," I said.

"I'm just checking. I'm just having a look, that's all. Turn off the porch light, would you?"

From my bedroom window I watched him set up the scope in the backyard. His white shirt caught the light from the Moon so that, moving against the dark line of trees, he looked like a ghost bobbing around at the rear of our yard. He hunched down to the eyepiece and then stayed there a long time, his hands resting awkwardly on his knees. He seemed to sigh occasionally, his shoulders rising and falling with his breath. *I'm here*, he might've been whispering to the comet. *I'm ready. I'm waiting.*

When I went to bed he was still there in the yard with my telescope, still waiting with his head bowed beneath the stars. Drifting off to sleep, I imagined a spark from the comet floating down, down like a mote of stardust, to land inside my father, where, settling in his belly, it rekindled the long-forgotten dreams and ambitions of his youth. I saw his white shirt glowing yellow in the moonlight, flames shooting from his fingertips, like he was a man set on fire.

And who knew then how great the flames would grow, how bright they would shine? Or how completely they would consume him? We couldn't have known, not then. Then, his comet was still little more than a joke to us all.

CHAPTER SIX

Groovy Science
by Alan Broussard

In a weekly special to the *Daily Herald*, local science teacher and astronomy expert Alan Broussard discusses scientific topics of interest to a general audience.

A Sunday morning a month into the start of the school year, my father trotted into the house in his pajamas and bedroom slippers carrying the newspaper. Megan, our mother, and I gathered at his elbows as he unfolded the paper on the table with a jerky excitement. On page three of the Fun section, just below my mother's horoscope column, was a black-and-white photograph of him. His glasses looked larger than in real life, and he wore a stiff, crooked smile.

"'Groovy Science'?" Megan said, frowning. "Whose idea was that?"

"The column was my idea. But the title, that's the editor's. They wanted to, you know, jazz it up a little."

We knew he'd been working on something for the newspaper but didn't know what, exactly. He told us he'd delivered this first piece just last week and everyone at the newspaper had liked it. "Careful you don't get butter on it."

I began to read the article aloud.

The Great Comet Kohoutek

Aristotle called them "stars with hair." Before the telescope was invented, people didn't know what to make of comets. They seemed to appear from nowhere in the sky, like strange stars with long hair. They would linger for a few days, weeks, or sometimes months before gradually disappearing. Early astronomers said they were rogue planets, or the exhalations of gas from the Earth, or even the smoke of human sins that rose into the sky and burst into flame. But no matter how they understood them, people throughout history have always been frightened by comets. They were bad omens. They portended disaster: wars, famine, the death of kings, even the end of the world.

Today, of course, we know that comets . . .

"Okay, okay, you don't have to read the whole thing," Megan said.

"It's just something easy. Something for families and kids," my father quickly explained. "I thought with the comet coming, this would be a good opportunity to raise awareness in the community about the importance of science in our everyday lives." He had already mapped out a bunch of ideas for future columns: the history of astronomy, early views of the solar system, the laws of gravity, the origins of the universe, the nature of time . . . "You could go on and on."

My mother looked at him with a peculiar expression of pride, envy, and disbelief. "And this is going to be in the newspaper every week?"

"Every week."

"Great," my sister said to me later. "Now everyone can know what a geek our dad is."

But I was impressed, seeing my father's name and picture in the newspaper. That afternoon he brought home a whole stack of them. And that same night he got to work on his next column, "Why Can't People Fly?" (*"Ever since Icarus strapped his waxy wings to his arms, men have stared at the birds in wordless wonder and envy, and thought,* Why can't I? *Groovy science tells us that according to the laws of gravity . . ."*) When I went up to bed he was still working on it, sitting at the table, consulting his old college textbooks and making notes in the light from the overhead lamp as the house creaked around him.

At school, my father's column was posted on the notice board in the entrance hallway with his name circled in red ink. Coach DuPleiss, seeing him out in the parking lot at recess checking the weather, couldn't resist poking fun.

"See any comets yet, Professor?" DuPleiss shouted. Mark Mingis and a handful of other football players standing around the coach chuckled.

My father lowered his eyes from the clouds. "If you're referring to Comet Kohoutek, not yet," he answered. "He's about halfway to Mars now. You'll be able to see him next month with a good pair of binoculars. By December, of course, you won't be able to miss him."

"I'll start digging my bomb shelter, Professor," DuPleiss said.

"Oh, I wouldn't worry about that. The chances that Kohoutek will actually strike the Earth are negligible."

"Negligible, you say?"

He could brush off the teasing easily enough, but the coach's nickname for him stuck. Students began to call out to him on the playground and in the hallway, in a half-joking, half-admiring tone: "Hey, Professor! How's it going, Professor?" Before long, other teachers picked up on it, too. "Any news on the comet, Professor?"

My father, far from shrinking from it, seemed to enjoy the attention. He answered all come-ons with a chirpy, self-conscious irony, as if to show that he was in on the joke. He'd pull his shoulders back and, smiling and twitching, say, "The Professor is feeling fine today, thank you," or, flipping open his notepad, "Latest coordinates are RA eleven hours, eighteen minutes, and twenty seconds; declination minus six degrees and six point two arc minutes. Distance two point two eight one astronomical units. Yep, Kohoutek's right on track."

Emboldened by the success of his newspaper column, he finally resolved to approach the school principal with a formal request for money to repair his department's crumbling science labs. He wouldn't be denied any longer, he told us at home over dinner. Didn't he deserve as much support as a football coach? Wasn't his work just as important? More, even?

He made a list of supplies and equipment, drew up a budget, and rehearsed his arguments with us at the table. It was, he said, "vitally important to engage students while the flame of their natural curiosity still burns." My mother said that he should try to be more forceful and less flowery in his delivery; he shushed her and went on: ". . . the space race . . . the reputation of our school . . . the health of our community . . . the future of our nation . . ."

In their meeting, Principal Lee agreed with everything my father said. He'd love to have new labs, too, he said, but he didn't have any more money in the budget for science that year. ("Tight. Tight tight tight this year," said Lee.) My father knew it was no use protesting that the principal had somehow found money for improvements to the football field. Instead, he said he'd be willing to start small—just the most basic repairs so that their labs could even do what labs were supposed to do. Lee said he'd help if he could. ("I'd build a, what do you call it, a launch pad right out there in the parking lot for you if I could.") But he really didn't have any more money. Those were the unalterable facts of finance. My father would just have to make do.

My father was disappointed, naturally, and came home grousing about the idiotic principal and his misplaced priorities. "'Tight tight tight!' What an ass. Don't tell anyone I said that." But his anger was short-lived. After he'd burned himself out complaining, he hunkered down and went back to work on his lesson plans and newspaper columns.

He didn't say so, not in so many words, but it was clear he was hitching his hopes to the comet. He fairly glowed with anticipation. *Just you wait*, he seemed to be saying. *Just you wait*. When the comet came, it would outshine all our expectations. It would dazzle, it would amaze; it would prove, to Principal Lee and to anyone else who had ever doubted him, the true value of science in our everyday lives.

And over the upcoming weeks, as the summer turned toward fall, and we continued to read his articles in the newspaper, and we saw the posters going up in the hallways, and we watched the foil-covered cut-out inching closer to the Sun, a similar feeling of anticipation grew among me and my classmates so that, in spite of our habitual teenage distrust of anything that adults claimed was true, and in spite of my father's reputation as a geek, a clown, Terrebonne High's most boring and ineffectual science teacher, we began to suspect that he could be right this time: something big could be in store with this comet of his.

From time to time I would see younger students, third and fourth graders, running across the playground. They'd see my father in his black raincoat standing in the parking lot looking up at the sky, and they, too, would slow, stop, and look up. Then they'd stand there a minute or two, rocking slightly back and forth, their mouths hanging open, their arms limp, gazing up at the heavens, hoping to catch a glimpse of something spectacular glinting behind a cloud.

CHAPTER SEVEN

WHO were we? Where did we come from? How did we get here?

Lying in my room at night during those early weeks of my freshman year, with my schoolbooks scattered on the floor beside my bed, and Gabriella's house lit up on the other side of the bayou, and the sharp, bright stars dotting the sky outside my window, I mused over my father's questions, the ones he said the comet might answer for us if we only listened closely enough.

My concerns weren't so much scientific or philosophical as they were practical. I wondered, for instance, why I was so damn timid and shy all the time. Why couldn't I just approach Gabriella in the cafeteria, say hello and introduce myself, like Mark Mingis had done that first day of school? Why was that so difficult? And what about this constant, aching longing I felt, the one that made me want to knock my head against the wall and roll around on the floor because I felt I was about to burst into flames out of loneliness and desire? What was wrong with me? Did everyone my age feel this way? Surely it was something you grew out of—"a phase" as our teachers put it—because the alternative, that I would be like this for the rest of my life, was too horrible even to consider.

I spent long minutes studying my reflection in the mirror above my dresser, searching for clues to myself. I turned from side to side, checked my profile, and adjusted my hair. I wondered if a girl like Gabriella could ever find me handsome. I doubted it. I had a head just like my father's, all square and narrow, as though cut from a block of wood. I saw his other features in my face as well. We had the same high forehead, the same thin eyebrows and long nose; if I'd put on a pair of black-rimmed glasses, I could've been his little twin. Whenever my classmates looked at me, they couldn't help but think of my father, and when they looked at him, they thought of me. That certainly didn't help my chances with Gabriella any.

And why, oh why, I wondered, had he named me after himself? What kind of a father would do that to his son? What could he have been thinking? Was it an excess of pride? Or was it, as my sister had once theorized, just the opposite, a deep-seated sense of inferiority that made our father want to double himself? He must've imagined we were just the beginning of a long line of Broussards: Alan the First, Alan the Second, Alan the Sixteenth, and so on, my father replicating himself forever into the future. Whatever his idea had been, I hated having to carry his name. When my classmates teased me, they didn't even have to invent new names for me; they only had to add a certain mean, twisty inflection to my own: "*June-yurrr!*" That said it all—the name contained not only my shortcomings but his as well. There was no escaping him; in the mirror, in the classroom, in the shops in town, he followed me everywhere. I dragged his name and reputation around behind me wherever I went: Alan Broussard, Jr.

For better or worse, I was my father's son, and I intuited, however unclearly, that my life was inextricably bound up with his. I was who I was because of him. His blood was in my blood, his history was my history. Even my future, the person I might one day become, depended on him, because everything he'd ever seen or done or thought or felt flowed up through him and into me.

And just who was he, that peculiar wooden man who lectured to us every day in class and then sat down beside me every evening for dinner? My father wasn't inclined to talk much about his past, and when he did—when I pressed him for details and he began to reminisce about his youth—he became so dull and long-winded that I soon regretted ever asking him anything. His storytelling lacked, as my mother said, "a sense of the dramatic."

Still, I already knew the basics. His background was part of our shared family history, told in bits and pieces over the years, embellished by my imagination, until it was almost as real to me as my own past.

And sometimes at night, if I squinted in just such a way at the black spaces between the stars, I believed I could see, as though through a crack in the sky, a glimpse of my father as he must've been: a boy who looked just like me, a boy who might've had the same doubts and yearnings as I did—a boy who, maybe just as I did, once stood gazing out of his bedroom window at a star-filled sky, wondering at the wild coincidences of time and space and desire that had made him who he was.

He came, so the story went, like a bolt out of the blue.

He wasn't even supposed to have been possible, but then, defying doctors' predictions, he appeared, just like that, *presto!* He was born a full decade after his next older brother, to become the last of three sons from the marriage of a Baton Rouge Broussard to a Baton Rouge Schexsynder.

"God's little surprise," his mother liked to call him.

"He must've gotten lost in the mail," his father quipped.

In early photographs my father-to-be appeared as a serious, frowning baby, with a full head of thick black hair and peevish eyes that seemed to say he was still angry about being yanked from the dark, peaceful universe he'd so recently inhabited and that, given half a chance, he'd gladly crawl back into that quiet place. They named him Alan, after, his mother later admitted, a picture she'd seen on a prayer card of Saint Alan of the Rock.

Even as a toddler he was a curious boy, always burrowing into the backs of closets and taking apart anything that could be taken apart. His older brothers, busy with their sports and scouting, stepped around him on the living room rug like he was a weird and troublesome new pet. It wasn't that they disliked him; they just didn't know what they were supposed to do with him, and so they shooed him out of their rooms when he was in the way and tossed him a ball from time to time when they wanted to distract him.

As he grew older, Alan retreated into his books about science, his model rockets and homemade radio sets. He became the studious one of the bunch, preferring indoors to out, and before he was even ten years old, he was wearing his first pair of eyeglasses. By the time he was ready to start junior high school, his oldest brother was already married and settled in his own apartment, and the other one was off in the navy fighting the Japs, leaving Alan alone with his parents, a single child in a suddenly quiet household, which, truth be told, suited him fine.

His mother he would always remember in a cooking apron with a smudge of flour in her dark hair. She was a thrifty, devout woman who said the rosary every night and who, even for years after other ladies had stopped doing it, continued to cover her head with a veil when she went to Mass on Sunday mornings. Alan's father was a practical-minded, vest-wearing man who worked for the post office—not as a carrier (a point of distinction for him), but as a manager in the big downtown branch. He owned one pair of shiny black shoes that he re-soled every two years for twenty years.

His father liked his work, so much so that he brought it home with him: he collected postage stamps, which he carefully mounted in thick gray albums that he kept locked in a glass-fronted cabinet. Alan would watch him handling his stamps with a pair of tweezers at the dining room table, his breath sighing in and out over his mustache as he inspected their watermarks with a magnifying glass. He spoke of finding the one rare stamp—an Inverted Jenny, or a good Confederate provisional—that would make his fortune. Alan's island-hopping brother, the one in the navy, sent stamps home to their father from faraway ports, exotic miniature landscapes embossed with the names of mythical sounding countries and kingdoms. At night in his bedroom in the quiet house, the young Alan would sit hunched over his home-made radio, pressing the headset to his ear as he listened for voices in the white noise, and imagine he was flying daring solo missions over Burma, Formosa, Trengganu, Syburi . . .

When he eventually graduated from high school and entered the College of Science at LSU, he felt, as he would later say, like he had died and gone to heaven. Biology! Chemistry! Physics! Astronomy! There were so many wonderful courses to choose from, he hardly knew where to begin; he wanted to take them all. Walking into his classes on the first day of college, he discovered rooms full of boys who were not so different from him, boys who even looked like him—young student scientists in glasses, their shirt pockets stuffed with mechanical pencils and slide rules, their arms full of books. He felt like he'd been waiting his whole life for exactly this.

He came to love everything about his department: the research, the camaraderie, and his professors, so decent and smart. Going to and from his classes in Nicholson Hall every day, he passed beneath a painted stucco relief set above the entranceway. Arranged in a line were the Greek symbols for the planets and above that, on a field of blue, golden emblems of the Sun, the Moon, stars, and, yes, a comet. It was, he thought, like walking into a temple. It gave him the feeling that he was doing something vitally important there, something almost sacred. Like he was working shoulder to shoulder with the gods. Really, he would've been happy to stay there for the rest of his life.

But during his last semester of his senior year, he happened to attend a recruitment fair for prospective schoolteachers held in the university field house. He'd only gone to accompany a friend and had no intention of even staying for the whole thing. But while he was there, just for the heck of it, he filled out some applications, sat for a couple of interviews, and a week later, to his surprise, he received a phone call from the Terrebonne Parish school district offering him a job.

Years later, he still found it hard to say why he even considered the offer. He had his sights set on graduate school; he'd never had much interest in teaching, and he wasn't even sure where Terrebonne was. Part of the answer, he knew, lay at home. His parents had supported him during his four years at LSU, and he couldn't help but feel indebted to them, even guilty, for having relied on their generosity for so long. And as for graduate school, his father questioned how practical an advanced degree in astronomy would be. A master's degree in star watching? Was that really necessary? Could it guarantee him a job? Sometimes his parents seemed to think there was something suspicious, possibly indulgent, even lazy, in all his study. After all, just look at his two older brothers. They didn't have any degrees, and they were doing fine, weren't they? Both of them had their own homes, jobs, nice families, cars. "Standing on their own two feet," as his father liked to say: a nagging expression of his that always made Alan think of his father standing at his manager's desk at the post office, the soles of his shiny black shoes slowly wearing away to nothing.

He talked it over with Dr. Brewer, his advisor in the science department, and decided that taking a year off from his studies—just a year—couldn't hurt. Lots of fellows took time off before graduate school. The teaching experience could even make him a better candidate for an assistantship. "Go have your *Wanderjahr*. That's what I would do," Brewer said, winking and patting his shoulder. "We'll still be here when you get back."

And so out of guilt, coupled with a desire to prove to his parents that all his book learning was useful—that, like his brothers, he could stand on his own two feet if he had to—Alan took the teaching job. He bought a secondhand car, filled it with books and clothes, plus five new ties, shook his father's hand, kissed his mother's cheek, and in late July of 1955, his temporary teaching credential in a brown envelope on the seat beside him, he drove south on Highway 1. Down he drove, down to the toe of the state, down to where the green land of his map tattered into blue patches of lakes and bayous and bodies of water too numerous to name before sinking into the Gulf. He felt, on that drive south, as the roads became narrower and the towns grew smaller and the land swampier (he ran over a black snake outside of Napoleonville), an unexpected sense of adventure, as though he were carrying the torchlight of science to the end of the world, bound at last for his own real-life Burma, Formosa, Trengganu, to a land called Terrebonne.

The town of Terrebonne, seat of Terrebonne Parish, had a population of about three thousand people then. It was surrounded by sugarcane fields to the north, marshland to the south. Bayous and canals crisscrossed the town and ran alongside roads and under bridges. In the middle of town stood the parish courthouse; it faced a square nicely laid out with walkways and benches sheltered by live oaks. Besides the handful of shops around the square, there were three churches, two grocery stores, two gas stations, and two schools, one for black students and one for the white. It took him less than ten minutes to see everything.

He settled into an apartment in a converted house near the square, went to introduce himself to his principal at the school, and before he quite knew what had happened, he found himself standing in his coat and tie on a dusty floor facing a roomful of rowdy summer-tanned teenagers. He was just twenty-one years old, barely past his teens himself, with no experience at all as a teacher—"as innocent as a Christian tossed to the lions" as he would tell it later.

His students were the sons and daughters of farmers and fishermen, trappers and oil-rig workers. Half of them, he was astonished to learn, came to school by boat. They clomped into his classroom with their shoes falling off, no socks or laces, like they weren't accustomed to footwear. Some showed up for only the first few days of lessons and never returned; others disappeared for weeks at a time during certain trapping or fishing or hunting seasons. Many spoke with accents so odd and thick that, in the beginning at least, he had trouble understanding what they were saying; he'd ask them to repeat themselves again and again until, judging by the laughter in the classroom, it seemed that the fault wasn't with the students but with him, and red-faced and stammering, he'd move on to the next topic.

Maybe he'd been sheltered for too long from the real world while working in the labs at Nicholson Hall, or maybe in his four years away from high school he'd already forgotten what teenagers were like, or maybe he was just hopelessly naïve; but he was honestly baffled to find that his students didn't share his love for science. He couldn't understand it; the field was booming, amazing new advances were being made every day. They should've been rapt with wonder: the DNA double helix, programmable computers, space rockets, radio astronomy, artificial satellites . . . Artificial satellites! Astrophysicists were drawing up plans to shoot small metal moons equipped with radio transmitters into orbit around the Earth. How could they not be fascinated by that? But the girls in his class just sighed and chewed their gum. The boys picked at their pimples and drew dirty pictures in the margins of their textbooks. They didn't care. He might've been standing in a field lecturing to rocks and trees for all the response he got.

He began to think he'd made a mistake in coming here. This teaching business was much more difficult than he'd imagined; in fact, he was pretty sure he hated it. After school he'd trudge home to his small apartment, annoyed and exhausted. He didn't know what the hell he was doing, but he didn't dare ask the other teachers for help, because he was afraid if he did he'd only reveal how incompetent he was. Never mind standing on his own two feet; he'd finish out his contract, and next year he'd pack up his car and go back to doing what he loved.

Except . . . except that from time to time, a boy would raise his hand and ask a genuinely interesting question, and Alan would see a spark of curiosity flickering in the eyes of his students as they waited for his answer. Or a girl—her name was Melinda, and she wore a wrinkled, dirty yellow dress and sniffed and looked generally friendless—would come to him after class and show him a rock she had found with markings on it. Was this a—*sniff*—fossil? How old did he think it was? And was it worth much money? Together they went to the library and found a book on geology that contained some nice line drawings of common fossils. They compared Melinda's fossil to the drawings and determined that it was likely from a kind of coral, possibly from the Paleozoic era, which meant that her fossil could've been, what? Three hundred million years old?

"Three hundred million years old! Gosh. Think of that," he said. "That's from before the dinosaurs. This whole continent was underwater, nothing here but a great big sea. . . . You're a lucky girl," he told her, carefully handing back her rock. "You've found something very special." Melinda went off sniffing and staring at her fossil like it was a diamond, and he felt a glow of satisfaction upon recognizing that, without hardly even trying, he'd won a convert: a girl who might lack for friends and clean dresses, but who from that day on would never lack for wonder in her life.

He gradually came to think of himself as a defender of students like Melinda. The girls who collected rocks, the boys with glasses who cringed when balls were thrown their way, the overweight, the underfed, the shy or awkward or stuttering loners who lingered at the edges of his classes: these became his favorites, the ones he gave special attention to, because in them he saw the image of himself as a boy, that lonely kid sitting in his room at night with his astronomy books and homemade radio.

Still, however much he began to feel useful at the school—a sense that he might actually be needed there—it would not have been enough to make him abandon his dream of graduate study and stay in Terrebonne.

That would only happen, as he would tell it later, after he met a certain girl in a certain drugstore one certain night.

CHAPTER EIGHT

MY mother, back when the new neighborhood behind us was first being developed, would sometimes take me and Megan there on Sunday afternoons "for a look-see."

I'd leave whatever book I was reading and we'd slide into the family Rambler, an economy model with a blue exterior, hot vinyl seats, and no air-conditioning—"a car that only a drunk door-to-door salesman would drive," my mother complained. She'd steer us out of our neighborhood, across the Franklin Street bridge, and past the handsome wooden sign planted in a bed of cedar chips: "Beau Rivage Estates." It was a glamorous name for a place that until recently had been a low wet field where people dumped old car tires and where Peter and I went to light fires and play soldiers. The windows down, we would roll slowly from one end of the neighborhood to the other along freshly paved streets, into cul-de-sacs and out, peering up at the large homes with their landscaped lawns and newly planted trees.

As she drove, I saw my mother's face take on the same covetous look it got whenever she brought us shopping at D. H. Holmes in New Or-

leans. In the cool lights and perfumed air of the department store, she
became like a starving animal searching for food. Her lips would go thin
and her eyes would dart from one side of the aisle to the other. If she saw
something she liked, a dress or a new kitchen appliance, she'd step
quickly to it and shoot out a hand to find the price tag. She'd peek at it,
tighten her face, and then tuck the price tag back into place before pulling us along to the escalators for the half-off discount racks in the base-
ment.

She was the same on our Sunday afternoon sightseeing drives.
"Don't gawk," she said as we stared out the windows with her. "Pretend you live here." But even her saying that made it plain that we
would never live there. We would only ever be tourists, gazing up at
the homes that we would never enter, dreaming of the luxuries we
could never afford.

After our tour of Beau Rivage Estates and a conciliatory stop at the
Tastee Freez, we'd return to our own nameless neighborhood. Bumping
along the asphalt road that crumbled away on either side into open
drainage ditches, seeing the mildewed clapboard houses with their
rusting pickup trucks in front, the tilting tin sheds out back, the broken toys in muddy yards, we could practically hear our mother sigh in
disappointment—at herself, at her husband, at our own shabby middle-
class existence. She tried, god knows she tried, but in spite of everything she did to keep up appearances, she still hadn't managed to scrape
the mud of this town off her shoes.

But just as the comet had begun to work its changes on my father, so
it began to affect my mother. A glimmer of possibility shone up there in
heaven—we all sensed it—and seeing the attention he'd begun to enjoy
on account of his comet, and reading his weekly column in the newspaper, and marking the new confidence in his step as he set off for school
in the mornings kindled in her the hope that our fortunes might still
improve, that our life could be better than what it was. And if there was
any model for what that better life looked like, it was the Martellos.

My mother started to linger in the backyard on the lookout for them as she rearranged her potted plants on the porch. She spoke casually about changes to their house or garden: "They're almost finished getting those lamps installed above the boardwalk. That'll look good, won't it?"

At the dinner table she began to wonder aloud about them: "I saw Barbara outside again today. I went down to the edge of the water and we had a nice long chat. She seems like really a very friendly woman." She'd heard from some ladies in town that Barbara was from a prominent Shreveport family, but you could tell just by talking to her that she came from quality. Very gracious, very well mannered. "Honestly, I'm ashamed I haven't bothered to introduce myself before now. I mean, I see her out there all the time."

About Frank, she hadn't heard so much. "Someone said he used to play football for that college up in Shreveport. What is it? Northwestern? Louisiana Tech? Anyway, he used to play football there, and then he worked at Shell for years and years before he was transferred down here." From what people said, she understood that Frank was pretty high up in the company—regional vice president or something like that. He was in charge of the whole area now.

"Have you met him yet?" she asked my father across the table.

He looked up from his plate. "Met who?"

"Frank. Frank Martello."

"Where would I have met Frank Martello?"

"I don't know. You go into town, you might see him around."

"Nope. Haven't met him."

"What about Gabriella?" she asked, turning to me. "What's she like? You must know her pretty well by now."

I blushed at the mention of her name. "Not really."

"But you're in the same class, aren't you? And you don't talk to her? Why not?"

What a horrible, awkward question to ask, I thought. Wasn't it obvious? Just look at the Martellos and then look at us. I would have liked to talk to Gabriella, sure, but in the one month we'd been sitting in classes together, we still hadn't exchanged two words. I doubted she even knew my name. It wasn't that she was standoffish; on the contrary, she seemed quite friendly. The problem was that I was still too shy, too much in awe to approach her. I could still only watch her from a distance, admiring the tilt of her head, her queenly walk around the school grounds at recess.

My mother went on wondering aloud about the Martellos like this for several days, speaking as much to herself as to the rest of us, sounding as if she was circling around and around some notion she had but was too timid to articulate: Didn't Barbara get bored in that big house all day long? It must've been hard for her, not knowing anyone here. She really would've liked to have gone on chatting with her that afternoon, but she felt like a hillbilly shouting across the water at her like that. . . .

Until my father, looking up from his lesson plans one evening, said, "Good lord. You should just invite them over if you're so all-fired eager to meet them."

"Oh, no, we couldn't do that," she answered reflexively.

"Why not? Just call them up, tell them to come over. They can come and fool around with the telescope some night. Come and check out the comet."

My mother dismissed this outright as a ridiculous idea. "You can't be serious, can you? Invite the Martellos to come here and play with your telescope?"

"Sure. Everybody likes that kind of thing. A stargazing party."

"A stargazing party. Where'd you get that idea? Good lord. That's the dumbest thing I've ever heard of." She shook her head at my father's hopelessness. "A stargazing party."

But later that same night, after she'd cleared the table and cleaned the kitchen and put away the dishes, she said that it might not be such a bad idea after all.

I looked up from my homework, my father looked up from his papers, not quite sure what she was talking about.

"I mean, why shouldn't we be friendly?" she said, standing in the doorway with a dish towel in her hands. "They're our neighbors, after all. Junior and Gabriella are in the same grade. You're her teacher. Why wouldn't they want to come over? People are people."

My father could set up his telescope—or rather, my telescope—in the backyard. They'd call the Martellos over, have cocktails, sit for some snacks and chitchat, and then we'd all go out and look at the comet. It could be fun. Just a small, informal affair with the two families, a chance to get to know one another. A stargazing party.

"Sure. Sounds fun," my father said, and bent back to his work.

She looked to me. "What do you think? Should I invite them?"

"Why not?" I said—although privately, I doubted the Martellos would want to have anything to do with us.

I was only fourteen, but even I understood that people who lived in Beau Rivage Estates didn't socialize with people who lived in our neighborhood. They joined the country club in Thibodaux, and played golf and tennis, or went fishing at their weekend homes on Grand Isle. The waterway between our houses marked a boundary as clear as the one between white and black, rich and poor. It was just like at the school yard, only with adults: the Martellos had their circle, my parents had theirs, and the two were never meant to overlap.

But regardless, over the next few days, my mother began making plans. There was some back and forth on the date. My father insisted that the viewing conditions had to be good. My mother said that it had to be on a weekend. He said you couldn't negotiate with a comet; it was guided by its own immutable laws, laws that human beings might never completely understand but about which we could at least make informed guesses. He checked with the LSU Astronomy Department, did some calculations, and proposed a Saturday in October when the comet should be visible as it crossed into the constellation Libra.

CHAPTER NINE

"I'M going," my mother announced that weekend, a note of defiance in her voice.

She spent the morning making cupcakes, and in the afternoon she asked Megan to go with her to deliver an invitation to the Martellos. Megan didn't want to. "Do this for your mother, Meg," pleaded our father. "Just this once, okay?"

As soon as they'd driven off in the car, I went upstairs to my room and uncapped the Celestron. In a minute they arrived at the Martellos' house. My mother pulled up on the wrong side of the road and parked the Rambler at the curb near their driveway. She got out, straightened her clothes, and then led the way along the sidewalk carrying the cupcakes while Megan slumped behind her in a white peasant blouse, the two of them looking like villagers bearing gifts for a king.

I swiveled the telescope and found Frank Martello sitting in his chair in their patio room. He was drinking a beer and watching a football game on TV, enjoying the kind of casually masculine Saturday afternoon leisure activity that my father never did. After a moment he raised his head, stood, and disappeared. Soon several pairs of legs appeared in the room, their bodies cut off from my view by the tops of the window frames. I recognized my mother's and Megan's legs. Barbara Martello was wearing a gold and paisley muumuu; her legs had a tanned, healthy, country club look. A blue-jeaned Gabriella joined them, and then she and my sister left, bringing the cupcakes to the kitchen, I assumed.

Eventually the glass door slid open and the adults came outside onto the patio. Frank led my mother around the swimming pool, through the tall iron gates, and down the boardwalk to their boat dock, talking and pointing. Barbara followed them. As they spoke and gestured, I could almost read the words on their lips:

I love your flowers.

I want to put some up there, too, hang them from the lamp posts.

We'll bring the boat right up here.

He thinks he's going to keep a yacht here. He thinks we live on the Riviera.

Sure. This goes straight out to the Intracoastal Waterway. You could take it all the way to the Keys. Are you and—What's his name? The Professor? Alan?—are you and Alan much into fishing?

Oh, no. We just sit at home. Look at the stars.

My mother's visit seemed to be going surprisingly well. She was right, the Martellos looked like friendly people, not at all snobbish. She shared a laugh with Frank and touched his arm. When Gabriella and my sister came out to join them, I tracked them with the telescope, their images bobbing in the lens. Gabriella was eating one of my mother's cupcakes—a good sign, I thought. She and Megan stepped down to the dock, and then my sister abruptly swung her arm around and pointed across the water to our house.

I jerked away from the telescope and pressed against the wall. Had they seen me? Could they see up here? I waited a minute or two before creeping back to the window. By then, everyone had disappeared from the Martellos' yard. Soon I saw Megan and my mother returning to our car. I went downstairs to the kitchen, where my father was busy repairing the toaster at the kitchen table, took a cupcake, sat, and waited for the report.

"They're coming," my mother said when she and Megan came in through the front door. "Frank said they'd be delighted to spend an evening with the famous scientist. They've seen your column, they know all about you."

My father barely looked up from the toaster. "Oh? That's nice."

"You should see their house. Good lord. They've got about a dozen rooms downstairs. Frank's got a billiard room with a fireplace and a whole bar set up in there, like something you'd see in a movie."

"I thought it was excessive," Megan said, unwrapping a cupcake. "Why do you need a house that big for three people?"

"But they're nice, aren't they? They're a nice family," my mother said.

"Gabriella has her own powder room," Megan said. "Can you believe that? A *powder* room. With a private phone line. Everything's *yellow*."

Even as she criticized them, my sister sounded as impressed as our mother was by the Martellos and their fabulous wealth. They went on talking about the house, comparing notes on things they'd spotted during their walk-through. The dumbwaiter: Did Megan see that? Or what about the intercom system with the two-way speakers in all the rooms? And the grand piano, and the walk-in closets, and the whirlpool tub in the master bathroom? Barbara collected porcelain dolls from around the world that she kept in a glass display case. Frank had a wine cabinet with a humidor for his cigars. They had a two-car garage with two cars, Frank's white Cadillac and a sky-blue Lincoln Town Car for Barbara. Frank's workshop was as big as our living room and dining room combined, and upstairs there were two—*two*—extra guest rooms.

"Gorgeous. Gorgeous home," my mother said, finishing. She paused to catch her breath. I saw her eyes dart around our own shabby kitchen, through the doorway to our living room, fly around the walls in there, and come back to land on my father, who was bent over the toaster with the coils and burnt crumbs and pieces of tin junk scattered on the Formica tabletop.

"Did you hear anything we just said? The Martellos are coming here next weekend."

"I heard. I heard! Good. Great. Frank has a workshop that's as big as our living room and dining room combined. What do you want me to do about it?" He looked up, a screwdriver in one hand, his glasses slipping down his nose.

My mother pressed her lips together. "Nothing. Nothing," she said—and she was right. There was nothing he could do. What she wanted, it was clear, exceeded what he could give her. Her ambitions were bigger than the room, bigger than the house, bigger than him, even.

CHAPTER TEN

THAT same afternoon she began cleaning. She scrubbed the bathroom and kitchen. She stood on chairs and dusted the tops of window and door frames. She vacuumed the cushions on the sofa and rubbed furiously at a large gray stain on the Mexican rug in the living room, a stain that had been there so long that it seemed an indelible part of our lives, something that, like our own stubborn middle-class poverty, could never be fully erased, only endured.

During the week she took the car and drove up to New Orleans and bought a new dress for herself, a shirt for me, and a dinner jacket for my father. She arranged with her old friend Dale Landry, a lawyer, to borrow his maid for the party. She had me trim the azalea bushes in the front yard, and she planted new mums around the back porch.

She was at a loss over what to do about snacks until she saw a fondue set in the window of a local shop. Saturday afternoon before the party, she and Megan cut fruit and melted chocolate. She got my father to tend to the Sterno, and he spent some time experimenting with the flame and the baffle to find just the right temperature to maintain the chocolate at the proper viscosity.

That evening, I went upstairs to get myself ready to meet the Martellos. I tried on my new shirt in front of the mirror. The fabric was a shiny polyester decorated with stars and planets—my mother's idea, in keeping with the theme of the party. In her bedroom next door, Megan played her Roberta Flack album over and over, the songs of love and longing thumping softly through the walls in an artful echo of my own chaotic churn of emotions.

Soon Gabriella would be standing inside our house. It was like my birthday wish come true, only the fulfillment of this wish left me more worried than happy. Her visit here was like a visit from a celebrity. Clearly, she didn't belong in our home, with its worn-out orange sofa and broken linoleum floor and dirty Mexican rug. My mother had over-reached in inviting them. So much could go wrong. I was tempted to lock myself in my room and not come out until the night was over and the Martellos had passed through and we could go back to being our normal sad selves again.

Leaning in to the mirror, I discovered a small bump on my forehead. I prodded it with my fingertips. It was hard and painful to the touch, like a BB pellet stuck under my skin. Over the last half year my body had taken on a life of its own, erupting with new hair and smells and fluids. This, I supposed, was what our teachers meant when they talked about "life changes" and "maturation." It sounded almost beautiful the way they described it, but it wasn't; it was ugly and unpleasant. They should've just said "You become like werewolves," and we would've had a better idea of what to expect from puberty.

I went to work excavating the pimple. The trick, I knew, was to press low and wide of the center, dig in below the bump with my fingernails, and squeeze. The pimple burst, spitting a satisfying speck of white goo onto the mirror. But then I kept squeezing, thinking there must be more of it in there, until a bloody fluid oozed out. I stopped and fingered the spot, afraid now that I had done some serious damage. I found a Cub Scout neckerchief in my drawer and staunched the blood, but my clumsy operation had left a button-sized welt on my forehead. "Damn. Damn damn damn."

I heard my mother coming up the stairs. She checked next door with my sister first. "Oh, Megan. You're not going to wear that, are you?" she said, her voice dripping with disappointment. They argued for a minute, my mother complaining, as she always did, about Megan's clothes, her hair, her room, her general disregard for manners and appearances, before giving up and coming to my room. She knocked.

"Are you almost ready? The Martellos will be here soon."

"Okay."

"Are you wearing your new shirt? Can I see?" She opened the door. "Hey, that looks good. . . . Oh, no. What happened, honey? Was that a pimple?" She reached to touch it. I flinched.

"Ouch. Don't."

"You sure made a mess of that."

"I know. I know."

"Oh gee, and your new girlfriend's coming over."

"She's not my girlfriend. Where'd you get that idea? I don't even know her."

"Say 'yet.' "

"What?"

"She's not my girlfriend *yet*."

"I doubt if she'll ever be my girlfriend."

"Hey, show a little confidence. Wait a minute." She ducked next door to Megan's room and returned with some rubbing alcohol and makeup. She pulled my chair around. "Sit."

She bent in and cleaned the spot on my forehead. Then she applied flesh-colored makeup with a tiny brush, narrowing her eyes and pressing her lips together as she worked. Silver hoop earrings rocked back and forth on either side of her face. With her orange minidress and buckled high-heeled shoes, she looked awkward and young. I could almost see her as the teenage girl she must've once been—the pretty, preening daughter of Bob and Dot Simoneaux, an only child, slightly spoiled, romantic and willful. "Terrebonne's undiscovered star," my father used to tease her.

"Did you ever have boyfriends? I mean, before Dad."

"Sure. I was quite popular once, believe it or not. Dale Landry—you know him, don't you?—he was one of my boyfriends, before I met your father. We used to go out. He had the raciest car in Terrebonne, a snazzy silver Corvette. Gosh, that was fun."

She talked about how they would go cruising around town, down to the courthouse square. Everyone would be out, boys leaning against their cars, couples strolling arm in arm, old folks sitting on the benches beneath the oak trees. Those were the days, she said.

"But then you met Dad in the drugstore."

She laughed—not a happy laugh, exactly, but one you might use in talking about an embarrassing incident from your past.

"Right. Then I met Alan. I was working at the McCall's Rexall, he was a new teacher in town. Fresh from LSU. A city boy, smart as a . . . smart as a book."

I'd heard the story of their meeting before in one version or another from both my parents. For me, it had always stood as a kind of lesson on the way love was supposed to work: for every boy, one special girl was waiting. She might be down the street, or in the next neighborhood, or even halfway around the world, but you could be sure she was there somewhere, waiting just for him—just as all those years ago, my mother had stood behind the counter of the McCall's Rexall waiting for my father to walk in the door.

I prompted her to tell it again. "It was late at night. You were working all alone in the store."

"He came in wearing his jacket and tie from school. He said he had a stomachache."

"And he came back every night for a week."

"He kept buying medicine. I think we went through every stomach medicine in the store before he finally asked me out."

"And gradually you grew to like him."

"Um hm."

"Why?"

"Huh?"

"Why'd you like him?"

"What a question." She blended the edges of the makeup into my skin with her fingertips, thinking. "I liked him . . . I liked him because he seemed nice, I guess. And smart. And neat. And determined. I liked his name, too: Alan Broussard. Very sophisticated."

"And soon you were dating."

"Soon we were dating. He came and met my parents, I went to Baton Rouge to meet his." She grabbed a comb and went to work on my hair. "And then we got married. Just like that—*Ka-boom*. Crazy, huh? I was just nineteen years old, Alan was twenty-two. Practically kids. Not much older than you are now."

"I think I've still got a few years."

"Yes. Yes, I think you do." She drew a careful part down one side of my hair. "For our honeymoon we took the Sunset Limited from New Orleans to Los Angeles. The train left at midnight, and we almost missed it because Alan was arguing with the taxi driver about the fare—"

"You had to run to catch it—"

"We had a tiny cabin in the sleeper car—"

"He sneezed all night because of the dust, and you were afraid to walk between the cars. You rode for three days and three nights, and when you got to Hollywood, you stayed in an ugly motel on Sunset Boulevard."

"Wowser, you remember it almost as well as I do. And then what happened? Turn this way."

"You went sightseeing? You met some famous movie stars."

"Not quite. We tried. That's the part I wished had happened but didn't."

"You went to the observatory after that."

"He had to see the Palomar Observatory. That was his big thing, the Palomar Observatory."

I had always thought that this was the most romantic part of their story. I pictured my parents young and in love, standing side by side beneath an enormous telescope on a dark mountaintop as stars streaked overhead. . . .

"The observatory," she said now. "Can you believe that? For a honeymoon?"

"You didn't like it?"

She sighed through her nose. "I shouldn't say I didn't like it. I mean, sure, we had some fun times together." She stood back and looked at her handiwork, frowning. "I just want to know who made the rule that you had to stop having fun once you got married."

I barely had time to consider this before she said, "Here, take a look," and stepped out of the way so I could see the mirror. She straightened my collar. "There you go. A handsome young man. She'd be crazy not to like you."

"You're just saying that because you're my mother."

"I'm not! Really. You're a good-looking kid. You're nice, you're polite. Any girl would be lucky to have you for a boyfriend." She brushed some dandruff off my shoulders. "You just need to put yourself out there a little more. Try not to be so shy. Take a chance now and then. Life only comes around once, you know."

She rested her hands on my shoulders and found my eyes in the mirror. "Follow your heart. That's what I always say. Follow your heart, and the rest will follow."

The doorbell rang downstairs.

"Oh, god. Here they are." She tugged at the hips of her skirt. "This looks ridiculous, doesn't it?"

"I think you look good."

"Aw, thanks, honey. I don't get to hear that much anymore." She shouted into the hallway, "Megan!" Then she stood up straight and pulled her shoulders back.

"What do you say? Are we ready for this?"

CHAPTER ELEVEN

"HERE he is. The famous Professor."

My father twitched and grinned as Frank Martello came in and shook his hand. Standing under the low ceiling of our house, blocking the narrow doorway, Frank appeared larger than I'd expected. He wore a beige safari suit over a white shirt with an oversized watch on one wrist. Barbara stood beside him smiling politely, stealing uneasy glances around our front room. She had on a stylish-looking black cocktail dress with a strand of white pearls around her neck. For the introductions, Gabriella slid up between her parents and stood with her hands cupped below her waist and her hair draped forward over her shoulders. Then Megan and I were obliged to come forward, too, so that we were lined up facing one another, the Martellos and the Broussards, like rival teams before a game. Seeing my mother standing bare-legged and nervous in her orange minidress, and my father shifting and sniffing in his new checked dinner jacket, and Megan in her bell-bottoms and frizzy hair and worn-out denim jacket, and myself in my psychedelic polyester shirt that suddenly didn't look so cool anymore,

I was certain that in any kind of competition, according to any kind of rules, the Martellos would win, hands down.

My mother led everyone the two steps into the living room, conducting herself with an awkward formality. She indicated where each person should sit and made showy requests to Christine, our borrowed maid: "Christine, could you take Mrs. Martello's purse?" "Christine, I forgot to put out the nuts. Would you mind looking after that?"

My father took drink orders and then repeated them, pointing to each person in turn. "We'll get to work on that pronto!" he said, and backed into the kitchen, where he'd set up a corner of the counter for his bartending. I could see him in there checking recipes in a guidebook and measuring out jiggers and ponies as carefully as if he were conducting a laboratory experiment.

Frank settled back on the couch and stretched his arm along the top of the cushions. His shirt collar flared opened over the top of his safari jacket and his sleeves were rolled up, showing skin that was the same golden shade as his daughter's. Barbara sat well forward with her hands clasped together on her knees, as if she was uncomfortable sitting on our dirty sofa and meant to signal that their visit here was only temporary, that any minute they might be called away to more important engagements. I spotted a brown cockroach crawling slowly along the top of the wall above their heads, and I prayed that no one else would see it.

My mother began by apologizing for not inviting the Martellos over sooner; she followed up with some small talk about the weather, and then the Martellos' new home, and the neighborhood. As though to draw out our families' connections, she reminded everyone that Gabriella and I were in the same grade at school. She appeared to be taking her role of hostess very seriously; she sat carefully upright, smiling stagily and speaking in full, deliberate sentences, as if she were reenacting a scene that she'd been rehearsing in her mind for a long time.

Frank, more at ease, turned to me and Megan, still standing there, and said loudly: "So! Tell us about yourself. What do kids your age do for fun in Terrebonne?"

I looked to Megan. My sister, as starstruck as I was by our guests, spoke about activities that we rarely participated in but that sounded exciting. We went to football games, she said, or to parties with friends or boating on the lake. She claimed to especially like water-skiing, which surprised me because I didn't know she'd ever done that.

Barbara said that they'd never tried water-skiing, but they'd recently taken up snow skiing, out in Aspen, and she asked if we had ever tried that. "Oh, but you should," she said when we shook our heads. "We just love it. It's the best thing. Gabby can tell you all about it."

Gabriella, standing beside my sister, agreed that snow skiing was wonderful, she loved it, she couldn't wait to go again.

My mother, flinging herself back into the conversation, said that she had always wanted to try snow skiing herself, and that she kept asking Alan to take us, but we never managed to find the time. "He's just so busy with his work," she said, nervously smoothing the hem of her skirt. "Especially now, with the comet and all."

"Speak of the devil," Frank said, and sat up as my father carried in drinks on a tray.

"At your service."

My father served the drinks around, apologizing fussily. He'd had to substitute bourbon whiskey for rye whiskey in Frank's Manhattan. He explained how there was an element of chemistry involved in bartending. You couldn't just throw things together at random; different liquors reacted to one another in certain ways in certain combinations. You might be able to approximate the result with substitute liquors, but without the proper ingredients, you could never expect to produce the perfect cocktail.

"We don't need a lecture, Alan!" my mother said, and laughed tensely. "Just give us our drinks."

"I'll be your guinea pig, Professor. Let's see how you did." Frank had thick sideburns that extended low alongside his ears, giving him a rugged, commanding appearance; he was the type of man you instinctively looked to for the final word on anything. We all watched him bring the glass to his lips, watched his throat move. My father waited for the verdict.

"That's not bad. Not bad at all. Man, that's got a kick," Frank said, and my father wagged his head in pleasure.

CHAPTER TWELVE

DRINKS delivered, we children were free to go. My sister brought Gabriella up to her room to listen to records. I slunk off to the kitchen, then went outside and checked on my telescope in the backyard, then wandered upstairs. Megan's bedroom door was closed, but I could hear the two girls in there talking and listening to music. I dropped down on my bed and leaned against the wall. It didn't seem fair that my sister should have stolen Gabriella away so quickly like that. They weren't even in the same grade. What could they have possibly had in common?

I picked up a book and tried to read. It was a science-fiction novel I'd been enjoying lately, a terrific, strange story about war and time travel and four-dimensional aliens, but I couldn't lose myself in the words, not tonight with Gabriella right next door. I let the book fall on my chest. Gradually, as if by accident, I turned my head until my ear was pressed against the wall beside my bed. I heard Joan Baez singing and my sister speaking. I strained to make out what she was saying, but it was like trying to find shapes in clouds.

My sister, I imagined, would've been trying to educate Gabriella about music, and Bob Dylan and the origins of the folk movement in Greenwich Village. I knew the talk; I'd heard it plenty of times myself. So much of the music they played on the radio was just awful, Megan would say. People here didn't even know good music when they heard it; you couldn't even find any good records here. All the decent music got left behind somewhere on the other side of Nashville. By the time it trickled down to us here in no-man's-land, all that was left were the Osmonds, and the Carpenters, and Tony Orlando and Dawn, and all that other insufferable sugarcoated crap. If you really wanted to hear good music, she'd say, becoming insistent and superior as she did whenever she talked about it, if you really wanted to meet the cool people, you had to go to the source: New York City. That's where she'd be right now if she had any choice in the matter. You could bet that as soon as she was old enough to travel on her own, she'd be out of here, away from these dismal swamps and the redneck boys with their Camaros, and the empty-headed girls who dated them and married them and wanted nothing more than to raise their own litters of more redneck boys and girls. . . .

I gave up and pulled away from the wall and gazed out the window. From my bed I could see the thin crescent moon hanging low in the sky. It looked like a tilted bowl filled with a bright, silvery liquid, ready to overspill. The sight of it gave me a strange, aching emptiness. As though the moonlight had rendered the walls of our house transparent, I could picture Gabriella sitting on the floor of my sister's room, not two feet away. She was listening politely to my sister, nodding her head in time to the music while turning over an album cover in her hands. Her luxurious hair fell around her shoulders. She was so close that I might have reached out and stroked her hair, taken hold of her hand. . . .

I groaned, grabbed a pillow, squeezed it to my chest, and rolled back and forth on my bed while whispering her name: *Gabriella. Gabriella. Gabriella.*

After a while I lay still. I turned my head on the mattress and let my eyes roam around my room. I'd tidied it up that afternoon on the off chance that she might want to visit me here. I wondered what Gabriella would think, seeing my room. I followed the slope of the low ceiling down to my desk. There were my schoolbooks, a wooden ruler, a metal compass. *A studious boy,* she might think. *An intelligent boy.* Opposite my bed was my bookcase, with my plastic model airplanes and old marble collection on top. The books were arranged on the shelves from the oldest at the bottom to the newest on top, like strata of the Earth: from *Winnie the Pooh* up through *Treasure Island* to *Huckleberry Finn,* to *The Hobbit,* to *Lord of the Flies. A serious boy,* she would think. *A thoughtful boy.*

Hidden behind the bookcase—she wouldn't have been able to see this—were old issues of my sister's *Seventeen* magazine. I'd stolen stray copies over the years, desperate to understand more about the mysterious world of women: bra sizes, tampons, electric leg shavers. "Are You a Flirt?" the story headings read. "First Date Do's and Don'ts"; "What Do Boys Want?"

My friend Peter would've had a ready answer for that last question. "It's all about the sex," he liked to say. "Sex sex sex. Who gives it, who gets it, who doesn't."

I believed he was right, and sensing Gabriella so close to me now, her living, breathing body just on the other side of the wall, only reminded me of how woefully inexperienced I was. At fourteen years old, I still had never kissed a girl. I had never even held hands with one. And the things Peter talked about, rubbing the photos in his father's *Playboy* magazines while he described what you could do with a woman like that, *mm-mm,* seemed so far off in the future as to sound like science fiction. It wasn't that I was naïve; I understood how sex worked, at least as well as Peter did. But such a great gulf lay between my understanding and my experience that I wanted all those things a boy was supposed to want in only the most abstract sense. When I tried to think of Gabriella as one of those women in the magazines, I couldn't. She was more than a collection of shiny body parts, and my attraction to her was something greater and more profound—more pure, I would've said—than Peter's *mm-mm.*

Sex sex sex . . .

How that little word troubled me. It suggested a whole other world still shrouded in mystery. I caught glimpses of this alien world from time to time, in the glossy photos in Peter's magazines, or in graffiti on bathroom walls, or in stray glances and odd chuckles that passed, like secret messages, between grown-ups. But these were only glimpses, and I knew there was more to it than that. Lately, I'd begun to suspect that this world of sex was even bigger and more pervasive than I could imagine. It might've been everywhere; it was going on all the time, all around me, like a parallel life that was being played out, half seen, on the other side of a thin curtain.

I remembered the first clear confirmation I had of its existence. It came from, of all people, my father. It had been on a night like this. I was nine or ten years old, sitting up in bed doing my homework, when he knocked on my door.

"Can I come in?"

Slipping into my room, my father asked what I was working on. He blinked distractedly, his hands on his hips. The white corner of an envelope stuck out of his left pocket.

"That's interesting," he said. "Mind if I talk to you for a minute?"

He carefully closed the door behind him. He pulled out my desk chair and sat near the foot of my bed. He began by questioning me about my classes, my friends. He talked about when he was my age and what fun that was: biking all over town with his buddies, annoying their teachers, teasing girls.

"Do you have fun like that?"

"Sure."

"I'll bet you do."

He slid the fingers of his hands together and squeezed them between his knees. He cleared his throat. When he spoke again, it was in a more serious tone. *Now we're getting to it,* I thought.

"Your mother suggested I speak to you. I agreed that it would be a good idea. You're getting older now, and typically it's around this age—nine, ten years old—that a boy begins to develop a natural . . . *curiosity* about girls. This corresponds to a growing awareness of the human body and a recognition of the differences between the sexes."

He took a breather, cleared his throat again, and pushed his glasses up.

"You'll get this information in school anyway, but you might as well hear it from me now. Get a jump on the other kids."

He began speaking generally about the life cycle of plants and animals in nature. He described the reproductive system of plants; he spoke about pollen, and a flower's stamen and pistil and ovule; and then he talked about fruits and their seeds and flesh, "like an apple, for instance." He spoke so thoroughly and carefully that he might have been delivering a lecture. Soon I became bored and confused and a little sleepy.

At last he arrived at his main topic, which was human reproduction. "In other words, sex," he said, and coughed. *Finally*, I thought, and perked up.

I already knew the basics by then. On the playground at school or squatting behind a neighbor's garage, boys like Peter would share what they had found out about girls. Some spoke confidently, some sneakily, some with a show of toughness, spitting down into the dirt at their feet when they said what a woman was and what you were supposed to do with her. But I didn't entirely trust their information to be accurate. Now at least I'd get my facts straight.

My father spoke about the parallels between the reproductive systems of plants and humans. Women were like flowers, he said, in that their bodies also contained eggs that needed to be fertilized in order to reproduce. He described the female reproductive organs: the uterus, the ovaries, the fallopian tubes, the cervix, the vagina—

He broke off, flustered, and cleared his throat several times in a row.

"Maybe a visual illustration would help," he said, recovering. He stood up, put his feet together, and spread his arms in a T.

"It's like a little man. Imagine a little man standing inside a woman's body. These are the ovaries," he said, cupping his hands into fists. "My arms are the fallopian tubes. My chest can be the uterus." He explained how egg cells formed in the ovaries and traveled down the fallopian tubes, where they were fertilized by the man's sperm, thus creating life.

He sat back down. He sighed abruptly. When he spoke again, he spoke slowly, almost sadly, as if he regretted what he had to say.

"Now. This is the important part. On the night of their wedding, the husband and wife lie together in each other's arms. And the man . . . carefully . . . impregnates the woman. This is natural. It's nothing to be afraid of. It's a very . . . very . . . lovely event."

He stopped and looked down solemnly at the floor. We were quiet for a moment. I held still. The air in the room was syrupy and warm. I felt myself sweating beneath my pajamas. Was he finished?

"Okay. I understand. Thank you," I said.

"You may hear people talking bad about this," my father cautioned. "Boys especially like to tell jokes and so forth. But I assure you there's nothing wrong or ugly or dirty about sex. It's perfectly natural. It's a part of life. I do believe, however, as most people do, that it is something that should be reserved for marriage. Something that occurs only between a husband and wife." He added, as if it were a point he'd almost forgotten, "Women are special. Always respect women. Women are like flowers."

I nodded.

"Do you have any questions? Anything. You can ask me. I'm your father."

"No. I think that's all clear."

"Good."

He sat back in his chair, relieved that he'd said what he had to say. He patted his hands together a couple of times and looked around my room. He picked up a model airplane from my bookcase, glanced at it, and set it back down. He seemed reluctant to leave now.

I was relieved, too. I didn't understand the actual how-to business of human reproduction any better now than when he first came into my room, but I was glad he'd stopped talking about it. Sex, in his telling, sounded like a kind of dark fairy tale, strange and a little spooky.

Eventually he got up to leave. He paused at my door. "I'm glad we had a chance to talk. If you have any more questions, I'm always here."

"Thank you."

"Thank you," he said, and closed the door behind him.

That's when I noticed the folded white envelope on the floor. It must've fallen out of his pocket when he stood to leave. I picked it up. On the back was written in neat, cursive pencil:

—teenager, curiosity, changes
—nature's life cycle
—reproductive system of plants: pollen, stamen, pistil, ovule
—   "   "   " humans // plants: uterus, ovaries, fallopian tubes, cervix, vagina
—lovely event
—respect for women

My father's notes on the science of love. I tucked the envelope into my desk drawer, where it stayed. I never consulted it again. But after that night, I could barely look at a girl without picturing a tiny man resembling my father standing inside her belly with his feet together and his arms outstretched, saying solemnly, *"Women are special. Always respect women. Women are like flowers."*

At fourteen, I still believed that this was true. But I also had the nagging suspicion that the natural, lovely event to which my father referred was more powerful, more dangerous and wild than his science would admit.

CHAPTER THIRTEEN

CHRISTINE was washing dishes in the kitchen when I wandered back downstairs.

"You've been quiet. Where've you been?"

"Upstairs. Reading."

I dipped strawberries in melted chocolate from a pot on the stove while I peeked through the doorway at the adults in the next room. The hi-fi played jazz, and they were talking animatedly, laughing loudly now and then.

"Sounds like they're enjoying themselves," Christine said.

"Sure does."

She was a chubby-faced black woman with rust-colored hair and oversized glasses. She wore a full-length white apron, like what a chef might wear. We'd never had a maid in our house before, and I watched her curiously as she ran water in the sink, adding dish soap and stirring it with her fingers to raise the suds.

"Your daddy's got that column in the newspaper, doesn't he?"

"Yes, ma'am. Groovy Science, that's right."

"I thought that was him. The scientist. Your momma said y'all are going to look at the comet tonight."

"We've got the telescope set up in the backyard."

"I heard about that comet. I haven't seen it yet, though."

"It's going to be huge."

"That's what I heard. That comet scares me. You're going to get sick, you keep eating all that chocolate."

I got myself a Coke and leaned back against the counter, listening in on the conversation in the next room. My father had started in on his old story about how he ended up in Terrebonne. He told about the accident of the recruitment fair at the university field house, and then his secondhand car with his five new ties and his temporary teaching credential, and the black snake in the middle of the road outside of Napoleonville. . . .

"Oh no, here he goes again," said my mother. "Mr. Marco Polo, to the rescue."

. . . and then his early days as a teacher, and how half his students used to come to school by boat, clomping into his classroom in their fishing boots. And the deplorable conditions at the school back then, with the doors falling off their hinges and the windows broken and the rain leaking in through the ceiling and dripping onto his papers . . . "Dreadful. Just dreadful. Even worse than it is now, if you can believe that." He was starting in on his usual complaint about the neglect of sciences in the Louisiana public schools when my mother cut him off.

"Okay, Alan, that's enough! Nobody wants to hear all that," she said, and laughed anxiously.

"No, no, I'm curious," Frank said. Sitting up, he asked my father if he'd seen much improvement in the local schools, because to be honest, they'd had some concerns about that when they moved here.

Barbara Martello, joining in, said that if it was up to her, they'd have sent Gabriella to a private school. It was a question of "standards," she insisted. Everyone knew that a private school had higher standards than a public school.

My mother agreed. She said something about my father's work being "charity," and if it were up to her, she'd do the same with her children.

Frank argued that the nearest private school was over forty miles away, and anyway, if public schools were good enough for him growing up—

"But things were different when we were kids," Barbara said. "Schools were safer then."

"Now they're just big zoos!" said my mother.

"Oh, let's just say it: my wife's afraid of the blacks," said Frank. "She thinks they're all savages."

"This has nothing whatsoever to do with race," Barbara protested. "I'm talking about standards."

I stole a peek at Christine to see if she was hearing any of this. She'd become very preoccupied with a spot on the edge of the sink, frowning as she scrubbed it with a washcloth.

"Ask him. Let's ask him," Frank said. "Hey, Junior!"

"Oh, no, don't bother him."

"Sure, why not? We've got an expert right here. I just saw him go into the kitchen. Junior!" Frank called again.

"Go see what they want," Christine told me.

"Yes, sir?"

The adults looked up as I stepped into the room. They all held drinks or had drinks resting on the coffee table. Except for a small mess of chocolate and strawberry stems in front of my father, the fondue hadn't been touched.

Barbara turned to my father. "I believe he looks just like you, Alan."

"That's why we call him Junior," my father said, and snorted a laugh.

Frank Martello bounced nuts in his right hand, like they were hot, before popping them one by one into his mouth. "Your folks and I have been talking about the local schools. My wife's worried about what kind of education Gabriella will get here. She's afraid the high school isn't safe. She thinks it's a jungle of sin and vice—"

"That's not what I said."

"That's not what she said," my mother echoed.

"Poor standards. You said you thought the school had 'poor standards,'" my father said, diplomatically.

"And I agreed," my mother said, nodding.

"And so what we want to know is," Frank said, going on, "from the student's point of view, whether you think you're getting a quality education."

They watched me expectantly. I hesitated, not sure what they wanted to know. I tugged my shirt from my chest.

"What kind of quality?"

"Well, you know, the school, the facilities, the curriculum . . ."

"The teachers," my father said.

"The teachers," said Frank.

"They seem all right, I guess," I said. "Not too bad."

"Would you call it a rigorous education?" Frank asked.

"Well—" I said.

"What about the students?" asked Barbara, sitting up. "How are they? Your classmates?"

"She means the blacks," said Frank.

"I do not. I mean all the students."

"They seem . . . fine. Mostly," I said. "They're friendly enough."

"A mixed bunch," my father put in.

"No student unrest, that kind of thing? Agitation?" asked Frank.

"No. . . . Things seem pretty quiet now."

My mother spoke up. "What about drugs? Do you see a lot of drugs at school?" She added in an aside to Barbara, "They all go to school high on drugs."

"Marijuana, for example," Frank said.

"You know what marijuana is, don't you?" my father asked me.

"Everyone knows what marijuana is!" said my mother.

"Well?" Frank asked. "You see much of that?"

In fact, I'd heard rumors that a few kids in my class smoked pot, but I had never seen it. I wasn't even sure what it looked like.

"Not much," I said.

"Not much?" Barbara asked, worried.

"I mean hardly any. None."

"There, you see?" my father said. "It's not as bad as you think, Barbara."

I expected that next they would ask me to look after Gabriella while she was at school—to take her under my wing and make sure she was safe there—but they didn't. Instead, they went on to talk about the problem with kids in general these days, and the generation gap, and who knew what the world was coming to. Soon they seemed to have forgotten that I was even there, but I stayed just in case I was needed to verify anything else.

The music played. My father nodded eagerly and dipped strawberries in the fondue. My mother's nervousness seemed to be wearing off; she became excited as she spoke, her hands fluttering up from her lap and then settling back down to play with the hem of her skirt. She looked overjoyed to finally have company in our house.

For her part, Barbara attended politely to my mother without appearing to actually hear her; I caught her glancing once or twice at the front door, like she was impatient to leave. Frank, though, looked genuinely happy to be here. He ate nuts, and hunched forward, and joked and argued with my mother, and teased my father about the difficulty of pleasing the womenfolk.

"Oh, Frank, you're terrible!" my mother said, and playfully slapped his knee.

I saw Frank's eyes drift to my mother's legs. They slid from the hem of her skirt, to her knees, down to her ankles, and back up again, as though he were painting her legs with his eyelashes. Then he looked up at her face and smiled, prompting my mother to redden and smile in return.

I felt hot-faced and queer for having witnessed such a thing, if indeed I had witnessed anything at all, because immediately Frank was again laughing and popping nuts into his mouth. My mother shyly touched her hair. My father, oblivious as usual, only sniffed and pushed his glasses up on his nose and checked his watch. But then he sprang up from his chair, and everyone leaned back to look at him.

"Oops! It's time. Let's go."

"What's time?" Barbara asked.

"The comet. It's here. Twenty-one hundred hours. We should be able to catch it in Leo now if we're lucky."

"Let's not keep the comet waiting, then," said Frank. "Hi dee ho."

CHAPTER FOURTEEN

MY mother clutched Frank's arm as he helped her down the wooden steps from the kitchen into the backyard.

"Wowser, what was in that drink?"

"Steady, girl."

"I can't see anything."

Barbara looked on as my father consulted numbers on a piece of paper and adjusted the telescope with the aid of a penlight. He had turned off the houselights so that we could see the sky better, and the darkness added an extra intimacy to our yard, causing everyone to huddle in closer and talk more softly, as though we were gathered around a campfire. The bayou lay still and black, and the water was filled with stars.

"That's an unusual-looking instrument you've got there," Frank said, leaning in.

"It's Junior's, actually. A Celestron C8." My father explained how the telescope worked, how you focused it. "What you really want is elevation. A high, dark place, away from the ambient light of the city."

"Reflection, refraction, half the time I have no idea what he's talking about," my mother said.

Barbara asked about the comet. "Will it really be as big as everyone says?"

"My opinion? I wouldn't be surprised if it was even more spectacular than what people expect. I haven't seen the scientific community this excited since the Moon landing." He explained how scientists were usually quite conservative in their predictions, so if they said that something was, to use the layman's term, "big," you could very well expect "enormous."

Frank gave a low whistle. Megan and Gabriella clomped down the steps to join us. Gabriella halted near me and shoved her hands into the back pockets of her jeans. She gave a quick smile. I smiled in return and immediately looked away. A swampy-sweet smell hung in the air, and the Spanish moss draping the trees waved in a slight breeze.

We all watched my father working the telescope for a moment, until he breathlessly announced, "Yes. Yes. Yes. There it is. I've got it. That must be it. Oh my goodness. Comet Kohoutek."

We looked from the telescope to the sky, expecting to see something moving up there. Even Frank and Barbara were excited by the sighting. They peered curiously at the stars while my father, hunched at the telescope, made small, panting noises of astonishment.

"Okay, okay, let someone else have a peek, Professor," Frank said at last.

My father pulled himself away from the eyepiece and helped each of us take a turn at the telescope. As he did so, he repeated a version of his classroom lecture on comets: their origins, their composition, their appearance and trajectories. He reminded us how Kohoutek was a relic from the birth of the solar system, likely older even than the Earth itself, and that already it had been traveling for millions of years across space to reach us. It was thought to be a virgin comet, he said, making its very first pass through the solar system, so we should get to see some really spectacular displays of outgassing as it came closer.

"A virgin comet, you say?" Frank said, amused.

"Now, Frank—" my mother warned.

"What? I wasn't going to say anything." He moved in for his turn, and my father helped him get adjusted at the eyepiece. "There? Is that it? That's the comet? That's just a little bitty sucker. You can barely see it."

"Don't let it fool you," my father said. "It's still over two hundred million miles away. That little sucker is about four times the size of our Earth."

If, as he expected, Kohoutek continued to grow in magnitude as it approached the Sun, and if its nucleus remained intact and didn't break apart, then by December it could easily outshine the Moon. It'd be the brightest thing in the night sky. At Christmastime we'd be able to read our newspapers at midnight by its light.

Barbara asked about the scary predictions some people were making: how the gas from the tail would poison our drinking water, or how the radio waves would disrupt electrical systems and shut down power stations. There could be blackouts all across the country. Trains would stop running, planes would crash to the ground. There was a preacher in Shreveport who was saying that the comet had been sent by God to wipe out sinners from the Earth.

"Seriously—we're not in any danger, are we, Alan?"

" 'And a great star fell from heaven to smite the sinners of the Earth! And the name of the star was Wormwood! Woe, woe, woe!' " My father laughed lightly and pushed up his glasses. "You always get that with comets."

The problem, he said, was when emotions overtook reason, causing people to behave irrationally. The same thing happened with Halley's. People went crazy, buying gas masks and stuffing wet towels under their doors. Some wackos even leapt to their deaths from the roofs of buildings, believing the world was coming to an end.

"People tend to become overly excited concerning things that they know little about," he explained. But there shouldn't be anything to worry about with Kohoutek. Its trajectory was such that as it crossed the Earth's orbit—twice, coming and going—it'd miss us by a long shot. At its closest, it'd still be some 60 million miles away.

"Of course," he added cleverly, his shoulders twitching, "comets have always been wildly unpredictable. No one ever quite knows what they'll do."

"Like women," Frank said. "Wildly unpredictable. Isn't that right, Lydia?"

"Don't say that," my mother said, and slapped his arm.

"She's always hitting me. Why are you hitting me?"

I finally got my turn at the telescope. I bent down to the eyepiece. The lens was dotted with points of light. In their center was a small, bluish star with a hazy bump on one side. It didn't move, only hovered there, vibrating slightly, as though it were charged with some great but restrained power. As I continued to stare at it, the comet seemed to come alive, slowly swelling and shrinking, like it was breathing. I realized that it was moving in time to my own breath, as though it were somehow connected to my body. When I pulled away from the telescope, I felt myself still thrumming in time to the comet. And when I looked at our two families standing in the dark in our yard, I could easily believe that everyone had been similarly touched by the sight of the comet, so that our lives were bound together now in some strong but as-yet indefinable affiliation.

"Someone go get Christine. She should see this, too," my father said, and Megan went inside to fetch her. The maid came down the steps, quietly excited.

"Good lord," she said, hunched in an awkward squat at the eyepiece; she was trying not to touch the telescope with any part of her body. "Look at that. I see it. Oh, my gracious. Great God in heaven, here it comes."

CHAPTER FIFTEEN

MY father was reluctant to leave the telescope, but eventually he was coaxed back inside to fix more drinks for our parents, leaving us teenagers alone in the dark yard.

Bullfrogs croaked. We could hear jazz music start up again in the living room as my mother put on another record. I rested a hand on the telescope and swiveled it back and forth. Stars hung all around us, as distant and close as heaven itself.

Gabriella stood not five feet away from me, standing on the same ground that I stood, breathing the same air that I breathed. I was almost paralyzed with nervousness to be so near her. This was another thing they failed to teach you at school: what to say, what to do when you were standing side by side with a beautiful girl. Gabriella broke the silence.

"Do you know how to work it?"

"Oh, yeah. Sure. I should. It's my telescope. What do you want to see?"

"No more comets. Please," my sister said. "I'm sick to death of comets."

Gabriella looked around. She pointed down the bayou to the left. "How about the Daigles' house? Can you do that?" Her voice was low, relaxed.

"Which one?"

"There at the end. The last one."

I aimed the Celestron at the house across the water. As I did, I explained about degrees of declination and ascension, the finderscope and the focus control.

"Oh my god, you sound just like Dad," said Megan.

"You guys must be really smart," Gabriella said. "I mean, with your father a science teacher and all."

"Our father's such a nerd," Megan said. "It's so embarrassing. I hate it."

I found the Daigles' kitchen window and invited Gabriella to have a look. I stepped aside as she bent to the eyepiece, looping her hair over her right ear. Her lips fell open; her lashes brushed the rubber socket of the eyepiece.

I felt a tug in my stomach. Everything about her was perfect. I wanted to reach out and trace her features with my finger: the fuzzy fringe of hair on her forehead, the rounded tip of her nose, the tiny dent above her chin. I wondered what she would do if I did touch her—just her hair. If I just touched her hair with my finger. She'd probably scream.

"Oh my god. You can see everything. They had pork chops for dinner. And mashed potatoes. And wait—Mrs. Daigle just came into the kitchen. She's talking to somebody in the next room. This is so cool. It's like you're right there with them. I can see the clock on the stove."

"Let me see," Megan said, and Gabriella moved aside.

We toyed some more with the telescope. The girls pointed out objects and I swiveled the instrument so we could examine each one: the lettering on the side of a batteau docked up near the Franklin Street bridge; the blinking red warning light on top of the water tower, its round tank rising like a pale green planet above the trees at the edge of our neighborhood. From inside the house behind us came a trickle of laughter. The water on the bayou rippled lightly, as if in sympathy with the sound. The reflected stars wavered and winked, and the moss in the trees swayed like seaweed in a current.

As though touched herself by the gentle mood of the night, Gabriella said, thoughtfully, "I remember you wrote that poem. 'I am the comet, far far away.' "

"Oh, right. That was dumb."

"I liked it. What was it? 'I am the comet, far far away . . .' "

"I don't remember."

"Yes you do."

"Junior wrote a poem?" said my sister at the telescope.

"We all had to. Come on. Say it."

"I don't—"

"Say it."

I recited quickly: "Far, far away, sailing pale and quiet past the stars, I am the comet, you are the Sun, beautiful Sun, unfreeze my heart and see me shine."

"See? That's nice." Her voice was soft, almost a whisper.

"Aw," my sister said. "He's the comet."

"Shut up," I said, and took the telescope back from her.

I stole a glance at Gabriella. She was watching me with a curious smile on her lips. Was it amusement? Admiration? Our eyes met for a second. I nodded quickly, as if to tell her, *Yes—it's you. You're the Sun,* and then ducked to the scope.

The moment had lasted only an instant, but it was ours, a private understanding between us. She knew. Of course she knew. How could she not? As I fiddled with the knobs, I sensed her looking at me, and I felt a confused, pleasant, swirling sensation in my chest.

Then she said, "Don't you dare spy on our house."

"What?"

"With your sneaky telescope."

"I wouldn't—"

She pinched my arm. "I mean it. Don't!"

I jerked away. "Ouch! That hurt."

She laughed, and I rubbed my arm, surprised but also secretly thrilled. My skin tingled where she had pinched me, a small, hot burn—our first contact.

CHAPTER SIXTEEN

"SHOULD be some good viewing next week, too," my father said, rocking on the balls of his feet.

The Martellos stood in the yard as our family crowded together on the front porch to see them off. Crane flies bounced off the yellow light bulb overhead. Down at the side of the porch, a cockroach inched along the wall of the house, and I wondered for a second if it was the same one I'd seen earlier, following us outside in one last attempt to ruin our evening.

My father promised Frank that he would come over tomorrow to take a look at his fountain; there was some electrical problem with the pump that he thought he might be able to fix. My mother repeated an invitation for the Martellos to come and visit us again. They were welcome anytime, anytime at all, she said. Just give a shout; we were always here, just across the water. In reply, Frank reached up and, in a teasing show of gallantry, kissed the back of her hand.

"Goodness, I feel like Juliet," she said, and my father, hugging himself, chuckled and slapped his own arms.

Barbara was already walking away across the yard. "Frank? Are you coming?"

My parents shouted more pleasantries as the Martellos headed to their car, their words trailing off into unfinished promises and gestures. Megan and I exchanged goodbyes with Gabriella until, reaching the road, she pivoted ballet-like on her feet. The streetlight shone on the glossy white finish of their Cadillac. I was reminded of the gulf between us, and as they receded from our porch and approached their car, they seemed not to diminish but to grow in size and stature until, opening the car doors and waving to us one last time, the spell that had cast us as equals was broken and they were revealed once again as our rich, distant neighbors. The whole evening was already beginning to feel like a dream—an unlikely visit to our home by a family of Roman-sized gods.

Standing in the open rear door of the car, Gabriella suddenly shouted, "Hey, Junior." I jerked my head up. "You are the comet!"

Then she dropped down inside the car, smiling, and closed the door. The headlights came on, the tires crunched on the gravel shoulder, and the night closed behind them as the Martellos drove away.

My parents were talking and cleaning up in the living room when I carried my telescope in through the back door and up the stairs.

"We should invite other neighbors over, too," said my father. "People like this sort of thing."

"See, I told you," said my mother. "Didn't I tell you? There's no reason why we can't be friends. They're our neighbors, after all, just—"

"—real friendly, real ordinary folks. No, no. You're right."

"All you have to do is ask, right? I'm mean, we can't expect—"

"—can't expect them to ask us, I know."

"I mean, it's only polite that we should invite them first. We're the locals, after all, they're the newcomers. . . . I think they had a good time, don't you? That Frank, he's a wild one."

"Are you taking Christine home or am I?"

I shut my door, turned off the light, and set up the Celestron at the window. I scanned the back wall of their house and found again what I believed to be her bedroom. The light was on but the curtains were closed behind the French doors. I adjusted the focus and waited.

Nothing happened for some time. Other lights came on and went off in their house. My parents' muffled voices seeped up through the floor as they continued to talk downstairs. Then there was a movement behind one of the French doors, the curtain was pulled aside, and suddenly there stood Gabriella. She hesitated a minute, looking out through the glass. Then she fiddled with the door, opened it, and stepped out onto her balcony.

She was wearing a ruffled yellow nightgown and her hair was pulled back from her neck. She rested her hands on the edge of the balcony and looked down into their patio, the light from the swimming pool casting wavering diamonds across her face and body. Slowly she raised her eyes and looked across their lawn down to the black water gliding between our yards. I could see past her into her room. It was like peering into a dollhouse; every object, every piece of furniture within had the charmed and distinct preciousness of a miniature: her yellow canopied bed, her vanity desk with its mirror and stool, a painted trunk, a nightstand with a lamp with a flowered shade. And in the foreground was Gabriella herself, standing on the balcony in her yellow nightdress, an exquisite doll come to life. My mouth felt dry; I could barely swallow.

She abruptly raised her face toward our house. I didn't think she could see me—my room was dark and the distance between us was too great—but I didn't dare move. I froze, holding my breath as I watched her through the scope. She lingered for a moment, as if she were remembering something. The corners of her lips rose slightly. Then she stepped back into her room, closed the doors, and drew the curtains shut.

I went to bed filled with a hot, restless energy. I couldn't sleep. I had witnessed something significant: she had smiled. Gabriella had smiled, and in that smile, a whole universe was born—stars and planets, galaxies and solar systems, blooming like flowers in the sky.

CHAPTER SEVENTEEN

Today: Do something for yourself for a change. Get out, enjoy the weather. Don't be shy—friends are waiting to hear from you. They'll be glad you called. Virgo rising says you're due for a streak of good luck, so be on the lookout for some exciting news around the middle of this week.

The Monday morning after our stargazing party, my mother, her face still puffy from lack of sleep, came out to the front step to see me and Megan off to school.

"Have fun!" she shouted, her voice cracking.

Seeing her standing there in her old pink bathrobe, clutching her coffee cup, I couldn't help but think that she would have gladly run down the steps and joined us if she could, so forlorn and abandoned she looked just then. Megan and I waved, got on the bus, and soon enough I forgot all about her, back there at home doing whatever she did all day while we were at school: cleaning up after breakfast, making our beds, sorting through the laundry, cooking our dinner . . .

But then again, later that week while sitting at the table doing my homework, I happened to look up and see her in the kitchen washing up after dinner. Her eyes drifted out the window above the sink, across the water to the Martellos' house blazing with light on the other side of the bayou, and she forgot the plate she was drying in her hands and stood there as though mesmerized.

What, I wondered, could she have been thinking? What made my mother so obviously unhappy with her life? Because now, more and more, I began to see evidence of her dissatisfaction everywhere I looked: it was in the way she hungrily scanned her horoscope at the breakfast table in the morning, and the way she called goodbye to us as we set off to school, and the way she sighed out loud every time she stepped through the front door into our living room.

Sometimes late at night, after everyone else had gone to bed, I would come downstairs to find her asleep in front of the TV, a half-finished drink tilting precariously in one hand. On the screen would be an old black-and-white movie, the kind where glamorously dressed couples were always strolling through plantation gardens and twirling parasols. I'd slip the glass from her fingers, sniff it, and dump it in the sink.

"Let's go. Time for bed," I'd say, urging her up from the sofa.

"Is that—? Oh, I'm sorry, sweetie. I just . . . What time is it?"

"Bedtime."

Had she always been this way? Or was it only now, with my own growing distraction, that I started to notice something similar in her?

Back in my room, I turned once more to the stars for answers. I didn't need a telescope; all I needed was a dark room, a quiet house, and a window. I rolled my head on my pillow and squinted up at the scattered lights outside until I found again that chink in the sky between the stars. In my dreamy half sleep I could see, as though it were a movie projected on the rear wall of heaven, a picture of my mother as she once had been.

Yes, look: there she was, sitting on the living room floor of her parents' house, having a tea party with her favorite doll, Missy. Her father had made the miniature table and chairs himself; her mother had sewn her dress, a fancy yellow costume trimmed with lace and tulle.

"Now, Missy," I could hear my six-year-old mother saying. "Don't slump over in your chair like that. Would you like some more tea? Yes? Just a little? Okay, I'll pour it for you."

The tea was warm water colored with blackstrap molasses. The dessert was day-old bread, toasted with butter and sugar and cut into small squares, "tea cakes," her mother called them.

Little Lydia Marie prattled on: "I think it'll be a gorgeous day, don't you, Missy? Oh, yes. Gorgeous. What would you like to do today? Would you like to ride ponies? Wouldn't that be fun? Oh, yes. We can ride ponies. Would you like to see my pony? I have a lovely pony. What's your pony's name? My pony's name? My pony's name . . . is Esmerelda. Esmerelda! What a gorgeous name for a pony! Oh yes, I think so, too. . . . "

Although she never admitted it herself, I believed my mother had always felt special—like she was destined for great things in her life, even though there was nothing in her childhood that might have promised her that.

Of the Terrebonne of her youth, she would most often remember the oyster shell roads, and the four paved blocks of downtown, and the smelly municipal dump that always seemed to be on fire, blowing black smoke over the ramshackle houses and shops and fishing piers that made up her hometown. And water, water everywhere. The ground squished beneath your feet whenever you stepped out of doors. Wooden planks were laid all around just so you could walk to the post office and back without drowning, and when it rained too much, she said, their neighbors would tie their boats up right to their porches.

Her parents were "not well off," as she would delicately describe them later. Her father, Robert Simoneaux—my Paps—had grown up in Terrebonne, trapping for fur and tending to his family's small holdings of oyster beds. When the oil companies started poking around in south Louisiana, he was one of their first guides, leading the surveyors through the maze of swamps and bayous that were like his own back-yard to him. Her mother, Dorothy Connor—my Grams—was from a large family of Irish Catholics who'd come south to help build levees and dig canals. Lydia Marie (born under the Sun in Aries, the Moon in Libra, and Venus in Pisces, "a very favorable alignment," she would claim), inherited her father's dark eyes and her mother's fair skin and red hair—features that set her apart from her playmates and made her feel, even as a child, distinguished.

Her father used to chuckle to see little Miss Lydia holding up the hem of her dress as she stepped carefully through the mud in their backyard. "Dainty as a princess," he teased her—but the phrase, he could tell, appealed to her. She refused to go barefoot, like the other neighborhood kids did, and would cry inconsolably if she got dirt on her clothes. Even at six years old, she began to complain that her mattress was too hard for her, that her friends were too rough, that even her parents should have been somehow better than they were. Sometimes she would stamp her foot and demand the impossible: "But why can't I have a pony?" And her mother and father would have to explain again how poor they were, how they couldn't afford this or that luxury, and the young Lydia would go to bed sobbing, mashing her face into her too-hard mattress and feeling, in a vague but powerful sense, the tragic unfairness of the world.

Nevertheless, my poor mother-to-be might've adapted easily enough and gone through life without any higher aspirations than those of her girlfriends, had it not been for a visit one Christmas to New Orleans and an unexpected encounter there. It was an event that she would tell about for years to come, repeating it so often that, for her and her listeners both, it began to take on the charmed and slightly unreal aspect of a fairy tale.

She was ten or twelve years old (so the tale began) when her daddy drove them up to New Orleans to see the holiday decorations along Canal Street. It was cold, or at least as cold as New Orleans could get at Christmastime. As they walked along the sidewalk, car exhausts blew clouds of steam past their legs, and the lights overhead stood out bright and sharp as stars, like constellations that had been dragged down from heaven and strung across the street for the holiday.

Lydia wore her best outfit, a dark green velvet dress that her mother had made for her, with black stockings, black patent leather shoes, and a green velvet bow in her hair. She carried herself with a proud, careful bearing, mindful of her dress, and of the specialness of their outing, and of the rich sophistication of the big city. She loved the department store window displays and insisted on stopping at every one. Resting her mittened hand on the glass, she stared at the miniature villages with their animated ice-skaters, and the electric trains winding through snowy landscapes, and the log cabins puffing real smoke from their chimneys, and she felt the scenes behind the glass were so beautiful, so perfect, so impossible that they made her want to cry.

At D. H. Holmes she indulged her parents by sitting on the lap of the Santa Claus, even though it embarrassed her, and even though she knew by then that he was just a fat man with a fake beard and smelly breath. She was rewarded with a candy cane, and she was still trying to figure out how to put her mittens back on and hold the stick at the same time when they stepped out the side door onto Royal Street and saw the car pulling up at the Hotel Monteleone.

Her father gave a low whistle at the enormous white Cadillac. It had a long hood, chrome bumpers, and rounded, winglike fenders, like some kind of spaceship from the future that had landed on the road in front of them. There was a flurry of movement at the hotel entrance, and Lydia and her parents crossed the street to see what was happening. Porters were ferrying out luggage on brass carts; other hotel personnel dashed in and out while a doorman tried to hold back sidewalk traffic. Then an important-looking man in a sharp gray suit stepped out of the lobby, escorting a woman holding a bouquet of flowers wrapped in tissue paper printed with the hotel's coat of arms.

The crowd jostled to see her. People murmured to one another. Lydia craned for a better view. Though she'd never seen a celebrity before, she knew such people existed, and she instinctively knew that this must've been one of them. The woman wore a red chesterfield coat with a black fur collar and large black buttons up and down the front.

Her skin was remarkably pale and white, her lips bright red, and her auburn hair fell in crimped waves over her shoulders. And her eyes: even standing at the rear of the crowd, Lydia could tell they were green as emeralds. She was, Lydia was sure, the most strikingly beautiful woman she'd ever seen.

Lydia's father had begun narrating the action: "There's no way they're going to fit all that luggage in that one car, I don't care how big it is. . . . That's one, two, three, four hatboxes . . . Look at that steamer trunk. You ever seen a trunk as big as that in your life? . . . There he goes, he's calling for another one. . . ."

The doorman stepped to the edge of the sidewalk and blew his whistle, causing the woman in red to grimace. A taxicab swooped up and the porters swarmed around. The man in the gray suit barked a few orders and then stepped in to help manage things, leaving the woman to wait alone on the rug in front of the hotel.

Lydia's feet had drawn her forward, away from her parents, until she was at the front of the crowd. She stared at the woman, studying her. Though she stood in the center of this whirlwind of activity, she appeared perfectly composed. It was as though, Lydia thought, she were enclosed in a glass bubble that kept her separate from the rest of the world—as though she had somehow contrived to live inside one of those beautiful, perfect scenes in the department store windows, and it was this extraordinary poise and containment, as much as her good looks, that set the woman apart and attracted Lydia to her.

Lydia was still staring when the woman turned and looked directly at her. She peered curiously at Lydia, and then she made a funny, bug-eyed expression, as if to say, *Yes? What?* Surprised, Lydia smiled. The woman waved, a quick, girlish motion of her gloved hand. Lydia tentatively raised a hand and returned the wave. The woman laughed, took three steps away from the carts and luggage, and squatted down in front of her.

"Aren't you a pretty girl. What's your name?"

Something about the woman's naturalness immediately put Lydia at ease. She felt like she was meeting an old friend, and she had no trouble at all answering her.

"Lydia," she said, but then corrected this: "Lydia Marie Simoneaux."

"What a lovely name. Lydia, my name's Ava." She took off a glove and offered her hand. "How do you do?"

Close up, she was even prettier. Her lipstick was perfect, like painted lacquer, and her eyebrows were dark and finely shaped. A rich, heady perfume wafted from her, a scent that suggested unimaginable luxury and romance.

"Are you from here?"

"No, ma'am. Terrebonne."

"Where's that?"

Lydia swung her arm around and pointed in the direction from which she supposed they'd come. The woman laughed.

"Small town?"

Lydia nodded seriously. "Very small."

"I'm from a small town, too, in Carolina. North Carolina. Do you know where that is?"

"Mm—not exactly."

The woman pointed over her shoulder with her thumb. "Back there somewhere."

This struck Lydia as enormously clever, and she laughed.

"Ava! We got it. Come on, let's go," the man in the gray suit called.

"Darn. I have to go," Ava said. "Here. Take this." She pulled a flower from her bouquet. "I like you, Lydia. You're a very special girl. You're going to have an amazing life, I can tell." Lydia took the flower. "Do you believe me? Do you believe Ava?"

Lydia wasn't sure what to say to this—it sounded strange—but the woman held her eyes until Lydia was compelled to nod her head and answer, "Yes."

The woman touched the palm of her hand to Lydia's cheek. "Merry Christmas, sugar."

And with that, she stood and left. The man in gray escorted her by the arm to the white Cadillac, waving off people's shouts for autographs. A photographer rushed in to take a picture. "Ava! Ava! Miss Gardner! Over here!" Ava smiled from the backseat of the Cadillac and dangled one bare, tantalizing leg out the door. The photographer got his shot, the door closed, and the cars roared off.

The camera flash startled Lydia back to her senses. The sidewalk, the cold air, the traffic fumes all began to return. Her encounter with the woman in red couldn't have lasted more than a minute, but Lydia felt as if she'd been away for days. Her parents appeared at her side, talking excitedly. They still weren't sure who the lady was.

"Are you kidding me?" a man said. "That's Ava Gardner!"

"Who?" Lydia asked.

"Oh, mercy me," her mother said. "I thought I recognized her. Of course. Good gracious. Can you believe that?"

As they resumed walking, Lydia's mother recounted in a rush all she knew about Ava Gardner, the famous Hollywood actress: her early marriage to Mickey Rooney, and then to Artie Shaw, and now the scandal with Frank Sinatra, how everyone said she lured him away from Nancy and now the Church wouldn't let him get a divorce and so he was petitioning Rome . . . "What in the world do you think she's doing here?"

Lydia's father recognized the name but was indifferent. "Probably getting married again," he joked, and then he opened a glass door and steered them into a noisy seafood restaurant with sawdust on the floor and shouting waiters. Her father embraced the cashier; the owner was called for. . . .

But for the rest of that night and well into the next week, Lydia was lost in a dream. Ava. Ava Gardner. She could've spoken to anyone, but she came to Lydia, knelt right in front of her, and gave her a flower. Lydia felt like she'd been touched by a goddess.

Back home in Terrebonne, she riffled through her mother's old *Life* magazines for photos and articles about the actress. When she exhausted those, she headed to the magazine rack at the drugstore. She begged her parents for money for the latest issue of *Movie World*, that week and then every week after. She learned all she could about Ava— her poor childhood, the sharecropper shacks, her tobacco-farming father, her homemade dresses, and her penchant for going barefoot, even after she'd been discovered and brought to Hollywood. She worried over the gossip she read and was dismayed by the studio's new label for her, "The world's most beautiful animal!" But she wasn't an animal at all, Lydia argued to herself. Anybody could see what a sensitive, intelligent woman she was—much more an Elizabeth Taylor than a Marilyn Monroe. She was being horribly miscast by the studios; she deserved so much better than the silly roles they gave her.

The movie she'd been filming that winter in New Orleans, *My Forbidden Past*, didn't come out until two years later, when Lydia was still in junior high school. As soon as it opened at the RKO in New Orleans, Lydia coerced her parents into taking her to see it. She dressed carefully for the outing, feeling in a way that it was her movie, too, and she was nervous when the lights went down and the film began to play in the half-empty theater. Her father shifted impatiently in his seat and gobbled his popcorn and guffawed. Her mother complained in a whisper that this movie really wasn't suitable for teenage girls. Even Lydia had to admit the film wasn't that good. But Ava—Ava, of course, was wonderful. Lydia attended carefully to every raised eyebrow, every sigh and gesture, chuckling with recognition and saying to herself, *That's just like her. That's just what Ava would do.*

"A special girl . . . an amazing life . . ."

The encounter would stay with Lydia all through high school, where she became a mediocre student, prone to daydreaming. She was impatient with her teachers and quickly grew tired of her classmates, too, especially the FFA boys in overalls who teased her for putting on airs. "Miss Nose-in-the-Air," they called her. "Miss Too-Good-for-You." When she thought about it sensibly, she knew that there was nothing at all for her to be smug about. And yet, the notion had taken hold that Terrebonne was just a way station for her. She'd been dropped off there by mistake, and if she only waited it out, the next train would arrive soon to whisk her away. Surely she wasn't meant to spend the rest of her life here in this muddy dump.

The summer after graduation she got a job at the McCall's Rexall. She'd been practically living at the shop anyway, going several times a week to read the movie magazines, and so when Trudy Arcineaux, the night girl, got pregnant and had to quit, Lydia barely had to turn around in order to take her place at the counter.

She loved the job; it made her feel grown up and important. Being right there on the town square, waiting on customers behind the large plate-glass window, was almost like being on stage. She took special care with her makeup and wardrobe, and she set herself the task of improving her deportment and elocution. "Yes, ma'am, we can certainly order that for you," she'd say, and, "If you don't mind waiting for just one minute, I'll ask the manager." Even during her breaks, eating her sandwich in the park, she was unfailingly poised and polite, as if (a boy once teased her) she was expecting someone to pop out of a bush and take her picture. Mr. McCall had nothing but praise for her.

She'd become a dedicated moviegoer by then, and on her nights off from work she drove with her girlfriends, or even by herself, to see the latest releases in Thibodaux or Houma. As she sat in the darkened theater, the dusty beam of light streaming over her shoulder seemed to cast her dreams up on the screen—dreams that were so private, so true, that she almost blushed to see them shown in public. Many times she had the overpowering conviction that it could've been her moving and talking up there in that silvery world. Indeed, she often felt that all it required was some intense act of concentration on her part—that if only she closed her eyes and squeezed her fists and wished it strongly enough, it would happen: all at once the beam would flip around to shine on her, and her life would be transformed. No longer just Lydia Marie Simoneaux from Terrebonne, she would become some greater, larger, brighter, more perfectly realized version of herself.

And yet, things did not look promising for her. All the wealthiest, smartest boys of her class had gone off to college, and the ones that remained in town were the poor boys who would always be there: the sons of fishers and trappers with their muddy boots and batteaus, and now the oil-rig toughs in their pickup trucks and greasy blue jeans. And then a year had passed, and while her classmates were getting married and having babies, she was still restocking dinner mints at the counter in the Rexall, staring out the window at the world passing by and wondering when, oh when, the amazing life Ava had promised her would begin.

Sometimes late at night before closing, when the store was empty and there was only the hum of the cooler and a faint buzz from the overhead fluorescent lights to disturb the silence, she would have the feeling that she was perched at the very edge of her dreams. She would stop whatever she was doing and lean on the counter, listening. A Gulf breeze rustled the leaves in the gutter; a train whistled on the outskirts of town. Possibility seemed to shiver in the air, like the electric sensation before a hurricane. Any minute now, she would tell herself, staring out the window, any minute now it would happen. It *had* to happen. She could feel it like a tingling beneath her skin. Any minute now, the bell would ring, the door would open, and her future would step in to greet her. He'd be wearing a suit and tie, and he'd ask in a polite, gentlemanly voice that sounded at once foreign but completely familiar, "Miss? Hello? Can you help me?"

CHAPTER EIGHTEEN

BY November we could spot Kohoutek easily near the head of Scorpio, visible in the lens of the scope as a faint blue teardrop-shaped smudge. From day to day it seemed not to move at all, but from week to week its progress was obvious. My father kept notes on its appearance and location, along with sketches to show the size of the coma and the shape of its tail. He compared his observations with those of other members of the regional American Astronomical Society, and he kept abreast of the more detailed scientific data available through regular bulletins issued by NASA. It had already passed Mars; around Thanksgiving it would cross the orbit of the Earth and brush past Venus and Mercury before looping around the Sun to begin its return pass through the solar system. Greatest magnitude was still predicted for late December and early January, when it would be nearest the Sun. Preliminary spectroscopic analysis revealed evidence of water in its makeup, and radio frequency radiation disclosed traces of hydrogen cyanide and methyl cyanide in its outgassing—discoveries that lent credence to the theory that Comet Kohoutek was indeed a relic from the origins of the solar system, "a messenger from the past," as my father called it.

Every night after his observations my father would fold up the telescope and return it to my room: "Night, son." As soon as he was gone, I'd turn off my lights, set up the scope at my window, and train it on Gabriella's house. I could spend an hour or more waiting for a glimpse of her. My back would ache, my neck would become sore; as I pulled away from the eyepiece, my vision would be blurry. But sometimes I was rewarded with a sighting, and that was enough to keep me watching.

I'd catch her crossing through the patio room, or see her sitting on the couch to watch TV with her parents. Other times I would find her in her bedroom, her shadow flitting back and forth behind the curtains of the French doors. Sometimes the curtains would be open and I could watch her sitting inside, talking on the phone, moving in and out of her powder room. She always closed the curtains before going to bed at night, however—evidence, I thought, of a certain polite modesty that must've been taught to well-bred girls like her. Or maybe, I thought, she suspected me; maybe she knew I was watching.

I felt vaguely uneasy spying on her like this, but at the same time, I reasoned, it didn't seem to be hurting anybody. I thought of it as a kind of scientific study; I saw myself as another Dr. Kohoutek, perched up in the lonely observatory of my room, dedicating myself not to the investigation of heavenly bodies but of earthly ones. Through careful observations I might uncover truths not only about her, but about me, about us, about the world we lived in.

I learned that she favored Tab cola in the can, for instance. I only once ever saw her eat ice cream, oddly enough, and that appeared to be strawberry. From five to six-thirty twice a week, Tuesdays and Thursdays, she attended ballet lessons; her mother drove her there and back, and afterward she wore her black tights for the rest of the evening in the house.

After dinner she usually watched TV for an hour or so with her father in the patio room. Two of her favorite shows were *Sonny and Cher* and *The Partridge Family*. When either of these came on, she would run from whatever corner of the house she was in and throw herself on the couch to watch. If her father made some comment or asked a question during the program, she would shush him with a wave of her arm. When the show ended, she'd stand and leave the room, jerking her hips and singing along to the closing theme song.

Regarding her study habits, she most often liked to do her homework at the same time as she watched TV. She had little patience for studying, though, and was easily distracted, so that as she sat on the couch in front of the TV with her schoolbook in her lap, she might not turn a page for half an hour at a stretch. But on nights before tests she would haul herself up to her room, close the door, and sit cross-legged on her bed with her papers spread around her, frowning and chewing determinedly on her pencil. She only read books that were assigned in class; otherwise, she read magazines. She subscribed to *Seventeen*, like my sister used to, and when she received a new issue she would lie back in bed and study it more seriously than she did any of her textbooks.

Her phone habits: She had a yellow Trimline Touch-Tone with an extra-long cord that allowed her to move it anywhere in her bedroom. I figured that she spoke about an hour a night for an average of roughly eight to ten hours per week on this phone. She made calls about twice as often as she received them. Once I saw her pick up the handset to call someone, then put it down, walk back and forth, pick it up again . . . She did this three times before making the call.

I learned to recognize the different attitudes she assumed while speaking on the phone, and from these I was able to make educated guesses as to probable conversation partners. She had one fairly upright, polite, but happy posture that she adopted for certain calls she received once or twice a week around eight o'clock in the evening; often at the end of these conversations she would report down to her parents. I took this caller to be a grandmother or an aunt—a close relative back in Shreveport.

When talking to girlfriends from school, however, she would bring the phone to her bed and lie down, sometimes hanging her head backward over the edge of the mattress so that I would worry about her becoming dizzy. Other times she would flop down on the yellow shag carpet to talk. Best of all was when she stood and paced the room. Holding the phone to her ear with one hand, she practiced ballet moves—walking pointy-toed, or dipping and rising in front of the mirror with one arm arched over her head.

Through these observations I began to see her as less of a goddess and more of a person. She was funny, thoughtful, at times awkward. She was, in fact, someone not so different from me: a human being trapped inside a teenager's body, waiting for the world to begin.

I came to learn more about Gabriella's parents, too. Her father, for instance, preferred the patio room for relaxing in at the end of the day. I reasoned that this was because the patio room was the most open and casual room in the house, and Frank Martello himself was an open and casual person. He drank his beer straight from the bottle, no matter how often Barbara brought him a glass, and on Sunday afternoons he took over in the kitchen, stripping down to T-shirt and trousers, to cook a large pot of spaghetti and meatballs for the family. Other afternoons he joined the gardener in picking up twigs in the yard, and from time to time he uncoiled the garden hose and washed down his driveway himself. He'd stand in his business suit spraying water on the concrete until Barbara came out to berate him for working outside in his good clothes; he'd finish his spraying and, reluctantly it seemed, recoil the hose and go inside.

Barbara's daily routine was still largely a mystery to me, but I knew that she always brought Gabriella to school in the mornings and picked her up in the afternoons in her sky-blue Town Car. Whenever I caught sight of Barbara, whether coming and going in the car or moving around inside the house, she was always nicely dressed, as though ready to meet company. She favored skirts and high-heeled shoes, and she spoke with an experienced, offhanded authority to their maid and gardener; she seemed to be a woman used to having things her way. On the weekends the whole family would sometimes disappear for a day or two, and then their house would stand quiet and abandoned, the shutters closed and the curtains drawn, the automatic pool sweep gliding around and around the sparkling blue water of their swimming pool.

The more I observed them, the better I knew them, until we seemed to be almost on familiar terms. I was, in a manner of speaking, a regular visitor to their house, following them home in the afternoon, and then settling in to watch TV with them in the evening, and then going upstairs to sit beside Gabriella on her bed as she did her homework or spoke on the phone. Soon I was spending more time with the Martellos than I was with my own family, and for good reason: their family was altogether more interesting and attractive than mine. I supposed the Martellos must've had their share of problems, but I never saw them; from where I stood, they looked all but perfect—like one of the charmed, well-lit families on the TV programs that Gabriella loved to watch.

Sometimes when Gabriella went out for the night with her family or friends, I'd turn the Celestron aside and pull my chair up to the window to wait for her return. During these long drowsy vigils, I would dream of meeting her again as we had on that night in my yard, but alone now, just the two of us. We would step out of our separate rooms and, like weightless astronauts on a space walk, wade through the air above our yards to meet in the dark sky above the bayou. Suspended there between the stars above and the Earth below, I would take her hand and we would soar together into the future, that unimaginable, that beautiful, perfect world.

CHAPTER NINETEEN

FOR our fall field trip to Baton Rouge, our class would visit the planetarium, tour the state capital, and see the museum before returning to Terrebonne in the afternoon.

The summer heat had broken at last and a clean, leafy scent was in the air. The change of seasons seemed to mark our own changes; we could all feel it, like a promise in the wind—the slipping away of our youth and the oncoming rush of adulthood. It caused students to talk more loudly and move more broadly. I'd noticed the change myself that morning when I went to put on my lightweight jacket and discovered that the sleeves were too short, as though I'd miraculously grown several inches overnight.

I'd been looking forward to the field trip as a chance to get closer to Gabriella, but Mark Mingis had gotten the jump on me. While we were boarding the bus at school, he slipped around everyone else, jogged up the steps, and dropped down next to her, as casually as if he belonged there. He sat beside her now, resting his arm along the back of her seat.

The wind tossed her hair around her shoulders. Creosote poles ticked past the windows, and the morning sun glinted off patches of water as our bus rumbled north along Highway 1.

"I can't believe she's with him," I said to Peter, sitting beside me.

"Who?"

I pointed to the front of the bus. "Mark and Gabriella. What's she doing with him?"

Coach DuPleiss was standing in the aisle beside the driver's seat, holding on to the vertical silver pole, like a captain at the helm of his boat. He leaned over to talk to Mark, who looked up and nodded, his face dumb and earnest beneath a red baseball cap. Gabriella held her hair back in the wind, attending politely to whatever they were saying.

"It's like you said, the universal law of attraction and all that."

"But they shouldn't even be together. They don't have anything in common."

"How would you know?"

"I just know."

Peter told me about Mark's new car, a Camaro Z28. He'd seen it when Mark came to his daddy's Conoco station the other day to fill it up. It was hot, Peter said: red with black racing stripes, a V8 engine, and a wind spoiler on the back. His father had bought it for him. Mark wasn't even fifteen yet, but he had his learner's permit, so he was practicing driving the car around town with his mother.

"To hell with him and his new car," I said. "Look at that, he's practically got his arm wrapped around her."

"You really do like her, don't you?"

"Everybody likes her."

"You should ask her out."

"Right."

"Why not? You're neighbors, she came over to your house. You talk to her at school. It's like you're friends now. You should just ask her."

"But she's sitting with him."

"You need to kick his ass. Show him who's boss. You've got to go up there and say, 'Step aside, punk. This is my girl.'"

"I suppose that's what you would do."

Peter shrugged. "I'm just saying."

Gabriella leaned across Mark Mingis to talk to the coach, looping her hair over her left ear, and I felt a painful squeeze in my chest. I continued to watch her, plotting how I might steal her away from Mark, as our bus rattled through Thibodaux, Supreme, Napoleonville. Islands of solid ground rose up out of the water as farmland replaced marshland. Students fell quiet; some dozed. My father sat at the front of the bus behind the driver's seat, trading jokes with the science nerds around him.

We passed farm shacks, and cheap new brick homes set on bare plots of red dirt, and a line of cars waiting at a gas station. We passed a broken-down old truck on the shoulder of the road with a black man in overalls working under its hood.

"Pete, it's your dad. It's Pete's dad!" someone said.

"It's not my dad. Moron," Peter answered, and bent back to his work. He was drawing something on the back of the seat in front of us. I leaned sideways to see.

"What're you doing?"

"Art."

The seat back was marked with old graffiti—curse words, sex words, obscure messages to unknown people: "LG + KP = ♡," "I love you Debbie Contreau." On the right-hand side, Peter was sketching a large penis. "*Homo erectus,*" he announced. He had to scratch the pen back and forth on the aluminum to make any kind of mark, and every time the bus hit a bump, his line went crooked. He laughed. "It's got an elbow now."

"Now for the woman," he said, and began scratching a new set of lines nearby. "Observe."

I stopped him. "Man. Someone's going to see that."

He pulled his hand away. "So?"

"So—it's not cool."

"This is human anatomy, Junior. It's perfectly natural. Better get used to it," he said, and went on drawing. As he worked, he sang to himself, "*Get back, honky cat, get back, honky cat, whoo!*"

"But that's not even right. That doesn't even look like anything."

"I'm not finished." He drew some more. "She's like a midget," he explained. "She's a midget with extremely long legs." He stopped and rubbed at the drawing with his fingertips. "*Mm-mm*, yeah. Ooh, baby. Touch me there."

"You pervert."

"Ooh, yeah. I love it when you do that."

Mark Mingis, his arm still resting along the back of Gabriella's seat, turned around and grinned smugly to one of his football buddies across the aisle, and I felt the time that I should've been spending with her slipping miserably away with each passing mile. When the bus banked into the air and crossed the bridge high over the Mississippi River, students jumped up to look out the windows at the muddy water frothing below, the sprawling refineries, and the capitol tower rising above the city. Peter stuck his head out the window and howled like a dog, and it was then, during the general whooping and hollering as we dropped down into the streets of Baton Rouge, that Gabriella swiveled around in her seat, caught my eye, and smiled. That was all the encouragement I needed.

At the planetarium, Coach DuPleiss herded everyone into groups outside the bus and began moving us toward the entrance of the building with outstretched arms, like a traffic cop. "Is it a good show?" a boy asked him. "Oh yeah, it's a great show," he deadpanned. "Spectacular. You wouldn't want to miss it." As Gabriella strolled with Mark to the lobby doors, I pulled Peter aside and asked for his help.

"He'll kill me," Peter protested.

"No, he won't. You're faster than he is."

"Only because you're my friend," Peter said. "I'll do it. I'll risk my life for you."

"Just go. Hurry," I said, pushing him along.

Peter hesitated, taking a bead on Mark. Then he ran around a clump of students, snuck up behind Mark, and tipped the baseball cap off his head. Mark spun around. Peter snatched his cap up from the asphalt, put it on his own head, and began dodging back and forth.

Mark went red in the face. He cursed and followed Peter, chest up, trying to keep his cool. "You little shit!" He lunged, but Peter screeched and slipped away. Students laughed. Encouraged, Peter bounced up and down on his knees and swung his arms, hooting like an excited ape: "*Hoo hoo! Hoo hoo!*"

I had my opening. I edged up beside Gabriella as she paused at the doors of the building.

"Comet Boy! What's up?"

I held the door for her. "Are you going in?" She glanced uncertainly at Mark, still chasing his hat in the parking lot. "Right this way, ma'am. Watch your step," I said, urging her inside.

The lobby was spacious and cool, with the echoing sound of a museum. We followed the other students around to the doors of the planetarium.

"You've been here before?" Gabriella asked.

"Lots of times. My father knows the guy who runs it."

"Oh, so you're the expert."

"I'm the expert."

"You'll give me a tour?"

"Sure. Here we have the clock. Here's the Coca-Cola machine. On your right, the water fountain . . ."

She laughed and, holding back her hair, bent in for a drink. I waited until she'd finished and then showed her into the planetarium. I steered us to a row near the back, explaining how if you sat too close, your neck got sore. We were just settling into our seats when Mark appeared in the doorway, his cap in his fist. He scanned the rows. Gabriella raised a hand to flag him; I pulled it back down.

"No!" I whispered.

"What?"

She raised her hand again. I pulled it down again. We wrestled briefly over her hand until someone sat on the other side of her. Mark frowned and took a seat at the front with his buddies.

"Why don't you want him to sit here?"

"I don't even know him."

"He's nice."

"I'll bet."

She pulled her head back and looked at me. "You don't like him, do you? You don't like him because he's a football player and you're not."

"That's ridiculous."

At the center of the planetarium, my father was trying to get everyone's attention. "Could I have your . . . Please . . . Settle down."

"All right, be quiet now! The Professor wants to talk!" the coach shouted, and students hushed.

"You don't have to shout. But thank you," my father said.

He had dressed for the outing that day in a corduroy sports jacket and a plaid walking hat with a small feather tucked in the band. Over the past month he'd started growing out his sideburns, too, so that with his jacket and hat, he looked like a TV game show host. He took off his hat to speak.

"We've got a really exciting program for you today. A little history, a little astronomy. A little philosophy."

"And fun," the man beside him said.

"And fun," my father said. "Let me introduce my friend Ed Elvert. He's in charge of the planetarium here. What do you call a person who runs a planetarium? Does anybody know?"

"A planetariumist," someone said.

"A dork," someone else said.

Coach DuPleiss stood up and turned around. "Shut up!"

"A person who runs a planetarium is called a— Well, you tell them, Ed."

He was a fat man with a brown vest, green trousers, and a neatly trimmed beard. He had wet lips and a fussy, complacent manner. He lifted his chin to enunciate it: "A *planetarian*."

"That's right. Ed's a planetarian. He's been operating the planetarium here in Baton Rouge for almost as long as I've been a teacher. He did his apprenticeship at the world-famous Carl Zeiss Planetarium in Stuttgart, Germany." My father turned to him, his face bright with admiration. "Wow. That must've been amazing."

Mr. Elvert nodded. "It certainly was."

"Ed's the president of our local chapter of the American Astronomical Society, and a well-regarded astronomer in his own right. And, I happen to know, he owns one of the finest telescopes around these parts, a Questar three point five. Kind of the Rolls-Royce of telescopes. Wouldn't you say, Ed? So if you're real nice to him, maybe he'll invite you over sometime to see his telescope. How about that?"

Mr. Elvert took the center of the room. "I don't think I can invite *everyone*. But thank you, Alan. I always look forward to having you here. Kind of a celebrity now, aren't you? Mr. Groovy Science." The two shared a chuckle. "But seriously, Alan has done a wonderful job of promoting science in the community, and for that we should all be thankful."

He quizzed us on Kohoutek and complimented my father on educating us so thoroughly. They'd been getting lots of phone calls about the comet, he said, so next week they were introducing a special weekly comet night there at the planetarium. They'd have a lecture, followed by a new light show, some music, wine and cheese for the parents, soft drinks for the kids. Something for the whole family. "Maybe we could get the Professor to come and speak for us, too. What do you say, Alan?"

My father twitched and smiled and said he'd be delighted.

"Fine. We'll try to arrange that." Mr. Elvert moved to a console and pushed a button. "It'll take several minutes for your eyes to dark-adapt, so in the meantime, I'll tell you a little about our planetarium. How many of you have ever been to a planetarium before?"

As the lights faded he introduced the projector, the large barbell-shaped machine looming up the dark behind him, "a Universal Projection Planetarium Type Twenty-Three Six, made in Germany by Volkseigener Betrieb Zeiss . . ."

Someone in a middle row made a snoring sound. Coach DuPleiss turned and glared at him. Mr. Elvert pushed some more buttons, and the theme music from *2001: A Space Odyssey* swelled from hidden speakers. A simulated sun rose over our heads, followed by a boom of timpani and a brilliant flash of light.

"The universe," Mr. Elvert intoned into a microphone. "Where did it come from? What does it look like? How will it end?"

Through all of this, I was acutely aware of Gabriella sitting beside me. This was the closest we'd ever been to each other, and in the cool dark of the planetarium, I imagined waves of energy emanating from her body—like radio waves, or X-rays, or maybe waves of beauty, radiating across the small space between us and warming the side of my face.

The show began with the birth of the universe in the Big Bang and then toured through distant stars and galaxies before arriving at the Milky Way. Mr. Elvert reviewed the major constellations and the stories behind them.

"Orion the Hunter," he said, as an outline of stars appeared on the right side of the ceiling. "See his belt, his shoulders, his sword. Luckless Orion, the handsomest of men, but he never got the girl. Every winter you can still see him chasing the seven daughters of Atlas, the beautiful Pleiades, across the sky. There they go. The Pleiades. Forever, always just out of his grasp."

I leaned sideways. "Look, it's you. The constellation Gabriella," I whispered.

"The constellation Junior," she whispered back. "I can see it."

As stars came and went overhead, I carefully slumped down until my shoulder brushed against her shoulder. First it was just cloth to cloth, my jacket touching her sweater, but I leaned in closer until I felt the press of skin and muscle beneath her clothes. I imagined a liquid warmth passing back and forth between us where our shoulders met. I raised my arm from my lap, inching it up along the side of my seat, and gently laid it next to hers on the wooden armrest we shared. The liquid warmth spread from our shoulders, down our arms, and to our elbows. I paused, excited by our arms touching like this. More stars came and went; eons passed. Gabriella sat still, not leaning closer but not pulling away, either. I searched for signals in the pressure of her muscles and bones against mine. Did she feel what I felt? Did she even know that we were touching? When she didn't withdraw her arm, I carefully shifted again until my forearm and then my wrist touched hers, so that, finally, our two arms were pressed together from shoulder to wrist—like lovers' bodies lying side by side. Her body swelled and shrank in time to her breath, and I paced my own inhalations and exhalations until my breathing matched hers.

A simulated meteor shower streamed overhead. Mr. Elvert spoke about how such meteor showers were the remnants of disintegrated comets, and how as the Earth crossed their paths, it was as though we were sailing through the dust of time itself, through glittering flashes of the past.

Gabriella bent her head to mine, brushing my cheek with her hair. "It reminds me of that night in your yard," she whispered, and then sat back up. As she did this, though, she slid her arm off the armrest and dropped it in her lap, leaving my arm lying by itself. *So, she doesn't love me after all*, I thought, and almost felt like crying.

Mr. Elvert was speaking now about the possibility of other forms of life outside of our solar system, and the solitude of human beings, and their long search for companionship in the universe. An image appeared on the ceiling, a reproduction of a plaque fastened to the side of the *Pioneer 10* spacecraft. In black lines etched on gold, it showed the location of the Earth in the solar system, and beside that, the figure of a naked man and woman, the man with his right hand raised, the woman leaning slightly toward her partner.

"A man. A woman. A modern-day Adam and Eve, his hand raised in a simple gesture of greeting," said Mr. Elvert, and Coach DuPleiss glared around from his seat in the front row daring anyone to laugh. In December, Mr. Elvert told us, *Pioneer 10* would pass Jupiter, from where it would continue on its trajectory into the outer reaches of space, bearing its message of peace and goodwill to whoever might find it—"a message in a bottle tossed into the sea of space."

When Mr. Elvert began to speak about the death of the Sun, I knew that the show was almost over. He said how billions of years from now, the nearby star known to us as our Sun would swell to become a red giant that would boil away the oceans and burn up all life on our planet in a fiery cataclysm of destruction.

On cue, the ceiling exploded in a wash of hot red and yellow lights. Cymbals crashed and music boomed from the speakers. Gabriella, startled, grabbed my wrist.

What was this? Her hand was surprisingly small and delicate but with a sure grip—like a bird perched on the back of my wrist. I didn't dare move for fear of frightening her away.

The planetarium faded to the dark blue of space again, and at once we were sailing back through the planets, past the Milky Way, past distant stars and galaxies. The drawing of the naked man and woman slid past over our heads and disappeared, "the relic of a once-proud race, gone and forgotten," said Mr. Elvert. The stars spread and dimmed. And still Gabriella held my wrist. I felt her skin warming mine; I felt the beat of her pulse against my own.

"Scientists now believe that the universe is a one-time event, never to reoccur. Since its origins billions of years ago in a mysterious Big Bang, our universe has been slowly expanding, growing bigger and bigger, thinning out, until, many billions of years from now, one by one the stars will all die, and all that will remain will be an unimaginably dark . . . vast . . . empty . . . nothingness."

The last star clicked off and the planetarium fell into darkness. Mr. Elvert was silent. Time passed. A few students sniggered and rustled, but the room stayed dark. Silhouettes of heads and shoulders materialized in the gloom as the exit signs spread a green glow through the air. I turned to look at Gabriella. Her face was inclined to the darkened ceiling, her hair hanging down around her neck. Her mouth had fallen open in an expression of sadness and disbelief, and in the glow of the exit lights, I was surprised to see tears glistening in her eyes.

I rolled my hand over so that my palm touched hers. I curled my fingers between her fingers. She returned the hold. I squeezed, and she squeezed. I closed my eyes, time slowed to a standstill, and there was nothing in the world but her hand in mine and the warmth of our touch filling the dark space around us.

How long did this last? A minute? Half a minute? Seconds? The lights faded up. She slipped her hand from mine, and I closed my fingers around empty air. Students began to shift and talk; the room, the walls, the ceiling and chairs all reappeared. Gabriella sniffed and wiped her eyes. She turned and saw me staring at her.

"I always cry at the death of the universe," she said, and laughed.

CHAPTER TWENTY

THEIR home was as still and picturesque as a color photograph from one of my mother's *Southern Living* magazines. The lawn was mowed and raked clean of leaves. The flowers in the flowerbeds blossomed. The driveway was white as sand, and the pool sparkled through the patio gates. The gardener had left for the day and so had the maid. I'd brought a book with me down to the rear of our yard, but I'd left it lying on the picnic table, unread. The real world was finally becoming more interesting than the ones in stories.

In the couple of weeks since we'd held hands in the planetarium, a bond had formed between Gabriella and me. This was more than just emotional; I felt it as an almost physical attachment. I'd read about such feelings before in novels but I'd always assumed they were romantic inventions, something along the lines of flying dragons or talking swords. Myself, I'd never experienced anything like this before. The warmth that had passed through our hands while sitting under the dome of stars had extended into what I pictured as an invisible golden cord joining our bodies. Through this cord I sensed her positions and movements throughout the day. As we traveled in our separate spheres, coming and going to classes, stopping to exchange words in the hallway or waving across the school yard, the golden cord might stretch or shrink, but it always connected us. Every word, every smile, every glancing touch as I handed her a pen and my fingertips brushed against hers only confirmed and strengthened our bond.

She was at home now, I sensed. Any minute she would come to her French doors and open the curtains, and I waited expectantly at the edge of the bayou, hoping for one last wave and hello before the end of the day.

The quiet was broken by a shout behind me. I heard my sister stomping through our house, yelling "Ruined it!" and "How could you?" Our mother told Megan not to raise her voice at her, but Megan shouted her down, ending with a furious "No! No no no no!" before storming out the back door and slamming the screen shut. She marched down the steps and across the yard while inside our mother trailed off into an ineffectual protest about ingratitude and respect.

"Oh. Hey. You," she said, pulling up short at the water.

"Nice to see you, too, sis."

Megan dug into the pocket of her jean jacket for her cigarettes. She'd only recently taken up smoking and came down to the water sometimes to sneak a cigarette when our parents were away. At the moment, though, she didn't seem to care whether our mother saw her or not. She fished a cigarette from her pack of Kools, lit it, shook the match and tossed it aside, performing the whole routine with the drama of someone intent on demonstrating her anger. She took abrupt, impatient drags, and soon she was coughing and rubbing at her contact lenses.

"What was that about?" I asked.

"God, she makes me mad. Look at that. Look!"

She turned sideways so I could see the back of her jacket. Drawn in colored ink on the denim was an oriental landscape of hills, rocks, bamboo, a river, and a tiny temple on the side of a mountain. Hovering above the scene, seated in clouds, were images of the Buddha and a couple of exotic Hindu gods waving their arms. She'd been working on it, I knew, since the beginning of the school year.

"What happened?"

"She put it in the wash. She said it was unintentional. She said she found it with my other clothes. . . . Bullshit. She did it on purpose, I know she did. She ruined it."

I didn't see how her drawing was ruined, exactly. I thought it actually looked better with the lines and colors a little faded, but I kept that to myself. I kept to myself, too, the thought that our mother might very well have thrown the jacket into the wash by mistake; she'd never been exactly scrupulous about the laundry.

"Mom obviously hates her life and so she takes it out on me."

"You can always redo that, can't you?"

"Not the point, bro. Not the point," Megan said, and took several more puffs of her Kool to calm herself.

I caught sight of someone moving past a downstairs window in the Martellos' house just then and snapped my head around to check. My sister eyed my book on the picnic table, the house across the water.

"Any sign of her?"

"Who?"

She nodded at their house. "You know who. Your little friend over there. The one you're always out here mooning over. You should try not to be so obvious. You might creep her out. She might think you're a pervert, spying on her like this."

"I'm not—"

"Relax. I'm kidding." She blew smoke out of the corner of her mouth and watched their house with me. "I like Gabriella. She seems very mature for her age. Very levelheaded. Cute, too. It must be hard being so pretty, though, don't you think? No one would take you seriously."

I had thought exactly the same thing about her. "I know, that's just it. You wouldn't expect it, but she is, she's very smart, very mature. She doesn't giggle all the time like the other girls. She sits at the front of the class taking notes. And she asks good questions, too, but then everyone laughs like she's trying to make a joke, but she isn't."

I'd said too much. Megan looked at my wryly. "Uh oh. Someone sounds like he's smitten."

I shrugged. "I just think it's interesting, that's all."

She snorted a laugh. She happened to have her cigarette in her mouth, though, and she swallowed a gulp of smoke, causing her to erupt in another fit of coughing. She coughed so much, hacking and bending over her knees, that I became worried for her.

"Are you all right?"

"Ouch. Damn."

"Those'll kill you, you know."

"Thank you, Doctor. I'll be sure to remember that." She straightened up and rubbed her eyes, recovering. "God, I'm so bored right now, I don't think I'd mind."

The air shifted and we could hear the marching band practicing on the football field at school. The sound drifted up the bayou and then fell back, drifted up and fell back, like waves at a beach. In front of us, the ground sloped down to a low muddy bank studded with cypress knees. The afternoon light flashed on the bayou. Water bugs skimmed and darted across the surface, tracing tiny golden wakes that glittered for a second in the spotty light and then vanished.

I wanted to go on talking about Gabriella, but Megan was staring at the water, her mind someplace else.

"If you could be anywhere in the world, where would you be?" she asked me. "Right now."

"I don't know. Texas?"

"Texas? My god, why would you want to go there?"

"It's just the first thing I thought of. Where would you go?"

"New York, for starters."

"Why New York?"

"Bob Dylan lives there." She brushed aside her hair with the fingers of her hand that held the cigarette; her nails were bitten and ravaged-looking. "I could. I've thought about it. I could pack my bags and leave tonight. Easiest thing in the world."

"Are you serious? How would you get there?"

"Hitchhike. Or take a bus. I figured it all out: New Orleans to Atlanta, Atlanta to Charlotte, Charlotte to Washington . . . I could be there in four days."

Driving into New Orleans we sometimes saw these kids, teenagers not much older than my sister, standing on the highway in ragged clothes and holding up cardboard signs scrawled with the names of improbable-sounding destinations: CANADA. CALIFORNIA. MEXICO. I pictured my sister as one of them, marching along the edge of Highway 1 outside of Terrebonne, a canvas bag on her back, a bandanna tied around her hair, angrily smoking her cigarette as she held out her thumb for a ride.

"And then what? Where would you stay? How would you live?"

"I'll find some room. I'll get a job in a restaurant or a drugstore. People do it all the time."

"Wouldn't you miss it here?" I asked—but I knew her answer before I'd even finished the question.

My sister looked around, taking in the dark bayou, our muddy yard, our little house, our small world. If she hadn't said it, the arch of her eyebrow would've been enough. She sighed a stream of cigarette smoke.

"God. Sometimes I hate this town. Hate it with all my heart. A great big world is happening out there right now and we're missing it. All of it. In Paris, right now, people are sitting down at cafés and drinking coffee and eating croissants and opening their morning newspapers. In China they're riding bicycles and rickshaws to work. In India they're waking up and making fires in their stoves and going to temples to pray. . . ."

She waved her cigarette at the water like a wand, and I could see the world she described floating there in front of us: Chinese men in coolie hats guiding water buffalo through rice paddies; an Indian boy in a turban bowing and praying to a blue-painted statue. Megan went on, gesturing more violently with her cigarette. She could really talk when she got herself worked up.

"And here—what do we do? We go to school, come home, go to school, come home. You get to do this every day until you're old enough to find a job and get married, and then you go to work, come home, go to work, come home. And then your little kids go to school, come home . . . It's like you're digging a hole deeper and deeper into the ground, and pretty soon you're miles below the surface of the Earth and you forget that there's even a world outside anymore. Paris might as well never exist. India, China—forget it. Your entire world is your hole. And people *like* this, apparently. They *love* it. They can't *wait* to dig. They're digging for all they're worth. They're digging like madmen, tossing out shovelfuls of dirt, digging their own graves as fast as they can. . . . My god!"

She broke off her rant, took another pull on her cigarette, and huffed twin streams of smoke from her nose like a dragon. Her eyes were red, her hair wild. There was no arguing with Megan when she got this way, so I didn't try.

Behind us, we heard our mother get into the car and back out of the driveway, off to do the grocery shopping. Megan looked over her shoulder to watch her go and then turned forward again.

"Not me. No thanks. I'm crawling out of this pit as soon as I can," she said, and flicked her cigarette away. It arched over the muddy bank, tumbling end over end through the air. The red tip flared up briefly before it landed with a *pfft!* in the water.

"Say hello to Gabby for me if you see her."

She turned, crossed the yard, and let the screen door fall closed behind her as she went back inside the house—to start packing her bags, for all I knew.

CHAPTER TWENTY-ONE

SHE was a tough one, my sister. In one way, I admired her. She was smart; she wasn't going to take any crap from anyone. No one could tell her what to do.

In another way, though, she alarmed me. She didn't look like a happy person, and I was afraid the same thing might happen to me soon. When I turned fifteen or sixteen, an irreversible change would take place in my personality and I would become like her—skeptical, mistrusting, holding a permanent grudge against a world that was wrong in ways too many and too obvious to even name. *This is what it means to grow up,* she seemed to say. *You stop believing whatever people tell you. You see things as they really are.*

I scraped up a handful of pebbles and began tossing them into the water one at a time, lifting my eyes now and then to check on Gabriella's house. The pebbles plopped into the water, sending concentric silver rings rippling across the surface.

For years, it seemed, our mother had tried to shape Megan into a polite, well-bred southern girl, and for years my sister had gone along with her, trying to live up to our mother's expectations. She dressed up Megan in ribbons and lace, with bows on her dresses, bows on her shoes, bows in her hair. She taught her how to curtsey and—god knows why—serve tea. She bought her an elaborate Junior Miss Makeup Kit, with an instruction booklet on "How to Be Attractive," and a fancy lacquer brush and comb set, and a jewelry box that played "Für Elise" when you opened the lid. She wanted, she said, to give Megan all the pretty things she'd never had as a girl—although whether or not Megan wanted those things herself was open to question.

Once—I remembered this particular incident well, even though I must've been very young at the time—our mother arranged to rent a pony for her birthday. In keeping with the cowboy-cowgirl theme of the party, Megan was costumed in a frilly yellow dress with boots and a straw hat. The pony, a snappish thing, was led around the front yard and up and down the street by an unfriendly woman in blue jeans and boots who kept warning us, "Don't tease her!" My sister was terrified of the animal and refused to go near it. Our mother, though, insisted: Megan looked so cute in her cowgirl dress, and all of her friends were here, and everyone was waiting. Our father, under orders from our mother, lifted Megan up, sat her on the pony, and held her in place, pleading, "Do this for your mother, Meg. Just this once"—words that would become a familiar refrain for her. How many times did my sister hear that growing up? A thousand? Ten thousand times? "Do this for your mother, Meg." And so she did, she clung to the pony as our mother told her to "smile, Megan, smile!" for the photograph, and tears burst from her eyes as my poor sister wailed in fear and misery.

The one thing that my sister loved unreservedly, on her own, without any prodding from our mother, was singing. That she should have this talent was somewhat surprising since no one else in our family had any musical ability. But she joined every choir and Christmas pageant she could find, and when she stood on the stage in the gym or in front of the altar of the church and opened up her mouth, her voice was like a butterfly, fluttering prettily up to the ceiling.

For her fourteenth birthday she begged our parents for a guitar. They bought her a Harmony Classic from Sears—a cheap thing, light as balsa wood, a starter guitar they called it, but Megan was thrilled to have it. She began taking lessons with a boy from school, Greg Barnett, a senior who played in bands. She practiced constantly, after school, in the evenings, even in the mornings if she had a few minutes between breakfast and the bus, picking out scales and chords in her bedroom.

Within a couple of weeks she was playing songs, mostly folk songs and songs about love: "Barbara Allen," "Scarborough Fair," "Blowin' in the Wind." After she had learned a new one, she would bring her guitar to my room. I'd sit on my bed, and she'd sit on my chair, her legs crossed, her left shoulder slumped low so she could see the frets.

"I'm still working on this one," she'd say. "I'm not sure about this part."

"That's a good one," I'd say. "I like that."

When she had three or four songs down, she gave a concert for our family. Our father moved the TV out of the way and set up a chair for her in front of the window curtains. We sat on the sofa to watch. "Wow, honey, that's wonderful," our mother said when she'd finished, and our father agreed: "You've got a real nice voice." She repeated the whole set, we liked it so much. "You should go on TV," I told her. "You could win a prize."

Her voice had a high, pure tone with a tentativeness to it that made it that much more lovely. At night when she stayed up late practicing I would hear her voice through the wall, and it was like having angels sing me to sleep.

That fall, the same year she got her guitar, she was invited to the high school homecoming dance. A boy she liked, a junior named Todd Picou, had asked her. The dance was open—you didn't need a date to attend—and so an invitation like this seemed especially significant. While Megan giggled and spoke on the phone to her friends in a corner of the living room, our mother paced the house trying to hide her own joy and anxiety.

She saw this date as a kind of a test, not only for Megan but for the whole family. She spoke earnestly at the dinner table about the importance of making a good first impression. She suggested that Todd Picou was just the beginning of a long line of beaux that Megan might expect to entertain as she grew older, and she explained how this date might be seen as practice for better, more serious dates in the future. "Everyone has to start somewhere," she said. In town, she found occasion to mention my sister's first date to old friends she saw in the grocery store or at the bank, and she managed to convey in the way she spoke about Todd Picou her opinion that while the Picous were perfectly decent and respectable people—she'd gone to high school with Todd's father, after all—they really weren't quite on the same level as the Broussards. Her daughter, she implied, could do better than Todd. This was just for fun.

A week before the dance, our mother brought Megan up to New Orleans for shopping and tea, "just us two girls." When they got home, she had Megan model her new dress for me and our father, coming down the stairs like you're supposed to do to show it off. The dress was knee length with poofy shoulders and a purple sash around the waist.

"We still have to find shoes," our mother said, worriedly fluffing the skirt. "It's not too long, is it? Do you like it?"

Our father whistled. "Man-oh-man, who is this pretty lady?" Even I had to admit that my sister looked good in the dress; she was suddenly taller and more graceful, more grown up, than the Megan I knew.

They got the shoes, they got everything ready. There were more phone calls to friends and relatives. On the day of the dance our mother made a plate of sandwiches, their crusts cut off, in case Todd was hungry when he stopped by to pick her up. ("He's not going to be hungry," Megan complained. "How do you know?" our mother said.)

Megan spent that afternoon strumming her guitar in her room, singing through all her songs, so I imagined, with special feeling. I had the idea she was rehearsing for him—that her dream was to play her guitar for Todd, sitting cross-legged on the grass with him while singing "If you're going to San Francisco . . ."

She got dressed early and came down to wait on the couch, sitting carefully so as not to wrinkle her skirt. She drank glasses of club soda to settle her stomach. Our father got the camera ready, and our mother chose the music that should be playing on the hi-fi when Todd came in, something young and jazzy and smart—"Take Five" with the Dave

Brubeck Quartet, for instance. ("You really don't have to do that," Megan protested.) Then we all tried to go about our usual business while we waited for Megan's date to arrive. But our only business that night was waiting for Megan's date to arrive.

By eight thirty, Todd still hadn't come. Megan refused to phone him; she said she didn't have his number anyway. Our father looked up the Picous in the phone book and said he would call him, then. Our mother, flustered and angry, put her finger on the cradle switch and said they would not stoop so low as to phone the Picous to beg them to send their son to our house. They fought about it over Megan's head until she shouted for them to "stop! Stop! Just please stop it!"

And so we waited. And waited. Our father offered to take her to the dance himself. At nine thirty our mother served dinner. Megan didn't want any, and she went upstairs to take off her dress. Our mother went up later to talk to her, and our father, to lend his support, put on an apron and washed the dishes.

For a day or two we moved about the house as if someone had died, everyone trying to be extra nice to Megan and watching her out of the corners of our eyes to see how she would hold up. Our mother offered bland reassurances and invented excuses for the boy: he probably just got cold feet, she said, or maybe he was sick and couldn't get to a phone, but there were plenty of fish in the sea, and besides, who cared about a rotten kid like Todd Picou anyway?

But Megan was too smart to be consoled. She knew the truth, and nothing anyone said could change it: she'd been stood up on her first date. That was it. That's what had happened. No further explanation needed. And if everyone would just stop talking about it, she'd appreciate it.

She got over it eventually, in a fashion. She went to school, did her homework, listened to music, and talked with her friends on the phone, like she always had. After several days had passed, though, I noticed she wasn't singing in her room at night anymore. She kept going to her guitar lessons for a few weeks, but after a while she lost interest. She put the Harmony away in the back of her closet, and that was the last we saw of it.

That Christmas, she redecorated her room. She pulled down her ruffled pink curtains and replaced the matching pink bedspread with a psychedelic tie-dyed sheet. She tacked up a black-light poster on the wall above her Panasonic stereo: LOVE it said in fluorescent red-orange letters against a rusty blue background, the word shot through with bullet holes, as though the poster had been sprayed with a machine gun.

And while I couldn't have said for sure that it was related, around this same time my sister began to gain weight. She threw off the frilly dresses our mother was still buying for her and began to wear big sloppy shirts with their tails untucked. She got round, oversized granny glasses, and she let her hair grow long so that it frizzed at the bottom, and before the school year was out, she barely resembled the girl I'd grown up with. Within a couple more years, she'd become the seventeen-year-old cynic who snuck cigarettes down by the water, the girl who chewed her nails and read *Ms.* magazine and serious-minded books with forbidding titles like *The Stranger* and *The Metamorphosis*, the one who spoke scathingly about all that southern belle–Miss Scarlett O'Hara–debutante crapola. The girl whose only wish was to flee.

And because of what? Because of one boy, one broken date? Surely there was more to it than that, but that's what it looked like to me, anyway. Dashed hopes had ruined her life.

Or maybe, I considered further, maybe Todd Picou hadn't ruined her life at all. Maybe he'd only given her the excuse to finally shrug off the expectations of our mother and become her own person. That disastrous first date experience had only knocked her life into focus, revealing, for better or worse, the true Megan, the one who had always been there.

Sunday afternoons—I knew this because I accompanied her once—she'd take the Rambler and go for drives around town, her cigarette dangling out the window. Around and around she'd drive, in ever-widening circles beginning at the courthouse square and spiraling outward through neighborhoods and farms until, bored with herself and the driving and the awful music on the radio, she'd stop the car at the edge of a field at the farthest edge of the town and sit there staring out at the road rolling north, as though readying herself for the day she might finally make her escape from the black hole of Terrebonne.

Behind me in her bedroom, I heard her record player start up. Electric folk music rattled out from her window, harsh and tinny sounding. She sang along in snatches, although you could hardly have called it singing. The words came out in whining, tortured phrases, like the song was being wrung from her throat: *"How does it feeeel? . . . on your own! . . . home! . . . stooone!"*

I looked up across the water at the Martellos' house, as grand and implacable as ever. A shadow moved behind the balcony doors of Gabriella's room. The curtains suddenly parted to let in the afternoon light, and I felt a sharp tug in my chest as I saw a hand, a slender arm, a flash of dark hair.

Forget it, my sister might have warned me. Not worth it. Quit while you're ahead.

Or, easier, she could've just turned and pointed to the poster in her room. That said it all: LOVE shot through with bullet holes.

CHAPTER TWENTY-TWO

IT came to her in a dream, my mother claimed. One Friday night, without even thinking about our father's labs or comets or anything like that, she went to bed and in her sleep she saw the whole thing as clearly as if it had already happened.

"A comet ball," Megan said, in a tone that plainly said how idiotic she thought the idea sounded.

"Sure. Like a charity ball. Like what they do in New Orleans."

Our father needed money for his labs, our mother explained. The school obviously wasn't going to help. He'd have to raise the funds himself, and what better way to do it than with a party?

She went on to describe her vision to us over breakfast, painting a picture in the air with her fingers as she spoke: there'd be a band, dancing, lights in the trees . . . costumed waiters bearing silver trays of champagne glasses . . . couples strolling arm in arm along the waterfront. . . .

"Where do you propose that we hold such a ball?" my father asked.

"And who's going to come?" Megan asked.

"We'll do it at the Martellos'. They've got that great big gorgeous house right over there. Everybody'll want to come," my mother answered.

"Do the Martellos know this yet?" my father asked.

"Well, no, not yet. I just thought of it."

"Let us know when you wake up," Megan said, leaving the table.

But my mother stayed seated, fleshing out the idea and answering all my father's objections. They could get the food and drinks donated and then charge a fee per couple. It shouldn't be that difficult really, she said. People put on these kinds of charity events all the time. Why couldn't they?

She phoned the Martellos that same afternoon to ask them about it. She spoke to Frank, he spoke to Barbara, and, surprising everyone but my mother, they agreed to host an event at their house. Frank said they were always looking for good charitable causes, and Barbara had been wanting to throw a party at their new house anyway. They'd be happy to help.

"See? I knew they would," my mother said.

"And you're going to organize all this?" my father said, peering at her over the newspaper.

"With their help, yes."

He shrugged, as though to say, *I'm not really sure why you're doing this or what's come over you, but if you want to raise money for the school laboratories, be my guest.*

I knew my mother well enough to know she didn't care about any school labs; she only wanted to have her ball. I supposed she might've been dreaming about just such a ball her entire life. It was a dream fueled by half-remembered scenes from half-read novels by F. Scott Fitzgerald; and pictures of feathered Mardi Gras kings and queens and their costumed courts that she'd seen in New Orleans newspapers; and scenes from the old Hollywood films she loved so much, where sleekly dressed movie stars spoke in vaguely British accents while descending grand sweeping stairways—all fantasies that for a woman stuck in a swampy southern town like ours must've seemed as remote and impossible as the stories of princes and princesses she'd heard as a child.

And yet, their impossibility never diminished the longing she felt to experience them herself. Now at last she would have her dream. She would conjure it up herself out of crêpe paper streamers, Christmas-tree lights, and the sheer force of her desire.

As for the Martellos, I was a little puzzled as to why they would agree to help. Maybe they really were interested in charitable causes, as Frank said. Maybe, as my mother once suggested, they were bored living all by themselves in that big house. Or maybe as newcomers to Terrebonne they were eager to make a good impression on the locals. But I couldn't help but feel that what really moved them to act was the strange, compelling power of that blue ball of fire in the sky, the one that had cast its spell over our two families as we stood in the yard a month ago watching it with my telescope—the comet that even now I felt hovering over our town, making us all do things that we might not normally have done.

My mother got herself a notebook and began working with the Martellos to plan the party. They had their cause, their venue, their theme. For the date they settled on a Saturday between Thanksgiving and Christmas—a good time for charity events, said Barbara, who apparently knew about such things. Over drinks one evening at their house they drafted a notice for the newspaper. My mother brought it home and, still giddy from her rum and Coke, showed it to my father, who checked it with his red pen. He corrected her grammar, trimmed a few sentences, and added a paragraph about himself, so that it came out like this:

Comet Ball Is Announced

Mr. and Mrs. Frank Martello, together with Mr. and Mrs. Alan Broussard, are announcing a party to raise money to refurbish the science laboratories at Terrebonne High School. THE COMET BALL, to be held Saturday, December 8, will feature music, dance, refreshments, and diverse entertainments. It promises to be the gala charity event of the season.

Mr. and Mrs. Martello, well-regarded newcomers to the community, will host the party at their residence in Beau Rivage Estates. Helping to organize the event is Mrs. Lydia Simoneaux Broussard, of Terrebonne. Mrs. Broussard says, "This Comet Ball is a great way not only to have fun, but also to raise money for a good cause."

Alan Broussard, familiar to readers of this newspaper from his weekly Groovy Science column, reminds us that the comet to which the event refers is Comet Kohoutek, due to light up our skies with a spectacular cosmic display at Christmastime.

Tickets are $40 per couple, and will be available for purchase prior to and at the event. For details, please contact Mrs. Lydia Broussard . . .

My father thought forty dollars was a lot to ask, but my mother disagreed, reminding him that if only a hundred couples came, he'd have four thousand dollars, less expenses, toward his science labs. Besides, she said, it was supposed to be a ball, not a barbecue. They didn't want just anybody to show up; the forty-dollar ticket price would help keep away the riffraff.

My father remained skeptical. But almost as soon as the announcement appeared in the newspaper, we began receiving phone calls. Women telephoned from as far away as Schriever and Montegut and Lockport to ask if they, too, could come with their husbands. My mother was proved right.

"Didn't I tell you?" she said. "People are dying for this kind of thing."

She agreed with Barbara, she said. The problem with Terrebonne was that there were just too few entertainment opportunities available for people with more sophisticated tastes. We might as well have been living in a jungle. There was no real social calendar to speak of; all we had were fishing rodeos, and oil company picnics, and those horrible, bloody, Cajun *courirs de Mardi Gras*, with drunken men on horseback flinging half-dead chickens in the air. Really, what chance did a lady have to get dressed up and put on her good jewelry and socialize in polite company? Without even quite knowing it, everyone had been waiting for an event exactly like this one.

But they would have to hurry; they needed a band, a caterer, bartenders, decorations. She and Barbara swapped ideas over the phone like two high school girls planning for a prom. Barbara had seen some cute Chinese lanterns in New Orleans they might be able to use. Frank was asking around town about the food and drinks. One day my mother rode with Barbara to Thibodaux in her Town Car to browse for party supplies. They stopped afterward for lunch at the Thibodaux Country Club, and telling us about it over dinner, my mother found opportunity to repeat the phrase "lunch at the club" several times. They ran into Connie Delaney there, of Connie's Gifts and Flowers, who agreed to do the flower arrangements. People were already talking about it, Connie had said. Everyone who came into her shop wanted to know who was going and what they should wear.

"Isn't that exciting?" my mother said, gripping her fork and knife. Her enthusiasm had a wild, stubborn quality about it, as if now that she had gotten a foot up on the ladder of society, she would hang on for all she was worth.

She began to spend more and more time with the Martellos. She would take off in the car in the afternoon, drive across the bridge to Beau Rivage Estates, and not return home until the evening. She sat making phone calls with Barbara in their patio room, or they drove up to Thibodaux, where after running errands they stopped off at the club or visited Frank's condo for "a little rest and relaxation," as my mother called it. Removing her scarf as she came in the front door, she talked breathlessly about who else they had lined up to volunteer this or that service.

My father followed her from room to room, the newspaper dangling from his hand, trying to keep up. He asked questions and tried to offer suggestions. The decorations, for instance. If they were going to have a comet theme, he might have some ideas for that. They could do something with lights, something to suggest stars and planets, maybe? Those kinds of touches were important, my father said. Maybe he should come over and talk to Frank about it.

My mother rolled her eyes. He really didn't need to worry himself, she told him. She and the Martellos had everything under control. My father could talk it up with the other teachers at school if he wanted, but really, there wasn't much for him to do.

At night when we were all getting ready to go to bed, my mother would still be up chatting in a whisper on the phone. She giggled and spoke in coded language, like a schoolgirl. "She did not!" she would say. "Well, you just tell her it's none of her business."

My father frowned behind his glasses, his face pinched and impatient. "Are you going to talk all night?"

"In a minute!" she answered.

He would close their bedroom door behind him, slamming it hard so that the walls shook and the living room windows rattled in their frames, prompting Megan to turn to me with raised eyebrows, as though to say, *Do you see this? Do you see what's happening here?*

What I saw was a growing rivalry between my parents, something I'd never noticed before but that manifested itself now in slammed doors, and muttered asides, and muffled arguments heard through the floor of my bedroom as my mother came and went on her various errands. But why it should appear now, I didn't know, and not knowing this, I turned to the comet. And then, as the comet winked and sparkled provocatively in the lens of my telescope, it became perfectly obvious to me: my mother was jealous of my father's comet, and like a jealous lover, she retaliated.

CHAPTER TWENTY-THREE

IT was only 160 million miles away now, fast approaching Earth's orbit. Day by day, my father relayed the latest news to us at school. Operation Kohoutek, set up by NASA, was coordinating the activities of hundreds of scientists around the globe. All the major telescopes, from Mount Palomar's 200-inch Hale on down, were on line to track it. Planes were being equipped with infrared telescopes to fly into the upper atmosphere to photograph it. Balloons would carry aloft packages of instruments to measure X-rays and gamma rays. *Mariner 10,* the *Orbiting Solar Observatory 7,* and *Pioneer 8* were all set to gather additional data, and the launch of *Skylab 3* had been delayed in order to bring the astronauts in for a close-up view of Kohoutek as it swept around the Sun.

Though as yet invisible in the sky without a telescope, the comet was everywhere in the media by now. It had made the cover of *Time,* and there were features in *Popular Science, Newsweek, National Geographic.* "The Comet of the Century," they called it. "The Christmas

Comet." "Kohoutek Cometh!" My father clipped all of these stories and taped them to a display board he set up in the lobby at school, under the heading "Countdown to Kohoutek."

"Got you a little bulletin board going there," Coach DuPleiss teased. But even he paused to read the headlines. "Seriously—we don't have anything to be afraid of, do we?"

The school astronomy club, which my father moderated, and which until recently had only four members, enjoyed an upsurge in popularity. They switched from monthly meetings to weekly ones, and a dozen students would gather after school in my father's classroom to rap with him about the stars. He sat informally on his desk, swinging his legs, and entertained them with stories of the more spectacular and terrifying comets in history. There was the Great Civil War Comet, for instance, that appeared over the Battle of Shiloh spurting flaming red jets from its head. Or the Comet of the Black Death that swept across the sky like a sword during a plague that wiped out half the population of the world. Or the famous Cheseaux Comet of 1744, whose tail split into six rays that fanned out across the horizon and then lingered for months, terrorizing cities all across Europe and driving men mad. Donati's Comet, the most beautiful comet of them all, hung in the sky for an entire year, expelling a series of shroudlike comas, like a woman casting off veils. Comet Encke dropped a piece of itself that exploded over Siberia with a blast a thousand times more powerful than the atomic bomb that flattened Hiroshima. The Star of Bethlehem: a comet? Could've been. Some scientists said it was.

Eager students rushed to buy telescopes at shops in New Orleans and Baton Rouge; when the shops sold out of telescopes, people bought binoculars. We would see them in the evenings, boys with their fathers, families who had never before had any interest in astronomy, people who had hardly ever noticed that there were lights in the sky, setting up their new telescopes in their yards or carrying them into empty fields at the edge of town, astronomy guidebooks in hand. My father, if he was passing on his bike, would stop to offer help. Sometimes he forgot the time and would come home long after dinner, burrs stuck to the cuffs of his trousers, apologizing.

Thanks to his Groovy Science column, he'd become known as the local expert on Comet Kohoutek, the go-to person for all things astronomical. He began to receive invitations to speak around the parish. During the day after his own classes, he visited schools in neighboring towns to talk to science clubs and student assemblies. In the evenings and on weekends he spoke at the Rotary Club, the Lions Club, the Ladies Auxiliary. He worked up a standard presentation for all these engagements, with ten-minute, thirty-minute, and forty-five-minute versions available. He practiced with note cards in the living room, until everyone in our family got to know his speeches almost as well as he did. They all followed the same basic outline:

1. *What is a comet? Where do they come from? Why are they important?*
2. *Famous comets in history*
3. *Kohoutek—The Comet of the Century*
4. *Viewing tips*
5. *Nothing to fear*
6. *Questions?*

CHAPTER TWENTY-FOUR

IN late November he appeared as a guest on Buckskin Bill's "Storyland Cabin," a morning show on WNGO-TV in New Orleans. He drove there early, and my mother, sister, and I watched from home before school as the show was broadcast. I was nervous waiting for him to come on. Half of Louisiana's youth would see him; some of my class-mates might even see him. What if he did something stupid?

Buckskin Bill was a middle-aged man in a fringed leather shirt and a coonskin cap. His Storyland Cabin was a small studio set designed to look like the inside of a log cabin, with a fake fireplace, deer antlers on the wall, and a rustic wooden bookcase filled with children's books. For the interview, my father sat on an upturned log across from Bill, who rested his hands on his knees and asked his questions in gentle morning tones, as if he were speaking to a sleepy child.

"We've all heard a lot about this comet, Professor. It sounds really exciting. Why don't you tell us a little bit more about it?"

In the tight frame of the camera, my father's head appeared larger and bonier than in real life. His skin had an orange-pinkish tint, like a pumpkin's. He sniffed and jerked a little at the start, but once he settled down he conducted himself with aplomb.

He spoke simply but knowledgeably about the comet, following his usual script. He illustrated his remarks with a prop that he'd begun bringing around to his lectures, a foil-covered Styrofoam ball. He had a variety of cardboard tails that he attached to the ball to show different apparitions of comets, and he moved the model around his head to demonstrate how Kohoutek would circle the Sun.

"Gosh. Look at that," said Buckskin Bill.

My father's presentation was interrupted by Señor Gonzales, Bill's puppet sidekick, who dropped down from above onto a stool between Bill and my father. He was dressed as a Mexican, with a thin black mustache and a sombrero, and he jumped and waved tiny guns attached to his hands. He acted the alarmist and wailed in a high, nasally Mexican voice, "The comet is coming! The comet is coming!" Buckskin Bill chuckled and patted Señor Gonzales on his sombrero. My father played along, saying to the puppet, "Now, now. There's nothing to be afraid of, Señor Gonzales." He brought the model comet down to show to the puppet, and together with Buckskin Bill they discussed what to expect and when the best time to view it would be. The puppet was mollified, and at the end pronounced Kohoutek *"fantastico!"* and did a jerky wooden-shoe dance on the stool.

"You didn't think it was silly?"

"I thought it was good," I said later that evening at dinner.

Megan said, "You should have strangled that little puppet."

My mother commented on his skin tone and suggested he might consider using a little powder before his next TV appearance. "Not makeup. Just a little powder is all I'm saying."

"It's just something for the kids, obviously," my father said, ignoring her. But heck, even Carl Sagan wasn't above appearing on *Sesame Street*. The important thing was that the astronomical community was finally getting the attention it deserved. He saw himself as a sort of emissary between the world of stars and the world of men. Ordinary folks tended to think of astronomy as something remote and removed from their lives, he explained, but with this comet they had the chance to bring it down to a personal level, to show people that all their stargazing really was relevant. Even Dr. Kohoutek recognized the need for this kind of public outreach.

Next month, my father told us, Luboš would be making his first visit to America. Everybody in the Astronomical Society was talking about it. For a man as notoriously lab bound and shy as Luboš Kohoutek, this was quite the venture. He'd be making the rounds: first he would speak at Harvard University, then he'd be the guest of honor at the biannual AAS conference, in Washington, and from there he would fly to Houston to visit NASA. But the thing that was getting the most attention was the Comet Cruise—a three-day comet-viewing excursion on the *Queen Elizabeth*, sailing from New York in early December. It had been sold out for a month, with East Coast socialites paying three hundred dollars apiece for the privilege of dining and dancing with the comet's namesake. Other celebrities sailing with Luboš on the Comet Cruise, our father had heard, were Hugh Downs, Buzz Aldrin, Carl Sagan, and Burl Ives.

"Not sure what Burl Ives has to do with astronomy," my father groused good-naturedly. "He'll probably bring his ukulele, sing a few tunes."

He spoke about the possibility of meeting Dr. Kohoutek himself—not on the cruise, of course, but maybe at the conference in Washington or while the scientist was passing through Houston. Who knew when he'd get another chance like this? It'd be like meeting a modern-day Galileo. Just to shake his hand, say hello, congratulate him on his discovery: that was all our father wanted. Oh, sure, he knew he was just a high school science teacher. But Luboš was just a man, like any other man, and besides, in his experience all astronomers shared a certain mutual respect for one another, no matter their standing. It was like with that Japanese fellow, the one who had found all the comets. No one cared that he worked in a factory, or that he didn't have a PhD after his name; he could sit at the table with the best of them. It was like a club, my father said, and the only requirement for membership was your love of the stars.

Because finally what mattered was the science itself. That was the main thing, and every astronomer understood this. Whether he was a professor at an observatory in Hamburg, or an amateur astronomer in Japan, or a teacher at a poor rural high school in Louisiana, any person who scanned the skies and felt that sense of wonder and shared it with his neighbor was making his contribution to the field, no matter how small. The comet might've held Kohoutek's name, but really it belonged to all of them. Its discovery was the outcome of years, centuries even, of study and stargazing by countless astronomers, famous and obscure, all over the world. Here, finally, was the proof of the value of their profession, and all the attention in the media was well deserved; for Comet Kohoutek, as everyone now acknowledged, was *the most important astronomical phenomenon of the century.*

He stopped and rested his hands on the table, as if the full significance of this was just sinking in. He had long fingers with wide white moons on the nails; they were the hands of a scientist, of a man meant to work quietly indoors—hardly the hands of a person who could stand up and meet the world blow for blow.

He shook his head, amazed. It was real. It was here. It was coming. Fifty times brighter than Halley's, the comet to outshine them all. Nobody at our dinner table seriously doubted him anymore. How could we? All the world's experts confirmed everything he'd been telling us for months. Even Megan had to admit he was right. He'd been right all along. We could practically hear his comet rumbling up there in the sky like a storm gathering above our house.

And perhaps it was only my impression, but as the comet raced nearer, my father seemed to be growing in size himself. He was slightly bigger than before, bigger than life. Seeing him now at home or at school—prepping his lessons, riding his bike, standing watch on the playground in his black raincoat—I pictured the glow of his certainty surrounding him like an aura, so that his glasses, his oiled hair, his white shirt and black tie became things not to jeer at, but rather the marks of his profession, things to almost admire about the man. It was as if he had finally fixed the focus on himself so that it was clear who he was. He needn't be ashamed of who he was; he was who he was. This comet, this lump of ice and gas, validated everything he'd ever stood for. It was evidence to the world that the life of Alan Broussard, high school science teacher and amateur astronomer, hadn't been a waste after all.

And for the first time in my teenage life, I began to feel a measure of pride for my father. For the first time since I was a boy, I wasn't ashamed to answer to my name.

CHAPTER TWENTY-FIVE

"COMET Boy! You are the comet!"

I stood at the kitchen window watching for her. The trees were bare and the weeds lay flat along the edges of the bayou. Five houses up, Mr. Coot was burning leaves in his backyard, sending smoke drifting in a low gray fog down the water. The afternoon light was clear, the air thin, the clouds high and white. In this cool, denuded landscape, the distance between her home and mine seemed to have shrunk. If I looked carefully, I could read the grain on the wood of their boat dock; if I listened, I could hear the click and thunk of their front door as the Martellos came and went during the day. Catching Gabriella as she passed from the car to the house or strolled up the drive to check the mailbox, I would call to her from our backyard. I hardly had to raise my voice for her to hear me. "Gabby. What's up?" She would answer, "Comet Boy! You are the comet!" And the invisible golden cord joining us would snap and twang, causing me to almost buckle over with joy and misery.

This feeling, this painful tugging in my gut whenever I laid eyes on her—was this what people called love? And did she feel it, too? How could I know?

My father stepped up beside me at the window and sniffed lightly to signal his presence. It was the Saturday after Thanksgiving Day. Megan had gone out and my mother had left for another visit to the Martellos, leaving just the two of us at home. My father peered up through the window to check the clouds.

"Should be some good viewing again tonight if the weather stays clear. I'm curious to see what that tail's doing."

I saw my mother arrive at the Martellos' house across the water. She parked the Rambler in the street in front, got out, and lifted bolts of silver cloth from the backseat; she and Barbara were working on some sort of costumes for the ball, only two weeks away now. Frank jogged up the driveway to meet her and helped her carry the supplies to the house.

"Friendly guy, isn't he?" my father said, but he didn't sound too pleased about it. We watched until they disappeared around the front corner of the house. "The women have abandoned us. We're on our own now." He stepped away from the window. "Hungry? Lunch?"

I cleared the table while he put on an apron and set about making sandwiches. The house was dim and cool, the lights off, the gas turned low to conserve energy, on account of the Arabian oil embargo. As he laid out slices of white bread on the countertop and methodically layered the components—mustard, turkey, lettuce, tomato, mayonnaise— he talked about the ball. He was still surprised people had responded as favorably as they had—seventy-two reservations so far and calls were still coming in. They probably didn't give a hoot about any science labs, he said; they just wanted their party. But no matter. With a couple thousand dollars he'd be able to do quite a lot for the department. He'd been talking with the other science teachers about how to best use the money, and everyone was drawing up their wish lists: new microscopes, spectroscopes, circuitry kits, centrifuges, topographical surveying equipment. With luck, they'd have the labs up and running again before the end of the school year; then we'd be able to do some really nifty projects in my class. "Wouldn't that be neat?"

He squared the sandwiches and cut them diagonally. "Pickle? I love a good pickle with lunch." He added some to a plate, and I poured apple juice for us and sat to join him at the table.

We ate our sandwiches, passing the salt and pepper. He wore a flannel shirt tucked into khaki-colored pants, his professorial formality set aside for the holiday. In spite of our differences—his short hair, mine long, his old-fashioned glasses, my new-fashioned bell-bottoms—I felt a rare sense of companionship with him. It could've had to do with the fact that I was nearly as tall as he was now, so that I sat higher in my chair, my head almost at a level with his. We had stepped away for the moment from father and son, teacher and student. We might have instead been a couple of guys on a camping trip, roughing it together without the women. The cool air batted the thin walls of our cabin, rattling the windows as we hunkered down inside, sharing our scrappy meal, one made that much more enjoyable by its improvised nature.

"This reminds me of when I was a bachelor," he said, pushing his glasses up with the back of his hand.

He told me how when he first moved to Terrebonne he lived on his own in a rented apartment in town. He used to do all his own cooking then. Washed his own clothes. Stayed up all hours of the night. Those were the days. Guys would come over and leave their beer bottles everywhere. "Your mother was appalled—*appalled*—when she saw that apartment." He chuckled at the memory.

To be reminded that my father was once a young man was always a little startling for me. Washed his own clothes? Up all hours? Beer bottles everywhere? That was hard to believe. To my eyes at least, he appeared to have been stuck at the same age, in the same body, for as long as I'd known him, as unchanging as a photograph in a school yearbook. But as unlikely as it seemed, I knew he'd been young once, too. Maybe he had even experienced the same confused longings and attachments that I felt now. Maybe he had had his Gabriella.

I edged up to the question between bites of my sandwich.

"How'd you and Mom ever, you know, get together?"

"You've heard this story before, haven't you? She was working in the drugstore. I was a new teacher."

"Right—"

"I had a stomachache, and I used to go there every night."

He began to retell it, his version of the scientist and the shopgirl story. Though I'd heard it before, I was eager to hear it again because it struck me as especially relevant just now. Maybe here would be some clue to my feelings for Gabriella, some guide to how I should act.

And so as the faint blue flames flickered in the gas heater and the winter scratched at the walls outside, I filled in the blanks in his story with my imagination until I could almost see my father as a hair-slicked, bespectacled bachelor, a young man who looked much like he did now only smaller, skinnier, a little jerkier: Alan Broussard as he once was, back before there was ever a thought of an Alan Broussard, Jr.

Back then, he told me, he never meant to be a teacher. He much preferred being a student. He loved everything about his department at LSU: the research, his classmates, the professors. Dr. Brewer, his advisor, always said he had the mind of a scientist, the ability to get inside a problem and visualize a solution. Not everyone had that. But then he happened to attend a recruitment fair for prospective schoolteachers at the university field house, and one week later, much to his surprise, he received a phone call from the Terrebonne school district offering him a job.

He didn't even know where Terrebonne was. But he wanted to prove to his parents that he could stand on his own two feet. "Go have your *Wanderjahr*," Dr. Brewer said. "That's what I would do." And so he bought a secondhand car and five new ties, shook his father's hand, kissed his mother's cheek, and drove south. Down he drove, down to the toe of the state, carrying the torchlight of science into the jungle. . . . He ran over a snake outside Napoleonville. . . .

"Okay, okay, I already know all that," I interrupted him. "I've heard it all before. As innocent as a Christian tossed to the lions. Everyone came to school by boat. There was a girl named Melinda."

"She found a fossil. . . ."

"Right, I know. You can skip all that. And then one day, after grad-ing papers all evening . . . ," I said, prodding him to move along to the important part of the story.

"Right. Okay. And so then one day, after grading papers all evening, I walked over to the McCall's Rexall. She was all alone in the store, the only employee working that night. . . ."

CHAPTER TWENTY-SIX

SHE was alone in the store, the only employee working that night he walked over from his apartment for some stomach medicine. The bell on the inside of the door dinged when he stepped into the shop. She didn't look up.

"What can I do for you?" she asked in a flat, sleepy voice.

She might have been one of his teenage students herself, so young and bored she seemed. She was leaning on the counter near the cash register studying the latest issue of *Movie World* magazine. The headline of the article she was reading, viewed upside down by my father-to-be, said "Is Debbie Waiting Too Long?"

Alan asked what she could recommend for an upset stomach, and when she finally raised her head to answer him, he was so startled by her appearance that he involuntarily took a step back from the counter. She had very white skin, a pointed nose, and red frizzy hair that surrounded her head like a nimbus of fire. She seemed an anomaly in this land of dark-skinned Cajuns. What was she even doing here? The tag on her pink smock said "Lydia."

Alan blinked. Had she said something?

"Excuse me?"

"I said, what kind of upset stomach do you have? Does it feel like gas? Heartburn? Nausea?"

"Burning. Like what I imagine an ulcer would feel like."

"Ooh. That can't be good."

She came around from behind the counter. Even in the dull glare of the fluorescent lights, she looked radiant. Beneath her frumpy smock she wore a snug gray skirt and low-heeled black pumps. And no stockings, which seemed to him wildly provocative at the time. He followed her to a shelf of stomach medicines. She walked with a wonderful lazy swish of her hips, talking over her left shoulder with a wonderful, lazy drawl.

"You're not eating right?"

"I don't think it's that."

"Do you drink? Smoke?"

"No. I'm, ah, a high school science teacher."

She laughed once, "Ha! That would do it." She bent to the shelf of medicines and handed him a bottle of milk of magnesia. "Try this."

He took the blue bottle. He didn't want to leave. He bought six dinner mints at the counter just to prolong his time with her for a few more seconds.

The next evening he returned to buy some aspirin, and the night after that some Vick's VapoRub, and then again for some more stomach medicine. He still had that burning in his gut; in fact, since he met her it only seemed to be getting worse. She asked about his classes and about his parents back home in Baton Rouge. He asked about her. She was vague about her family. But she loved the movies and talked about Hollywood actors and actresses as if she knew them all personally. Debbie Reynolds had bought a new house for her and her mother in Brentwood. Cary Grant was going quail hunting with his friends that weekend in England. Hedda Hopper, in her gossip column, was still calling Ava Gardner a home wrecker, but anyone who looked at her could tell it wasn't true, and didn't Alan think she was just divine?

The Barefoot Contessa, that new film with her and Humphrey Bogart, looked like a good one. Ava played Maria Vargas, a poor but proud

Spanish cabaret dancer who gets discovered by a rich Hollywood pro-
ducer and then goes on to marry a real live count. It was supposed to be
very sad and romantic—the movie opened and closed with Ava's death,
which in Lydia's opinion sounded like a terrible way to begin and end
a story. "But I'd love to see it just for Ava and Bogart. What a great pair.
Don't you think?"

Alan agreed with whatever she said. Yes, that did sound like an interesting movie. He wouldn't mind seeing that himself. When was that
showing? Did she know?

Finally, on the sixth night as he lingered at her register, she slapped
his small wrapped package of cough medicine down on the counter and
said with something like exasperation in her voice: "Look, if you want
to ask me out, just ask me."

He would always remember that as the moment he definitely, irre-
vocably fell for her. The sensation was like dropping into a bed of feathers. He felt his stomach relax, and the burn in his gut vanished in a
wisp, *pfft!*

That weekend he drove her to Thibodaux to see the movie. As they
walked together along the sidewalk, he was struck by how carefully
upright she carried herself, as though, with her high heels and erect
posture, she was making a studied effort to raise herself above her
peers. He bought them popcorn and Cokes in the theater and they took
their seats. When they showed the preview trailer before the newsreels
and cartoons, Alan didn't have high hopes for the movie; it looked like
the kind of overripe story that he normally avoided: "*The world's most
beautiful animal! Spanish gypsy! Café society dancer!* The Barefoot
Contessa *will shock you, provoke you, excite you, as no other film ever
has!*"

But when the film began, Lydia was instantly caught up in the story.
She sat so still that she appeared spellbound. He looked back and forth
from her profile to the screen, wondering what she was seeing there.
The light and colors flickering across her pale skin seemed to him to be
the projection of her own secret dreams and thoughts playing out
across her face. He imagined that this must've been what Lydia looked
like when she was asleep, and seeing her so unguarded, so exposed,

moved him in unexpected ways. When the pregnant Ava got shot at the
end, Lydia gasped aloud and grabbed his arm in genuine shock and dis-
may, so that he wanted to hug her shoulders and kiss her hair and
whisper, *There, there. It's only a dream. It's only a dream.*

After the lights came up and they stood from their seats and started
up the aisle, the effect of the film lingered. Even as they left the theater
and began walking along the sidewalk, it felt as if the movie hadn't
ended but instead was continuing with another reel, one that now fea-
tured them and the town they were in, and the stores they passed, and
the people and cars on the sidewalks and streets. When Lydia took his
arm and squeezed it, he knew she must've been feeling the same thing.
That oak tree with its autumn leaves lit by a streetlight; that orange
neon sign above a clothing store; that man in the hat lighting a cigarette on the corner; and that woman they passed with the red lipstick
who tossed her head back when she laughed: they were all in the
movie, too, a romantic story about a scientist and a shopgirl out on
their first date in a small southern town. Alan wouldn't have been surprised to find that when he next opened his mouth to speak, his words
came out in song, and the passersby, the man in the hat and the lady
with the lipstick, lined up for a dance number and joined in at the chorus.

He brought her to dinner at a restaurant up the street, and as they
settled into the padded booth and picked up their menus, the feeling
persisted that everything they said and did was preordained and perfect. Over their hamburger plates they discussed *The Barefoot Contessa.* Lydia claimed that the movie's story paralleled Ava Gardner's
own life, and she told Alan all about the actress's dirt-poor childhood,
and the scandal with Frank Sinatra, and her affair with Howard
Hughes. . . .

"Huh. I did not know that," he replied.

They talked about Ava's and Bogart's characters in the movie. Lydia
insisted that they were meant for each other, and that this was the
tragedy at the heart of the film—the barefoot contessa was desperately
searching for what could only be a substitute for the true love she was
denied. Alan, enjoying the discussion, argued that while they might

have looked good together on the screen, those two characters could never have been happy with each other. Bogart—or rather, the fellow Bogart played—was just being realistic about the potential difficulties of a relationship between two people as different as they were. Besides, they were both already married, and they couldn't very well just—

"So you think they were better off that way? Each of them stuck in their own miserable lives?"

"I'm not saying—"

"Even if they belonged together? Even if they were so obviously *perfect* for each other?"

"Well, yes, I suppose—"

"Don't you think she's an attractive woman?"

"Why, yes. Yes, of course I do. She's a very attractive woman. Anyone can see that."

While gesturing nervously with a french fry, Alan accidentally got ketchup on his silk tie. Lydia ordered him to take it off immediately, called for soda water, and sprinkled his tie with salt and dabbed away the stain with paper napkins. When she'd finished, she held up his tie for him to see. "There. Good as new, Mr. Broussard," she said, and he thought that this, too, was perfectly executed, a moment arranged by some not-so-subtle director in the sky to demonstrate their compatibility. He was already beginning to see them as a team, not so very different from Humphrey Bogart and Ava Gardner in the movie: he with his good sense, she with her sensitivity.

They went out again after this, and he visited her every day at the drugstore, but she never allowed him to pick her up at home; she always met him in town for their dates. Alan didn't press the issue, but her evasiveness about her family did seem odd. Finally, on their fourth date, she invited him to her home. When he arrived she jogged out to his car to meet him. "My father . . . ," she tried to warn him as she led him along the broken sidewalk to her front door, but then she let it drop.

The house was a tiny Depression-era cottage with slope-roofed add-ons and a barking dog on a chain in the backyard. When they walked in, her parents were standing stiffly side by side on a square of vinyl laid atop the worn carpeting in the middle of the front room, as though she had posed them there and told them not to dare move until she and her beau had left. She introduced them rather formally as Robert and Dorothy Simoneaux.

Her mother had Lydia's Irish-red hair and pale skin. But her father . . . That was when Alan saw what she'd been afraid to tell him: her father had only one arm. Or, more precisely, he had one and a half arms. The right sleeve of his white shirt flapped loose below the elbow. Alan hardly had time to register his surprise before Bob quickly proffered his left hand. Alan shook it in his right hand, their fingers gripping each other's awkwardly but firmly, like the couplings of two railroad cars jammed together.

Lydia didn't give them time to talk and hustled Alan out of the house minutes later. She seemed ashamed of her parents. "Bob and Dot," she complained. "It sounds like a drive-in diner. It sounds like a laundromat."

But Alan thought they seemed like decent enough people, and over the next few visits he learned what a good gumbo Dot could make, and he learned from Bob himself about his job as a salesman with a local drilling supply company, and how he got his start as a guide leading surveyors in a pirogue through the swamps and bayous around the parish, and his wildcat years as a tool pusher on rigs in the Gulf, up until the time a stupid new roughneck lost his grip on the tongs and the chain came whipping around and snatched his hand right off. He'd been fitted for a prosthetic, but he hated the damn thing; it just got in the way. One weekend Bob took him fishing out on Lake Boeuf, and Alan enjoyed it more than he ever thought he could. He liked the man's quiet, sneaky humor, and he felt touched when Bob stopped him and showed him the proper way to scale and filet a fish, flipping and slicing it with a delicate, unselfconscious ease using the shiny callused stump of his right forearm to brace it down on the cutting board. . . .

No, in spite of Lydia's embarrassment about them, he didn't have any problems with her parents. And that summer, as soon as he finished his first year of teaching, they were married. Just like that. They took the Sunset Limited to Los Angeles for their honeymoon, returned, and soon they were busy with all the work of setting up a home.

He signed on for another year at Terrebonne High, and then they had their first child; and so he signed on for another year, and then they had their second child. Before he knew it, he'd become that middle-aged schoolteacher he'd never wanted to be, lecturing forever from the same old textbook, himself apparently unchanging even as the years hurtled past and his students rotated in and out of his classroom so quickly that they became a blur, giving him the impression that he was standing still while the rest of the world spun faster and faster around him.

From time to time he would look back on that night at the drugstore and wonder what might have happened if he hadn't stopped—if instead of stepping inside for medicine, he had walked on, taken a turn around the square to settle his stomach. In his dreams he would actually sometimes see that other Alan, the one he might have been, wearing a white coat and goggles and working in a sophisticated-looking research laboratory. Or he would spot him, that other Alan, while watching another Apollo launch on TV with his family: look, there he was, sitting in front of an oscilloscope, twirling knobs and listening on a headset as Mission Control began the countdown.

But that other Alan, he knew, was just a fantasy, as distant and irretrievable as his own childhood. There was no going back. He was who he was. Life had delivered him here, where, twenty years later, he was winding down yet another semester of freshman Earth and Space Science. He was a schoolteacher now. Now and forever.

CHAPTER TWENTY-SEVEN

"AND that's how it happened," he told me, ending his story. "As fast as that. *Ka-boom!* Here we are. Mr. and Mrs. Alan Broussard. For better or worse, till death do us part."

My father gave a quick, stiff smile across the table. He picked up his turkey sandwich and resumed eating. The lettuce crunched between his teeth; a dribble of tomato and mayonnaise fell to the plate. I picked up my own sandwich and took a few bites.

I liked my father's version of the story well enough, but hearing it now left me oddly unsatisfied. It sounded almost too neat, too easy to be true. And what was that note of regret I thought I detected at the end? I got the feeling he wasn't telling me everything.

Besides, his story didn't really answer my questions about Gabriella. What about that mysterious attraction that drew people together in the first place? How did that work? And how did he know that he loved her? And that she loved him? How could you ever be sure?

When I asked him this, he stopped chewing. We had never talked seriously about these things before, and he seemed to recognize the urgency in my voice.

"What is love, basically? Is that what you're asking?"

"Right."

He set down his sandwich. "Hm. That's a good one, all right. Well, okay, let's see."

He began by saying how, in biology, there was actually a whole science of attraction. Those who studied this could explain it better than he could, but basically, it involved hormones, pheromones, estrogen levels, things like that. Looking at it in terms of evolution, he said, it was well known that females of a species were attracted to partners whose physical features and behaviors indicated that they would be good providers and protectors, whereas the male preferred females who looked like they would produce healthy offspring. When one met a potential mate, he or she communicated his or her interest through certain signals, certain sounds and gestures. He talked about courtship rituals among animals, such as the bird-of-paradise in New Guinea, which spread its feathers and danced and hung upside down from a tree in order to lure females. . . .

He must've seen he was losing me, because he stopped talking.

"That doesn't help, does it?" he said.

"Not really."

He sighed. He took off his glasses and began cleaning them with his handkerchief. Without them on, he looked naked and vulnerable. Gray purses of flesh hung below his eyes, and his nose appeared thinner, bonier. A paler, older version of my father had taken his place across the table—a man almost a stranger to me. He grimaced slightly, as though he were experiencing again the indigestion he'd felt all those years ago in the drugstore. When he spoke again, it was with effort.

"Look, I'll be honest with you, Junior. It's difficult, this business of love. When you're young, your head's filled with all these romantic notions that you get from songs and stories and movies, telling you how great and magical and mysterious love is. How it's going to last forever. Love love love. And sure, that's good, that's fine. That's part of being young. You need that kind of . . . kind of belief."

He grimaced again, a single twitch on the left side of his face.

"But as you get older . . . as you get older, you realize that those are just, you know, stories. They're kind of like fairy tales that we tell each other, tell our kids, to keep us going. Because they're not real, you know. Not really. Real life isn't like that, not like in movies and songs. Real life is about hard work, and family, and responsibility. So as you grow older, you buckle down, you get busy with your job, you try to do good work, try to take care of your family. And pretty soon you don't worry about love so much anymore. Maybe you stop thinking about it altogether. And I'm not saying that's bad. That's just the way it is. That's part of growing up. That's what they call becoming an adult."

What was my father saying? That the story about the boy and the girl in the drugstore wasn't true? Or that he didn't love her? Or she him? Or, worse, that love didn't even exist? That it was just a made-up story for children and fools?

I felt queasy. It was like he had led me to the edge of a bottomless pit and pointed over the side. I could feel the chilly air rushing up from the black depths, smell the rank odor of death. *Take a good look,* he might've been telling me. *See? There's nothing there. Nothing at all.*

He put his glasses back on and gave a quick sniff as he settled them into place on his nose. When he lifted his head, the light coming in from the window fell on the lenses so that they were like two small, flashing shields.

He stood up and brought his plate to the sink. He stopped behind me and quietly rested a hand on my shoulder.

"But hey. Don't worry about all that. You're still young. You've got your whole life ahead of you. Now's the time for you to be having fun. Right?"

"Right," I said.

But too late: the damage had been done. He'd taken that white worm of doubt and planted it in me. He might have called it a healthy dose of skepticism, or even objective reality. But his worm would stay with me, and even though I could tamp it down, forget about it for weeks at a time, the worm would always be there, a wriggling reminder of my worst fears:

That life wouldn't get any easier as I got older. If anything, it would only get harder as I grew up to the realization, as he apparently had, that all our beliefs were built on a flimsy scaffolding of stories, and that happiness was nothing but a wish and love was only a lie.

CHAPTER TWENTY-EIGHT

MY mother closed the front door behind her. She wore a scarf over her head and carried a shoe box full of paperwork. It was late in the evening. Megan was upstairs in her room, the kitchen was clean, the house quiet and cool. I sat with a magazine in the corner of the couch.

"What took you so long?" my father said, looking up from his papers at the table.

"We had to go into Thibodaux," she answered.

"You did? Who? What for?"

"We had to see about the lights. The lights for the decorations."

"That took you all day?"

"Guess who might come? The mayor."

She shoved my father's papers aside and set her box on the table, talking all the while about their arrangements for the ball. Frank had spoken to the mayor—he knew him, naturally—and the mayor said he would talk to his wife. Now Barbara was worried that the party might get too big, but my mother figured the Martellos' house could easily accommodate three hundred people. They could open up the yard, have tents and gas heaters out there in case it got cold.

She took off her scarf and shook out her hair. "We should've done tickets and invitations, I know. I'm always thinking too small, that's my problem."

Frank, she went on, was going to get a crew to lay a dance floor in front of the gazebo. He had sketched out some plans while they were chatting in the living room, *zip zip zip,* just like that.

"Thank god for Frank," my father said.

"What?"

"Frank Frank Frank. What would a party be without Frank?"

"What in the world are you talking about?"

"You know what I'm talking about. Your playboy across the water there."

"Oh, come on. Don't be absurd. He's been very helpful. In fact, you should be thanking him. We're doing this for you, you know."

"I don't need any favors."

I left my magazine and sat down beside my father at the table. "What about the dancing?"

"What's that, honey?"

"Who's going to dance?"

"Everybody, I hope. It's a ball. That's what you do at balls. You dance. Which reminds me, we still have to find clothes for you and Megan." She went to the kitchen to fix herself a drink, turning on lights in the house as she moved. I talked to her through the doorway.

"What kind of dancing?"

"Hm?"

"What kind of dancing will there be?"

"Any kind. Every kind. You do know how to dance, don't you? Don't you?"

"Where am I going to learn how to dance? School?"

"Oh, but every young man should know how to dance. It's a requirement. Women expect it. Society demands it. A man who can't dance is like a . . . like a horse without a saddle. I'll have to teach you."

"When?"

She came back into the living room. "How about right now?"

"The lights," my father said, pointing. "You left the lights on."

"Oh, pooh." She switched off the lights in the kitchen and came back. "Stand."

"What?"

"You can't dance sitting down. Get up. Help me move this."

My father stayed seated while we pulled the sofa back and cleared a space in the living room.

"When I was your age everyone knew how to dance. We went to dances all the time. Every weekend. Gosh, it was fun. Boys lining up to get inside the gym . . ."

"Your mother's golden years," my father said. "Hundreds of boyfriends, lining up for their turn."

"Thousands," she said, snapping her chin at him. She positioned herself in the middle of the floor. "Come on. I'll be the girl. You be the boy."

"Good plan."

"Wowser, you're getting tall. Okay, first you should politely approach the girl and ask, 'May I have this dance?' "

"May I have this dance?"

"Oh my god. Nobody does that," said Megan, coming down the stairs.

"Shh," said my mother. "Why, of course you may. I'd be delighted. Now, left hand up . . . like that. Your right hand goes here on my back. Stand up straight."

"I am."

"Straighter. We'll begin with something easy. A waltz."

"That's useful," Megan said. "Why not teach him to jitterbug, too?" She went to the kitchen for leftover pumpkin pie and ice cream.

"Ignore the armchair critics," my mother said. "We'll start slow. One-two-three, one-two-three. Just like that. Follow my feet. Ready? Here we go."

I mouthed the numbers with her as we shuffled around on the stained rug. Gabriella, of course, would know how to dance. She studied ballet, after all. I imagined she danced like an expert—waltzes, jitterbugs, anything.

"Oops. Sorry."

"That's okay. You're getting it. One-two-three."

I concentrated on the steps until I was able to see them in terms of geometry, invisible squares and diagonals traced on the floor.

"Oh my god, you dance like your father. Try not to look so grim. Smile! It's supposed to be fun. Girls like boys who smile." She stopped to take a swallow of her drink. "Okay, here we go again. Stand up straight. Relax. Don't look down."

After a while I could do it without tripping up too badly, but it wasn't what I would have called fun, exactly. While we practiced, my mother offered more advice about girls. Girls liked boys who took the lead, she said—men who showed confidence and acted like they knew what they were doing, even if they didn't. It was best to be forthright, too; I should just come right out and say what I was thinking. Girls were gifted with many amazing powers, but telepathy wasn't one of them. Also, I should look for opportunities to be polite, to offer small favors whenever I could. I could offer to get a girl a glass of punch, for instance, even if she said she didn't want one. Girls loved to be waited on like that. I'd be surprised how much could be achieved with one well-timed glass of punch.

"Oh, and by the way—don't be put off by the competition," she said.

"What competition?"

"Well, you know—pretty girls are always popular at dances. There's no getting around that. That's why you need to be especially polite and friendly. Polite and friendly beats out the competition every time."

"What competition?" I asked again.

"Don't worry, you'll be fine."

She taught me how to break in on a couple, and what to say to the girl while we were dancing. "Compliments. Nothing but compliments. Try it. Say 'I like your dress.'"

"I like your dress."

"I like your hair."

"I like your hair."

"I like your nose."

"I like your nose."

"Will you marry me?"

"Wait. What?"

"Just kidding on that one. You don't want to get too far ahead of yourself."

She pulled away, brushing stray hair from her mouth. "Not bad. You're getting the hang of it. Now when you're finished, you're supposed to bow and say 'Thank you for the lovely dance.' "

"Thank you for the lovely dance," I said, and she cracked up. "What?"

"No, no, she'll love it."

She told Megan to run upstairs and get some of her records, the fun ones, the ones you could dance to. Megan came down with a stack of 45s and they shuffled through them. "Try this," our mother said, and they put a disc on the turntable. I recognized the song immediately; it'd been playing all fall on the radio. It began with a few pleasant notes in the upper registers of an electric piano, like something a girl would pluck out at a recital. She turned up the volume.

"The speakers—" my father complained.

"Forget everything I just taught you," my mother said over the music, slipping off her shoes. "The only rule to dancing to music like this is that there are no rules. Anything goes. If it feels good, do it."

She grabbed my hands and twisted with me, humming and singing along to the record. "That's it. You've got it." She drew away, danced to the end of the sofa, did a kind of shimmy, turned, and came back. I watched, amazed. She didn't look stupid, she didn't look like someone's mother trying to dance. She looked . . . she looked lovely.

"Don't just stand there, silly. Come on. Move! It's fun."

I closed my eyes and made a few tentative steps. The song had a ridiculously simple arrangement, just a single piano, guitar, bass, and drums. It told about a party where everybody came together to have a good time. The Moon was bright; they danced, and people felt warm and alive. Then the whole thing repeated itself, and then again—there was almost nothing to it. But when the chorus broke in, the bounce in the rhythm and the invitation in the words was so irresistible that I felt myself lifted up on the swell of its refrain and soon I was dancing along with everyone in the moonlight. This, I understood in a flash, was why people liked to dance. It made you forget who you were and at the same time remember who you were always meant to be. You became more than yourself. You became, as the song put it, *su-per-na-tu-ral*. You flew.

"Oh my god," said Megan.

When the record finished, my mother stepped back clapping. "Wowser. Honey, that was great. You'll slay all the girls."

We played the record again, and then again, until Megan gave up sitting and joined us. Our father refused to stand, however, saying that he didn't understand this kind of dancing.

"Fuddy-duddy. Fuddy-duddy, you had your chance," my mother said.

So we danced without him. We stomped on the ruined rug, we turned circles between the sagging furniture and bumped against the old TV. This room, these things, didn't normally inspire celebration, but tonight it might've been Christmas in our home, or New Year's, or a holiday that none of us had known until now but were inventing at that very moment: the Holiday of Hope with the Dance of Possibility on the Eve of the Comet.

CHAPTER TWENTY-NINE

BY late November it had crossed the Earth's orbit and was speeding toward Venus, traveling at 250,000 miles an hour. Its coma had already grown to more than 100,000 miles across, its tail 5 million miles long. We still couldn't see it with our bare eyes, but with the telescope we could find it hanging just above the southwestern horizon, hovering near the archer's hand in Sagittarius. In the lens it appeared as a flickering blue flame giving off a wispy trail of smoke. From night to night the tail moved and changed, fanning out, coming together, corkscrewing, breaking in half and then restoring itself. It looked, I thought, powerful and determined. Inexhaustible. Indomitable.

My father kept up his nightly vigil in the backyard. From my window, I watched him shivering in his Sears McGregor raincoat. He'd zipped in the synthetic wool liner, but he didn't think to put on a sweater, and late at night the air off the bayou could be chilly. His right eye glued to the lens of the telescope, he moved his lips as he muttered under his breath, as though he were whispering into the ear of a lover:

Yes. Yes. There you are. I see you. Come on. Come on, you beautiful thing. . . .

While downstairs, in her room below me, his wife, my mother, sat at her vanity, cleaning her face with cold cream and tissues. Her hair would've been tied back, her legs crossed under her nightgown, one slippered foot bobbing up and down. *You're not that old yet,* I could imagine her telling herself. *You've still got some looks.* She smiled to remember the movie stars of her youth, glamorous women leaning their heads back, their pale throats curving forward as they closed their eyes to receive the lips of their leading men, and in an instant she became all those women, leaning her head back to kiss the man who was all those men. . . .

While in her room next door to mine, my sister was biting her nails and studying the liner notes on a favorite album. I pictured her rocking back and forth on the rug below her black-light poster, LOVE shot through with bullet holes. She grabbed a fistful of her hair, frizzy and thick, and frowned at it. She thought of Joan Baez, how sleek and straight her hair was—like her face, her body, all sleek and long and dignified. She sighed, dropped her hair, and returned her thumb to her mouth. With her front teeth she chewed at a sliver of flesh at the corner of her cuticle until, giving a good yank, she ripped it free, drawing blood. . . .

While I, her brother, backed away from my window to resume practicing dance steps. I didn't have a record player so I had to imagine the music in my head. I bent my knees and dipped my shoulders to a rim shot, then sprang back up, strutted, and turned. I thought I had it for a minute, felt I must've been dancing, but then I caught sight of myself in the mirror, a gangly fourteen-year-old kid jerking around in his tiny room, and I lost whatever confidence I had. I looked like a damn idiot. She would take one look at me and laugh out loud.

I stopped, caught my breath, and averted my eyes from the mirror. Then I started the record playing again in my head. I stood up straight, pulled my shoulders back, didn't look down.

Gabriella, I asked, *do you know this song? May I have this dance?*

CHAPTER THIRTY

"AN auspicious night," my father called it.

The sky was clear and speckled with stars. A full moon climbed up from the horizon. Mars was high, a faint red pinpoint hanging overhead. As we walked along a line of parked cars to the party, he pointed out constellations to me, tracing their outlines with his finger: Gemini, Orion, Aquarius.

He reminded me that Luboš and his high-society pals were on the Queen Elizabeth right now, sailing out of New York Harbor for their comet cruise. Maybe they were looking at these very same stars, he said. We were luckier, though; we didn't have to go out on a ship to see them: we got them for free. That was one advantage of living in a small town. "The greatest show on Earth, playing nightly. All you have to do is turn your eyes up."

He talked about organizing some kind of town-wide comet viewing here in Terrebonne. Astronomers were planning these events all over the country, and there was no reason why we couldn't have one, too.

"Wouldn't that be fun? Get everybody to turn off their lights for a night and come out to watch the comet. Parents, kids, everybody out in the streets. Like the Fourth of July, only better." He was trying to work out the best date for it now.

I agreed that it did sound fun. I could picture it: kids on bikes, lawn chairs on the sidewalks, everyone gazing skyward with the silvery light of the comet falling on their faces.

"Where is it now?"

He stopped, took my finger, and pointed with it to a spot below Orion. "Crossing through the orbit of Venus. Right about . . . there." He stood up straight and squinted sideways at the sky, trying to see it with his peripheral vision; he might've been listening for it. "It's close, it's awfully close. It's sneaking up on us."

I listened, too. I didn't hear any comet, but there was something, a suggestion of music in the air: notes from an electric piano, a guitar string being tuned, the *thump thump* of a bass drum.

Ahead of us stood the Martellos' house. It was set back across a deep lawn, lit with spotlights and decorated for Christmas. Behind the house we could see lanterns in the trees and the white peak of a canvas tent. As we continued walking, I had the feeling of approaching a circus at night, that same sense of expectancy. The air was brisk but not too cold, and as my father and I turned down the walkway to their house, around the lit fountain, and up a flight of low stone steps to their porch, the stiff cloth of our winter coats brushed back and forth on itself with a whispered *yess, yess, yess, yess.*

Don't gawk, my mother would've said, but when we stepped through the front door it was hard not to stare.

The entrance hall opened up into an unexpectedly high ceiling lit by a crystal chandelier. A curved stairway led to a second floor balcony. On the walls on either side of the hall hung large, gold-framed portraits of the family: Mr. Martello standing beside a desk with one hand resting on a book, Mrs. Martello sitting regally in a high-backed chair, Gabriella as a girl holding a yellow bouquet of flowers and gazing off into the sunshine.

Below her painting stood the real Gabriella in a purple velvet dress, her hair tied up with ribbons, welcoming guests.

"Mr. and Mrs. Daigle. How are you? It's great to see you. Thank you so much for coming," she said, and the Daigles smiled and gushed in return. She was the perfect hostess: gracious, poised, friendly. Just seeing her made you glad you'd come. She passed the Daigles on to my sister, who sat at a white-draped table with a money box, dutifully ticking off names in a notebook.

While my father spoke with the girls about party arrangements, I looked back and forth from Gabriella to her painting, marveling again at her and the extravagant wealth of her family. I might've been easily intimidated by it all, but before we moved on, Gabriella reached out and tugged my sleeve.

"You're looking sharp, Junior."

This wasn't true. My suit was an old two-piece from my eighth grade graduation, the jacket ridiculously small, the pants high-waters. But when Gabriella said I looked good, I could almost believe it was true, and my hopes for the evening were given a boost. We promised we'd see each other later, and I walked away rehearsing tricky dance steps in my mind.

We met Christine, our one-time maid, in the library. "They got me taking coats," she said. We chatted as she hung ours up on a long rack. She asked my father about the latest comet news.

"Soon. Real soon," he promised. In a few more weeks she'd have to duck her head to miss it.

"I'll start saying my prayers."

He chuckled. "No need for that. No, no."

He paused to take in the room. A floor-to-ceiling bookcase covered most of one wall. There was a fireplace, leather chairs, a writing desk, antique maps in frames, a globe in a wooden stand: it was so handsome, so picture-perfect, it might've been a display room from D. H. Holmes—"Gentleman's Study"—bought whole, taken apart, shipped here, and reassembled exactly as it appeared in the store.

My father gave a low whistle. "Man-oh-man." He reached out and touched the spines of a few books in the case and then retracted his hand, as though he'd caught himself doing something he shouldn't have.

He went off to find my mother, leaving me to wander on my own through the rooms. There was more to the house than I had imagined; my telescope had never taken me this far inside. Opposite the library was a living room with plush furniture, flowers in vases, picture books on a table, and a cart with a silver tea set. A large, elaborately decorated Christmas tree stood at the window. Farther on was a dining room, the table gone and the chairs pushed back against the walls. I peeked into a billiard room, a music room, a breakfast room, a sun room, and other rooms and passageways whose functions I could only guess at. It was like walking through a museum, and as in a museum, I felt wary of touching or standing too close to anything.

At the rear of the house I found the patio room with its familiar armchair, sofa, and television. The sliding glass door stood open to the pool and yard, where lights were shining, music was playing, and people were moving.

"Gorgeous. Gorgeous home," my mother had said. Seeing it myself, I understood why she liked visiting here so much, and why she always seemed so disappointed when she returned home to ours. It was obvious, wasn't it? Who wouldn't have wanted to trade their lives for this dream?

CHAPTER THIRTY-ONE

"JUNIOR. Over here."

Mark Mingis, my blond-haired, blue-eyed rival, was standing at the edge of the patio, a glass of cola in his hand.

"Cool party," he said.

"What are you doing here?"

"I can't come to the party?"

"I didn't think anyone else from school would be here."

"I'm not supposed to say. It's kind of a secret." He took a sip of his Coke and looked away mysteriously.

I had no interest in talking to Mark, but we were the only two boys at the party, and so I stepped up beside him. We watched the yard fill with guests while we sipped our Cokes. He stood half a head taller than me and wore a crisp blue blazer over a white turtleneck sweater.

"You live somewhere around here, don't you?" he asked.

"Over there across the water."

He glanced across the bayou. "Over there?"

"Yeah."

"Huh." He nodded, as if the matter was settled.

The band had begun playing in the gazebo in the corner of the yard. People stood in small groups, talking and drinking. Others carried plates of food from the buffet under the tent and sat down at tables lit with candles and warmed by gas heaters placed around the lawn. At a bar near us, a slim black man in a white jacket snatched up bottles and poured out drinks, murmuring, "Yes sir, yes sir! What'll you have? Yes, sir!"

I recognized a few locals from town, but the rest, men in suits, women in furs, were people I'd never seen before. They belonged to that privileged class of people who lived and moved in the golden sphere, playing golf at the country club in Thibodaux and spending their weekends at second homes on Grand Isle. Mark, I was surprised to see, knew many of them. He gestured with his glass as he pointed them out in a dull, bored manner.

"There's the mayor. That's the manager of the bank. That's a friend of my dad's—he's in oil, Ted Freely. There's another one, Mr. Burns. He's in oil, too, from Lake Charles, I think. Him, too. It's a good turn-out. All the oil folks.

"Gabby's dad, over there," Mark said, nodding. "He's cool. He's buying new jerseys for our team."

Frank Martello stood with a group of men all about his age, all sharing his same rugged handsomeness. He squeezed the shoulder of one, relit the cigarette of another. He turned to shake the hand of someone who'd been waiting to introduce himself. You could see the party gathering and circling around Frank; people recognized his importance and instinctively gravitated toward him.

Barbara stood in another corner of the yard talking to a clutch of wives. She wore a dark navy-blue outfit trimmed with black fur. She might've stepped from the pages of a magazine, so rich and elegant she looked—the perfectly turned-out woman of the house.

And there—over there was my mother. I caught sight of her flitting around the edges of the party in a new lime-green dress with a kind of short yellow cape. She looked like a parakeet escaped from its cage, fluttering excitedly around the yard and bouncing off people's shoulders. She spotted her old friend Dale Landry and swooped in to say hello. She put her hand on his arm, leaned in to exchange some words, and then threw her head back and laughed. I could hear her laughter all the way across the yard, bright and startling.

She fluttered over to Frank's circle and landed beside him. Frank slid an arm around her waist, pulled her in close, and introduced her to the men gathered around. They raised their eyebrows as my mother talked and gestured animatedly. Frank bent over and whispered something in her ear. She slapped his arm, and the men all chuckled and shook their shoulders.

Beside me, Mark had begun talking about football. He looked straight ahead, not at me, as if he were addressing an invisible roomful of people. He said what a fine team they had this year, and how Coach DuPleiss really knew his business. The man was tough but fair, and the players respected him for that. Mark was just a freshman, but the coach had seen his potential and given him a shot at outside linebacker in their last game. He had the weight, he had the strength; now he just had to work on his speed, he said.

"Who do you like?" he asked, turning abruptly to me.

"What?"

"Who're your teams?"

I didn't know anything about football, so I said LSU.

"LSU!"

Mark cursed the team and said he used to like them, too, until they got their asses kicked by Alabama. Then it was like they just rolled over and played dead. There was no excuse for a team like that, he said, a team that had everything going for it, a team that could win all season and then toss in everything at the end. He couldn't believe they'd lost their last game to Tulane.

"Can you believe that? Tulane."

He shook his head disgustedly and let out another string of curses against LSU.

If there had ever been any doubt about my feelings for Mark, there wasn't anymore: I couldn't stand the guy. There was something mean

and stupid in his nature. It showed in his thick nose and blunt forehead, and in the way his eyebrows lowered when he swore. He was
only talking about a football team, but he could as easily have been
cursing the blacks, or the Communists, or anybody else he took it into
his mind to hate. He was strong and unforgiving, a bully, and I saw that
he would be that way for the rest of his life; and for this same reason I
suspected that he would always be successful in whatever he did, and
I despised and feared him for that.

I was glad when my mother swooped up from the lawn and interrupted us.

"Boys! Boys!" she said breathlessly. "Are you having fun? Did you
get something to eat? Isn't this fabulous?" She had a drink in one hand;
her eyes were bright, her face flushed. She grabbed Mark's arm. "I need
you now. I need you right now. Are you ready?"

"Yes, ma'am."

Mark finished his Coke in a swallow and looked around for a place
to put his glass. My mother took his glass and handed it to me.

"Where're you going?"

"You'll see. In a minute," she answered, and spirited Mark away
into the house.

The band finished a song and started another one. Guests mingled
on the dance floor in front of the gazebo; they crossed the lawn, passed
in and out of the house, and stood at the edges of the swimming pool,
looking around as though waiting for something to happen. I saw my
father lead the mayor out through the gates of the patio and down the
yard toward the Martellos' dock. They stopped on the grass, and my
father took the mayor's arm and pointed up at the sky. The mayor, a
short man with a white crew cut, nodded and pointed along with my
father.

Right there, you say? the mayor might have been asking. *And we'll
see it when? You bet. That is exciting. Sure, we might organize something like that. A town comet viewing. I like that.*

Overhead, the stars winked in reply: *An auspicious night, an auspicious night.*

I bounced my knee in time to the music and kept an eye on the back doors of the house, waiting for Gabriella to appear. I could see the evening unfolding as beautifully and simply as a story. We would dance together in front of the gazebo, turning arm in arm beneath the lights as the band played. Between songs I would fetch her something to drink from the bar and then escort her to that white-draped table over there in the corner of the yard. Maybe we'd take a stroll along the edge of the water. Later, toward the end of the evening as guests were leaving, we'd talk quietly in a dark corner of the porch. I would hold her hand, and before the night was over, if all went as planned, we would kiss.

Up on the gazebo, the band was playing a song I didn't recognize, but in the snatches of lyrics floating over the heads of the guests, I caught an echo of my own hopes for the evening:

> *Tonight* (dah dah dah) *lonely*
> *Tonight* (dah dah dah) *only*
> *Tonight* (dah dah dah) *show me*
> *Tonight!*

CHAPTER THIRTY-TWO

FOUR songs later, there was a drumroll and an electric fanfare from the band.

People turned toward the corner of the yard as Frank, Barbara, and my mother stepped up onto the floor of the gazebo. My father hustled up to join them, and they arranged themselves in a crowded line in front of the microphones.

My sister slid up beside me to watch. "Hey, little bro. Are you ready for the big show?"

"What show?"

"Oh, boy," she said.

Frank spoke first. He bent over and lightly touched the side of the microphone with the fingertips of one hand, his other hand resting in his trouser pocket. He was poised, relaxed—a man used to addressing large groups.

"Is this on? Good evening. I want to thank everyone for coming. It's really great to see so many people I know here tonight. Barbara and I are delighted that we finally had this opportunity to open up our home to all our new friends, and we look forward to hosting many more events like this in the future."

He gave a special thanks to the mayor and led a round of applause for him. Then, "I think Lydia has a few words to say to you now."

Frank adjusted the stand as my mother stepped to the microphone. She jerked her head back, startled at hearing her voice so loud when she first spoke. Then she went on quickly, holding her hands away from the microphone as if she were afraid it might shock her. Talking more loudly than necessary, she thanked the Martellos for hosting the party and said how without them, none of this would have been possible. They were only newcomers to Terrebonne, but already Barbara and Frank had shown themselves to be wonderful, caring, involved citizens of the community—the kind of neighbors anyone would be happy to have. And wasn't everything just so . . . so . . . so gorgeous tonight? Like a dream come true.

"Now about the party," she said. "Why we're all here."

She turned the microphone over to my father, who came forward unfolding a piece of paper.

"Oh, god," said Megan beside me. "Here he comes."

Our father reminded everyone that the party was named after Comet Kohoutek and spoke about what a momentous occasion this was in the history of science, and how that soon, very soon, we'd be able to see the comet for ourselves, growing bigger and brighter every night until Christmastime, when it would outshine all the stars in heaven. . . .

My mother stood erect, hands clasped below her waist, a smile fixed on her lips, as he went on to explain how the proceeds of this party would go toward refurbishing the science laboratories at Terrebonne High School. Consulting his notes, he listed some of the equipment they'd be buying. Then he spoke about the importance of science education in schools. He said how public schools provided the workforce for the industries and businesses that helped our cities grow. Without science in the schools, there would be no engineers, no technicians, no workers to man the oil rigs or run the refineries. . . .

As he spoke on and on, my mother's smile began to waver. She touched her hair, readjusted her posture, until, overcome by a spasm of impatience, she bobbed forward and yanked the sleeve of his jacket. He snapped around, spoke sharply to her, and then turned back to the microphone. He finished by thanking everyone for their generosity, and said how by supporting public education, they were ensuring a better future not only for themselves, but also for their children, their children's children, and for all the future generations of people living on the planet.

"Thank you," he said, and folded away his notes.

Frank Martello leaned into the microphone. "End of lecture. Class dismissed."

"Wait, wait! It's not over yet."

My mother edged back to the microphone. She spoke again in her too-loud voice, holding her hands out and batting the air.

"Okay, okay. Everybody! You all know this is called the Comet Ball. And of course, no ball would be complete without a king and queen. And so now—"

She nodded at Frank, and he leaned in to the microphone with her: "We present to you—the Comet King and Queen!"

They both gestured with their right arms to the patio. The band struck up a march. There was a spark of light and a stir of movement at the rear of the house.

Then Mark and Gabriella stepped out, costumed in silver robes. Gabriella wore a crown that had golden rays shooting up from the back of it, and Mark wore a silver turban with a cut-out golden comet arching across the front. Over their heads he held a Fourth of July sparkler that hissed and sputtered as it threw off silver and gold shards of light.

People moved back, laughing and clapping as the two began a slow procession around the yard. Gabriella smiled and nodded, looking embarrassed, but Mark walked tall with a proud, dumb grin on his face.

"What is this? You knew about this?" I asked Megan.

"I know, I know. It's retarded," she said. "Mom wanted a pageant. She had to have one. This is what they do at balls, apparently. They actually rehearsed this, believe it or not."

"No, I mean Mark and Gabriella. What are they doing together? Why didn't anyone tell me about this?"

"I guess Mom didn't want to discourage you."

"But then why didn't you tell me? You could've warned me at least."

"Oh, come on. It's just a stupid show. It doesn't mean anything. They needed a boy and girl. It could've been anybody."

"Great. Thanks. That helps a lot."

As Mark and Gabriella promenaded and the band played, my father came forward and repeated a more dramatic version of his lecture on comets, sounding like Mr. Elvert at the planetarium—"What strange light hails yonder?" and so on. He ended with Comet Kohoutek, the Christmas Comet, the Comet of the Century, "mightiest and most beautiful comet to ever grace the skies of our humble planet."

At this, Mark and Gabriella mounted the steps of the gazebo. Barbara bent in to adjust Gabriella's gown. The Fourth of July sparkler had gone out, but Mark still held the burnt-out stick above his head. The band stopped playing.

Frank greeted them with mock formality. "Welcome, Your Majesties. Thank you for coming."

"Welcome," said Mark.

Frank bantered for a minute with his friends in the crowd while Mark and Gabriella shifted and whispered to each other on the platform. Then Frank turned to my mother, wondering about the rest of the ceremony.

"Aren't they supposed to say something now?"

"No, we cut that."

"That's all they do?"

"That's all."

"Well—all right, then." He turned back to the crowd. "Won't you please join me in welcoming our very special guests for the evening, the Comet King and Queen."

The band played a fanfare. Gabriella curtsied, Mark bowed, and people cheered.

My mother took the microphone again. "And now everyone, it's time to have fun! Dance! Enjoy yourself!"

"The night is still young," Frank prompted.

"The night is still young!" she shouted, and the band launched into a song.

Mark led Gabriella down onto the floor, and people cleared a space for them as they began dancing. Mark danced the same way he spoke, holding his head high and staring straight ahead, like a dog sniffing the air. But Gabriella danced beautifully; she steadied her cardboard crown with one hand and swished the hem of her silver robe with the other. Someone lit sparklers and passed them around. My mother urged others to dance, too, and then she grabbed Frank and began dancing with him. She moved dramatically, holding both of Frank's hands in hers and staring intently at his face, as though she was trying to hypnotize him.

Not to be outdone, my father shouldered his way onto the floor. He gave a shout and began doing a ridiculous Russian-style dance, folding his arms in front of him and kicking his legs out one after the other. He kicked, spun around, lost his balance, and fell over backward into some people. They helped him up by the shoulders and he bounced back onto the dance floor, his face red and determined as he leaped and shouted. People clapped and laughed.

"Oh my god. I think I have to go kill myself now," said Megan, and slipped away.

And how did I feel, seeing all this? Miserable. Horrified. I might have been witnessing a scene from my worst nightmare: Gabriella the queen and Mark the king, the most beautiful couple in the world, turning coolly at the center of the dance floor while my parents bumbled and crashed pathetically around them like two furious, crippled birds.

CHAPTER THIRTY-THREE

THE stars stretched and wavered in the black water. I stood at the edge of the Martellos' dock with my back to the party. The band was taking a break. People were wandering around the yard, ice tinkling in glasses, voices murmuring. From time to time I heard my mother's shrill laughter flutter up above the hubbub and then settle back down again. Gabriella and Mark, the king and queen, had disappeared somewhere.

I looked up across the bayou to our house. It squatted there like a fishing shack behind the trees. The lights were off, the windows dark. I saw my own window, a tiny black square jutting off the roof. I turned to look over my shoulder at Gabriella's room up in her house. Her balconies were decorated with Christmas lights, her bedroom lit behind the yellow curtains. I looked back and forth between our two rooms, and they seemed farther apart than ever tonight.

What was I thinking, imagining there could've been something between us? Some cruel god or fate had set me down on one side of the water, her on the other side, and no wish, no prayer could ever alter that unfair fact of life.

That was the problem with expectations: they were good only as long as they lasted. Better not to expect anything at all. Better to join the cold-blooded, big-eyed creatures slithering in the mud at the bottom of the canal, animals that didn't have to worry about love and hope and expectation. Because as soon as you grew two legs and learned to walk upright, you were pretty much doomed to a lifetime of disappointments.

I looked down at the water, black and slick as oil. The stars blinked invitingly at my feet. How easy that would be, to throw myself in and slip away from all this. I imagined myself tipping over the edge of the dock, tipping, until I fell, plunging head first into the stars. The night sky splashed around me, cold and dark as the sea, and then the black, airless space rushed in to fill my mouth and lungs—

"Don't jump!"

I looked up from the water, startled out of my reverie. Giggles came from a clump of skinny pine trees at the corner of the yard.

"No, no, no."

"Shh. Leave him alone."

I stepped down off the dock and walked along the edge of the water toward the voices. A group of shadows huddled in the grove, their bodies barely distinguishable from the tree trunks.

"Who is that? Who's there?"

"Oh, man. Why'd you have to—"

As I came into the trees, the shadows revealed themselves to be my sister and the members of the band. A faint red dot floated between them, and a sharp, sweet odor hung in the air.

"Is he cool?" one of the boys asked.

"Never," Megan said.

"What are you doing here?" I asked.

"Oh, man," one of the boys said.

"It's okay. We're just enjoying a little smoke," another said. I recognized him as the leader of the band. "You want some?" He held out what looked like a twisted-up cigarette.

"Is that— No. No way. I don't think so." I took a step back.

They laughed. "He thinks we're demons."

"If you tell anyone, I swear I'll kill you," Megan said.

"Aw, he's cool. You're not going to tell anyone, are you, man?"

I'd only ever seen marijuana in movies and in documentary films at school, so to come across it here, in real life, with my sister and this shadowy band of college-aged musicians, was frightening and strange. They passed the joint, sucking on it in long, deep breaths and clamping their lips shut. I glanced over my shoulder at the Martellos' house.

"Relax, man. It's safe," said the leader.

"You remember Greg, don't you?" my sister said. "My old guitar teacher?"

"Oh, right."

Greg had wavy, shoulder-length hair parted down the middle. He held out his hand for a soul shake. "Hey. Little Alan, right? Junior. How've you been? What's up, man?"

I was introduced to the other members of the band, the bass player, the keyboard player, the drummer. In the dim light, they were little more than long hair and pale faces bobbing above skinny bodies hunched in jackets.

"You enjoying the party?" Greg spoke gently, his voice fluid.

"It's okay," I said, but then added, more truthfully, "Not really."

"You're like the only kid here."

"I'm not a kid, exactly."

"Your age, I mean."

"It's like an old folks' home," agreed the bassist.

"Rich old folks," said the keyboard player.

"There were those two comet kids," said the drummer.

"That was kind of funny," said Greg. "The Comet King and Queen. With the sparklers." They joked about the march they had to play for the procession—*pah-rum pah-rum pum pum.*

"Junior's in love with that girl," my sister told them.

"What?" I said.

"Gabriella."

"Really? That's cool," Greg said, nodding and taking the joint. "She

looked kind of cute. I mean, it was hard to tell with the crown and all."
He took a hissing drag and then asked through pinched lips, "Where is
she?"

"Who?"

"Your girlfriend. The comet girl. You should bring her over."

"She's not my girlfriend."

"Oh. I thought you were being serious."

"He wishes she was his girlfriend," explained another.

"That's tough, man," Greg said, shaking his head. "That's a hard
one. Watching from the sidelines." He offered me the joint again. "Sure
you don't want any?"

I hesitated. We'd been warned in school about just such a situation:
a friendly older fellow would try to offer us drugs, and before we knew
it we'd be hooked, addicts.

"No?" Greg shrugged, and the red dot floated to my sister.

He asked Megan if she still played guitar. "I remember you used to
have a real sweet voice."

"Used to," she said.

"You don't sing anymore?"

"Nope."

"That's too bad."

Megan brought her hand to her lips; the red glow lit her face, then
she pulled the joint away suddenly from her mouth and stifled a cough.

"Dude's freaking out," the bassist said, eyeing me.

"He's waiting for her to do something crazy," the drummer said.
"Start speaking in tongues."

"Spitting fire."

"Levitating."

"No, I'm not," I said.

"We're just teasing you, man."

Noise from the party spilled over the wall around the backyard, but
in the trees it was quiet. The joint went around. Although I knew what
they were doing was criminal and quite possibly dangerous, these boys
didn't strike me as threatening. They seemed quite friendly, actually.
They asked me and Megan about our father. "The science dude," they

called him. They all read his newspaper column, apparently. Greg
asked if they'd seen his last one.

"All about Pythagoras and the music of the spheres. What was
that?"

" 'Do You Hear What I Hear?' " said the drummer, remembering the
title.

"Oh, right. That was dumb," I said.

"I thought it was pretty interesting," said the keyboard player.
"Like, there's music in space only we can't hear it." They talked about
that for a while. Greg wondered if he could tune his guitar to a Py-
thagorean scale, what that would sound like.

"Tune it to the stars, man," said the drummer.

"No, I'm serious," Greg said. "I'm going to try it."

"I like astronomy," the keyboard player said. "I wish we had a telescope right now." He shaped his hands into a tube and looked up at the
sky.

"I have a telescope," I said.

"Yeah? You do? That's cool."

They asked me about the comet. I told them what I knew.

"You know a lot."

"Not really."

I'd been keeping my eye on the joint, and when it came around again
I impulsively reached for it. I glanced at my sister. She acted surprisingly unconcerned about this, my momentous decision.

"Just a little puff," Greg said as I brought it to my lips. "That's
right." I coughed, spitting out all the smoke. There were some chuckles.

"You've got to do it easy," said the drummer, and demonstrated how
I should inhale.

I tried it again. They watched. "Hold it . . . hold it," they said, but I
coughed out all the smoke again. I shook my head and passed the joint
along.

"Takes some getting used to," the drummer said, and they went on
talking and smoking.

I swallowed, tasting the residue of the smoke in my mouth. I waited for some strange sensation to take hold of my body—weightlessness, maybe, or dizziness. I thought I might go crazy and start laughing uncontrollably; I would see giant spiders, or run and leap off the dock, believing I could fly. Nothing seemed to be happening, though.

The others had shifted and were looking up at the stars between the trees, talking about space.

"You ever wonder what's behind the stars?" Greg asked.

"Nothing, man," said the drummer. "More space."

"I mean, what's behind the space?" Greg wiped his hand across the sky, like he was cleaning fog from a window.

"It just ends. Stops," my sister said. "Like a . . . like a crystal ball."

"Heaven. Angels."

"Demons."

"We are stardust. We are golden," said Greg.

"We are billion-year-old carbon," replied my sister.

I looked up with them. There was a quiet pause as we all considered the possibilities. The Moon had lifted higher and it hung cool and familiar above our heads. I experienced a peculiar sense of déjà vu just then—like I'd stood here before, with these same people, in this same configuration of time and place and sky.

"Maybe there's another universe," I said. "Behind the stars. Exactly like this one, occupied by people exactly like us, only doing what we wished we had done but never did. A universe filled with people's wishes."

"I like that," Greg said.

"That's trippy," my sister said.

"Junior's stoned," the bassist said. "He caught a, what do you call it, sympathetic buzz."

We all stood looking at the stars for a minute longer. I had been ready to go home, but now I wanted to run back to the party, into the lights and people, and find Gabriella. Maybe it wasn't too late. Maybe I wasn't just imagining things; maybe there was something between us. Hadn't we held hands? Hadn't we promised to meet each other tonight? Hadn't she tugged on my sleeve and said, "See you later, Junior"? The stars winked and chimed overhead, *An auspicious night, an auspicious night.*

Someone let out a breath. "Man, I'm baked."

"Is it finished? Where is it? I'm holding it." The drummer inspected the joint and stuffed the nub into his jacket pocket.

"How long have we been here? We've been here forever. We should check the time."

They all began straightening themselves, sniffing and rubbing their eyes. "Rock and roll," they said, and started shuffling toward the patio.

"You guys sound good," I said, walking a little off to the side.

"Hey, thanks, man," Greg said. "You should come and check out a real show sometime." At the gate, he stopped and shook my hand again while my sister waited beside him. "Be cool, man."

"I'm cool," I answered.

My sister laughed out loud at this. But then she did something she hadn't done in years—she reached out and rubbed my arm.

"Little bro," she said, her eyes glassy. "Wishes he was cool. Go find your girl."

CHAPTER THIRTY-FOUR

I hurried back to the party. I made a pass through the yard; I walked through the tent, circled around the patio, and went through the yard again, but I couldn't find Gabriella. I did, however, run into my grandparents. They were putting on their coats in the library, getting ready to leave.

"We haven't talked to you all night," Paps said. "Are you having fun? Isn't this a nice party?" Grams asked.

Paps helped her on with her coat, using his one hand to hold it up while Grams slipped her arms into the sleeves. My grandmother wore rouge and jewelry; my grandfather wore a tie, the knot crimped and off center, his hair combed flat with stray strands sticking up in the back. Outside of their own home, under this high ceiling, against the tall bookcase, they appeared small and awkward. They looked like two hunched, friendly rodents.

"How about this house, huh?" Paps said as they started for the door. "Your folks are keeping some mighty impressive company these days," Grams said. "Nobody's hurting here, no sir-ee," Paps said.

I was opening the front door for them when Gabriella appeared at the top of the stairs. She was wearing her purple dress, her hair done up in ribbons again, looking resplendent.

"Here she is, the belle of the ball," Paps said. "The princess," Grams said.

"You're not leaving, are you?" she asked, and hurried down the stairs to them.

I hovered nearby while she chatted with my grandparents. I was surprised she knew who they were. She held my grandmother's hand and said how nice it was to meet them. My grandfather told her how much they'd enjoyed the evening and what a fine Comet Queen she made.

"Don't be a stranger, *petit garçon*," Paps told me, starting off. "Come visit," Grams said, and she slipped her hand into the crook of Paps's good arm as they turned and ducked out the door. Gabriella and I stood in the doorway and watched them shuffle arm in arm up the sidewalk, Paps's empty coat sleeve waving a little as they walked.

"When I'm old, I hope I shuffle just like that," Gabriella said. "They're charming, aren't they?" It was a word I never would have used to describe my grandparents, but hearing her say it, I saw how, in a certain light, it might apply. They disappeared between some parked cars and then she abruptly turned to me.

"Where've you been?"

"What? Nowhere. Right here."

"I thought you were avoiding me." She spun on her feet, and I followed her back inside.

"Avoiding you? No! I was looking for you."

She smiled and greeted guests as we passed quickly through the house. At the back door she halted and looked out at the party, her hands resting on the doorframe. She sighed dramatically. "I don't think I can talk to another soul. I'm absolutely exhausted."

She swung around and her eyes went to the kitchen. "Are you thirsty?"

"Not especially."

She rolled her eyes. "Say yes."

"Okay: yes."

I followed her into the kitchen, where Christine and another woman were washing glasses at the sink. Stacked against the walls were cases of liquor. Gabriella slipped a green bottle of champagne out of one of the boxes and shoved it at me. "Psst. Here, take this."

I caught it under my jacket. "Hey—"

"Mm-hm," Christine said. "I see that."

"Come on. Quick."

Gabriella pulled me by the jacket through the house, looking for an empty room, but we kept running into other people, men and women in nice clothes standing around talking in groups. "In here . . . Wait . . . No, here . . . Excuse us . . . Mr. and Mrs. Daigle, how nice . . ." We came around again to the front hall and she jogged up the stairs ahead of me. "Up here. Hurry."

I followed her up the stairs, down a hallway, and through a door. She closed the door behind us, and then I stopped short, staring at the room.

I knew her bedroom well, I'd studied and admired it, but to see it here from the inside was like tumbling into a photograph in a picture book. There were the French doors, the canopied bed, the painted trunk, the telephone, the door to her powder room, all of it very familiar but also slightly unreal, precisely because it was real and I was standing inside it now. Her silver costume and golden cardboard crown lay on the bed.

Gabriella kicked off her shoes and followed my eyes around her room. "What's wrong?"

"Nothing. Nothing, it's nice. You have a nice room."

"Why thank you, *petit garçon*. Sit down, you're making me nervous." I sat in an armchair. She took the champagne bottle from me, went into her powder room, and came back out. "No glasses. Can you open it?" She handed the bottle back to me.

"How do you do this?"

"You don't know how to open a champagne bottle?"

"No."

"You're a boy. Aren't you supposed to know how to do things like that? The twisty thing—"

She sat by me on an ottoman and together we wrestled with the bottle until the cork popped out. "Yay," she said.

"You first."

"Cheers," she said, and took a hefty swallow. "Oops. Too much. I might burp." She handed it to me.

I got a big mouthful and felt it sting my throat and swell up into my nose and eyes. "It's bubbly," I agreed. We passed the bottle, trading sips.

"Is this your first drink ever?"

"Not *ever.*"

"It is, isn't it? Oh, no. I'm corrupting you."

"I guess you have champagne all the time. You probably drink it for breakfast."

"How'd you guess?"

"You probably wash your hair in it. You probably bathe in it."

"I swim in it. Every morning, for exercise. The swimming pool is full of it," she said. "If you swim too long, you get drunk and you drown."

There was an abrupt lull in our conversation, as if the burst of energy that had carried us from the front door, to the kitchen, through the house, and up the stairs had run out, and now we were both a little surprised to find just the two of us sitting alone in her bedroom passing a bottle of champagne.

She smiled quickly, suddenly bashful, and took the bottle from me. I rested my hands on the arms of the stuffed chair. My wrists stuck out of my jacket sleeves, bony and funny looking. I saw that the cuff of my jacket was missing a button, and I folded my arms over my chest to hide it.

Nervous now, I got up and went to the French doors. I looked out through the curtains. The band played and the music thumped lightly against the panes of glass. People turned and mingled on the lawn. From this perspective, the party, with the lights, the people, the tents, appeared distant and magical, like it was an event that might have happened once long ago and I was seeing it not as it was now, but as I remembered it.

I spotted Mark Mingis on the patio. He was talking to Gabriella's father and a group of his business friends. His costume was off; he had one hand in his trouser pocket, his other hand holding a drink, the mirror image of the men standing around him—a junior oil man in training.

"Someone might see you," Gabriella warned.

Trying to keep my voice steady, I asked, "Someone like your boyfriend?"

"Who? Mark?"

"Yes."

"How'd you know he was my boyfriend?"

"He looks like your boyfriend. I always see you with him. He is, isn't he?"

"I guess so."

So it was true. I'd suspected it all along, but to have it confirmed made me angry and sick to my stomach. Speaking as though it barely concerned her, Gabriella explained how she'd known Mark for years. Her father and his father were old friends. They were doing some oil business deal together—Mr. Mingis was a contractor or driller or something important like that. When they needed a boy for their ball tonight, Mark was the obvious choice. The Comet King and Queen: their parents all thought it was the cutest thing in the world.

"The whole king and queen thing has kind of gone to his head, though," she said. "He seems to think we're practically married now—which is a little creepy, considering we're only in high school. But that's how Mark is. If I don't phone him every night, he gets mad at me."

She phoned him every night: so that's who she'd been talking to all those times I'd seen her with my telescope. Of course. I looked down at Mark through the window, in his blue blazer and turtleneck, and if I could have, I would have vaporized him with my eyes.

She sipped from the bottle. "He's got a new Camaro. Did you see it? It's outside. He just got his license. He's going to teach me how to drive as soon as I get my permit."

"Oh, really? Gosh, that's great. That's great news. Thank you for sharing that with me. I can't wait to see you and Mark driving around town in his new Camaro. I'll be sure to wave." I took the bottle from her and paced the yellow carpet.

She laughed. "Oh my god, you hate him, don't you? Why do you hate him so much?"

I couldn't think of a polite way to say "He's a mean, dumb, smug son of a bitch," so I just said, "He's boring. All he ever talks about is football."

"Well. That's kind of true. But he's a nice boy. Really, he is. Everyone likes him. Everyone but you."

"You probably go to the country club together. Play tennis, go horseback riding."

"We do."

I stopped. "Really?"

"In Thibodaux. Something wrong with that? Give me the bottle."

"Really?"

"Yes! Give me the bottle."

"He goes to dinner with you?"

"Sometimes."

"And tennis? You play tennis together?"

"You've never played tennis?"

"No!"

She shrugged. "You should. It's fun."

"I bet it is."

She drank from the bottle, then looked at me shrewdly. "You're jealous."

"I'm not," I said.

"It's true. You're a jealous boy. You're burning up with jealousy."

"Well—why shouldn't I be?"

She shook her head. "Don't be. Where is he now?"

"Mark? He's down there talking to your dad."

"And where are you?"

I looked at her. She smiled and nodded. "See? Aren't you glad you're you?" She raised the bottle to me and took another sip.

Dear god, I thought. *How did any girl my age get to be so cool? So clever! So pretty!*

She hiccupped. "Whoops. Excuse me. Too much. Here, take this." She handed the bottle to me and then slid off the ottoman, lay on her back on the floor, and flung her arms out.

"Oh my god, I think I'm drunk now."

CHAPTER THIRTY-FIVE

THIS was turning into a night of surprises. It was like walking through her house: there's a room . . . there's a room . . . there's another room. And look, around this corner, what's this? A girl lying on her back on the floor. She looked like an angel lying there. She'd crashed in through the French doors and landed on the floor, her purple velvet dress rumpled around her bare legs, her dark hair scattered extravagantly around her head.

She opened one eye and peered up at me. "Don't stare at me like that."

"Sorry."

I dropped down onto the floor and sat with my back against her yellow trunk. My head felt heavy and the edge of my vision was blurry. I stretched my fingers out and looked at them. "Ooh. Look at that. I can feel everything. I can feel my bones under my skin. I can feel my teeth."

"Junior's drunk, Junior's drunk."

I crawled over and lay down next to her on my back, and then turned my head on the carpet to look at her. Her ear! Her ear was small and perfectly formed, like a pink seashell. A white pearl pendant earring dangled from the lobe, trembling slightly with her breath.

"Are you staring?"

"No."

I reached out and touched her earring. It reminded me of Christmas, like a miniature Christmas tree ornament. On her left jaw was a small, pale birthmark, the size of a nickel. It was exquisite.

"You are the queen."

"That was dumb, wasn't it? The costumes?"

"But you looked good. You looked very royal."

"It wasn't my idea."

"I think it was my mother's."

Electromagnetic waves of beauty emanated from her body and spread across the carpet to warm my face. I peeked down and saw her hand resting inches from mine on the carpet. Her fingers moved up and down, like her hand was signaling to my hand to hold it. I was scooting closer when she began to talk again. She spoke as though she were thinking aloud.

"Do you ever get the feeling . . . Do you ever get the feeling that you're just acting out a part in someone else's play?"

"What do you mean?"

"I mean, everyone's got these ideas about what you should do and how you should act—go here, do this, wear that. It's like your whole life is arranged for you by someone else. Never mind what you want."

"We're only in high school. We have no choice."

"My mom, for instance, I swear, she has my whole life planned for me: who I'll marry, where I'll live, how many kids I'll have."

"Really? Who will you marry?"

"A rich college boy from a good family in New Orleans. Preferably a doctor or a lawyer. We'll live in the Garden District, halfway between Uptown and Downtown, not directly on St. Charles Avenue but on a quiet, respectable side street. We'll have two kids, a boy and a girl, both in private schools. They'll wear uniforms."

"Wow," I said. "That's—"

"Her plan, not mine. She wants to send me away to a boarding school. Did I tell you that?"

"No. Wait. What? You're going? Where? When?"

"Not yet. She's just talking about it. There's a Catholic girls school in Grand Coteau. She says it'd be better for me there. She hates Terrebonne. She never wanted to move here in the first place. She'd rather be back in Shreveport where all her society friends are, with their hats and dresses and garden clubs.

"My dad, on the other hand, he likes it just fine here. He's got plans for me, too. He wants me to marry a good old boy like Mark, someone he can go into business with, preferably. They'll go fishing together, join a hunting club. Go to all the football games. He can hardly wait. If it was up to him, we'd be married tomorrow."

I might've been discouraged hearing all of this, but she was speaking with such intimacy and trust that I only felt closer to her. She was sharing her secrets with me, telling me things she wouldn't have told anyone else.

"What do you want?" I asked.

She rolled her head on the carpet to look at me.

"See, that's just it. How can I know what I want? Or what I'll want ten years from now? How can I know anything? I can barely even decide what clothes to put on in the morning. Everyone says, 'Oh, you have to think about your future,' but that's ridiculous. It's too soon to be worrying about the future. We should be having fun, enjoying ourselves. Don't you think?"

I would've agreed with anything she said just then, if only because she looked so pretty saying it. But I was impressed by her thoughtfulness; her life, her problems seemed altogether more serious and sophisticated than mine. The band outside was playing a song, a gently rocking number that seemed to have been going on for ages. I found her hand on the rug, closed my fingers around it, and squeezed. She squeezed back.

"Comet Boy, Comet Boy," she sighed, and turned her face back up to the ceiling and shut her eyes again. "I never want to grow old."

We lay there holding hands and floating on our backs on the floor of her bedroom. The warm feeling flowed back and forth between us. Old age seemed impossible, nothing but a scary story told to frighten children. We would never grow old, obviously. We would be young forever.

After a while I heard a strangely familiar voice drifting on the air. It seeped in through the windows and filled the room around us, like water fills a pool.

"Listen. Do you hear that?"

"Mm. Someone's singing."

"That's . . . It's my sister."

"She's got a pretty voice."

I wanted to explain how my sister used to sing but she didn't anymore, not since her ruined date with Todd Picou, and how she redecorated her room and put up a poster that said LOVE shot through with bullet holes, and how she hated everything, but tonight I'd found her smoking pot with the boys from the band down by the water, and they seemed really cool, not like criminals at all, and so I had tried it, too, yes I did, just a puff. . . .

But it was too much and too complicated to explain, and anyway, it hardly seemed necessary. We held hands. My sister's pretty voice washed down on us like liquid gold, singing, *"Ooh love . . . Ooh love . . ."*

"If you could be anywhere in the world, where would you be?" I asked her. "Right now."

She thought about it. "Florida. Miami. I'd like to be in Miami. I'd like to be lying on the beach in Miami. On the sand. In the sun."

We both lay there in the sun for a minute, enjoying that thought.

"Where would you be?" she asked.

"Nowhere."

"Nowhere?" She rolled her head and looked at me.

"Nowhere else in the world. I'd like to be right here, with you, just like this. Forever."

Her eyes changed and her face went soft. I saw something there that I'd seen that afternoon in the planetarium, a certain tenderness tinged with sorrow—a depth of feeling that seemed at odds with her youth and beauty, but that also seemed to mirror my own feelings, feelings I hardly recognized in myself until I saw them in her.

I drew my hand up and traced a finger along her hairline. I touched her forehead, and then her eyebrows. She didn't flinch or move away. I touched her nose; she wrinkled it. I touched her birthmark on her cheek, and then her chin, and then her lips. She puckered them.

I knew then that I could kiss her if I wanted to. I lifted myself up on one elbow and leaned over her. She looked up, studying my face, her eyes curious and trusting. I bent down, and as our lips came together, I understood why people made such a big deal about this. First there was the novelty of it: the weird sensation of my lips pressed against hers, and the warm air sighing in and out of our noses, and the mysterious dark hollows behind our teeth. After that came the disappearing. The walls of the room fell away, the ceiling vanished, and we floated up, up to the stars, suspended in a clear crystal bubble while my sister sang a lullaby in our ears. Our kiss contained us, it contained all of our hopes and fears and wants, and even more. It contained the world: Indians praying to painted gods, and skinny Chinese men pedaling their bicycles to work, and the glossy black water of a bayou at night, where, above it in a soft yellow room, a boy kissed a girl for the very first time while the silver-and-gold sparks of a comet rained down on them. . . .

Gabriella twisted her face away. Her chest rose and fell as she stared at the ceiling, catching her breath.

"Oh, boy," she said. "Oh, no. Oh, wow."

"What?"

"Oh no, no, no, no."

"What? You didn't like that?"

"I did. I liked it. I liked it a lot. But—"

"But what?"

I leaned in and tried to kiss her again, but she slid out from under me. She got up and went to the French doors. She opened the curtain and peeked out.

"What's wrong?"

She worked her feet on the carpet. "Nothing. I just—" She glanced at me and then back. "I don't want anyone to get hurt."

"Nobody's going to get hurt."

"Somebody might."

"Who's going to get hurt?"

"Can't we just be friends?"

"We are. We are friends."

"Good. Good, because I like you. I like you a lot."

"I like you, too."

What the hell, I thought. *A minute ago we were kissing, everything was great, and now—!*

I got up and stood beside her. I tried to kiss her again, but she wouldn't let me.

"No. Wait. Stop. Look at the party with me." She rested a finger against the windowpane. "Look. There."

My sister stood on the floor of the gazebo with the band, both hands shoved down into the pockets of the jacket she'd borrowed from Greg. Her head was tilted back, her eyes closed as she sang into the microphone. The white lights in the trees around the gazebo looked like low-flying stars snagged in the branches.

"Pretty," Gabriella whispered.

I took some of her hair in my hand and twirled it in my fingers like I'd seen her do. She leaned sideways against me and slid her finger along the windowpane to point across the bayou.

"There's your house. Which room's yours?"

"Who cares?"

"Don't be like that. Which one's yours?"

"The one on the right."

"Can you see me from there?"

"No. . . . Maybe. Sometimes."

"With your telescope, I bet. Were you spying on me? You were. You were, weren't you? I knew it! I'm going to keep my curtains closed from now on, so you can't see me."

Leaning against her, I had begun to shiver. My legs shook, my arms shook—I didn't know why.

"What's wrong? Are you cold?"

"No. I don't know. It's nothing."

"Ooh, you're shaking all over." She briskly ran her hands up and down my sides. "Is that better?"

"Not exactly."

I rested my head on her shoulder, burying my nose in her hair and smelling her perfume. We stayed like that for a while, leaning on each other and sighing in and out. "We should go back down," she said at last. "People will wonder where we are."

She pulled back, straightened up, and put out her hand, official-like. "Friends?"

I took her hand. "How long do we have to be friends before we can kiss again?"

She laughed, as if I were making a joke, and then she became quick and serious. "You go down first so no one sees us together. I'll wait here and then come down in a minute—"

I pulled her back to me, but in doing so I yanked her off balance and she fell over the ottoman. I tumbled on top of her, and we laughed, rolling together on the carpet. We stopped, and I was just leaning in to kiss her again when we heard someone in the hallway.

"Gabby! You up here?"

We jerked apart. Footsteps clomped toward her door. Gabriella scrambled up from the floor and looked wildly around the room.

"Gabby?" Mark called again. He rapped twice on her door.

"I'll—" I whispered.

"Go!" she whispered, and then shouted at Mark through the door, "What? Yes! In a minute!"

I tried to open the balcony door but it was stuck. "How do you—?" I whispered, shaking the handle.

"Go! Go!" she whispered. "Coming!" she shouted.

I was diving behind the bed when her door opened and Mark walked in. "Hey, Gabby, what're you—" Mark stopped short, seeing me. "Hello?"

"Hey," I said, straightening up.

"What are you doing here?" He turned to Gabriella. "What's he doing here?"

"He was just . . . nothing. We were talking, that's all."

"What're you doing over there behind the bed?"

"Nothing. I'm just— I was going over there." I pointed at the side window and went to it.

Gabriella began bustling around. She grabbed her shoes, slipped them on, and then checked her hair in the mirror, talking all the while.

"I was showing him my room. That's all. He wanted to see it. He's never seen it. Did you know Junior lives right across the water? Right over there. Where've you been? What's everybody doing?"

"Everybody's looking for you. Why was the door closed?"

"I can't close my door? My god, don't be so suspicious." She brushed her hair a few strokes.

Mark went to the champagne bottle sitting on the table next to the armchair. He tilted it back with his fingertips and looked at me.

"I brought that," I said.

"You brought this?"

"He was being all sneaky," Gabriella said. "He stole it from the kitchen. He wanted to get me drunk."

"You want some?" I asked Mark.

He glared, and for a second I thought he might snatch the bottle up and hurl it at me. But Gabriella dropped her brush on her dresser, went to the door, and slapped her thigh, like you would to call a dog to go for a walk.

"What're we waiting for? Let's go. Let's go, boys!"

I slunk behind them out of her room. In the hallway, Gabriella gave me a quick apologetic look over her shoulder. But then, just to make it clear who belonged to whom, Mark draped his arm around her, pulled her close, and planted a kiss on her temple.

The bastard. I wanted to jump on his back and wrestle him to the floor; I wanted to beat his head against the wall. I squeezed my hands into fists and pressed them against my thighs, feeling miserable and angry and elated all at once. Gabriella took her hair in her fingers and began worrying it with both hands as we started down the stairs back to the party. We passed her portrait on the wall, Gabriella in a white dress holding a bouquet of yellow flowers and gazing off into the sunlight—

No wonder people wrote songs about this, I thought. No wonder people fought and killed and died over this. I could still feel her kiss tingling on my lips. I was like a man on fire. I was shot through with bullet holes. I was in love; I was in love, and I was dying.

Rooms, rooms, and more rooms. The night wasn't over yet.

As I was passing a little later through the front hallway to get my coat and leave, I bumped into Frank Martello coming out of the library.

"Ho ho ho!" he said, and laughed oddly. He clapped a hand on my shoulder and asked how I was enjoying the party. His face was red, his manner blustery. He asked if I'd seen my father. I said I thought he was out back.

"Out there?" he said, pointing.

"Yes, sir. I think so."

"All righty, then. We'll see you later."

He clapped me on the back again and headed to the rear of the house, stuffing his hands in his pockets as he hurried away.

I paused beneath the chandelier. The hall was quiet. The tall double doors of the library stood half open. Something was up. Some strangeness in the air, a whiff of deceitfulness trailing in the wake of Frank Martello, drew me toward the library. I peeked in through the doors.

The room was empty—just the racks of coats, the leather armchairs, the desk, the globe of the world . . .

And my mother, standing at the floor-to-ceiling bookcase with her back to the room.

"Hello?"

She turned around. "Oh. Hi. I was just looking at the books. They sure have a lot, don't they?"

She gave a quick, stiff smile. Her eyes glanced off mine as she moved away from the bookcase, touching her hair and walking shakily. Her shoes clicked across the polished wood floor and then were muffled by the corner of the oriental rug.

She wasn't looking at any books. The realization came to me slowly and then all in a rush. An hour ago I might not have even noticed it, but now her condition seemed as obvious to me as her red hair and green dress, as obvious as her yellow cape dropped on the floor over there at the base of the bookcase.

My mother was a woman on fire. She was shot through with bullet holes. She was miserable and angry and elated, all at once. Her lips— I could practically see it as she drew nearer—her lips were still tingling from where he'd kissed her.

CHAPTER THIRTY-SIX

OOH love . . . *Ooh love* . . .

In the morning the sky was low and yellow. A white fog rose up from the bayou and crept across the yard, transforming the scene outside my bedroom window into someplace strange and only vaguely familiar. Lines were blurred; trees had lost their shape, the ground its solidity. Here and there objects stuck up out of the fog, like junk floating in a flood: the corner of the picnic table, the side of the garage shed, the handlebars of my bicycle. Looking up, I imagined the comet hidden behind the yellow sky, streaming its vapors down onto the Earth, spreading its mysterious outer-space gases in a white cloud over our town, our home, our lives.

Downstairs we shivered and paced through the rooms, looking at sections of the Sunday newspaper and then dropping the pages to the floor. My head hurt, my stomach ached. Our house seemed dimmer, grayer, more cramped than usual. At the Martellos', workmen arrived early and began breaking down the tents and tables. We could hear the clank of metal and the exchange of voices on the other side of the bayou. My mother stood at the kitchen window with a cup of coffee, hugging her bathrobe around herself and staring across the water. Her eyes darted back and forth in her pale, sharp face; her red hair stood out messily around her head. She puckered her lips and blew across her coffee, complaining about the cold.

In the afternoon it rained. It splashed on the sills outside the windows. It spread in sheets across the surface of the bayou, and beat the leaves in the yard into the mud, and streamed in rivulets under the house, sending damp cold drafts up through the floorboards. My mother turned up the gas heaters, my father turned them down. She turned them up again. He started to protest, but then he tightened his lips, sighed through his nose, and spread his student papers out on the table. He picked up his red pen and went to work, the fuzzy black cloud of frustration settling over his shoulders.

My mother changed into old clothes and began fitfully cleaning the house. She shoved the vacuum around the living room; she snatched up pieces of newspaper from the floor and threw them on the couch and bent over to pull pine needles out of the carpet below the Christmas tree. When she knocked the vacuum cleaner against a leg of the table, sloshing my father's coffee onto some papers, he snapped his head up and shouted furiously at her.

"For crying out loud! Can't you see I'm trying to work here?"

"And can't you see I'm trying to clean!"

None of us wanted to be there that day, in our house, as we were. We'd seen joy and happiness and celebration, and the memory of that, the knowledge of how rich life could be, didn't linger to warm and cheer us. Rather, it did just the opposite. None of us wanted to be us anymore. I wondered how long we'd be able to sustain ourselves, and I imagined, dramatically, the fumes of our dissatisfaction building up inside our house until they exploded, blowing out the roof and walls, leaving nothing but the burnt empty shell of a home.

Upstairs in my room, I played and replayed the evening of the party in my mind, turning it this way and that, chipping off the rough edges and polishing my recollection of it until it took on the gemlike glow of a fable. It was like my parents' own scientist-and-the-shopgirl story, except that mine and Gabriella's began not in a drugstore but with a kiss in a yellow room floating above a black bayou.

I squeezed my pillow between my knees and rolled back and forth on the mattress moaning her name, hot and sick with my desire to hold her again as the winter rain pattered against the window.

The bad weather carried on into the week. The rain overflowed the ditches along the road and turned potholes into small ponds. At school the driveway was flooded up to the front door; the floors were tracked with mud, the classroom windows fogged over. Students slammed lockers and ran in the hallways; they shouted across the cafeteria and piled coats on tables and knocked chairs around. Everyone was wet and restless. We had only a week of classes left before the holiday, and everything—teachers, lessons, schoolwork—seemed like a tired and overly complicated joke, a great waste of our time.

"You dog! You goddamn dog," Peter said when I told him about the party. He banged his fist on the table and leaned in over his lunch tray. "You got her drunk and made out with her on the floor of her bedroom? At the party? Right there? When everyone was downstairs? Man."

Across the cafeteria, Gabriella sat with her usual group of friends at her usual table. Mark sat directly across from her. She turned her hair over her ear and picked up her fork, yanking the cords to my heart.

"It wasn't exactly like that," I said.

"That's sure what it sounds like to me. It sure as hell does. You and Gabriella. You're like my hero now. Tell me everything. Details, I need details." He asked if when I'd gotten Gabriella on her back, I'd felt her up.

"Not quite—"

"Not quite? Not quite? What the hell does that mean? Man, I would've been all over that. I would've gotten me a handful of that."

I tried to tell him again how it wasn't like that, exactly.

"Then how was it, exactly? You made out with her, right? Or are you just making all this up?"

"No, it happened, it did. It's just hard to describe. I can't describe it. You have to experience it for yourself."

"Well seeing as how that's not likely to happen to me anytime soon, I just have to rely on you to enlighten me. Mr. Hugh Hefner. Mr. Playboy of the Western World."

But I couldn't do any better than that for Peter. How to explain it to him? How to explain the thrill I had felt when I touched her eyebrows with my finger? Or how the walls had vanished when we kissed? Or how I had shivered all over just to stand near her? How could you talk about those things with anyone? You couldn't, not unless you lied and embellished and changed things, and so I didn't even try.

"She said she just wants to be friends," I admitted at last.

Peter sat back. "No. Oh, no. She didn't say that, did she? That's the last thing you ever want to hear from a girl."

I told him about Mark, about how her parents were friends with his parents, and how they went to the country club and played tennis together, and how she phoned him every night. Peter listened, and then dismissed it all with a wave of his hand.

"You know what? To hell with that. Don't worry about that. Girls always say that 'friends' thing. They have to. It's like a test or something. She wants to be sure you're serious about her before she sleeps with you."

I didn't ask Peter how he knew this. His father's *Playboy* magazines? He went on.

"Sure. Look at the facts of the situation. Did you or did you not get drunk and make out with her on the floor of her bedroom? I ask you: did you or did you not? That beats tennis any day. It's a clear and obvious sign. She wants you. She needs you. She's saying, 'Please, rescue me from this asshole Mark Mingis.' That's what she's saying."

I knew Peter wasn't the best person to take advice from; still, I was glad to hear him confirm what I already believed in my heart was true: that it didn't really matter what Gabriella or I said. We could say whatever we wanted; all that mattered was our kiss. Our kiss—that golden, glorious kiss—told the real story. There was no doubt in that kiss, none at all. It was our pledge, and the proof finally that what I felt, she felt, too.

"I'm going to ask her out."

"You'd better. That's what you're supposed to do. She's probably waiting for you. She's probably wondering what the hell's taking you so long." He shook his head and grinned at me across the table. "You goddamn playboy. There is hope in the world yet. You and Gabriella. Man. Go get her, you dog."

But try as I might, I couldn't get near her. Mark trailed her everywhere she went now. He hovered at her side before and after classes; he escorted her down the hallway and then stood by while she changed books at her locker. All Gabriella and I could manage were quick exchanges in passing—innocent-sounding pleasantries about the party, the weather, our holiday plans. But even during those brief encounters, I felt our connection. We were like two spies who shared a great and thrilling secret. I marveled at her ability to move her lips, those lips I had kissed, and laugh and touch her hair, that hair I had stroked, and carry on as if we were just two ordinary people, talking and breathing and doing the things ordinary people did. But I was sure that anybody who looked at us would've seen what impostors we were. Even Mark could see it; that was why he was keeping her from me. There was no hiding it; our love shone all around us like a spotlight.

In Earth and Space Science, my father turned off the lights for a slide show on cloud formations. He was excited about the bad weather; it coincided fortuitously with our unit on atmospheric precipitation, he said. As he clicked through the color photographs, I watched Gabriella from my desk at the back of the room, attempting to read her thoughts in the tilt of her head, the slope of her shoulders, the movement of her fingers in her hair. She turned to gaze out the windows at the rain, beautifully.

"Cumulus," my father said as a slide flashed onto the screen. "Look familiar? That's what's responsible for our rain today. Warm air rises up to meet a cooler layer of air in the atmosphere, where it condenses to form these thick, cotton-shaped clouds. . . ."

This, I supposed—watching Gabriella in a darkened classroom, with the rain streaming on the windows and my feet growing cold in wet socks—this was what it meant to be in love. It was a wet, miserable, blissful feeling. I wondered if everyone who had ever loved had felt the same.

A new slide. "Stratus. Got those today, too. Low, flat, hazy formations. It's basically high-altitude fog. When we say 'a cloudy day,' this is usually what we're talking about. . . ."

I saw again my mother touching her hair as she walked shakily across the floor of Frank Martello's library. Was this what she felt, too? This same wet, miserable, blissful feeling? I'd never thought it was possible for adults, parents like mine and Gabriella's, to fall in and out of love like teenagers, at least not in any world that I knew. But what if they could? Then what?

"Cirrus. What does that look like to you? What do you see there? . . . That's right. Comes from the Latin word for 'curly hair.' Mares' tails, they're sometimes called. . . ."

At the front of the classroom my father lectured on, crossing back and forth in front of the images on the screen, as though he were walking in clouds.

CHAPTER THIRTY-SEVEN

THE comet was halfway between the orbits of Venus and Mercury, less than two weeks from perihelion. Scientists all around the world were tracking it, collecting data that had never before been obtained from a comet. Infrared photography showed that its temperature had increased dramatically as it approached the Sun, from -94 °F to 900 °F. Electrographic cameras revealed an immense, healthy hydrogen halo, and observatory photographs recorded a well-defined double tail (both type I plasma and type II dust tails), extending 20 million miles behind it in a graceful arc. In one recently published article that was attracting some attention, "Comet Kohoutek and Penetrating Rays," a Russian physicist hypothesized that this was the first known visible specimen of an antimatter comet—a comet composed entirely of antimatter that, were it to come in contact with matter, would instantly annihilate both objects with an explosion more powerful than the most powerful of hydrogen bombs. It was suggested that more gamma-ray observations be made to test this hypothesis.

Meantime, noting that the comet was coming from Leo and entering Aquarius, astrologers were forecasting cataclysmic events across the globe for the new year—international unrest, unusual weather, famine, blight, epidemics. In Egypt, bands of hippies had gathered at the Pyramids to welcome the comet, hailing Kohoutek as the Starseed that would bring an advanced new civilization of peace and love to the world. In Nevada there was a rash of UFO sightings, and in New York a cult called the Children of God gathered on the steps of the United Nations wearing red sackcloth to warn Americans to flee from the cities, the Doomsday Comet was coming.

We saw them on the evening news the Friday night before the start of our Christmas holiday. Long-haired, skinny-armed, and staring, they waved signs for the cameras: THE GREAT DAY OF HIS WRATH HAS COME (REV 6:17)! BABYLON THE GREAT IS FALLEN. THOU SHALT KNOW VENGEANCE!

"Crazies," my father said, looking up from his work at the dining room table. "The Doomsday Comet. What idiocy."

He shook his head and went back to his writing. He'd gotten approval from the mayor for a town-wide viewing event. He'd already announced the date in the newspaper: January 6, the first Sunday in the new year. The Moon would be in a good phase then and the comet in optimal position for viewing. He was busy now with all the practical work of organizing the event: enlisting the cooperation of the various municipal departments, getting the word out to civic groups, and so forth. Never mind that we still couldn't see it without the telescope; my father assured me that the closer it got to the Sun, the brighter it'd become, until by the end of the year it'd be shining like a giant star, the brightest light in the sky.

I headed upstairs to my room, repeating to myself, "The *Dooms*-day Comet. The *Dooms*-day Comet." I liked the ominous sound of it. I knew, because my father had said so, that there was no danger from this comet. I knew, too, that the astrological predictions and supernatural expectations surrounding the coming of Kohoutek were all nonsense—just crazy people saying crazy things, as my father put it. But all the same, I couldn't help but feel that this comet was something more than just a comet. Changes were in the air. A jittery rest-lessness hummed through the streets of our town. Even the wind had a peculiar moan to it tonight. It whistled through the cracks around my window; it blew across the yards behind our row of houses, rustling leaves along the ground and rattling the loose side of the garage shed. Dogs barked, as though they, too, sensed a disturbance in the atmosphere—the penetrating rays of antimatter, perhaps, trickling down from the comet.

In her room next to mine, Megan was singing along to her stereo. Our mother had gone out for last-minute Christmas shopping with Barbara in Thibodaux, and Megan was waiting for her to come home so she could take the car to go see Greg's band rehearse. Since the party, Megan had been talking to Greg nightly on the phone. She'd begun singing in her room again, too, for the first time in years. She was har-monizing now to an old song about love and promises. Her voice floated up and down above the melody, pleasant and light, sounding an odd contrast to the wind and noise outside.

I turned off my light, stepped up to the window, and uncapped the Celestron. My heart jogged in my chest as Gabriella came into view in the lens. I was surprised to find her at home tonight; I was sure she would've been out with Mark or her friends, but there she was, cross-ing back and forth behind the French doors. I did a quick survey of her room. Clothes were scattered on her bed and furniture; two suitcases lay open on the floor. I knew the Martellos were leaving that weekend to go to Colorado; she must've been packing for their trip.

I focused in tight with the Celestron until I was hovering right at her side. I followed her to her walk-in closet and waited while she disap-peared inside. She came out with a blouse, changed her mind, and ducked back into the closet. She reappeared with another blouse and carried it to her bed, almost bumping into me as she passed. It was like being back in her room with her as I'd been on the night of the party, except that now she couldn't see me. I was invisible to her, a ghost. And yet, I saw her so clearly, I felt so close to her that it seemed impos-sible for her not to know I was there. I wondered if in some special way she could sense my presence. Holding the focus tight to her shoulder, I whispered in her ear, "Hello, Gabby. Hello. I'm here. Can you hear me?"

She turned and went back to the closet. I decided that if she came to the balcony doors and looked out, that would be a sign that she was thinking of me; that would be my signal to go visit her tonight. I would throw on my coat, hop on my bike, and in five minutes I'd be standing beside her in her room, not as a ghost but for real. Enough of my damn timidity. What was I waiting for? Peter was right: we had made out on the floor of her bedroom, we were practically lovers already. We could at least share a goodbye kiss before she left for the holiday.

"Follow your heart," as my mother said, "and the rest will follow."

Just then our phone rang downstairs. My father went to pick it up. I heard his muffled voice coming through the floor as he talked with whoever was on the line. He sounded confused.

Prompted by I didn't know what, I swung the telescope down to check the patio room of the Martellos' house. The lights were on, the TV was playing. And there was Barbara Martello standing by their couch, talking on their phone. I watched her speak, and I heard my father answer in our living room below me. This was odd; Barbara was supposed to have been out shopping with my mother. But I figured that my mother must've been on her way home now, and so I thought little more of it.

I tilted back upstairs to Gabriella. She was still moving around in her bedroom, laying out her clothes. In my mind's eye I was already pulling my bike from our garage shed and heading down the driveway. I saw myself standing up on the pedals as I raced out of our neighborhood . . . and then I was halfway over the Franklin Street bridge, with the red light of the water tower blinking over my shoulder, the stars blinking above . . . and then I was turning in past the Beau Rivage sign and speeding down her street to her house. . . .

Junior! This is a surprise, her mother would say, opening the door. *Of course, come in. Gabby's right upstairs. Can I get you something? A Coke?*

From the corner of my eye, I caught the flash of headlights as a car turned down their driveway and into the garage. I swung the scope down in time to see Mr. Martello walking into the patio room down-stairs. Barbara met him and then followed him as he went out of the room and returned with a bottle of beer. They stopped near the patio doors. Barbara pointed once toward our house. Frank spread his hands, explaining something. She crossed her arms, unconvinced by whatever he was saying.

I left them there and looked again upstairs, where I found Gabriella standing now directly behind her balcony doors. She leaned in and put her face against the glass, cupping her hands around her eyes. Then she pulled her head back, shaped her hands into a telescope, and made as if to search in the direction of our house.

My lights were off so it was impossible for her to see into my room. And yet she acted as if she knew I was watching her. She became play-ful. She hid behind the yellow curtain on one side of the door and poked her head out. Then she wrapped the curtain around her like a dress and began doing a kind of striptease. She snaked her arm out from the edge of the curtain, rolled her shoulder around, and then snapped the curtain up to her chin, hiding herself. She put a leg out and slowly slid the curtain up to reveal her foot, and then her calf, and then her knee, before dropping the curtain again over her leg. She laughed. I laughed, too. She was fully dressed, wearing blue jeans and a T-shirt, so her show was more silly than serious, but all the same, I found it wildly exciting.

While watching her, I heard, as though from far away, my mother return home. The car door slammed outside, and then the front door opened and closed behind her. In a weird mirroring of what I'd just seen at the Martellos' house, I heard my father following my mother around downstairs. They came to a stop directly below my room, talking in tense, hushed voices. I could only make out a few of the words, but the tone was clear enough. They were arguing.

Thibodaux! . . . Barbara! . . . Not an interrogation, a simple ques-tion . . . Frank . . . You admit it now . . . Because I knew what you'd say . . . I'm supposed to believe that! . . . Yes! Yes! What's so hard to believe about that!

I blocked out their voices and kept my eye on Gabriella. She had moved out from behind the curtain and was standing behind the balcony doors again. She wagged a finger in the air, as though scolding me. Then she looked down slyly and gripped the bottom of her T-shirt in her hands. She slowly raised it, sliding it from side to side, and then she flashed her chest at me and yanked her T-shirt back down.

I almost knocked over the telescope in my excitement to leave. That was more than just an invitation; it was like an offer. I grabbed a sweater and shoes. Sitting on my bed to tie the laces, I heard my parents' voices growing louder downstairs. Next door in her room, Megan had turned off her stereo and stopped singing.

Answer me . . . No! . . . You're lying to me . . . Don't you talk to me like that . . . Admit it . . . The children . . . I don't care! I don't care!

There was a sharp yelp from our mother, followed by a muffled thump.

"Stop it! What are you doing?"

The thought of meeting Gabriella vanished into the air as I ran to the door. My sister lurched out into the hallway at the same time I did. We hesitated, looking at each other, and in the dim light of the hall I saw that she was as worried as I was. I saw, too, that we both knew what was happening; at some level, we must've been expecting this moment for months. We went to the stairs, me in the lead.

Our father stood over our mother, gripping her arm. She was buckled halfway to the floor. A drinking glass lay on its side on the rug. The room was dim, the colored Christmas lights blinking on the tree in the corner. Both our parents were breathing heavily, their faces red and distorted; they appeared to be vibrating all over. Our father snapped his head around when Megan and I stopped on the stairs.

"Oh good, here they are," he said.

"Let go of me!" our mother said, trying to squirm free.

"No, wait." Keeping a tight hold on her arm, he spoke in an unnaturally loud, halting voice, as though he was restraining himself from shouting, or crying.

"Children. Sorry to disturb you. Your mother and I are having an argument. Obviously. She lied to me about going out tonight with Frank Martello—"

"I didn't—"

"No, no, you did. You certainly did. You lied. She said she was with Barbara, but she wasn't. She was with Frank all evening. Frank Martello—"

"Shopping! I told you, we were shopping for Christmas presents."

"—in Thibodaux, with Frank, doing god knows what. What do you think? Is that okay? Should we worry about that or not?"

"Let go of her," Megan said evenly.

"Stop it. Just stop it! This is ridiculous," our mother said. "They don't have to hear this. We can go to our room."

"Oh, I think they're old enough to hear this, don't you? They're old enough to know what's going on in this family."

"Let go of her!" Megan repeated.

Our mother glared up sideways at him. Biting off her words, she said, "It's *nothing*. I told you. He's my *friend*. We *talk*. We enjoy each other's company."

"Is that what you do? You talk. What do you talk about? What can you and Frank possibly have to talk about?"

"I don't have to put up with this," she said, and tugged away from him. He snapped her back and shook her roughly.

"You think I don't see what's going on here? You think I don't know?"

"You're hurting her!" Megan said.

"My god, you must think I'm an idiot. You must think I'm as dumb as you are. But I'm not. Oh no, I know exactly what's going on—"

Our mother grunted, twisted around, and bit his hand. He hollered as she stumbled away from him.

This wasn't happening, I thought. This couldn't be happening. Our parents didn't fight like this. They didn't even look like this. We'd all been swallowed up into some dark, alternate universe where these two impostor parents had taken the place of my own and were battling it out on the floor of our living room. I felt queasy and hot; I wanted to run and hide but I was stuck on the stairs, unable to move.

Our father had stopped on the rug, his legs apart, his hands squeezed into fists, huffing. Our mother stood with the corner of the sofa between them, her head thrown back. When she spoke next, it was with a wild, vindictive sneer.

"Okay, yes! You're right! You're right, I see him all the time. And you want to know what me and Frank do when we're alone together? You want to know? We laugh at you. The Professor. Oh boy, oh boy, we laugh! Yeah, we have a grand old time. We think you're hilarious. And then when we finish laughing at you, we do things you can't even imagine . . . wonderful things . . . beautiful things. He takes me in his arms and he—"

He shot a hand out and struck her face. For one startled second, no one moved. Then she opened her mouth and let out a sound I'd never heard from her before, a pained, animal-like yowl.

She ran to their bedroom, shouting over her shoulder, "Leaving! . . . Gone! . . . Finished!"

Megan shoved past me on the steps and ran after her, hissing at our father as she passed, "How dare you do that! How dare you!"

I stayed frozen on the stairs. I heard my mother sobbing and knocking around in the bedroom while Megan tried to console her. My father paced below me in the living room, rubbing the hand he'd hit her with. He wheeled around and shouted at the bedroom.

"Where're you going? Frank's house? What do you think's going to happen? He's going to leave his wife? Leave his wife and daughter? For you? Oh, that's brilliant. That's great. It's good to see you've thought this all the way through."

She shouted back through the doorway, her voice teary and unclear. "Yes! Yes! You find that so hard to believe? That somebody actually cares for me? That somebody could love me?"

He rushed into their bedroom, shouting something incomprehensible. Megan shoved him out. "Leave her alone!"

My mother went on crying and shouting from the bedroom. "No, because you don't even know what love is! You stopped loving me fifteen years ago. You don't even like me. You despise me."

"Don't put this on me! I'm not the one slutting around with the neighbor."

She stormed out of the room, a suitcase in her hand. Megan followed. He blocked their way, and they all three wrestled clumsily over the suitcase. The Christmas tree was knocked sideways, ornaments fell to the floor. "Where're you going? Huh? Where do you think you're going?" he grunted.

My mother broke free and stumbled to the front door with the suitcase. Then she stopped and swung an arm around to point in the direction of the Martellos'. There was a smear of blood below her nose. Her face was a crumpling mask.

"He loves me. Do you understand that? *He—loves—me.*"

She turned and banged out through the front door and down the steps.

Megan went after her. Our father tried to grab her arm. "Don't you touch me!" she spat, and ran out to join our mother.

He caught the door and shouted into the yard, "Fine! Go! Leave!"

A dog began barking. The car backed up the drive. The red taillights crossed behind my father's figure in the doorway and then rolled out of view down the street.

After a long, stunned moment, my father turned around and came back inside. He walked stiffly to the middle of the room and, raking his hand through his hair, looked helplessly from side to side, as though he'd forgotten something.

The room was silent but the air still echoed with the violence of their fight. The colored lights on the toppled tree blinked on and off. He stopped and looked up at me. His hair stood on end; a swollen, crooked vein running down the middle of his forehead throbbed in time with the blinking lights.

"What the hell just happened here?" he said hoarsely.

CHAPTER THIRTY-EIGHT

WHAT in the hell just happened?

How to explain the sudden and calamitous turn of events that left my parents separated, Megan and my mother living with our grandparents on the other side of town, and my father and me pacing alone through the cold, dim rooms of our house? It didn't seem possible, and yet it was.

Christmas Eve, my father stood on the muddy ground of the backyard in his black raincoat, desperately scanning the sky for signs of the comet. From my bedroom window he looked like a large, sad, sagging crow. He straightened up to stretch his back, sighed visibly, and then bowed back to the telescope.

Across the bayou, the Martellos' house shone as brightly as ever. They'd left for the holiday, but the lights were on timers so that the decorations blazed to life every evening at dusk, like a promise that their absence was only temporary, they'd return soon.

While above us, hidden behind the stars, the comet hurtled toward the Sun. Although we couldn't see it, the comet, I was sure, could see us. Gazing down from its lonely circuit through the planets, it couldn't have helped but feel sympathy for me, my sister, my mother and father, and all our baffled, battered hearts.

Who were we? Where did we come from? How did we get here?

Somewhere out beyond the invisible crystal sphere that surrounded our solar system, beyond the most distant, distant star, was the place at the edge of the universe where dreams were born and people never died and all that had ever happened was still happening. There, in that impossible place, my parents were still young and in love, newlyweds setting out on their honeymoon together.

Squinting my eyes at the sky, I could almost see them myself. Look, there they were again, Alan and Lydia Broussard, hurrying along the line of passenger cars of the Sunset Limited at New Orleans Union Station. He was just twenty-two, a skinny boy with high-waisted trousers and Thom McAn loafers, struggling to carry both their bags. She was nineteen with a navy-blue polka-dotted dress that she thought looked like the one Audrey Hepburn wore in *Sabrina*; she carried a neat, sky-blue cosmetic travel case, a wedding present from an aunt. It was the middle of the night, and the air was spiced with the smell of diesel and tar, cigarettes and perfume. They were running late—Alan had had some dispute with the taxi driver over the fare. Steam hissed, announcements blared overhead: *"Departing now from track nine . . ."* As they trotted along they glimpsed wedges of sky and stars between the roof of the platform and the tops of the train cars.

"Here it is! Here's our car," Alan said, and heaved their bags up into the doorway. He climbed aboard and held out a hand for his new wife. She was nervous; she'd never been on a train before. The gap between the step of the train and the edge of the platform looked enormous. Whistles were blowing, conductors were shouting. She hesitated.

Who was this man, after all? And what did either of them know about marriage, or living with another person, or raising a family? Nothing at all. But they were in love, and love made people do crazy things, and—good god, the thing had already started moving.

"Come on! Quick, give me your hand," he shouted, and hauled her up into the train, where they fell into each other's arms, laughing with relief and trepidation as the train pulled out of the station. . . .

. . . and then, all too soon, the train was pulling back into the station and their honeymoon was over. They settled into the happy business of setting up a home. Lydia shopped for towels in town, Alan wanted a good lamp for his reading chair. He became handy with a paintbrush, and she learned how to gut and bake a chicken. A year quickly passed, and then suddenly one night Alan found himself pacing in the dim corridor of a hospital.

From a radio at the nurses' station in the corner—he would always remember this—came the mysterious signal of the *Sputnik* satellite as it passed overhead. *Beep . . . beep . . . beep . . . beep . . .* He was summoned to a room down the hall, and he dashed in to find his wife waking groggily in a bed. Lydia was sore; she hardly knew where she was; she remembered she was dreaming about . . . something. Stars and planets, a Russian robot beeping in space. She was handed a thing in a blanket, and when she looked down and saw the baffled, angry little person squirming and shaking her fists in the air, she laughed and cried with motherly recognition. . . .

And then three more years somehow quickly passed and she was nursing a second baby, a son, in a corner of her bedroom while trying to keep an eye on Megan screaming and kicking her wooden blocks around the living room floor. "Alan!" she pleaded. "Can't you do something?"

Life rolled on, carrying our young family through countless changes of diapers, loads of laundry, summer flus and winter colds and middle-of-the-night upset stomachs. . . . There was our mother making a lunch of peanut butter and jelly sandwiches for us at the counter. . . . There was my sister Megan sitting on a pony at a birthday party, crying her eyes out. . . . And there was my father reading aloud to me in bed at night from an illustrated anthology of Jules Verne. I pressed against the wall, snuggled beneath the sheets, while he lay beside me with the book tilted to the bed lamp so he could see the pages. He read about Captain Nemo and his voyage twenty thousand leagues under the sea in search of the mysterious sea monster, and the two astronomers who chased a golden meteor across Nebraska, and three bold adventurers who fired themselves to the Moon from a giant cannon on a beach in Florida. . . .

A couple of years later, and now he was teaching me how to play baseball. It was a bright afternoon in early spring. My father had a library book propped open on the picnic table, consulting it over his shoulder as he tried to arrange my limbs to match the stance of a tough-looking blond-haired kid in a photograph.

"Feet shoulder width apart . . . forty-five-degree angle . . . relaxed but secure grip . . . Right, good. Like that."

He jogged to the other side of the yard with the ball. He was dressed in shorts and a plaid shirt, his legs embarrassingly white and bony. In place of a mitt he wore a gardening glove. He tried an overhanded pitch. The ball flew wildly off course as I swung the bat around at empty air. We tried again, and again, my father mumbling about wind speed and arc and trajectories and "getting a feel for the thing." He called words of encouragement as he jogged back and forth in the grass to retrieve the ball. "You almost hit that one. I think we almost got it."

My mother, delighted to see us finally doing the sporty kind of activity that fathers and sons were supposed to do, brought out glasses of Kool-Aid on a tray. Megan joined her, and they yelled advice as they watched. "You have to throw it straight! You're not doing it right! You're swinging the bat too soon!" I added my complaints. "How can I hit that? That's nowhere near where I'm standing. Throw it this way!"

My father, sweating by now, was getting fed up. "I know! I know! You think I don't realize that?"

We all saw it was hopeless. The ball landed on the picnic table and knocked over two glasses of Kool-Aid. Megan laughed out loud. My father shouted at her that it wasn't as easy as it looked and if she thought she could do better, then she was welcome to try. "She probably could," our mother muttered. His next pitch dropped the ball into the bayou.

"Great. Thanks, Dad," I said. "That's perfect. You've been a big help. I think I'm ready for the big leagues now."

"Stuff it. Just stuff it then," he said, and ripped off the gardening glove and stomped back inside. . . .

Where in the morning he shaved at the sink, slicked his hair, and knotted his tie, sighing out through his nose as he got ready for another day of work. He lined up the pens in his shirt pocket, three colors, red, blue, and black. He repacked his brown leather case, finished his coffee, handed off the cup to his wife with a kiss on the cheek, and headed out the door to his bicycle. He wobbled a bit on the drive before catching his balance and turning down the road to school. Our mother watched him go, waving goodbye from the front step. Then she turned and went back inside to wash the dishes, make the beds, do the laundry, and cook our dinner. . . .

And then again: he shaved, slicked, knotted, lined up, repacked, and headed out the door. She waved, turned, and went inside to wash the dishes, make the beds, do the laundry, and cook our dinner. He shaved, slicked, knotted, lined up, repacked, and headed out the door. She waved, turned, and went inside. He shaved, slicked, knotted; she waved, turned, went inside. Shave, slick, knot, wave, turn, go inside; shave, slick, knot, wave, turn, go inside . . .

Good god. They had no idea adulthood could be so tiresome. Sometimes they wondered how they could stand another day of it. Sometimes they wondered why they even bothered.

Life chugged on, picking up speed. The weeks and months whipped by faster and faster. Dust gathered on windowsills, sinks clogged, weeds sprouted, furniture sagged, curtains faded. A cabinet door fell off, it was missing a screw or something, and the toilet was backed up and spilling onto the floor. The children needed new clothes, yes, of course they did, but the house needed painting, and the roof needed repairing, and there was a crack running through the front porch step that was getting bigger and bigger every year—and, no, we couldn't afford a new car, and why would you even ask that?

Someone should've told the newlyweds, back before they boarded that train, that this was what it would be like. Someone should've told them that married life would not be filled with years of honeymooned bliss, but with an endless parade of chores and clutter and routine annoyances that over time would begin to make them feel older, slower, less buoyant.

No doubt a part of them did know this; they were sensible people, after all, and they'd grown up in families themselves, so they understood what domestic life was like. But another part of them, the part that hopped aboard the train that night, clung to the belief that their lives would be different, that theirs would be better than average—because, really, who didn't believe that?

A dozen or more years after the start of that ride—years that sped by so fast and then faded so suddenly and absolutely into the past that they might have never happened at all—a dozen years later, and my father dropped into bed at night, exhausted. Soon he was asleep and dreaming, but even in his dreams, he was still hard at work. He was standing, in his dream, at the front of the classroom writing on the chalkboard. He needed to explain some critical piece of information— without this information, the whole lesson would be lost—but it wasn't coming out the way he wanted it to. He wrote and wrote, but even he couldn't understand what he was writing. It looked to be a different language, but not any language that he knew—Czechoslovakian, maybe. He looked up and saw that the whole board was filled with his scribbling. He heard his students growing restless at his back. They whispered and growled like waves at a beach. He wrote, erased, wrote, erased, but the baffling words kept reappearing on their own; they wouldn't go away, and his students were laughing now. They were roaring with laughter. They thought he was hilarious. . . .

While in bed beside him, his wife, my mother, turned her head on her pillow and saw him twitching in his sleep. The Moon shone in through a crack in the curtains, casting shadows on the sheets. Her husband's mouth fell open and he began to snore, a wet, nasal rattle. In the dim light, with his glasses off, he looked completely alien to her— like a stranger who had wandered in off the street and lain down beside her. Was his nose always that big? Was his forehead always that bony? Who was this man who called himself her husband, anyway? A breeze stirred a tree outside the window, and the house creaked around her. In the distance, she heard the whistle of a train at the edge of town, and she felt very far away from herself.

She remembered that dreamy teenager in the drugstore, leaning on the counter and staring out the window at night, waiting for her future to walk in the door. Whatever happened to that girl? she wondered. So young, so expectant, so full of hope? She puzzled over the mysteries of time, memory, and space. She imagined that girl, her younger self, still waiting there in the drugstore, as though the store itself and she in it were suspended in some timeless, heavenly blue place where bright flowers bloomed in endless green fields in an eternal spring. . . .

Her husband snored. She shivered. Her feet were cold. She pressed her bare, bony knees together under the sheets and stifled a sob. What was wrong with her? She should've been happy. She *was* happy, she told herself. It had just been a long day, that was all. She had everything she needed. Her husband didn't beat her, her children weren't hoodlums. Nobody was starving and they had their health, thank god. They were tremendously fortunate, she knew that. And yet . . . and yet in those long, lonely hours between one and three in the morning, when everyone was asleep and the house creaked around her, she couldn't help but feel that she was already half dead, so slight and inconsequential her life had become. She was a ghost, trapped inside a tiny, rickety home, stuck in a world she never foresaw.

She sat up and, careful not to wake her husband, slipped out of bed and into the living room. She hugged her gown around her as she looked out the back window at the night. Across the bayou, the trees had been cleared for a new house. Above, a wash of stars and—good lord, but it was bright tonight—the Moon.

A Gulf breeze blew, rustling the trees. She rubbed her arms and hugged her gown tighter around herself. She felt a familiar burning sensation in her gut, one she realized she must've had for quite some time now. It seemed to come and go, flaring up especially at night. What was it? Hunger? Heartburn? Loneliness? Regret? She'd go get a glass of water and lie back down. She was just tired, that was all. What was she doing anyway, wandering around the house like this in the middle of the night?

She could not have known then, my young mother, that you couldn't just ignore an ache like that and expect it to go away. Such a burn, unattended, could grow and spread, laying waste to entire villages—trees, homes, cars, and families up in flames.

Nor could she have anticipated a future when, a few years later, she would surprise even herself by leaving her husband on account of another man—a man who, to be honest, she barely knew, but whom she loved with such a blind, needy love that she was ready to throw over everything she had for him.

She couldn't have known these things, not then, but as she stared out the window that night, in some dim, prescient corner of her mind, she could almost already see her husband standing abandoned in their yard in his raincoat, surveying the sky with a telescope, wondering what the hell had happened to their marriage; while their son, a teenage boy who looked just like him, stared sleepy eyed and puzzled from his bedroom window upstairs, wondering how such certainties could collapse so suddenly; while arching over them all, a comet, grand and mysterious, disappeared behind the Sun.

CHAPTER THIRTY-NINE

ON Christmas Eve, Comet Kohoutek dipped behind the Sun, disappearing completely from view. In the lens of the telescope now there was nothing but black space between the stars. The celebrated Comet Cruise on the *Queen Elizabeth*, I read, had been a bust; the skies were cloudy, the water choppy, and no one could see anything; Dr. Kohoutek became seasick and stayed in his cabin, refusing to attend any of the events. A few newspaper editorials were already starting to call the comet a hoax, going so far as to raise questions about its discoverer's motivations and nationality. Meanwhile, astronomers at institutes and observatories everywhere struggled to explain why the comet had so far failed to dazzle.

Some attributed the lack of visual magnitude to its chemical composition, speculating that Kohoutek was a relatively clean comet with not enough dust particles in its coma to properly reflect sunlight. Others said that maybe Kohoutek wasn't a virgin comet after all, and that it must have exhausted most of its volatile gases in a previous passage, perhaps millions of years ago. Still others blamed the media for over-hyping the comet and building up public expectations to far beyond what anyone in the scientific community had actually promised.

Whatever the explanations, many astronomers began backpedaling on their earlier predictions for a postperihelion apparition. Reminding us that comets were notoriously capricious, they advised a wait-and-see attitude now. Nobody, not even the comet's namesake, could safely say how big or bright this one would eventually appear once it rounded the Sun and began its second pass through the planets.

The curtains were closed, the living room dim when I went downstairs on Christmas morning. The only light was a murky flickering from the TV. My father sat on the sofa in his pajamas, a blanket wrapped around his shoulders. His hair stood on end, his face was unshaven. Scattered on the sofa around him, on the floor, and on the dining room table, were all his magazine articles and newspaper clippings about Kohoutek.

"What're you watching?"

He answered as though from very far away. "Huh?"

"What's on TV?"

He pointed. "It's the, ah, *Skylab*. They're having Christmas now."

On the screen was a fuzzy video feed of astronauts in orange jump-suits floating around inside a spaceship cabin. They were decorating a spindly silver tree made from empty space-food tubes. One of the astronauts pointed to three socks taped to the side of a metal cabinet, each marked with a set of initials, and gave a thumbs-up sign. I watched for a minute over my father's shoulder before backing away into the kitchen.

"Are you hungry?"

"What?"

"Hungry? Do you want something to eat?"

"Okay," he mumbled.

In the cupboards we had only a couple of cans of vegetables, cooking oil, and some Cream of Wheat. In the refrigerator, some carrots, wilted celery, and butter.

"We need more food," I called to my father.

"What?"

"We need more food!"

I boiled water for the Cream of Wheat, but there was barely enough for both of us; two servings' worth made only a thin gruel. I carried a bowl to my father and cleared a place on the table for myself. We slurped our breakfast. On the TV was a commercial for Norelco electric shavers, with an animated Santa riding a silver rotary razor over hills of snow, ho-ho-ho-ing and waving his arms. Our Christmas tree had been restored to its base in the corner of the room, but neither I nor my father bothered plugging the lights in; even the thought of blinking Christmas tree lights here, now, in this house, seemed too sad to bear.

This was yet another one of those things that school failed to prepare you for: how to deal with the unpredictable behavior of real people in the real world. My father had always been the model of responsibility. He was never sick. He never missed a day of work and was never late for class. The only time I normally ever saw him in pajamas was before bed or on Sunday mornings, when he liked to linger with the newspaper and coffee in his armchair. So to see him like this, as he had been for the past several days, was frightening.

Midmorning, my sister let herself in the front door. She carried a grocery bag of food and an empty suitcase.

"*Brrr.* It's freezing in here," she said, coming around the corner into the room.

It was her first visit since our parents' fight the week before. There was an awkward moment when she met eyes with our father. He looked like he might say something, but then he closed his mouth, stood up from the sofa, slipped past her into the bedroom, and shut the door behind him.

"I guess he doesn't want to talk to me."

"I guess not. You're in the enemy camp now."

She set the grocery bag down on the table and began unpacking it. "It's not much, but it should tide you over until the stores open again. Got bread, eggs, milk . . . I need to pick up some more of my clothes and things, too, while I'm here."

She stopped to take in the rooms—the paper and clutter, the dishes piled in the sink, the stray pieces of clothing. "Jesus, it looks like a train wreck in here." She asked quietly, "How's he holding up?"

"He's holding up fine!" our father answered from inside the bedroom.

I shook my head: *Not fine.* My sister mimed smoking a cigarette and pointed to the backyard. I took some bread, grabbed my father's blanket from the couch, and, still wearing my pajamas and slippers, followed her outside.

The day was crisp and sunny. We settled on top of the old picnic table at the rear of the yard, resting our feet on the bench. The table wobbled precariously under our weight. The light off the water was so bright that it made us squint.

"Did you do something to your hair?" I asked.

"I got it cut," she said, holding up the ends of it. "And I brushed it."

"It looks good."

"A compliment! How unusual." She pulled her Kools out of her coat pocket. "You want one?" she asked, offering me the pack.

"No, thanks."

"Strictly a dope man."

"Ha."

As she lit up her cigarette, I ate a piece of bread and watched the Martellos' house across the water. Yellow leaves littered the yard and boardwalk. The curtains were closed, the patio furniture rolled out of sight. I knew they were gone for the holiday, but I couldn't help watching the house anyway, half hoping to see an arm, a head of black hair flashing behind a window.

Megan said, "Mom said to be sure to tell you hello and that she misses you and she wishes you would talk to her."

"I did talk to her. She telephoned."

"She said you were angry and wouldn't say anything."

That was more or less true. My mother had telephoned, more than once, in fact. But what was there for me to say to her? That I understood what she was doing? That I didn't have any problem with her running out like she did?

"You might try calling her back, you know," Megan said.

I shrugged and didn't say anything, and Megan let it drop.

"So how's he doing?" she asked. "The same?"

"The same."

I told her how our father still wasn't leaving the house; how he spent his days rereading all his notes and papers on the comet, or watching the *Skylab* on TV, or just lying in bed like a sick man. "I don't think he'd bother to eat if I didn't bring food to him. I don't know what to do. I've never seen him this way before."

"Paps and Grams invited you all for Christmas dinner. You should try to get him to go."

"I don't think he will."

"No. No, probably not," my sister agreed. "Not with Mom there."

In the distance we could hear neighborhood kids shouting and playing outside with their new Christmas toys. I felt suddenly older than I'd been a week ago. I pulled the blanket around my shoulders.

"What's going on with you guys?" I asked.

Megan said that she was still sleeping on the couch, our mother still in her old bedroom. It was awkward staying with our grandparents, my sister admitted, because our mother hadn't told them the whole story yet, only that she and our father had had a fight, and so they didn't realize how serious the situation was. Grams and Paps treated her like she was just some hotheaded teenage girl who'd run away from home for the weekend; they seemed to think that if she'd only go back and apologize, everything would be all right. That didn't make it any easier on our mother, naturally. Megan wanted to get her out of the house later this week, maybe drive up to New Orleans for the after-Christmas sales and help her shop for new clothes. . . .

As my sister rambled on about living arrangements, the Martellos' house didn't just disappear. It squatted there unmoving on the other side of the water, a reminder of what had led us to where we were now.

I hated to even think about it myself, but I needed to know. When Megan stopped talking, I finally asked her.

"Has Mom told you anything about Frank? Do you know what's going on between them?"

She sighed. "It's complicated."

"Just tell me."

She took a long drag on her cigarette before saying, matter-of-factly: "She says she loves him, and he loves her, and no matter how uncomfortable that might make some people, she has to do what she knows in her heart is right."

"So it's true? They really were, you know—"

"Having an affair? Apparently so."

"She told you that?"

"We've talked about it, yes."

Megan took another puff of her cigarette and blew out the smoke, coolly, as if she encountered this kind of thing every day. I'd suspected it myself, ever since the party at their house, but having our mother's affair with Frank Martello verified, brought out into the daylight and stood up naked in front of us, was still shocking.

She went on to tell me how after our parents' big blowup last week, the first thing our mother did was drive to the Conoco station and call Frank from the pay phone. Megan had been with her in the car, so she'd witnessed the whole thing. Frank couldn't talk just then—he was having dinner with his family—but he promised our mother that when he got back to town after New Year's, they'd discuss everything like rational adults and find some solution. He only wanted what was best for her, he told her. Our mother was counting the days now until Frank's return.

One good thing to come out of all this, Megan said, was that she and our mother were finally getting to know each other better. Since spending more time with her, Megan had come to see what a strong, independent-minded woman our mother really was. Lydia's only problem, my sister said, was that she'd been trapped for all these years in an unhappy marriage. As our mother described it, she felt like she'd been standing under a dark cloud while everyone else was enjoying the sunshine.

But Frank had helped her to see that she had as much right to happiness as anyone; he'd been really wonderful for her that way. If she didn't like a situation, Frank told her, she should change the situation. It was as simple as that. She was an adult, after all; this was her life, and she should be able to do with it what she chose. The only thing that kept her standing under that dark cloud was habit and fear. There was the sunshine; all she had to do was step toward it. "We make our own happiness," was how Frank put it.

My sister paused to take another pull on her cigarette. I didn't see how she could be so calm talking about all this. She seemed to be overlooking the whole sleazy aspect of it—the fact that our mother had actually been sleeping with our neighbor behind our father's back. But when I thought of this, when I pictured Frank Martello cupping my mother's head in his hand and whispering to her, *We make our own happiness, Lydia*, it made my stomach clench.

"That guy's a snake," I said.

"You don't think our mother deserves to be happy?"

"What? No, of course she deserves to be happy. I'm not saying that. I'm just saying I don't trust Frank Martello. All this 'sunshine' and stuff. What's he up to? How well does she know him, anyway? What does she think's going to happen? He's going to leave his wife and family for her? And then what?" I slipped my sister's cigarette from her fingers and tried to smoke it.

"You sound like Dad now."

"Well, maybe he's right. This whole thing is crazy. It's like our mother's been brainwashed or something." I coughed on the cigarette smoke. "And what about us? What're we supposed to do? She can't just abandon us like this."

"See, you're not even thinking about her. You're only worried about yourself. You're worried about who's going to clean and cook and wash your clothes for you. That's why you're feeling so anxious. But we're all adults here. We can take care of ourselves." I started to say something but she went on. "We need to be thinking about our mother right now. Lydia's going through some very challenging times, and she needs all the support we can give her."

"What about Dad? You think this is fair to him?"

"You think he'll even notice she's gone? He's practically ignored her for years. What difference could it make to him now? All he cares about is his precious comet."

"Yeah, but . . ."

"Honestly, did our parents look like a happy couple to you? Did they? I'm surprised they lasted as long as they did. Lydia probably should've done this years ago. I applaud her. I think it's very brave of her. For the first time in her life, she's doing what she wants and not what everyone else wants. At last she'll be free to pursue her own dreams."

"You *applaud* her?"

My sister must've been listening to too much Joan Baez—"We Shall Overcome" and "I Shall Be Released" and all that. She was enjoying this whole separation mess much more than she should have been. In fact, hearing her go on about "free to pursue her dreams" and "doing what she wants," I got the feeling Megan was speaking more for herself than our mother: it wasn't our mother's freedom that my sister was so excited about, it was hers. And since when, by the way, did she start calling our mother by her first name, like they were best friends from school?

I swallowed a gulp of cigarette smoke and had a fit of coughing. The picnic table creaked beneath us. Megan took her cigarette back from me.

"Those'll kill you, you know," she said.

"Thank you, Doctor. I'll be sure to remember that."

I felt dizzy, either from the cigarette smoke, or from everything Megan had told me, or from both. This was all happening too fast. One day we were a regular family, maybe not exactly delirious with happiness, but normal enough, and the next, my mother had fallen in love with our neighbor and run away with my sister, who was coming now to deliver food and collect more clothes.

I looked around our scrappy yard: the trees along the bayou, the rusted chain link fence, the tilting garage shed, my bike resting on the ground over there. Though I'd never held any special affection for it, the place at least had a dependable familiarity. I felt a version of the same sentiment for our household. Our family was like the wobbly picnic table Megan and I were sitting on: four legs supporting some planks, a simple enough structure, nothing remarkable, but it did its job. If you altered it in any way, broke away a leg or pried off the top, it hardly qualified as a table anymore. Then it was just—what?—a pile of scrap wood, something to haul away to the dump, and then only the memory of a table. Maybe soon you were even missing the rotten table.

I adjusted the blanket around my shoulders. I was beginning to shiver; it was colder outside than I'd thought.

"How long do you think this is going to last?"

Megan looked at me curiously. "How long?"

"Yeah."

"I hate to tell you, little bro, but I don't think this is just a temporary situation." She confessed that she wasn't sure how our mother's relationship with Frank would turn out; we'd have to wait until he got back after New Year's to see how he arranged things with his family. But regardless, Megan didn't see how our parents could stay together after this.

She squinted dramatically through her cigarette smoke. "I do believe we are witnessing the end of Mr. and Mrs. Alan Broussard as we knew them."

"You mean like . . . divorce?"

"Don't act so shocked. It happens all the time. Why not them?"

I protested. Maybe it looked bad now, I said, but in a couple of weeks, a couple of months at the most, they'd find a way to get back together. Then things would return to normal. They had to. We couldn't go on living like this. This was impossible. This was . . . this was a disaster.

"Or what other people might call real life. Better get used to it, Junior. You've got decades of it ahead of you."

She bent over and stubbed out her cigarette on the picnic bench, then tossed the butt toward the bayou. And with that, she got up to go back inside. I stood by while she packed clothes in bags, took her old guitar, and said goodbye to our father through the bedroom door. Then she got in the car and drove back to our grandparents' house, leaving me to stumble and shiver through the ruins of our home, washing dishes, picking up clothes, wondering how we could even begin to build a new life out of this rubble.

CHAPTER FORTY

PETER opened the door for me and my father, and a wave of warm, smelly air washed out from inside the house.

"Come on in!" Mr. Coot called.

The heat in the living room was turned up so high that it was like wading into a warm pond. And the smell—it was a rank, shut-in odor that made me instinctively close my nose and breathe through my mouth.

Mr. Coot hobbled around the corner of the couch to greet us. "You made it," he said, and put his hand out for my father.

"Merry Christmas, Lou. Thanks for having us."

Lou—Mr. Coot—was around my father's age, with a large belly, a thick neck, and dirty blond hair that he wore slicked back in a flip from his forehead. He walked with a kind of waddle, on account of his hip, and when he wasn't dressed in his gas station uniform he liked to wear blue jeans with suspenders, as he did now.

"You didn't have to get all dressed up," he said, eyeing my father's tie.

My father shrugged and said he wasn't sure, it being Christmas and all.

"Oh, hell no. We take it easy here. Casual attire required."

We happened to be there because I'd mentioned my parents' separation to Peter, who told his father, who invited us over for dinner. We all bumped into the small front room behind Mr. Coot, who went on talking loudly, not looking at any of us.

"Told Pete, you know, it's a shame, they're there all by themselves, we're here by ourselves. I said, Pete, go ask them. We're neighbors, after all. No need to be strangers. People are people."

My father proffered the bottle of whiskey he'd brought. "Sorry, I couldn't find the wrapping paper. It's, ah . . . Well, that's all we have."

"I'm a Wild Turkey man myself, but I like Dickel, too," said Mr. Coot, taking the bottle and looking at it. "Mix that with a little Coke, you got yourself a nice drink. Take that to the kitchen, will you, Pete?" As Peter carried away the bottle, Mr. Coot called after him, "And get the sodas and stuff out, too. See what all our guests want."

Mr. Coot moved a TV tray out of the way and snatched up a half-eaten bag of potato chips from the sofa, moving with a breathy effort. "We meant to clean up here but didn't get around to it. You know how that is."

The Coots' house was almost identical to ours except that everything was reversed left to right, like in a mirror. There was a kitchen, a small dining room, a living room with a TV against the wall; one bedroom downstairs, two attic bedrooms upstairs—all the same. Also like at our house, the Coots had a Christmas tree in the corner of the front room. Theirs, however, was artificial.

"Let me show you," Mr. Coot said, and pulled off one of the wire-and-plastic branches and handed it to my father. "We used to have a real tree but you know what those are like. You've got to water them, clean up after them, the needles falling off. Fire hazard. This one, you finish, you pack it up, throw it in the garage. No fuss, no muss. It's clean, that's why I like it."

He began to look around. "We've got the, ah, the scent." He hollered to Peter, "Where's that spray? The tree spray?" Peter shouted something back from the kitchen. "Here it is," Mr. Coot said, finding the

can on top of the TV. He read the label aloud for us: " 'Real pine scent.' "
He shook the can vigorously and sprayed the tree. "Smell that? It's just
the same. Better, maybe. It lasts ten, twelve hours. You spray it on one
time every day, and that's all." He set the can back on the TV.

My father had turned to look at a narrow table against the side wall.
On top was a kind of shrine to Peter's older brother, who'd been killed
in Vietnam. There were framed pictures, a set of medals, a folded
American flag.

"Oh, yeah. That was Tommy. You remember him, don't you?" Mr.
Coot said to my father, coming near. "I don't guess you've been here
since then."

I paused with them in front of the table. The centerpiece was a
framed portrait of Tommy in a dark blue uniform and a white hat,
standing beside a flag. In front of the picture sat a bowl of dusty red,
white, and blue plastic flowers. On either side were two candles in
silver holders. On the wall behind it was a framed poem written in old-
fashioned script on antique-looking paper; it began, *"Here lies a man
once known . . ."*

"I remember he used to ride his bike . . . ," my father started to say.

"Just four years ago," Mr. Coot said, suddenly reverent. "He would've
been twenty-four by now."

We stared silently at Tommy's things for a minute. His death seemed
to hang over this side of the room like a heavy cloud, the source of the
sad, oppressive air that filled the house. Mr. Coot wheezed softly beside me.

"They say you get over it? That's a goddamn lie. You never get over
it." Mr. Coot sniffed wetly and then let out a string of obscene curses
against the government.

Peter came in carrying a large tray of beer and soft drinks, and we all
backed away from the shrine, quieter and sadder now. "Set it there,"
Mr. Coot said, and Peter put the tray on the coffee table in front of the
couch. He waved at us. "Sit, sit."

Mr. Coot sat painfully in a large blue recliner, lowering first his right
hip to the cushions and then allowing the rest of his body to drop. He
coughed and gasped. It was the pleurisy, he said. The doctors told him

he had to have his fluids drained, but he'd be damned if he was going to let anyone stick a spigot in him, no thank you.

My father and I sat on the couch, which was covered by a green bedsheet that kept slipping down. "Just tuck it back up there," Mr. Coot said. We grabbed handfuls of potato chips while Mr. Coot leaned forward to try to manage the drinks. "Help us out here, Pete." I took a Shasta cola, and my father and Mr. Coot started with cans of Budweiser.

"Hell no, it's not too early," he said. "This is a public holiday. One of seven days a year the station's closed. Time I get to celebrate." He proposed a toast: "The lonely hearts club. Four lonely men, all alone on Christmas. Making the best of it."

He lifted up his hip, pulled the remote control out from under him, and turned on the TV. They had a larger, newer TV than we did, and Mr. Coot described its features to my father while he switched through the channels. He found a program—"*A Christmas Carol,*" he announced—and left the TV tuned to that. Then he abruptly began talking about the challenges of living alone without a woman.

"You've got to get you a routine," he advised. The hardest thing for him, when Patty left, was coping with the responsibility of taking care of the house. "Me and Pete, we divide up the chores. One day he'll do the cleaning, the next day I'll do. That right, Pete?"

"I remember when I first moved to Terrebonne," my father said. Holding his beer can on one knee, he started to tell about how he used to live alone in an apartment downtown during his bachelor days, and how when Lydia came over she was appalled—absolutely appalled—by the condition of that place. . . .

He trailed off, as though forgetting the point of the story.

Mr. Coot nodded. "The first days are the worst. You'll get used to it. . . . How about cooking? Do you cook?"

He talked about the best places for takeout in Terrebonne. Ralph's Restaurant had a good Monday night buffet, he said. All you can eat. You go in there, fill up one of those cardboard boxes—lima beans, baked ham, macaroni and cheese, vanilla pudding, everything. ("Sounds good," my father said, nodding.) He talked about spaghetti sauce. Ragú.

That was something they had discovered as of late. ("Chef Boyardee?" my father asked. "That's another one," Mr. Coot said.) He said how, himself, he was happy with hamburger. Him and Pete could eat hamburger eight days a week. Little ground chuck. What you did was—here was a tip—you mixed in instant onion soup powder with the ground meat. No, really. You put that in there, mix it in real good, you got a delicious and satisfying meal. . . .

I looked out the front window to the street, where neighborhood kids were riding their bikes back and forth in the slanting afternoon light, and I wished that I was outside with them.

"That's the Ghost of Christmas Past."

"What?" my father said.

Mr. Coot pointed at the TV with the remote. "The first ghost. The Ghost of Christmas Past."

"Oh, right."

We all turned and stared at the TV for a moment. A cartoon Scrooge was cringing on his knees while a flaming blue ghost rattled his chains and pointed a finger at him. *"Mercy! Dreadful apparition, why do you trouble me!"* cried Scrooge.

"Another thing is, Green Stamps," Mr. Coot said, going on. "S&H Green Stamps. People laugh at that, but I tell you, you can get a lot of practical things with those. Toast ovens. Coffeemaker. Our station gives them away, and sometimes people don't even want them. I take them myself—I can do that legally—and save them. . . ."

Peter asked if I wanted to see his new gun. I got up to leave with him, relieved to go.

"You boys run along, have fun," Mr. Coot said, waving a hand. "Us tired old bachelors'll be down here discussing things of an important nature."

Climbing the stairs to Peter's room, I gradually allowed myself to breathe again through my nose. On the couch, my father stared dully at the TV and took another swallow of his beer, as though he'd already succumbed to the sad, suffocating air of the place and could barely move his body.

CHAPTER FORTY-ONE

"CHECK it out," Peter said, lifting his new rifle down from the rack.

Except for a long, high window in place of a dormer window, the layout of Peter's room was exactly like mine. Same size, same low slanted ceiling, even the same furniture—bed, bookcase, desk, chair. His room, though, was dirtier and more cluttered than mine. Clothes and junk covered the brown carpet; cookie and cereal boxes and soda cans lay everywhere. On the nightstand beside his bed sat a bag of cough drops, a jar of Vaseline, and a roll of toilet paper. In an aquarium on his desk, a gerbil ran round and around on a squeaky metal wheel.

"Browning semiautomatic," he said, bringing the gun to the middle of the room. "Sweet piece, huh?"

He turned it back and forth under the light. It had a polished wooden stock and a blue-black metal barrel. He pointed out its features for me: the flip-up sight, the loading slot, the safety button, the firing chamber.

"Is it loaded?"

"Nah." He reached into a desk drawer, pulled out a box of bullets, and dropped them on his bed. "Twenty-two longs. That's fifty rounds there." I asked if they were dangerous. "Hell, yeah. Those can kill a man." But really, a twenty-two was best for small game, he said. Rabbit, foxes, squirrel. You'd have a hard time bringing down a deer with a twenty-two.

He showed me how to sight with it, and we took turns standing on his bed and aiming at distant objects through the window. He said his daddy was going to take him hunting with it as soon as he got the time. They'd go out to Lake Boeuf, maybe. He explained the hunting seasons: deer was fall to winter, duck was winter, turkey was spring, and squirrel and rabbit were basically anytime—nobody really cared about squirrel and rabbit.

"Have you shot it yet?"

"Man, I've been shooting all day. You haven't heard me?" He'd been doing target practice down by the water, he said. "We'll take it out again before it gets dark."

He took the gun back from me, protectively. He sat down on the bed and had me time how long it took him to break the gun apart and put it back together.

"How fast?" he asked when he'd finished.

"Twenty-one seconds. But that's just three parts. That's nothing."

"I can do it faster," he said.

He tried it a couple more times and then got a rag and oil and began polishing his gun. As he did, he talked about the next gun he wanted—if not a Winchester thirty-thirty, then a shotgun. In fact, a shotgun might even be a better choice because it would make a nice companion piece for his twenty-two. He could buy it himself, he said. His daddy was going to let him start working part-time at the gas station. He figured twenty-five dollars a week, one month, that's a hundred dollars, six months, that's six hundred dollars . . .

I watched him as he talked and rubbed his gun. He'd been letting his hair grow out so that now it hung limply over his ears almost to his shoulders. Since Thanksgiving he'd been trying to grow a mustache, too, but the brown fuzz above his lip only made him look rattier. He had a cold, and whenever he sniffed the brown fuzz wiggled up and down. As he spoke he looked not at me but at his gun, which he stroked lovingly in his lap. Behind him on his desk I saw something that looked like a dead animal, and then I realized it was the rabbit pelt that Peter was trying to make a hat from. The gerbil ran like a maniac round and around on its squeaking wheel.

I looked out the window and wondered what Gabriella was doing right now. How could anyone stand to live or speak or move in a world like this, knowing that a girl like her existed? I pictured her skiing down a white mountain slope, a furry hood encircling her face, cutting back and forth in the snow. The air would be clean and cold, and she would be laughing, smiling. I remembered our kiss, and the warm, dark, mysterious hollow of her mouth. . . .

"My BB gun and now my twenty-two," Peter said, replacing his new gun in the rack below his old one. He peered out the window. "What're you looking at?"

"Nothing."

"Look what I got," he said, and pulled two *Playboy* magazines out from under his mattress. "I swiped them from my dad. You can see this one. I'll look at this one." He tossed one to me and sat down in his desk chair with the other.

I tried to enjoy the magazine, but I couldn't, not with Peter there. "Oh, man, look at her. She is hot. *Mm-mm*," he said as he turned the pages and stared intently at the pictures. He talked about the various attributes and faults of each girl, and what he would do with each one if she was his girlfriend. After a minute he fell silent. His mouth dropped open, and he began breathing and squirming in his chair so that it made me uncomfortable to be near him.

I closed my magazine. He looked up. "Are you finished? You want to trade?"

"Maybe we should go back downstairs."

"Wait a minute, you have to see my black light," he said. "This is cool. You've got to see this."

He pulled a tube-shaped black light from underneath his bed. He had me plug the cord into an outlet, and he pulled the shade down over the window and turned off the overhead light.

We shined the black light on our teeth and our clothes, and waved our hands under it, seeing how our skin and fingernails looked like X-ray photos. On the wall opposite his bed was a fluorescent poster of a laughing red devil's head with horns and yellow teeth. Peter held the light below the poster, and then he held the light under his own face and laughed maniacally. "Ha ha ha ha! Ha ha ha ha!"

"Look at this one," he said. He knelt on his bed and shone the light on another poster tacked to the wall above his bed. It was the image of a woman's naked body wrapped up in red, orange, and yellow flames. He moved the light back and forth.

"Look. It looks like it's moving," he said quietly.

"No, it doesn't."

"Wait—you have to lie down on the bed." He showed me how I should lie down and look up. "Put your head here, your feet there, just like normal. That's the best position."

I lay down on the bed, and in his eagerness to show me, he lay down next to me. He slowly waved the black light back and forth at the poster on the wall above us. He began to speak in a low, excited whisper.

"See? It's like it's moving. Look at that. You can see everything. She's a naked lady. She's completely naked."

Peter waved the black light, and the image seemed to rise up off the poster. Shadows shifted eerily around the dark room. The light cord slapped with a ticking noise against the side of the bed. Beside me, Peter began to breathe damply. He pressed his leg against mine as he kept up his low whisper.

"You can imagine it's Gabriella. That's her, that's her naked body. She's in the room with you. She's dancing. Look at her dance. She's right there. You can almost touch her. Her hair, look at her hair. Her body, look at her body. Her legs, her breasts. Here she comes. Come on. Come on, baby. Ooh, yeah. Gabriella. Gabriella, Gabriella . . ."

"Cut it out, man."

"What?"

"Stop it! Don't do that."

I scrambled up off the end of the bed and turned on the overhead light. "What're you doing, man?"

Peter looked up at me from the bed, his dark eyes piteous and imploring. "Nothing."

I was suddenly furious at him, for his damp breathing, and his creepy *mm-mm*, and for dragging Gabriella into his dirty room. She didn't belong here; even saying her name aloud here was wrong. She was too good for this. She was too good for any of us.

"I'm leaving. I'm going downstairs."

"Wait!" he cried.

"No, that's it, that's enough. I'm going," I said, and opened the door.

"I'll get my gun," Peter said, and hurried to follow me.

CHAPTER FORTY-TWO

"IT'S those damn cats," Mr. Coot said, kicking aside the cats that were jumping up onto the back porch. "Pete keeps feeding them."

"No, I don't."

The cats meowed and swarmed as we stepped through the stacks of newspapers and broken grill pieces and other junk on the porch and followed Mr. Coot down into their backyard. He carried the opened bottle of Dickel; both he and my father held plastic cups full of whiskey. They'd been drinking quite a lot, apparently. They stumbled out to the middle of the yard. Mr. Coot asked about the comet.

"I've been watching for it. Where is it? I don't see nothing yet."

We all looked up. The sky was gray and violet. The water tower loomed pale and blue above the bare trees off to the right. My father, slurring his words, spoke confusingly about pre- and postperihelion apparitions, and moon phases, and visual magnitude relative to distance to the Sun.

"It's here. It's here, but we just can't see it."

"I saw it," Peter said.

"When?"

"Last week. Saturday or Sunday night, I forget which." It was the middle of the night, he'd gotten out of bed, looked out his window, and there it was. It was yellow and white with a long, skinny tail, Peter said.

"You were dreaming," I said.

"Could be, could be," mused my father.

"That was a cat you saw," said Mr. Coot.

It was a question of light and elevation, my father insisted. Light and elevation. In Hawaii they saw it. In Alaska they saw it. Problem here was that we had too much light and not enough elevation.

"It's gonna come around the Sun," he said. "Then you'll really get it. Then you won't be able to miss it. No, sir!"

Mr. Coot and Peter began walking back and forth, tacking paper targets to trees along the bayou. As they did, my father talked about his plans for a town-wide comet viewing. He'd been discussing it with the mayor. They were going to set up a viewing station at the courthouse, get the city to shut off the lights, get everyone to come out to see it. Like the Fourth of July only better . . .

"Put that one up there," Mr. Coot said to Peter. "Little farther on."

"Light up the night like a new moon," my father said, waving his arm at the sky.

Mr. Coot stopped and rested his weight on one hip. "Have you ever considered the existence of a higher power in your life? A power greater than yourself?"

My father looked at him blankly.

Mr. Coot began talking about his men's club, the King Solomon Lodge. My father should come for a meeting sometime, he said. They always welcomed any interested party, any man who valued brotherly love, relief, and truth in his life. He showed my father his ring. My father bent in to look at it.

"What? What?"

"Freemasonry is what I'm talking about. Look at that. The square and compass."

"Hm."

"Lots of famous people throughout history. Presidents, astronauts, scientists . . ." He poured more Dickel into their cups. "They help me find the light in my life. Ever since Patty and Tommy are gone, they've been a constant source of love and inspiration to me. Love and enlightenment."

"Ready," said Peter.

"You think about it, let me know when you're ready," Mr. Coot said confidentially to my father. He gestured. "Y'all back up now. Stand back."

Peter stepped forward with his rifle. He wore a too-large green army coat with the name Coot on the breast. He made a show of adjusting the parts of the gun, loading the bullets, and checking the chamber. "Clear the line," he said, and shook the sleeves of the coat away from his hands and raised the gun to his cheek.

There was a light pop; my father and I jerked. Peter fired several more times at a target on a tree. A neighborhood dog began to bark.

"Check it out," he said, and he and I went to inspect the target. He tried to pry a bullet out of the bark of the tree behind the target with his fingernail but he couldn't.

As Peter was getting me set up for a turn with the rifle, the Martellos' house blazed to life across the bayou, the automatic timers turning on the Christmas decorations. Our fathers began talking about them.

"Look at that. No worries there. Money to burn."

"Hell, what do they care?" Mr. Coot said. "They're dancing and singing all the way to the bank. Oil embargo's best thing ever happened to them."

Mr. Coot spoke about OPEC, and Henry Kissinger, and the worldwide Jewish conspiracy to raise the price of oil to twenty dollars a barrel. He talked about the Louisiana mafia, and how they had their fingers in the pockets of every station owner in the state. They set the price; there wasn't nothing he could do about it. And now President Nixon calling for gas rationing, wants him to voluntarily—*voluntarily*—close for business on Saturday and Sundays.

"The world is unfair," my father said, suddenly moody.

"People like you and me—" Mr. Coot said, and poured more whiskey for them. "Gotta stick together."

I fired, and the rifle knocked against my cheek, surprising me.

"You missed completely," Peter said. "Try again."

The sky had lowered to orange at the horizon, bringing out shadows around the trees, so that it was hard to see things clearly. I kept shooting until I hit a target, then I handed the gun to Peter to reload.

"Give it a whack, Professor," Mr. Coot said.

My father stumbled forward to take the gun, but then, remembering, turned and carefully handed his plastic cup of whiskey to Mr. Coot before turning back and taking the rifle from Peter.

"Rest it there against your shoulder," Peter said, helping him.

"I don't have a permit. Do I need a permit?"

"Hell, no," said Mr. Coot. "It's a free country."

"Where is it? What am I looking at? I can't see anything."

Peter positioned him facing the target. "Hold still. Squeeze it easy."

The gun went off. "Did I get anything?"

"You went wide."

"About a mile wide. You were in the next parish. You have to hold steady." Mr. Coot gestured with one of the cups. "Pete, help him."

Peter gave him more instruction and helped him line up the sights. My father concentrated. His lips spread back from his teeth and his face took on a wild sneer as he fired off several more rounds. "Yeah!" he shouted, like he was punching somebody with each shot he fired. "Yeah!"

Mr. Coot started telling dago jokes: Why did birds fly upside down over Italy? Because there was nothing worth shitting on. How many dagos did it take to grease a car? Just one if you hit him right. How could you fit twenty-five dagos in a Trans Am? Make one the boss and the rest would crawl up his ass. . . .

My father laughed oddly, a kind of hiccupping sound. His shoulders shuddered; he fired wildly and missed the target again.

Then Mr. Coot began a complicated dirty joke about a prostitute, a chicken, and a dago. He lost the thread of it, slurred over the middle part, and jumped to the end: "And then Luigi said, 'My wife-a no whore!'"

"Damn him. God damn him," my father cried angrily, and wheeled around with the rifle and pointed it at the Martellos' house. "The next time I see that greasy dago I'm gonna shoot his head off!"

Mr. Coot caught my father from behind. "Whoa! That's a loaded weapon you got there. Pete, take the gun."

"Okay, Mr. Broussard. Take it easy."

Peter got the gun, and in their fumbling, my father fell to the ground.

"Oh . . . I'm sorry," he muttered. "Screw me. Goddamn screw me."

"That's what I feel like sometimes," Mr. Coot said.

My father sat up in the dirt, his legs splayed out in front of him, his chin hanging down on his chest. He rubbed his oily hair. He began talking about my mother, his words coming out sloppy.

"I knew she was flirting with him, I knew that. But she does that with everybody, doesn't she? I never expected . . . I mean, how? That's what I want to know. How'd they do it? Just like that, right under my nose. I didn't even see it. I didn't see a goddamn thing!" He hit the dirt with his hand.

Mr. Coot patted his shoulder. "Okay, okay. Take it easy now."

"No. No! I need to know. How'd they do it? Where? When?" he cried. "Were they at his house? His condo? A hotel? Was she drunk? Is that it? Did he lock the door and take off her coat? Was she wearing perfume?"

"Hush. You stop that. You're just gonna make yourself crazy."

"No! I need to know! How long has this been going on? Were there others before Frank? She's at home all day. What the hell do I know what she does? Dale Landry. Coach DuPleiss. Who knows? I don't. I don't, because I'm a goddamn worm. I'm a goddamn blind little worm and I can't see a goddamn thing. I probably deserve it. Oh, who cares? To hell with it. I might as well be dead. You might as well shoot me now, get it over with. See if I care. Where's that gun?"

He swung around clumsily and bumped Peter's rifle with the back of his hand. Peter, startled, stepped away, but my father lunged and grabbed the barrel of the gun with both his hands and yanked it toward himself. For a moment, he and Peter tugged back and forth on the gun, both of them shouting, my father trying to press the mouth of the barrel against his forehead, shouting, "Here! Here! Shoot me here!"

Mr. Coot knocked the barrel of the gun up in the air with his arm. It went off with a bang, and my father fell over sideways onto the dirt, collapsing into his raincoat.

"Oh . . . oh . . . oh," he whimpered.

"Holy shit," said Mr. Coot.

"I thought . . . the safety . . . ," stammered Peter.

In the confusion I believed my father had been shot, and I dropped down onto my knees behind him. I tried to get him to sit up. "No, no," he moaned, clutching his stomach. His glasses had fallen off, and I looked around on the ground until I found them. The left earpiece had snapped off, and I found it, too.

"Let's get you inside," Mr. Coot said. "You're messed up. You need something to eat. We'll get you something good to eat. Pete, help him up."

"No, no, leave me," my father moaned, but Peter and I tugged at him until we got him to his feet. I carried his broken glasses, and we helped him across the yard and up the porch steps.

Inside, Mr. Coot went straight to the kitchen to make hamburgers. He began knocking around in there; he got out the ground beef, a bowl, and the instant onion soup mix.

But my father kept walking unsteadily through the house. He bumped into the couch and stumbled across the living room. I caught his arm as he fell against the TV. *A Christmas Carol* was still on, and Scrooge stood shivering in a graveyard as the Ghost of Christmas Future pointed a bony finger at a tombstone. *"No, Spirit! Oh no, no!"*

A thought flashed through my mind then that this—a stumbling father, a smelly house, rooms full of sorrow and neglect—this was my future. In a year from now, maybe less, my father and I would be living exactly like Peter and his father. It seemed unavoidable; this was our fate, the only possible ending to a lifetime's worth of crippled hopes and bad fortune. An artificial tree, a dirty sofa, dusty plastic flowers: this was all we had to look forward to for the rest of our lives.

"They're leaving," Peter called to his father in the kitchen. "They're leaving!"

Mr. Coot waddled out of the kitchen, a mess of red ground beef in his hands. "Where're you going? I'm making dinner for us."

But my father was already out the door. "I think we're leaving now," I said, and hurried out to help him before he fell down the steps.

Mr. Coot came to the door. "Y'all don't want to stay? Come on back. It's Christmas. I got the chuck." He held up the meat in one hand. Peter came up behind him to look out.

"Some other time. Thank you, good night," I said.

"It's Christmas!" Mr. Coot hollered sadly.

I tried to take my father's arm but he shrugged off my hand. At the end of the Coots' driveway he stopped, looked up at the sky, and shook his fist at the stars. Then he lurched left, aiming himself out of the neighborhood.

He walked quickly, leaning forward over his feet and letting momentum carry his body so that with every step he seemed to be just catching himself before he pitched over flat on his face. He stumbled like this to the end of the block, his raincoat flapping behind him, and turned right on Franklin Street toward town. Off the side of the road stood the water tower, the red warning light on top blinking on and off. I stopped at the edge of the pavement as he swerved in across the grass to the tower.

He stopped and rested a hand against the nearest support, catching his breath. The thing loomed above him, four round legs reaching up to the dark belly of the tank. On the leg he leaned against, a metal ladder ended a few feet above his head. He clumsily tried to hop up and grab the bottom rung a couple of times.

"Where do you think you're going?" I called. "You can't go up there."

He muttered something about light and elevation, if only he had the proper light and elevation.

"There's nothing up there!" I said.

I looked around, hoping there might be someone nearby to help, but there wasn't. It was just me with my father staggering around under the water tower. He seemed to be disintegrating, crumbling to pieces before my eyes, and I couldn't do anything about it.

CHAPTER FORTY-THREE

THE reception was poor. Through the fuzzy blue and white snow, I could make out the figures of two men floating around inside a cabin, moving as though in slow motion. Radioed voices sputtered on and off as the astronauts spoke back and forth with Mission Control. An off-screen announcer described what was happening:

"*You can see them checking their equipment. . . . Gibson and Carr, suiting up as they prepare to leave* Skylab *for another space walk . . . their second of this mission . . .*"

The program shifted to the inside of a bright blue and yellow TV studio, where a NASA scientist in a white shirt and black tie held up a toy-sized model of *Skylab*. Pointing to various parts of it with a pencil, he explained how the astronauts would attempt to attach a new camera to a telescope mount on the outside of the spacecraft during their space walk.

I sat on the couch, hugging a blanket around me. Outside the day was chilly and damp; inside, chilly and damp. In the three days since our sad Christmas with the Coots, my father had gone from bad to worse. He barely stirred from his room now. When he did come out, he spent most of the day sitting on the couch, distractedly watching TV, not even bothering to open a journal or magazine. I could hear him through his bedroom door now, snoring through his nose.

So this really was it, I thought. Two sad, lonely men shuffling around in blankets in an underheated house. My sister could say what she wanted about our situation being perfectly typical for families of our age and generation, but clearly, this should never have happened to us. Something had gone very wrong in the universal scheme of things. I still half expected to see my father come bounding out of his bedroom, dressed and ready for the day, and announce that there had just been a slight mix-up, an unexpected kerfuffle in the cosmic order, but all that was straightened out now and we could go back to our regular, uneventful lives.

On the TV, two white shapes floated and bumped around inside a tiny cabin, like a couple of divers trapped inside a sinking ship.

I thought about what Megan had told me regarding our mother and Frank Martello. If what she reported was true, and if there really was the possibility of a future relationship between our mother and Frank, then what did that mean for us, their children? Maybe, I thought, there could be some good news here, too. I tried to envision different configurations of our families, the Broussards and the Martellos. If my mother married Frank, she might move into the house with him across the bayou. Maybe I would move in with them. Gabriella and I would be stepbrother and stepsister then. We would sit together at breakfast in the morning. We would ride together to school; maybe my mother— Mrs. Martello now—would drive us in Barbara's own sky-blue Town Car. After school, we'd sit together for dinner, and then Gabriella and I would watch TV while doing our homework. At bedtime, Gabriella would go up to her room, and I to mine next door. . . .

That scenario was so fantastic, so appealing, that I was afraid to even think about it for very long, for fear that by wishing too earnestly for it, I might also somehow wish away the likelihood of it happening. Even entertaining the possibility of it for more than a few minutes made my stomach twist in worry and anticipation.

I remembered then that I hadn't eaten any breakfast yet. I was just getting up to fix something for myself when I heard a mention of the comet on TV.

" . . . *track and gather information on Comet Kohoutek. Although we haven't been able to see it much here from Earth, the astronauts are in line to get a clear view of the comet as it comes around the top of the Sun. . . .*"

On the TV, murky white shapes drifted slowly past a confusing backdrop of panels and equipment. There was a head, an arm, a leg.

"*Gibson and Carr. There you see them exiting the air hatch now. . . .*"

I ran to my father's room and knocked on his door. When there was no answer, I went in. He was sprawled crookedly across the bed, half covered by the sheets. I shook his shoulder.

"It's the comet. They're talking about the comet."

"Huh?"

"Get up. I think they're going to look for it." I shook him again. "Come on. Hurry up."

He pulled himself up. I found his broken glasses on the nightstand and handed them to him. He staggered into the living room and stopped in front of the TV, adjusting his pajamas around himself.

An astronaut was clinging to the outside of the spacecraft, his feet floating free as he crawled with his hands along industrial-looking pipes and rails. Far below, the edge of the Earth was just emerging from shadow.

"They're going to attach a camera to the telescope mount," I explained.

My father, his hands shaking a little, quickly tried to adjust the controls on the old Zenith to bring in the picture better. He fiddled with the antenna, a complicated add-on device with a nest of metal hoops, and then we both backed up and sat on the couch to watch.

Voices crackled. Nothing much seemed to be happening. But then through the static, their voices sounding tinny and distant, we heard the astronauts begin to talk to Mission Control about Kohoutek.

"*Have you got visual yet? You should be able to see it . . . just above the horizon. . . .*"

Beep.

"Hey, look! It's right out there."

Beep.

"Do you see it?"

Beep.

"Oh, man. Oh, man, I tell you, it's one of the most beautiful cre-ations . . . beautiful creations I've ever seen. It's so graceful. I'll try to aim the camera around. . . ."

"There it is. There it is," my father whispered. His hands, resting on his knees, began to tremble.

"Can you see it now?"

Beep.

"Roger. We see it sharp and clear."

Beep.

"It's yellow and orange, just like a flame. Man, will you look at that? It's just . . . it's just spectacular. Unbelievable."

I looked at the side of my father's face and was surprised to see that he was crying. I had never seen my father cry before. Thick tears ran down alongside his nose. He snatched off his glasses and rubbed his face roughly with one hand.

I swallowed and stared down at the stain on the rug. He sniffed. We didn't speak for a long moment. When I looked back up at the TV again, an astronaut was drifting away into space. A white tube trailed after him, and his body was bent in a peculiar manner, as though he were tumbling. Far below him was the curved rim of the Earth, blue oceans and white clouds. Behind him, against the black backdrop of space, just visible above his right shoulder, was the bright yellow smear of the comet.

"Beautiful. So beautiful!" my father croaked.

He pressed both his hands over his face and began to rock slowly back and forth on the couch. An odd noise escaped him.

"Dad?" I said.

"Fine . . . fine," he said, and made another strangled noise.

The astronaut continued to move in slow motion, floating peace-fully above the Earth, looking as though he might happily fall forever.

CHAPTER FORTY-FOUR

KOHOUTEK hadn't failed us after all. It had returned, just as my
father had promised, rising spectacularly over the rim of the Sun.

With that postperihelion sighting from *Skylab*, his spirits were re-
vived. He threw off his bathrobe, shaved, and dressed, and that same
afternoon he sat down at the dining room table and went back to work.
His recovery was so sudden, so unexpected, in fact, that I didn't entirely trust it to be genuine.

He rechecked his almanacs; he looked again at the bulletins from
NASA, the National Weather Service, the AAS. He might've been off
by a week or two in his predictions for a Christmastime apparition, he
explained, but he'd just been overeager, that was all. Historically speaking, it was a fact that most comets became brighter after they circled
the Sun. There was no reason to believe that Kohoutek wouldn't behave the same. Over the next week, he told me, it should continue to
draw energy from the Sun, so that by the sixth of January, the night he
had set for our town-wide viewing, its coma would be swollen to maximum size, its tail fully extended. For the rest of the month we'd con-

tinue to see it blazing above the southwestern horizon, hanging like a giant flaming sword in the sky.

Never mind all the naysayers in the media; never mind that my father had been promising virtually the same thing for the last six months. Hadn't we seen it with our own eyes right there on TV, as magnificent as the astronomers had said it'd be? There was no longer any doubt in his mind, he said, none at all. Kohoutek was still coming, we could be sure of that. And we should be ready for him when he arrived—to greet him, as my father said, with all the pomp and ceremony due to a visitor of this importance.

The breakup of his marriage, the flight of his wife and daughter, our disastrous Christmas with the Coots: all that was shoved behind him. It might never have happened. My father lived only for the comet now, and in the days leading up to the new year, he turned his attention back to it with a feverish, single-minded intensity—as though believing that the very strength of his devotion might help fan the flames of the comet brighter. If he only loved the comet enough, it couldn't help but love him back.

For the night of the viewing, he had Kohoutek in Capricorn, becoming visible half an hour after sunset. The Moon wouldn't be up yet, and the tail would be in a horizontal position relative to the Earth, allowing for maximum visibility.

But there were so many local atmospheric variables, and these were what concerned him: cloud cover, temperature, humidity, wind speed, air pollution, skyglow—all these could affect viewing. So many contingencies, so much to consider, so much to try to understand. He filled pages and pages with charts and notes peppered with arcane-looking symbols and equations:

Given resonance light $A2\Sigma$ – $X2\,\Pi$ for the radical H, at 0.6 AU, production rate of QOH = 4 xsx 1028 moleculesec –1sr –1 . . .

Sometimes he mumbled aloud to himself: "Come on. We got you. We got you now. Where do you think you're going? Huh?"

He became especially excited when, a few days after their space walk, the *Skylab* astronauts spotted an antitail on the comet, a long yellow spike extending from the head of the coma, like the golden horn of a unicorn.

"You see?" my father said. "You don't get those often with comets, no sir. Kohoutek's getting dressed up. He's going to put on a real show for us."

Afternoons, he stuffed his papers in his briefcase and rode his bike downtown to organize the viewing. The mayor had given his okay, and announcements had appeared in the paper, but logistical details still had to be coordinated between the different municipal services—the fire department, the police, the public utilities, the chamber of commerce. My father was overseeing everything. They were going to block off the streets around the square. Everybody would come out, they'd bring their kids and grandkids . . . balloons, ice cream . . . couples standing arm in arm . . . children with their faces lifted to the sky. And then, at precisely six o'clock, the air-raid siren would sound, the streetlights would be extinguished. The town would go dark, and—*Ahhh!*

Something we would remember for the rest of our lives. Something we could tell our children and grandchildren about. *We were there,* we could say. *We were there when Kohoutek came.*

The week before the event, he printed up fliers and began distributing them to shops and businesses. He biked all over town, out to the black grocery stores on the north side, to the fishing and tackle shops along the canals to the south. Late in the day, when people were getting off work, he stood at the edge of the square and handed out sheets to passersby. I sat on my bike around the corner from the drugstore and watched him. In his black raincoat and taped-together glasses, he looked like one of those comet crazies we'd seen on TV. But people stopped and took his fliers; they nodded and asked questions. Almost everyone knew my father from the school or from his column and his talks around town, and they didn't seem to find it especially odd that he should be standing on the street corner handing out fliers. If anything, many seemed eager to hear more about the comet; he was our local astronomy expert, after all, and if he said it was still coming, then it must be coming.

*And we can see it when? This Sunday? The whole town? Sure. Will
do. Sounds interesting. Thanks.*

In the evenings, I set the table for takeout dinners from Ralph's Restaurant. We had fried chicken and coleslaw, baked ham and lima beans.
Between bites of food, he updated me on the progress of the comet and
told me what all he'd accomplished that day. "I think we'll have a good
crowd for it. Folks are getting excited," he said. Community cooperation was vital if we hoped to achieve a full blackout, and so far things
looked promising. He'd been in touch with the various civic organiza-
tions, the Cub Scouts, the Lions Club, the Rotary Club, to be sure they
knew about the night of the comet. He'd sent announcements to the
TV and radio stations, too. "I think I'll bike out to the churches next
and make sure they have some fliers. They can talk it up with their
congregations, encourage people to come."

Growing expansive, he said that this kind of positive public response
just went to show how much one man could accomplish with enough
well-focused effort. He talked about the possibility of writing up a report about his experience and presenting it at the next American Astronomical Society conference. Lots of members would probably be
interested in hearing how he'd been able to generate enthusiasm for
astronomy in Terrebonne: his cross-curricular projects, his newspaper
articles, his visits to clubs and schools. Town-wide viewing events.
Heck, if he could do it, anybody could. "Shoot for the Stars: Stimulat-
ing Support for the Sciences at the Local Level"—something like that.
He'd have to think about it some more; that could be his next project,
as soon as he finished with Kohoutek.

And then—but this was still down the line, just a notion he had—
he'd been thinking of speaking with Dr. Brewer about returning to
graduate school at LSU. There wasn't any reason that he couldn't start
up there again during the summers.

"I mean, sure, I'm forty years old and I've been out of college for a
while, but that's not necessarily a strike against me. I've kept up with
developments in the field, more or less, and now that I've made something of a name for myself, I don't see why they wouldn't admit me—

"Hey! Think about that." He stopped and looked up across the table
at me; his broken glasses wobbled on his nose. "Maybe by the time you

finish high school and start at LSU, I'll be teaching undergraduates by then. Wouldn't that be neat? Alan and Alan Junior, together at college. Running across the quad to our classes. You could take my Introduction to Astronomy course. . . ."

After dinner, after I'd cleared the table, he'd pull out his books and papers and go back to work. When I went up to bed he'd still be sitting there beneath the weak bulb of the overhead lamp, the darkness of the room hanging around his shoulders like a cloak. I'd wake in the middle of the night to hear him stirring downstairs. The back door would carefully open and close, and his footsteps would creak across the wooden porch and down to the yard. I didn't need to look out my window to see what he was doing; I knew what he was doing. In the morning when I came downstairs, he'd be as I left him the night before, sitting at the table, shirtsleeves rolled up, pen in hand, dried mud on his shoes. He might've never gone to bed at all. He'd look up and blink, as though surprised to see someone else in the house.

Maybe, I thought, his comet would still shine as brightly as he said it would. Maybe it would light up the sky day and night like a blazing fireball. Just because it hadn't happened yet didn't mean that it still couldn't. What did I know, after all? This was the first comet I'd ever seen, so I hardly knew what to expect.

And yet, something was obviously not altogether right. There was a desperation to his conviction, as though he feared that if he admitted any doubt at all, the whole castle of his belief would crumble to the ground, and as the night of the comet approached, I watched him with a growing apprehension.

Sometimes while scribbling at his papers, he'd put down his pen, pull off his glasses, and press his hands over his eyes. He'd hold this pose for a long minute, jamming his palms so tightly to his face that his arms would begin to tremble. He'd make a pained sound, like a dog's whimper, and then slide his hands away to reveal wet, bloodshot eyes. Then he'd blink, replace his glasses, take a deep breath, and resume his work.

Every time he did this, I wondered what he was seeing behind his covered-up eyes, what dark vision of the past or the future he was trying so hard to obliterate.

CHAPTER FORTY-FIVE

Groovy Science
by Alan Broussard

He's here at last. Our long nights of waiting are over. We can put aside our spyglass, step out into the street, and greet our guest with open arms. I refer of course to Comet Kohoutek.

By now readers of this column are well acquainted with our cosmic visitor from outer space. Discovered last spring by Dr. Kohoutek, tracked by astronomers of every nation as he approached the Earth, our friend will put in a stunning farewell appearance this week as he begins his return journey to . . .

Late Sunday afternoon I sat at the kitchen table with the newspaper. My father had already left with Mr. Coot to go set up for the comet viewing. I was to meet Peter soon, and together we would bike downtown to join our fathers in the square. Outside, the light was low and silvery, making mirrors of all the windows at the Martellos' house. They were due back home from their vacation today, but I hadn't seen any sign of them yet.

Like my father, I had high hopes for the evening. Three days ago I'd received a postcard from Gabriella, sent from Colorado. I'd already studied it exhaustively, but I looked over it again now while I waited for her family to return.

The front of the card was a color photograph of skiers coming down a mountainside; above them on the slope was a rustic lodge where more skiers were gathered. A chairlift cut across a backdrop of pines. Gabriella had playfully drawn a circle around one of the skiers, with an arrow and a label saying "Me!" She'd also drawn a tiny stick figure of a deer peeking out of the trees, with another arrow: "Deer!"

On the reverse was her message:

Junior!

Hey, it's me. Are you surprised? Snow is great. We skied skeid skiied? in Vail yesterday and saw a whole herd of deer on the mountain. How's your Christmas? See you soon!

Your friend,

Gabriella

xoxo

Here, finally, was the proof I'd been waiting for. She missed me; she'd been thinking of me during her vacation. Perhaps she'd even thought of me at the same time I was thinking of her, skiing down the slope in her hooded jacket. She'd seen the deer gathered against the trees, lifting their heads as she sailed past, and in that very moment she'd said to herself, *I'll bet Junior would like this.* Later in the lodge— perhaps the same lodge in the photograph—her cheeks stinging from the cold, she'd stopped off at the gift shop, looked through the cards, and chosen one especially for me.

But most important was her message on the back, and I examined it again to see if there was anything I'd missed. I loved the offhanded intimacy of her greeting, and the self-deprecating joke about her uncertain spelling skills, and then her expression of concern for my own holiday. "See you soon" with an exclamation mark was obviously another way of saying "I can't wait to see you again." But I puzzled long and hard over that word "friend." Was it meant to be ironic? Another joke? Or was it sincere, a reminder of how much our friendship meant to her? Either way, the subtext of her entire message was revealed in the last thing she wrote, down at the very edge of the card, an impulsive admission of her true feelings for me, and a private reference to our magical night together: *kiss-hug, kiss-hug.*

Or maybe not.

Maybe I was misreading everything. Maybe her words and scratchings were just the ordinary conventions that a teenage girl used when she jotted a quick postcard. Or maybe Gabriella herself was confused about her feelings for me, and thus the confusing messages that I read in her card.

I propped her card up against a drinking glass and reviewed again all the evidence of our love: the smiles and whispers we'd shared in the corridors at school, the pinch she'd given me that one night, our hand-holding in the planetarium, her appearances on her balcony, our kiss (our kiss!), and now her card from Colorado with its closing "xoxo." The facts seemed indisputable; it all added up. And yet, the closer I looked at it, the less clear it became. Despite all the evidence, I couldn't get rid of a nagging doubt that told me I was only wishing into existence something that wasn't there at all.

This, I saw, was where science failed you. All of my father's talk about the "objective observation" and "trusting the evidence of your senses" was of little use when it came to trying to understand other people. People, I was beginning to believe, didn't so easily conform to the rules of science. With people, it was all just guesswork. You might think you knew someone perfectly well, and that she knew you, but there was still that wall of flesh between you. And it wasn't as if you could pin someone down on a laboratory table and cut her open like a frog to find out what was going on inside her. You could never know what was going on inside another person, not really.

Follow your heart, my mother would say, and the rest would follow.

That was the best you could do. In the uncertain seas of human rela-
tionships, the only reliable compass was your heart. And the heart—
the heart never lied. Did it?

I checked her house again. Still no sign of them. Feeling inspired, I
found some typing paper and wrote a note for her; I had to redo it three
times before I was satisfied with it. I welcomed her home and said I
hoped she had a good holiday. I reminded her about the comet viewing
in the square and said I hoped I'd see her there. I would look for her
tonight, I wrote, adding that there was something important I needed
to tell her. I signed it "Your friend, Junior. xoxoxo." Then I tucked the
paper into an envelope, along with one of my father's fliers, and wrote
her name on the outside.

I stood and looked out the window to see how the weather was holding up. A scattering of low, well-formed clouds drifted under a blue-
gray sky. They moved slowly, like cardboard cutouts being thoughtfully
arranged here and there by an invisible hand. What were they? Stratus?
Cumulus? Cirrus? My father would've known; he knew how to read
clouds, could say exactly what they meant and what weather they portended. I tried to decipher them myself, looking for a sign that would
tell me how the evening would turn out. One cloud looked like a
mountain on fire. Another looked like a rabbit hiding behind a bush.
Still another, if I squinted in a certain way, looked like Gabriella lying
back on a pillow, her hair scattered extravagantly around her shoulders. . . .

I grabbed my coat, went out the back door, and was just pulling my
bike from the side of the shed when a movement across the bayou
caught my eye. I turned to see our Rambler roll up and stop at the curb
in front of the Martellos' house.

What was this? The light fell on the car windows so that I couldn't
make out who was driving. Sensing something odd about it being there,
though, I stepped behind the corner of the garage shed to watch. Our
car sat there for some time. When another car passed behind it on the
street, the driver quickly turned her head as if to hide her face, and
then I saw that it was my mother. She studied our house for a moment,
shifting to see it better through the trees. Then she turned forward
again, put both her hands on the steering wheel, and stared straight

ahead, like she was sitting at an intersection waiting for a light to change.

By then I had an idea of what she was doing at the Martellos' house, and seeing my mother waiting in the street like this for Frank to come home from his vacation—so hopeful, so vulnerable—made my heart go out to her.

Fifteen minutes later, my legs were tired, I was beginning to shiver from the cold, and she was still waiting there. Brown leaves tumbled across the Martellos' driveway. Nearby in the trees, two crows had begun arguing back and forth, their caws sounding sharp and angry in the winter air.

At last the Martellos appeared. They rolled up in their white Cadillac, coming from the direction of the Beau Rivage Estates sign. Their car turned into the driveway, crossing in front of our Rambler, and then stopped with two tires on the drive, two in the street. I could just make out Frank and Barbara in the front seat. They looked sideways through their windows at our car; they exchanged some words with each other, and then Frank resumed driving down to their garage. I hid myself more carefully behind the shed as the automatic door opened and he turned in.

A moment later, the Martellos all walked out of their garage. Gabriella wore sunglasses and carried a blue airline travel bag over one shoulder. Mr. and Mrs. Martello both wore alpine-style sweaters and dark pants. The whole family looked tanned and fit, the picture of health and prosperity. They stood in their driveway staring up at our car. Mr. Martello pointed for Gabriella to go inside. She hesitated. He repeated his order, and she turned and slumped into the garage, looking back over her shoulder.

Frank and Barbara argued briefly at the bottom of their drive, the wind blurring their words so that I couldn't hear what they were saying. Then my mother stepped out of the car, closed the door behind her, and began walking down the driveway. The Martellos stopped arguing and turned to watch her.

She wore an outfit I'd never seen on her before, an attractive navy-blue suit with a snug skirt and a matching jacket trimmed in black fur.

On her feet, black high-heeled shoes. Her hair was freshly styled, and she wore a white pearl necklace. She looked, I thought, not quite like herself, but rather the self she wished to be. As she walked down the concrete drive toward the Martellos, she carried herself with an erect, shaky determination.

Ooh love, I thought: *look at what it had done to her.*

I felt queasy with dread. I hated to see this, but at the same time I couldn't pry my eyes away. I leaned into the side of the shed, scratching at flakes of old paint with my fingernail while I watched the scene play out across the water like it was a movie with the sound turned off. Only this movie, I feared, wasn't one of those old-style Hollywood romances that my mother loved so much, but a bleaker, more modern movie, one featuring imperfect people making bad decisions that led to endings that weren't guaranteed to be happy.

Frank left his wife and walked up to meet my mother halfway down the drive. Her face, I could see as she came nearer, was made up, her lips bright red. Frank acted puzzled to see her; he shook his head and opened out his hands. She nodded and spoke seriously to him for a minute. Frank pointed to his house, where Barbara stood watching from the bottom of the drive. Gabriella was watching, too; I saw her standing just inside the garage door, peeking out.

My mother kept talking. At one point she looked like she might begin crying. She put her hand on Frank's shoulder and touched her fingers to the back of his neck. He grabbed her hand and moved it away. Then he took my mother by the elbow and steered her up the drive, away from his house.

That was it. That was all it took—that one public gesture of Frank's, him removing my mother's hand from his shoulder and leading her away from his house—to show everyone exactly where she stood. He put her in the Rambler and closed the door, returning her, as it were, to her place. He stepped back . . . but then my mother stubbornly opened the door and got out again. He went to put her back in the car, but as he grabbed her, her knees went sideways and she crumpled like a broken doll onto the sidewalk.

My poor, poor mother. I wanted to do something to help her, but what could I have done? Shouted to Frank to leave her alone? Swum across the bayou and carried her home? Frank tried to pick her up by the arm, but she yanked it away from him and refused to move. He started to walk away, shouting something at her. She dropped her head pathetically over her arms. Then Frank came back and tried again. He hauled her up from the sidewalk and managed to get her seated in the car. He closed the door and pointed for her to go, like you would point for a stray dog to get out of your yard.

He waited for her to leave. She wouldn't. She rolled down her window. He put his head down near her face, said something, and stepped back. He slapped twice on the hood of the car, *bam bam*. Finally she started the engine and, her humiliation complete, she drove away, fallen leaves rippling sadly in the wake of the car.

Gabriella by now had given up hiding and stood beside her mother near the garage. Mr. Martello turned and gave them an over-the-head wave with both his arms from the top of the drive, as though to signal, *It's safe. She's gone. It's all right now.* Barbara didn't wait for him but, putting her hand on Gabriella's back, turned and headed inside with her daughter.

And although the distance was great, and although my eyes by now were clouded with outrage and shame, I could've sworn that before they disappeared into the garage, I saw Mrs. Martello's face relax into an expression of satisfaction.

CHAPTER FORTY-SIX

SOME more of history's most legendary and fearsome comets, as described to our class by my father and recorded by me in my notebook that year:

Moses's Star: At the birth of Moses, a moving star streaming long radiant tails of light was seen by the Magi of Egypt; they read it as an omen for the Pharaoh, who ordered that all male Jewish babies born under its sign be drowned in the River Nile.

The famous Comet of Carthage: Shone over Hannibal's armies as he marched his elephants across the Alps and into Italy to defeat the Romans. Twenty years later, the same comet reappeared and shone for eighty-eight days over Asia Minor with such a furious, horrible luster that Hannibal the Great drank poison and killed himself.

Mithridates's Star: Upon seeing this dreadful comet that was so bright it eclipsed the noonday sun, Mithridates, King of Pontus, conqueror of Asia Minor, drank poison and then had his eldest son decapitate him with his sword.

Caesar's Comet of 50 BC: Lit Julius Caesar's way as he crossed the Rubicon River into Roman Italy, initiating a great civil war from which there could be no return. Caesar's wife Calpurnia saw another comet in a dream and warned Caesar of the omen, but this could do nothing to forestall its appearance on the Ides of March, when Caesar was murdered by Brutus in the Roman senate. The comet lingered for seven nights, rising always at midnight, and was visible to all the citizens of Rome, who recognized it as the soul of Caesar ascending to heaven.

St. Peter's Comet hung like a sword over the city of Jerusalem, portending the destruction of the Temple in the year 70 AD.

Vespasian's Comet in 79 AD accompanied the eruption of Mount Vesuvius, which covered the city of Pompeii in lava and ash. Emperor Vespasian himself was warned of the dangers of this comet; he scoffed at the warnings, and then died a miserable death.

Constantine's Comet, seen burning in the shape of a cross above the battlefield, prompted Constantine the Great to kneel on the ground and become a Christian. 312 AD.

In 410 AD, under an immense sword-shaped comet that shone over Italy for four months, the Visigoths sacked and plundered Rome, bringing an end to the Roman Empire.

Attila, King of the Huns and Scourge of God, was overthrown in a great battle against the Romans on the Catalaunian plains under a terrible comet that appeared as a brilliant white angel brandishing a fiery sword; Christianity was saved. 451 AD.

Mohammed's Star: A great scimitar-shaped comet that appeared over Arabia in the year 570, heralding the birth of the Prophet.

Charlemagne's Comet: A torch-shaped comet seen above Germany in 814, foretelling the king's death. Upon sighting the comet, King Charlemagne divided his empire among his successors, made his confession, and died.

In January of the year 1000, the Great Millennial Comet was observed all over Europe. Many feared it heralded the end of the world. The comet was shaped like a horrible dragon, and its mysterious light was said to be able to penetrate walls, illuminating the interior of homes and palaces with a sinister red glow. Followed by floods, famines, earthquakes, and universal panic.

The Easter Comet of 1066: A seven-rayed comet that shone for forty nights, waxing and waning with the Moon; it guided William the Conqueror across the English Channel to his victory over King Harold at the Battle of Hastings.

Genghis Khan's Star: In 1222, appeared as a demon's head with a crown of fire as the Great Khan slaughtered 1 million people in the city of Herat. When the comet retreated, Genghis Khan took it as a bad omen and also retreated. He soon died.

In 1453, Constantinople, the magnificent capital of the Orient, succumbed to the fire and sword of the Turks under the illumination of an immense, terrifying comet that resembled a fire-breathing snake.

In 1519, the Aztec emperor Montezuma witnessed a bright, white-bearded comet that foretold the end of his empire and the return of the god Quetzalcoatl; that same year, when the Spanish conquistador Cortez appeared from the eastern sea, the emperor Montezuma fell to the ground to welcome his white-bearded god.

The Great Parisian Comet of 1528 appeared over Paris as a bent arm holding aloft an enormous sword, as though ready to strike the city; at the point of the sword shone three bright stars, and on both sides of the sword were visible a great number of knives, axes, and blood-colored pikes. The air all about the comet was filled with a ghostly hoard of hideous faces with silver beards and bristling hair. The Seine River overflowed. Fires, famine, pestilence.

In 1556, upon seeing a terrible blood-red comet in the sky, Charles V abdicated his throne and became a monk. There followed widespread wars over Europe, the Turks ravaged Hungary, and Bloody Mary, Queen of England, began her persecution of Protestants, burning thousands alive at the stake.

The Great Comet of 1607: Seen all over Europe. Floods, plagues, massacres. Called "the Red Knife in the Sky" by American Indians, it incited them to war against the English settlers; by its light, they captured John Smith, who escaped with his life only when the Indian maiden Pocahontas laid her head across his own as the fierce Chief Powhatan, her father, raised his club to murder Smith.

Napoleon's Comet glowed with a ruby-red luster at the birth of Bonaparte. Later, the Great Comet of 1811 blazed for a full year and a half like a giant torch on the horizon, lighting the Emperor's invasion of Russia. The Comet of 1821 shone for only one night over France and the island of St. Helena, the night Napoleon died.

Halley's Comet, in its 1835 apparition, was shaped like a giant red whale in the sky. Bloody wars erupted throughout Central and South America; bubonic plague wiped out the population of Alexandria; the Great Fire of New York burned for three days and three nights, reducing much of the city to ashes; and in Texas, under its red glow, the Mexican army massacred Jim Bowie, Davy Crockett, and hundreds of American soldiers at the Battle of the Alamo.

The Great Sun-Grazing Comet of 1882 appeared suddenly one morning in September above the Southern Hemisphere. It shone so brightly that it could be seen alongside the midday sun, until, six months later, it exploded into five pieces and faded from view.

The San Francisco Comet of 1906: It flared for one night only over California as the earth shook, buildings fell, and San Francisco burned to the ground.

CHAPTER FORTY-SEVEN

THE sky was a gunmetal gray with low bundles of pink-lit clouds. The air smelled damp, like wet leaves, and here and there smoke snaked up from a neighbor's chimney. Some houses already had sheets of newspaper or pieces of cardboard taped up inside the windows, per my father's suggestion. Squirrels skittered around to the sides of trees and froze on the bark, their tails flicking, their eyes alert, as Peter and I pedaled our bikes through the neighborhood and turned onto Franklin Street.

We rolled down the sidewalk toward the square, cars passing us on the road. Peter wore his oversized army coat, along with the hat he'd made from his rabbit pelt; it looked like a furry swim cap with flaps covering his ears. Swerving back and forth on his bike beside me, he talked excitedly about what we might expect from the comet tonight.

Lots of people had seen it already, he said. You just had to know where and when to look. His cousin Trent, in Napoleonville, he saw it three days ago. They were at his farm, they walked out into the field, and it was hanging right in front of them like a burning spear. Some people were afraid to even go outside at night now. They were buying up food and water. His daddy said his tanks were almost dry and soon there wouldn't be any more gas left in town. Since Peter had begun working at the Conoco, he'd seen people coming in every day to fill up their cars and generators, just in case. . . .

I was barely listening. I was still thinking about the horrible scene I'd just witnessed between my mother and Frank Martello. I knew that marked the end to any association between my parents and the Martellos; they wouldn't be crossing the bridge to visit one another again anytime soon, I was sure of that. But what about me and Gabriella? What did this mean for us? Despite this complication with our parents, and despite the fact that I hadn't been able to deliver my note to her, I clung to the hope that I would still see her tonight, and as Peter and I approached the center of town, I kept my eyes open for her.

Two blocks before the square, the traffic backed up to a crawl and the sidewalks became crowded with people. Peter and I hopped off our bikes to walk them. We passed Mr. Coot's Conoco; the lights were off, the bay doors closed, and Mr. Coot's truck was parked out front. Across the street, the McCall's Rexall had stayed open late; a teenage boy stood to one side of the entranceway filling helium balloons from a tank as folks passed in and out of the store. At the end of Franklin Street a policeman stood next to his car, directing traffic around the square.

Seeing all the cars and people, I felt a surge of confidence in my father. I hadn't expected to see this kind of turnout; I hadn't expected to see much of anything, really—maybe a handful of people in a near-empty square. But he'd pulled it off, hadn't he? Everything was just like he'd said it would be.

Peter and I pushed our bikes between cars and across the road. We saw some of our classmates from school, as well as some teachers, parents, and a young mother pushing a baby stroller. Coach DuPleiss raised a hand in greeting as we passed him on the sidewalk; he was accompanied by a thin, anxious-looking woman with her arms crossed tightly over her chest.

We found my father in front of the courthouse. It was a square, modern building with a broad concrete porch and a low flight of steps flanked by two lamps. He stood beneath one of the lamps, giving instructions to three or four Cub Scouts and their den leader. One scout wore binoculars around his neck; another rested his hands on a long cardboard telescope box propped up between his feet, listening carefully to my father. The rest of the scouts were busy carrying folding chairs out from inside the courthouse. Mr. Coot directed them, waddling and huffing as he showed them where to set up the chairs.

"Line it up. Line it up," he said. "Pete, Junior, give these kids a hand."

We left our bikes at the side of the porch and helped the scouts arrange the chairs in rows facing the courthouse. Looking up from under their caps, the boys asked if we had seen the comet yet and how big we thought it'd be tonight. Peter told them about the sighting by his cousin Trent in Napoleonville. One kid insisted that he wasn't afraid of the comet, he just wanted to get a good look at it, that was all. They hoped to earn their astronomy pins tonight, and they told us what all they needed to do for that.

My father, meanwhile, had started helping people set up their telescopes near the bottom of the steps. He was an unmistakable figure in his black raincoat, plaid hat, and glasses, and as he hustled back and forth, people seemed drawn to him. "Hey, Professor!" they called, and he turned and waved, pointing repeatedly to the southwestern sky for anyone who asked.

"Look who's here," Peter said, and pointed to Mark Mingis cruising along the edge of the square in his red Camaro. He had his window down, his elbow resting on the door, the radio playing loudly. Peter said that since Mark had gotten his driver's license he came by the station two or three times a week now. He always ordered full service, and if Peter was working he had to wait on him. "Hey Pete-Pee, use your premium. None of that watery stuff," he'd say. "Hey Pete-Pee, don't get any grease on my car."

"Asshole," Peter said. "I hope he wrecks his damn car."

Mark disappeared behind the courthouse as he looped around the square, and just then I had the notion that he was looking for Gabriella, too. Like me, he must've come here tonight expecting to meet her. Maybe she was already here, out strolling with her girlfriends. I scanned the crowd, searching for her dark head of hair. Dusk was lowering in the square, swelling the sky with orange and pink. Suddenly I was sure that our whole future together, my and Gabriella's, depended on who would be standing beside her when the comet came.

"Where're you going?" Peter asked as I turned to leave.

"I have to find Gabriella."

"Is she here?"

If she was, I was determined to reach her before Mark did. As I hurried off, the lamps at the courthouse were just coming on. Their white globes glowed in the air like small moons floating above the heads of Peter and the scouts.

I circled the square on the outside walkway, looking for her face among the crowds of people. I passed a hippy couple, an older boy wearing a floppy hat and a long purple coat with his arm around a girl in a psychedelic miniskirt and purple stockings. I must've been staring, because the girl puckered her lips and blew me a kiss, making her boyfriend laugh. I kept walking, past a black family gathered around a park bench.

"You're not going to say hello?"

It was Christine; I hadn't seen her. I stopped and she introduced me to her family—her sister, her aunt, her mother and father, a few kids. "Wouldn't miss it for the world," she said. "I said we've got to go see that comet. I told them how your daddy showed it to me on the telescope."

A little boy standing at my knees waved a cardboard tube. "I got a telescope."

"That's my littlest one, Jeremy," said Christine. The boy put the tube against his eye and looked up with it. "What do you see? You see anything?" she asked him.

"The Moon," the boy said, and everyone laughed. The boy looked around worriedly, not sure why this was funny, and hid his face against Christine's legs.

She opened a picnic basket beside her on the bench and invited me to stay and eat with them. They had chicken, biscuits, everything. "Peppers? You like peppers? That's from my garden last summer." I begged off, saying that I had to meet someone.

"You're in a hurry, that's okay." Christine returned the jar of peppers to the basket. "Tell your daddy I said hello. Tell him we were here."

I thanked her and said goodbye. The little kid waved his cardboard tube in the air at me as I moved on.

I'd lost sight of Mark and his red Camaro; I didn't see any sign of Gabriella yet, either. But cutting through the middle of the square, I heard music and turned around to see my sister. She was sitting cross-legged on a tie-dyed sheet on the ground in a corner of the square, playing guitar with Greg. She wore a tiara of yellow and white plastic flowers. Greg slouched beside her in a winter coat. The other members of the band lounged back smoking cigarettes and listening, glassy-eyed. I stepped across the grass to them.

"What're you doing here?"

Strumming her guitar, Megan looked up. "Same as you. Came to see the comet."

"Alan Junior," said Greg, and reached up for a soul shake. The drummer took a suck of gas from a helium balloon and said in a high, funny voice, "What's up, dude?"

I asked my sister if she'd seen Gabriella. She hadn't. "The Comet Queen," Greg said. "I remember her."

"You think we'll see it?" the drummer asked, squinting up at me from the ground.

"My dad says so."

He nodded. "That'd be cool."

Greg began strumming his guitar along with Megan. They got up a tune, and my sister took the high part, her voice sounding light and pretty. I looked over their heads to the end of the square. Night was falling fast; the streetlights had come on and the store signs were all lit now. On the corner, people were going in and out of the Rexall—

A ridiculous hope, I knew, but it was worth a try.

"Rock on," the drummer said as I rushed off.

The kid with the gas was still filling balloons at the front of the store, tying them off and attaching strings with a bored expertise. I held the door open for a woman coming out, and as I waited for her to pass I saw one of my dad's fliers taped up inside the window. Across the top of the flier was a poorly reproduced black-and-white photograph of a comet; around the edges were hand-drawn stars and planets:

> Come See Comet Kohoutek! The municipality of Terre-
> bonne will host a public comet viewing, to take place Sun-
> day evening . . . Alan Broussard, local science teacher and
> astronomer, will be on hand to . . .

Inside, then, and up and down the aisles. The lights were white, the air medicinal. The store couldn't have changed much since my parents met here almost twenty years ago: same magazine racks, same shelves of stomach medicine. Coming around to the front of the store, I half expected to find, through some magical repetition of time and events, Gabriella waiting for me behind the counter. Instead, there was a thin black girl wearing the shop's pink smock, her hair combed out into a large, well-shaped Afro. She leaned across the counter flirting with a black fellow about her age, one foot extended behind her rocking from side to side on its toe.

"I'm not going to give you a discount. Why should I give you a dis-count?" she said.

"Because I'm your friend," the guy teased. "I'm your special friend."

She laughed. "Shoot. You think you're my special friend."

No Gabriella, though. I went back outside. A damp, cutting breeze blew along the sidewalk as the last traces of daylight bled from the sky. I stuffed my hands in my coat pockets and was about to cross the road for another pass through the square when I noticed the front fender of a blue car peeking out from the alleyway beside the drugstore.

I stepped closer. It was our Rambler. My mother sat behind the steering wheel, her eyes on the square. I knocked on the passenger-side window and she jerked back, startled. Then she leaned over and unlocked the door to let me in.

CHAPTER FORTY-EIGHT

"IT'S cold out, isn't it?"

She still wore the navy-blue jacket and skirt I'd seen her in earlier at the Martellos' house. Her pearls were gone, though, and her eyes were red and puffy. The motor was running and the heater on. I didn't want to embarrass her by asking what she was doing here, and she didn't seem inclined to offer any explanation, so instead we both pretended that it was perfectly normal that I should find her hiding in our car in the alleyway.

I warmed my hands in the heat from the vents and watched the square with her. Policemen had begun blocking off the road around the square with sawhorses. Red brake lights winked on and off; above, soft blue comas haloed the streetlamps.

My mother sniffed and wiped her nose with a tissue. "I'm surprised to see so many people."

"Me, too."

She peered up thoughtfully at the sky through the windshield. "Can it do that? Just appear all the sudden?"

"I guess so. It's supposed to be a good night for it."

"But it's cloudy."

"I know."

"Where's your telescope?"

"With Dad." I told her how I'd come with Peter, and how we'd been helping the Cub Scouts set up chairs. "I saw Megan."

"Was she with Greg?"

"With him and his friends, yeah. Over there playing guitars."

"I like Greg. He seems like a nice boy. He probably smokes pot, but at least he's polite."

My mother and I hadn't spoken to each other since her phone calls to me the week before, when I'd hung up on her. Having witnessed her horrible humiliation at the Martellos' that afternoon, though, I was finding it hard to stay very angry at her for abandoning us. Still, I wasn't ready to just forgive and forget everything yet.

Three of Gabriella's girlfriends from school passed directly in front of us on the sidewalk. They were followed by some older boys who teased them as they walked. The girls jutted their chins and pretended to ignore the boys, which only provoked them more. The girls turned sharply to cross the street, and the boys chased after them.

My mother smiled. "Look at them go. . . . Reminds me of when I was a teenager. We used to come here all the time. It was just like this. Families and kids, people out walking. Boys circling in their cars, chasing after the girls. You hardly ever see this anymore."

"Why not?"

"I don't know. People like to stay inside and watch TV, I guess. Or maybe they're afraid to go out at night now."

I fooled with the heater vents as she went on, her voice taking on a wistful, sentimental tone.

"Do you remember when we used to take you and Megan to see drive-in movies? At that place out on Highway One? You got so scared the first time, I don't know why."

I had a vague memory of huddling in blankets in the front seat between my parents as brightly colored giants went crashing and leaping across the night sky in front of our car.

"It was something like *Mary Poppins*. You were so afraid!" She laughed.

"I didn't know it was just a movie," I explained.

"Probably not. You had nightmares for weeks after that. Because of *Mary Poppins*." She laughed again, and I chuckled with her. She sniffed and wiped her nose, and then asked, "How's your father?"

"He's all right, I guess."

"Did you two have dinner tonight? What'd you eat?"

"Leftover chicken."

"He cooked it?"

"No. God, no. Are you kidding?"

We sat there a minute, looking out the windshield. I got the feeling we were both working up the courage to start in on what we really needed to talk about, which was the whole complicated issue of where we stood now as mother and son, and what would become of the Broussard family.

Off to the right, I saw the guy who'd been flirting with the counter girl come out of the drugstore. He bought a balloon and ducked back inside.

"It's your famous drugstore," I said.

She looked across me out the window. "My famous drugstore."

"The one where it all began."

"Ha."

"It was on a night like this. You were working all alone," I prompted. She didn't say anything. "He was a new teacher, fresh from LSU. . . ." Still nothing. It suddenly felt important to hear the story again, as a reminder, for both of us, of how love was supposed to work.

"Tell it," I urged her.

"No, not now."

"Why not?"

"It's too sad."

"How's it sad?"

"It just is."

"You should come home."

She looked at me and sighed. "Oh, honey."

"Why don't you?"

"There's so many problems now."

"No there aren't." I poked at the heater vent. "He misses you."

She bit her lip and turned forward. In the dim light of the alley her face was gray and shadowed. She was looking through the windshield, but she wasn't seeing the scene outside anymore; she was seeing something else entirely, perhaps peering down into her own heart.

"I think I might've made a terrible mistake," she said softly.

"What?"

"It's like I wasn't thinking right. I believed something was true that wasn't true, and then I . . . and then I . . ." She shook her head, as though to shake away the thought. "God, I'm such an idiot. I'm so stupid. I'm so stupid. What did I do? Look at the mess I made."

"Maybe you can still fix it."

"I don't know, it might be too late for that." She looked at me. "Am I a terrible mother? Do you hate me?"

Her eyes were damp, her brow wrinkled and pleading. An honest answer might've been, *Yes, sometimes you are a terrible mother, and yes, sometimes I hate you for that.* But now, I sensed, was not the time for honest answers.

"No. No, of course not," I said.

Across the square, someone was checking the microphone on the podium. *"Test. Testing one, two."*

She wiped her nose. "He's a stubborn man, isn't he? Your father. He never gives up. He just keeps on going. I don't know how he does it. He stands by his beliefs, no matter . . . no matter what other people think. You have to admire him for that, I guess. Even if sometimes he does seem a little . . . a little, I don't know what. Cuckoo."

At the courthouse, the mayor had begun speaking at the microphone.

"It's starting," my mother said. "You should go watch. He'd want you to be there."

I hesitated before leaving her. We hadn't really resolved anything, but the mayor was introducing my father now, and Gabriella was somewhere out there, maybe watching and waiting for me.

I turned once more to my mother. It could've been the way the light in the alley fell on her face, but she looked suddenly older. She might've aged twenty years since that afternoon. I thought of her as that teenage girl staring dreamily out the window of the drugstore, and then the nervous young newlywed boarding the train for her honeymoon, and now the sad, mistaken lover dropping to her hands and knees on the sidewalk in front of our neighbors' house—

She leaned abruptly across the seat, grabbed me by the shoulders, and gave me a strong kiss on the cheek. Then she pushed me toward the door.

"Go. Go watch it, sweetie," she said. "Once in a lifetime chance and everything. You wouldn't want to miss it."

CHAPTER FORTY-NINE

THERE was a smattering of applause in the square as my father came forward and laid his notes on the lectern. The wind riffled the pages. He adjusted his broken glasses and thanked the mayor, thanked everyone for coming out this evening. Then he stood up straighter, cleared his throat, and began his speech.

"Tonight, we are gathered here to witness a truly remarkable event, one whose importance will be recorded not only in the history of science, but also in the broader history of civilization. As inhabitants of the planet, we are fortunate indeed . . ."

The sound system was weak, and from where I stood at the edge of the square it was difficult to hear what he was saying. But the audience was attentive. People shushed one another. A woman beside me stopped her child from running and held him at her legs in front of her and told him to be quiet, the scientist was talking now. I moved to a spot nearer the chairs where I might hear him better.

He said how, for as long as men had wandered the Earth, they'd looked to the stars for guidance. He spoke about celestial navigation, and how ancient men used the stars to find direction on land and sea. Then he spoke about guidance of another sort, referencing the Greek myths and the stories of bravery and love we found memorialized in the constellations. From there he moved on to astrology. . . .

It was a carefully thought-out speech. I knew how much time he'd spent writing and rehearsing it, and I knew how important it was for him. As he spoke, he gestured woodenly, raising a finger to emphasize his main points and making broad sweeping motions with his right arm.

Halfway through his speech, a breeze lifted his hat off his head. It tumbled away across the porch. A Cub Scout chased after it, and as my father turned from the lectern to receive his hat from the scout, his papers fluttered to the porch. Two more scouts ran up to help, and as the three boys and my father chased the flying papers around in a circle, it looked for a minute like the program was going to turn into a comedy. Some people in the audience chuckled, but others upbraided them for laughing during what was obviously meant to be a serious lecture.

Settling his papers back on the lectern, my father resumed his speech. He spoke now of the human condition, and about how life as we knew it was mostly an unpleasant experience. He mentioned the commonplace disasters that awaited us all: loved ones might leave us, our families break apart, our houses slide into disrepair. Objects we treasured fell to pieces in our hands. Everything raced toward its dissolution. For proof of this we only had to look in the mirror and see our skin sagging on our face, our hair turning gray. Like it or not, we were all dying, every day and every minute of our lives.

And then, he went on, if we looked around us, we saw that others suffered the same fate as we did, often worse. We turned on the television or opened a newspaper to see a seemingly endless parade of daily disasters: floods . . . famines . . . earthquakes . . . whole cities washing into the sea . . . men shooting each other with guns . . .

"What's he talking about? Can you hear him?" a man near me asked his friend.

"About the comet," his friend answered.

"I could've guessed that."

"About nature and the comet. How they go together."

My father turned at last to the consolations of science. Becoming emotional, he said how in the midst of all this misery and decay, science gave us reason for hope. Yes, it did. Science revealed to us the beautiful order hidden within the natural world.

Consider the comet, he said. He spoke about its origins in the invisible crystalline sphere that surrounded our solar system, and how the comet itself was a relic of the same swirling cloud of dust and gas that, billions of years ago, gave birth to our Sun, the Earth, and all our familiar planets. Indeed, when we looked at the comet, we could not help but be reminded of the common origins of all creation.

"Look, here, in this tiny piece of dust," he said, and touched his finger to the lectern and held aloft an invisible mote. "Some carbon, silicon, sulfur, maybe some water . . ."

"What is it?" whispered the man near me.

"Don't know. Can't see it," his friend answered.

My father went on to say how this very speck of dust might well have come from the tail of a comet like Kohoutek. This same species of dust filled the universe. It floated in the space between stars, it combined with gas to churn in the fiery furnaces of nebulae to produce yet more stars and planets and comets. It was, he said, the elemental fluff of life.

A thousand tons of this cosmic dust fell to the Earth every day. It was in our water, our soil, our food, our blood. We ate it and breathed it. It was us. We ourselves were made out of this cosmic dust. He wasn't speaking metaphorically, my father insisted; it was a simple scientific truth: when we traced the origin of the elements out of which human bodies were made, we discovered that we all ultimately were, in fact, stardust.

This, he said, was the message of the comet. This was what Kohoutek had come to remind us of: that we were a part of everything, and everything was a part of us.

And seeing how we were all so intimately connected in this way, he concluded, we couldn't help but feel sympathy for our fellow human beings. And from this feeling of sympathy, we couldn't help but feel compassion, and from this compassion, we couldn't help but feel . . .

But we would never know what it was that the comet was supposed to make us feel, because just then the air-raid siren wailed to life, drowning out the end of his speech.

Everyone knew this was on the program, but it was nevertheless startling to hear. The sound began at the fire station on the corner, was echoed by another siren four blocks up Franklin Street, and still another one atop the water tower. The sirens swelled, increasing in pitch and volume until they became a sustained cry filling the air above the square. My father shouted out something over the noise, but it was impossible to hear what he was saying anymore.

And then right on schedule, the streetlights around the square went dark. After that, one by one, the lights in the shops along Franklin Street blinked off, and then their marquees. The policeman standing at the edge of the square saw that the blue flashing lights on top of his car were on, and he reached in the door to turn them off. Finally, as though they'd almost been overlooked, the lamps flanking the courthouse steps clicked off.

With that, the night became suddenly, surprisingly dark, like a blanket had been thrown over the town. My father vanished, the courthouse vanished, the square and the benches and the trees all vanished. I couldn't see the people standing beside me, or even the tips of my own shoes. The sirens trailed off, leaving an absolute and profound silence. No one talked, no one moved. We might've all disappeared from the face of the Earth, leaving nothing but an empty square and the distant stars winking between mountains of clouds.

We stared up, bodiless, and watched. For the moment, all our town's hopes, all our aspirations, were focused on that one patch of sky above our heads. I could hear the unspoken wishes of my neighbors swirling and rustling around me like leaves stirred by the wind: wishes for love, for happiness, for peace; wishes for a new car, a friend's toy; the safe return of a son, an end to illness, the cure of a habit; respect from a spouse, success at work, a more certain future. Our wishes rose together into one great silent prayer of longing sent up to the stars, where, as if in answer—*Ahh!*—a thin streak of fire shot into the clouds from the east.

Everyone gasped as the streak burst into a shower of sparks. And then another streak shot into the sky, and then another. . . .

Fireworks. Someone was shooting off bottle rockets, that's all it was. In the distance, a boy whooped. The crowd chuckled in response.

"Huh. Thought it was the comet," someone said.

People began to shift and look around themselves, somewhat embarrassed. They scanned the sky and whispered to one another.

"Do you see it? I don't see anything."

"Give it time."

"Maybe we missed it."

I could feel the spell that had held us in such breathless suspense already beginning to slip away. We looked up, we waited, but there was no comet, not tonight, not that we could see. There was nothing up there but clouds and stars in the same sky that we had always known. A man—it might've been Coach DuPleiss—shouted from the rear of the crowd: "Hey, Professor! Where's your comet?" This elicited a good round of laughter from those standing near me.

The evening, I feared, was turning into a colossal failure, a great joke at the expense of my father. I was glad it was so dark because I wouldn't have wanted anyone to recognize me as the son of the man up there on the steps with his ridiculous coat and hat and his crazy talk about balls of fire falling from the sky. What could he have been thinking anyway, bringing everyone out here tonight if there was nothing for us to see? Why go on and on about his marvelous comet? Couldn't all his charts and calculations have predicted something like this might have happened? Or was he honestly expecting some sort of miracle tonight? Whatever his idea had been, I hated him for building up everyone's hopes like this, and then I hated myself for allowing myself to believe for even one minute that my father could've been anything like a great man, a hero.

I pushed my way through the square so I could get my bike and resume my search for Gabriella. As I drew near the courthouse, I saw Mr. Coot, Peter, and the scouts clustered anxiously at the bottom of the steps, staring up not at the sky, but at my father—

Who stood at the edge of the porch, his dark figure silhouetted against the pale front of the courthouse. His whole body trembled as he extended his arms to the sky, as though he were trying to reach up and pull down the comet from heaven.

CHAPTER FIFTY

THE streets around the square were dark and quiet. Most of the houses had complied with the blackout, making it difficult to see much of anything, only the dim outlines of homes and buildings, the traces of trees and telephone poles. Here and there figures floated along the sidewalk, and I peered at them as I rolled past on my bike, looking for Gabriella's hair and shape.

After circling through downtown and still not finding her, I headed back up Franklin Street. Here, too, the lights were off, the houses dark. In the distance I heard the popping noise of firecrackers, or maybe gunshots. Dogs barked and howled. A gang of junior high school boys came flying past me on their bikes, whooping and hollering like wild Indians before melting again into the night.

I passed the dim legs of the water tower, crossed the bridge, and turned in at Beau Rivage Estates. As I pedaled through the blacked-out neighborhood, I could make out folks standing on their lawns, talking and visiting one another. The Martellos' house loomed at the end of the block, its walls and roofs elongated into shadows so that it appeared even more imposing than usual. I stopped half a block away and straddled my bike. I heard the voices of Frank and Barbara Martello; I saw their figures crossing their drive to greet a neighbor, heard the tinkle of ice cubes in drinking glasses . . . but no sign of Gabriella.

I set off again, thinking to circle the block and approach their house from the other side, out of sight of her parents. If she was at home, I would find her; a force as irresistible as gravity drew me to her. For every boy, one special girl was waiting, and every cell in my body, every star in the sky, told me she was the one. As I stood up on the pedals of my bike, I was already halfway up the stairs to her room, taking the steps two at a time . . . and then Gabriella and I were falling into each other's arms . . . and then we were rolling on the carpet, lost again in our kiss, that golden kiss that would rescue the day and make everything better. . . .

I pedaled past new homes, past half-built homes, past vacant lots in dark cul-de-sacs. I turned, and then turned again onto the road at the far side of the neighborhood, heading back toward the bayou. Overhead, the clouds had shifted to reveal more stars, sharp and bright in a moonlit sky. I'd never seen them so bright before. The Milky Way was a wide, luminescent band arching up from the horizon, and the constellations appeared as plain and obvious as a child's line drawings: Cancer, Gemini, Pegasus. Looking around, I was surprised to see that the road and sidewalks, the homes and vacant lots were all lit up by a diffuse, silvery skyglow. Beneath my bicycle tires, the asphalt itself seemed to sparkle, like a pathway of stars laid out before me.

I must've missed the last turn, because all at once the road ended. I bumped over the curb and came to a stop in the weeds of a vacant lot, almost toppling off my bike. To either side were dim mounds of bulldozed dirt and stumps. Dirt tracks led through the weeds and disappeared around a line of bare trees. I was backing up my bike when I saw, ahead through the trees, a faint yellow ball of light.

Was it curiosity that drew me to it? Intuition? Fate? Or did the stars overhead tell me this was the place, command me to get off my bike, lay it on the ground, and walk forward through the weeds?

A small animal rustled in the brush to my right and shot across the path in front of me. Past the line of trees, the track opened up into a clearing. It was the site of someone's future home: ribboned stakes in the dirt, stacks of lumber to one side, and a pole with a circuit box propped up in the ground. Straight ahead was the bayou, and tucked into a stand of evergreen trees at the edge of the water was Mark's car.

I recognized it immediately on account of the low, curved shape of the body and the wind spoiler on the back. The motor was running and the radio played. The yellowish interior light lit the trunks of the trees around it, giving the impression that the car itself was surrounded by a soft golden glow. I squatted down in the weeds to watch.

They were in the backseat, their heads and limbs bobbing in and out of view through the rear window. A pale arm flashed past, and then a foot, and a shoulder, and a head of dark hair. Then the car rocked and Mark reared up. His chest was bare, his face red and wild-looking. He began violently jerking up and down, and I immediately became afraid for Gabriella. I heard her cry out. I sprang up from the ground, and in my mind I was already running to the car to save her, already dragging Mark out the side door and wrestling him to the dirt . . . when I heard her laugh. It was a low, throaty chortle, nothing like the laugh I was familiar with, but unmistakably hers.

I squatted back down in the weeds, breathing heavily, and continued to watch.

Mark dropped out of sight and Gabriella rose up to take his place. She was shirtless, and her lush hair spilled forward over her bare shoulders to partly cover her breasts. She pulled Mark up and clutched him to her chest, digging her fingers into his hair. She shuddered and lifted her eyes up, and in the dim light of the car, her face glowed with a terrible, radiant joy.

In that light, in the moment of her ecstasy, the girl I loved appeared more beautiful, more angelic, than ever before; and as I watched her bend down and kiss his mouth, I knew I was witnessing nothing less than the end of the world; and as he raised up and wrapped his arms around her, I heard my father's voice at my ear, solemnly reminding me: *"Nothing to be afraid of, son . . . It's perfectly natural . . . a very . . . lovely . . . event."*

And with that, it was as though a curtain had been ripped aside, revealing a truth that had been hidden from me for so long.

As I pedaled back through the neighborhood, I was shaking so hard that I could barely steer my bicycle. The air had become colder, and the light, too, had changed; the stars looked dimmer and farther away than they had moments ago. It was only gradually that I realized that the streetlights had come back on, and that was why the stars were so faint, and why I could see all the objects of everyday life clearly again—the houses and sidewalks, the fire hydrants and stop signs, all restored to their stubborn ordinariness.

On Franklin Street, cars rolled in a steady trickle from the square, people returning home from the failed comet viewing. I turned in at my street and passed Peter's house. Mr. Coot's truck was parked in front and their house lights were on. My own house was still dark, but I barely registered this as I got off my bike and pulled it around to the backyard, where I saw—but I could hardly believe it—my father with the telescope.

He was bent over the eyepiece, still wearing his hat and raincoat. He slowly straightened up when he heard me come into the yard.

"I was just giving it another look . . . ," he said, and made a pathetic gesture toward the sky.

This was too much. I couldn't take it anymore. All the misery and confusion, all the hurt and humiliation that I'd ever known welled up inside of me and sent me charging across the yard to my father.

I grabbed the telescope from him. He tried to hold on to it, and as we tugged back and forth, I cursed him and his damn comet. I cursed him for my mother and Frank, and for Gabriella and Mark, and for every damn thing that had ever happened to us . . . but I hardly knew what I was saying anymore.

"Wait. Wait, no, please—"

I wrested the telescope from him and, taking it by its legs, swung it around into a tree. The thing smacked the trunk with a satisfying crack, followed by a tinny clatter as pieces fell to the ground. I swung it around at the tree again and again, shouting, "There is no comet! There is no love! There's nothing, you idiot! Nothing! Nothing! Nothing! Nothing! Do you see? Do you see now?"

I threw what was left of the scope to the ground and then kicked it for good measure. Then I wheeled back around to my father. He cringed, and had he not looked so pitiful at that instant, I would've lunged in and ripped him apart.

"This is all your fault, you know," I said, panting. "Everything. You did this. You did this to us!"

"I know. I know," he said, and spread his arms helplessly. "You're right. I'm sorry. . . ."

"I hate you. I want you to know that. I hate you for everything you've done. I hate you. I hate you. I hate you! Is that clear? Is that perfectly clear?"

"Yes," he said. "I know, I know, son."

"You're useless. Absolutely useless. And I wish . . . I wish to god I'd never been born."

CHAPTER FIFTY-ONE

BUT Kohoutek hadn't left us yet. The comet was still there, flickering yellow and faint as a candle above the clouds as our town settled in for the night.

In the empty square, a scrap of paper tumbled down the steps of the courthouse, rested against the leg of a park bench, and then fluttered free. Bare tree branches creaked back and forth beneath the streetlights, casting waving shadows on the pavement. Moonlight silvered the narrow canals that crisscrossed the fields and farms and wound under bridges and behind rows of quiet houses. . . .

While at home upstairs in my tiny room, I tossed on my bed, unable to sleep. I felt like a stranger to myself, overgrown and monstrous. My bed was too small, the walls were too close, the ceiling too low. I thought of the comet, and of Gabriella, and of my father and mother, and of the whole miserable wreck of our family. I hugged myself beneath the sheets, shivering with sorrow and regret, and wished that I could undo this night, undo this entire mistake-riddled year, and send myself back in time to start over again from my fourteenth birthday.

In his room below me lay a man who looked very much like me, my
adult twin, tossing sleeplessly in his own bed. From time to time I
heard a groan escape him. I pictured his broken glasses on the nightstand beside him, his clothes scattered around the floor. He sweated
and grimaced; he clenched his hands into fists. Rolling back and forth
on the mattress, he knocked a fist against his bony forehead, as though
trying to dislodge whatever thoughts were stuck there in his brain.

If I could have, I would have sent him back in time, too: back to a
time before there was any thought of this family, this house, this difficult life. In my prayer for my father that night, I turned my eyes once
more to the sky outside my window and found again that heavenly
place beyond the stars where dreams were born and memories never
died and people lived forever. And there, floating in a cloud of cosmic
dust, I saw my father as he used to be: a bespectacled, carefree young
man, back during a time when his future seemed to roll out before him
like a smoothly paved road on a sunny day.

He was steering a rented DeSoto along the Pacific Coast Highway.
One hand rested on the wheel, his elbow propped up in the opened
window. His new wife sat beside him wearing a pleated white skirt
with a road map spread on her bare knees. The air was dry and light, so
unlike the swampy heat of southern Louisiana. As they rounded a
bend, a pleasant, woody scent blew through the windows of the car.

"What is that? Pinyon?" my mother-to-be asked.

"Desert cactus," my father-to-be answered, although in truth, he
had no idea what it was.

"It's nice."

He looked at her and smiled. She caught her hair and laughed for no
apparent reason, and in that instant he felt himself buoyed up on the
wave of her smile, her hair, the golden sunlight on the hills and road.

Did my father, in that long, lonely midnight of his soul, remember
that day? Wouldn't that have been enough to pull him back from the
brink? Or was not even that smile, that skirt, that sunny road enough
to overcome a lifetime's worth of disappointment?

The sun warmed their faces as he piloted the car between the glittering blue-and-white ocean on the one side, the dry green hills on the

other. Already the newlyweds were planning other trips they could take out west, a seemingly endless summer of holidays: The Grand Canyon. The Rocky Mountains. Pike's Peak, Yosemite Valley, Yellowstone Park . . .

So much to see, right here on Earth, the best of all possible earths. Who in the world would ever want to leave it?

They drove through Newport Beach, Laguna Beach, and Mussel Cove. At Capistrano Beach he turned inland—Lydia wanted to see the swallows at the mission, and Alan was quick to agree. They could stop and stretch their legs, maybe have some lunch, before continuing on the road to Palomar.

Their guide at San Juan Capistrano, a tanned, bearded man, led them through the ruins of the old church, pointing out the mud nests of the birds clustered up among the crumbling stone arches. The newlyweds followed, he squinting up with his hands clasped behind his back, she listening attentively as their guide explained how the swallows flew six thousand miles from their winter home in Argentina to arrive like clockwork every year on the Feast of Saint Joseph. "What do you know about that," Alan said, impressed. "Like a miracle," Lydia said, and the guide smiled indulgently and folded his hands across his belly like a priest.

At the mission gift shop, they spent some time looking through a stack of handmade rugs. The one they ended up with was a garish thing, with bright Mexican colors and a rough weave, not even the one they really wanted, but the woman who sold it to them was so sweet and insistent—she didn't have any teeth—and they had already spent so much time bargaining with her over the price, that when she folded it up and shoved it into their hands, they really had no choice. "For our new home," Lydia said. "So we can always remember this day."

For lunch they had real Mexican food at the El Adobe restaurant.

"Honeymoon," they told everyone, and four mariachis in sombreros came to serenade them at their table. The window was open; pink bougainvillea frothed in around the wooden frame. The skinny mariachi shook a pair of red maracas and threw his head back and sang something high and plaintive in Spanish, prompting Lydia to find Alan's hand and squeeze it under the table. Budget be damned, Alan thought, and when they left the restaurant, he tipped the singers and the waiters and everyone much more than he should have.

From San Juan Capistrano the road wound up through the Santa Ana Mountains, cutting switchbacks along a high, narrow ridge, through forests of fir and cedar, pine and spruce. The air became cool and misty. Huge green ferns hung from the sides of steep rocky walls. There wasn't a service station in sight, and Alan worried whether the rented DeSoto would make it up the next bend. But the old car proved sturdy enough, and late in the day they rolled into a high green valley and found the lodge where Alan had made reservations.

The Palomar Mountaintop Lodge was a picturesque, rustic resort surrounded by wooded hills. Tidy cabins and stables were tucked against the trees, and a mountain spring ran down along one edge of the pasture. The peak of Palomar Mountain rose up dramatically behind the roof of the lodge house.

The owner, Mr. Lundgren, met them on the porch and showed them to their room on the second floor. From their balcony they could look down the mountain and see the coastline stretching all the way from Santa Monica to Mexico, with a chain of low gray islands far out in the water, like a school of giant whales. Lydia leaned over the railing and breathed in the clean air. She felt lighter, larger, on top of the world.

"Alan," she said. "Come see the sunset. Isn't it gorgeous?"

He joined her on the balcony, and she held his arm in both her hands. The Sun was a giant ball of fire lighting the sky with a fantastic smear of colors. As they watched, the gap between the rim of the Sun and the edge of the sea slowly narrowed, although without any perceptible movement of either. Lydia was impressed by the grave drama of the event; she pictured planets like massive iron spheres creaking past one another, and the thought of this almost frightened her. When the Sun touched the horizon, the sea swelled orange and red, like it was catching fire. She tugged urgently on Alan's arm, and he looked down sideways at her, smiled reassuringly, and patted her hand.

They had just time to get cleaned up and eat dinner before going out again. Alan got directions from Mr. Lundgren and then waited outside on the porch while Lydia ran back up to the room to grab a sweater. The night was dark and brilliantly clear. And the stars—more stars than he'd ever seen in his life. "Look at that. Look at that," he kept saying to Lydia as they walked to the car. "Gosh. Have you ever seen anything like that in your life?"

It was a short drive up the hill to the observatory. As Alan turned into the research complex, they were both hushed by the sight of the white dome rising grandly above the top of the mountain, like a perfectly realized emblem of science. Getting out of the car and approaching the observatory, they spoke and treaded more softly than usual, feeling like they were walking on sacred ground.

Dr. Greenstein from Caltech was waiting for them, just like he'd written Alan that he would. The professor was a genial, gray-haired man dressed in a white shirt, dark pants, and narrow tie. On his nose, black-rimmed glasses. Alan was only a jittery first-year high school teacher from Louisiana, but Dr. Greenstein welcomed him with all the courteous respect of one scientist meeting another. As the professor showed them around the various outbuildings and facilities of the observatory, Alan felt a warm sense of brotherhood swell in him, and Lydia, recognizing the importance of the occasion, linked her arm in his, the proud wife of the promising young scientist.

Arriving at the white dome, Greenstein led them through a set of doors and a dark vestibule that opened up into the dim, cavernous interior. He guided them past a mystifying array of scaffolding and equipment that looked like something from a science fiction movie, and then—good lord, it was as big as people said it was: the two-hundred-inch Hale Reflector, the world's largest telescope.

The shutters were open and they could see a band of sky through the parted ceiling of the dome. They climbed a flight of metal stairs to a platform and then stepped up under the enormous bowl-shaped mirror of the telescope while Dr. Greenstein spoke about its design. He pointed out to Alan the mirror support mechanisms and the small springs he'd installed to preserve the alignment of the panes. "What is that, a spring gauge?" Alan asked, curious. "A fish weight scale," Greenstein said. "I found a bunch of them at a tackle shop down in Long Beach. They work perfectly." "Huh. What do you know about that. Honey, come look at this."

Two men in lab coats passed carrying important-looking equipment. "Oh, good. You're in luck," Dr. Greenstein said. They'd been taking exposures of a white dwarf that night, but just now they were changing the plate. Did Alan want to go up to the cage? The prime focus cage?

This, Alan knew, was a rare invitation. Only well-vetted researchers were normally allowed to go up inside the telescope. But it was a slow night, the professor said, and after all—here he winked at them—it was Alan's honeymoon.

"Give you something to remember," Greenstein said. "Something you can tell your kids about."

And so, while Lydia waited on the floor below, Alan rode with Dr. Greenstein in an open elevator up along the side of the dome. He followed the professor across a short catwalk and then down into a metal capsule suspended above the telescope's mirror. There was barely enough room for three or four men to crowd shoulder to shoulder around a steel tube that came up through the middle of the grated floor. Engines groaned and the giant telescope began to move. Holding on to the side of the cage, Alan tried not to show his excitement, but he felt like a boy on a carnival ride.

Below, Lydia crossed her arms and watched the machinery tilt into place. It looked very serious and impressive to her. She didn't especially mind being left behind for the moment; the men were doing science, talking about things she couldn't have possibly understood. Besides, she recognized that this was Alan's adventure now, and so she was content to stand on the sidelines and cheer him on.

As she waited, something made her think about the swallows back at Capistrano, how they returned to the same place at the same time every year. How did they know how to do that? she wondered. Maybe she would ask Alan about it later; he might be able to tell her. Those tiny birds, flying thousands of miles over land and sea, mountains and valleys—it didn't seem possible. She pictured them in dark, cloudlike swarms, the Earth far below, the stars above, beating their little wings determinedly through the night. The guide had laughed when she called it a miracle, but really, what else could you call something like that?

Inside the focus cage, Dr. Greenstein was showing Alan where the photographic plate screwed into place. They'd been using a spectrograph designed by Dr. Page for nebular work, he explained, a really fine instrument with a 390-millimeter dispersion. The engines quieted to a low hum as the telescope locked into tracking mode. Dr. Greenstein bent to an eyepiece angling out of the side of the tube. He adjusted some knobs and then scooted to one side.

"Go ahead," he said. "Have a look."

Alan held his breath as he bent to the eyepiece. Dr. Greenstein stood at his shoulder describing what he was seeing.

"I love this star. It's one of Luyten's white dwarfs. We found some really pronounced hydrogen lines, very broad and shallow. I mean, they're so obvious, you can't miss them. Kuiper classified the spectrum as 'continuous,' but he doesn't know what he's talking about. Okay, to be fair, we've got a better telescope. But anyway, what we're finding is that there's a rough correlation between spectral class and color index—which is no great surprise, really, given that the DA-zero-two stars, as we've always known, are bluer than the DA-three-seven stars."

Alan hardly knew what Dr. Greenstein was talking about. But it didn't matter. He was lost in his own wonder at what he was seeing. The doors of heaven had opened to show him this star, this white dwarf, a small dot of light couched in a luminous blue halo. It was, he knew, a star in the last stage of its life. How appropriate, how beautiful, he thought, that it should die this way, reduced to the pure white core of its being.

"How far?" Alan whispered.

"About seven thousand light-years, give or take."

"How old?"

"Hard to say. Maybe ten billion years?"

Ten billion years. Good god. He might've been peering down a tunnel into the past, billions of years before any of this—he, the telescope, Dr. Greenstein, the Earth, the Sun, the Moon, the planets—even existed.

Alan lifted his face from the eyepiece, staggered by the thought. He looked up through the crack in the ceiling at the star-filled sky, dizzy with a sense of the vast expanse of time and space within which he stood. His position in the universe felt so, so . . . *tenuous.* So unlikely. So very, very fortunate.

He looked down over the edge of the cage. His wife, standing eighty feet below on the concrete floor, smiled and waved up to him. What more could a man ever want than this? And with tears starting to his eyes, he thought: I could die now and be perfectly happy.

CHAPTER FIFTY-TWO

MIDNIGHT, I was awakened by a stirring in the house.

I sat up in bed to listen. The night was quiet; the Moon shone in at my window. I heard a rattling noise outside at the garage shed, and got up and went to the top of the stairs. As I did so, I was seized by the peculiar sensation that I'd done this before, sometime once long, long ago.

"Dad?"

But his bedroom door was ajar and the house was empty, as I knew it would be. There was the tilting Christmas tree in the corner, the TV set, the couch, the rug, the chairs. My broken telescope, the pieces that were left of it, sat on the floor near the back door. *Light and elevation,* I thought. *Light and elevation.* I paused just long enough to pick up the phone in the living room and dial a number.

I asked Megan if she'd seen our father. Was he there with them? No? I told her where to meet me and to hurry. "Something's wrong. Something terrible is happening."

Outside was cold; I hadn't stopped to put on a coat over my pajamas, and I could see my breath rising in front of my face. Up above, stars and a bright wedge of moon. I jogged out of our driveway and down the street. A breeze stirred the trees, and a dog barked from a nearby backyard. Here and there a neighbor's house was still blacked out, with the curtains drawn and the lights off. Some still had sheets of newspaper taped up behind their windows, giving them a ruined, desolate air. The streetlights, though, those were back on, and as I ran below them I passed from light to dark and light to dark again.

I came out of the neighborhood at the end of the block and turned right toward town. There were no cars at this hour on Franklin Street; there was no sign of life anywhere. The street, with its cement sidewalk, the drainage ditch along the side of the road, the overgrown weeds, the dark trees—the street looked strange, at once very familiar but also foreign, as though it were a street I'd visited once in a dream, and now I was running down the same street in what was either real life or, quite possibly, another dream. The wind rustled the leaves of the trees, and I looked up to check that everything was where it was supposed to be, that the stars and planets were all still in place.

Up ahead, the blue-green tank of the water tower rose on its four spindly legs above the trees like some alien spaceship that had landed at the edge of our town. I was still some distance from it, half a football field away, when I spotted the wooden stepladder from our garage toppled on the ground below it. That's when I looked up and saw—

But I knew he'd be there. He was wearing his black Sears McGregor raincoat over his blue-striped pajamas, his coattails flapping behind him as he scaled the tower. His bony white ankles flashed above his shoes. His elbows jutted out, his head was twisted to one side, his glasses hanging at the end of his nose. I halted in the road to watch, hugging myself as I stepped from one foot to the other. I still didn't quite believe what I was seeing, although at the same time, I knew exactly what was happening.

When my father reached the top of the tower leg, he disappeared under the belly of the tank and reappeared seconds later standing on the catwalk. He steadied himself with a hand on the railing and began walking carefully to the left. At the hip of the tank, he stopped, turned, and looked directly at me.

"Hey!" I shouted, and jerked a hand up to signal to him.

But he quickly began moving again, looking back from time to time over his shoulder as he circled around to the dark side of the tower.

I stepped to the left, tracking his orbit from the street. When I caught sight of him again he was no longer standing on the catwalk but was hanging on the outside of it. He had somehow crawled under or over the railing so that he was now balanced with his toes on the edge of the catwalk, gripping the handrail and leaning in awkwardly toward the water tank.

All at once he threw out his right arm and leg, flipped around, and grabbed the rail behind his back so that he was facing the air with his heels hooked on the edge of the catwalk. I gasped; at the same time, my father made a small exclamation, as if he was pleased and a little surprised at having been able to execute this tricky maneuver: "Ha!"

But the abrupt motion had jarred his glasses from his nose. We both watched them fall end over end through the air. There was a faint cracking sound as they landed on the sidewalk below the tower.

When I looked back up, he was staring out at the night sky. For a moment we were both perfectly still, my father watching the sky, me watching him. An unnatural charge began to fill the air, an electric premonition that raised the hairs on my arms. I wanted to cry out a warning, I wanted to do something, but I couldn't move or speak, struck dumb by the awful knowledge of what was about to happen.

My father leaned out from the railing and lifted his head, like he was trying to touch his face to the sky. He stretched out his arms behind him, opened his mouth wide, and squatted. Just then the wind stirred, lifting his black raincoat behind him, and for one breathless instant he appeared not to fall, but to float up into the air, hanging as if suspended between earth and sky, between the past and future, between wish and reality, between all that we want and all that we can't have. . . .

"No!" I screamed. "No! Don't!"

I ran across the grass and stopped directly below him, shouting and waving my arms, trying to rouse him from whatever nightmare he was trapped in. He leaned out from the rail, a hundred feet over my head, and looked down at me.

"Get away! Go home!"

He swung around so that he was facing the tower again. Then, hanging on to the rail, he began sidling around to the back of the tank. I followed him below. When I ran into some bushes, I pushed through them and kept going, me shouting up for him to stop, he shouting down for me to get away, go home, leave him alone.

When I came around to the wooden stepladder on the ground, I grabbed it and propped it against the nearby leg. It was a difficult stretch from the stepladder to the ladder on the side of the leg, and then the metal rungs were awkwardly spaced and hard to climb. The tower was much higher than I'd thought, too; I stopped once to look down and saw that I was only halfway to the top. I kept climbing, shivering in my slippers and pajamas and trying to keep an eye on my father, who was watching from the rail, hollering at me to go back down, it wasn't safe.

By the time I reached the top, he'd crawled back under the rail and was crouched on the catwalk. He watched just long enough to see that I made it up okay, and then he ducked out of sight around the side of the tank.

"Hey—!"

I pulled myself to my feet and jogged around the catwalk after my father, keeping one hand on the rail. The tower felt as if it was swaying in the wind; the platform seemed to float above the town spread out below—the lights along Franklin Street, the red sign of the drugstore, the dark trees of the square, the black patches of swamp and sugarcane fields beyond.

I found my father at the back of the tower, starting to climb yet another ladder that ascended the curved belly of the tank.

"Jesus. What the hell—"

I grabbed at his pants. He tried to kick me away, and so I hugged him around both legs, pinning him to the ladder. He looked down at me with a sickly, guilty expression as he groped for the rungs above his head.

"You think this is a joke? You think I'm kidding around?" he said.

"I don't think it's a joke."

"Let go of me, damn it!"

"I'm not letting go."

"We'll both fall."

"Fine, we'll both fall then. That'd be good."

"I'm warning you—"

I gave a heave and pulled him away from the ladder. We teetered on the catwalk for one heart-stopping second before collapsing together onto the metal grating. Then he got to his hands and knees and began to crawl to the edge of the catwalk.

"Jesus Christ. What the hell's wrong with you?" I grabbed his leg, dragged him back, and threw myself on top of him. We lay there belly to belly, our heads pressed together, panting into each other's ears. I could smell his aftershave, his hair oil, his body odor—all scents as familiar to me as my own bed.

"Where do you think you're going, huh?" I kept saying into his ear. "Where do you think you're going? You're not going anywhere. I'm not letting you. You're staying right here, damn it. Right here."

After some time, after he'd calmed, I rolled off my father and lay on my back beside him, holding on to his shirt with one hand just in case. We both rested there, recovering. The red warning light pulsed on and off above our heads. A light breeze blew. All around, stars shone in ridiculous profusion, like someone had taken handfuls of diamonds and scattered them across the heavens. And close—so close I might have reached out, plucked one from the sky, and put it in my pocket. Beside me, my father let out a long, heavy sigh, as though he were resigning himself at last to a life on Earth.

A few minutes later our Rambler came rolling down Franklin Street. It swerved in, bumped over the curb, and braked to a stop on the sidewalk. Megan got out from the driver's side, my mother from the other, and they ran around to the front of the car and stood in the beam of the headlights, calling our names.

"Up here!" I shouted down.

"Alan? Alan! Where is he? Is he up there? Is he with you?"

"Yes!" I answered, and my father added his own grim "I'm here."

We lay there a moment longer, enjoying our nearness to the stars, until my mother's worried shouts roused us from our backs. And with that, we both pulled ourselves to our hands and knees and crawled carefully to the ladder.

"Light and elevation," he used to say. Those were the two most critical factors when it came to stargazing: light and elevation.

Riding home in the car that night, sitting in the backseat with my father, I told Megan and Mom everything that had happened. I explained how you needed to get above the ambient light of the city to see the sky. I told how we'd taken the stepladder from the garage and carried it to the tower, Dad and I. Yes, it had been stupid of me to go out with no coat, but it was all kind of last minute, and anyway, we hadn't planned on being out long, we just wanted to get one last look.

I didn't think my mother believed a word of it. How could she? She knew everything that had preceded this; she'd witnessed her husband's awful public humiliation in the square earlier that evening. She must've realized right away what he was up to, and had there been any doubt at all in her mind, she'd only had to look at our stunned, frightened faces as we climbed down the ladder to know the truth.

But she didn't challenge my story, not then, and Megan, driving, held her tongue. My father didn't say anything either, only stared straight ahead as I weaved my clumsy story, hastily inventing bits and switching other bits around, adding details and explanations, until I had almost convinced even myself that what I was saying could've happened.

And through some unspoken family understanding, my sloppy lie became the version of events that we all agreed upon. It was the story that we would repeat to friends and to one another, not just over the following days, but for years to come—at birthday parties, holidays, weddings, anniversaries: how, on the night of the comet, my father and

I had been so eager to see Kohoutek that we climbed the town water tower to look for it, and, good lord, what a shock it had been for my mother to find us up there in the middle of the night. "Crazy," she would say, shaking her head. "These two . . ."

An outright lie, yes, but it was easier than trying to explain what had really happened. Because that could've only been a long, sad tale that implicated us all, and involved sex and betrayal, failure and despair, and ended with a forty-year-old man running to a water tower in the middle of the night to kill himself. And, really, who wanted to hear that? And which one of us would have had the courage to tell it? Certainly not me, not then.

As Megan turned into our driveway, my mother had one last question, and despite what we all surely knew to be the case, I believed I detected a lingering note of hopefulness when she asked, in a soft voice:

"And did you see it? The comet?"

I glanced at my father, sitting beside me. With his glasses missing, his hair disheveled, and his pale, scrawny neck jutting up from his rumpled raincoat, he looked old and frail, like someone's grandfather. I answered for us.

"Yes. Yes, we did. We saw it."

"And what . . . what did it look like?"

"It was . . . it was amazing. One of the most beautiful things I've ever seen."

Beside me, my father began to blink rapidly. I rested my hand on his leg. His Adam's apple bobbed up and down. In the dim light of the backseat of the car, he put his hand on top of mine and pressed down hard.

SOMETHING we would remember for the rest of our lives, he used to say. Something we could tell our children and grandchildren about. We were there. We were there when Kohoutek came.

I still watch for it. I know I'll never see it; it's 5 billion miles away by now, won't return for another 10 million years. But even today, a quarter of a century later, I find myself scanning the dark spaces between stars, half hoping I'll catch a glimpse of something unexpected flickering up there in the sky. It's what draws me out into the backyard on a night like this, when the neighborhood is quiet, and the stars are clear, and my wife and boy are getting ready for bed inside the house.

"Alan! Are you still out there?"

It's Miriam, calling to me from the house. Her voice hauls me back to the here and now. There's the familiar ditch, the barb-wire fence, the pasture, the gleam of the cow pond in the distance.

"Yes! I'm still here!" I call back over my shoulder.

"Are you going to be out there all night?"

"Nope!"

A breeze stirs the leaves of the sourgum tree in the corner of the yard. The half moon has traveled halfway across the sky by now, and the Big Dipper has tilted up on its end, spilling out all its stars.

What was it he used to say? "The fault, dear Brutus, is not in the stars but in ourselves"?

I've thought a lot about that night since then, trying to understand what made my father do what he did. The most obvious explanation is that he did it because of the comet. He'd already lost everything he had to Kohoutek, after all: his wife, his son, his daughter, his reputation in town, his faith in himself, and his hope for the future. He was ruined. With nothing left for him in this world, there was only one place left for him to go. And so he snuck out of the house in the middle of the night, climbed to the highest spot in town, where, with one glorious leap, he would free himself from the awful burden of life on Earth and join his beloved comet in the sky.

Or maybe, I've thought, it wasn't the comet that sent him to the tower that night, but the desire for revenge. His wife's affair with Frank Martello had humiliated him beyond anything that anyone could've imagined, and in his tortured mind, he believed the best way to punish her would be by taking his own life. After that night, she would never be able to forgive herself; her life would be destroyed, just as his was.

And I've blamed myself, too, of course. When I smashed the telescope he'd given me and cursed him with the worst words that any child could ever utter to a parent, I had effectively driven him to the tower myself and pushed him to the edge.

But the way I prefer to see it now, after all these years, was that my father did what he did out of love. Yes, love. As crazy as it might sound, I believe it was love for his family that sent him running to the tower that night. He knew how completely he had failed us, as a husband, a father, a provider, a teacher. Our lives, he felt, could only be better without him. And so, on that disastrous night of the comet, he set out to do the bravest, most selfless thing a man can do.

And I, moved not by logic or understanding or even obligation, but by something much more elemental, something I'd like to think of as instinctual to all human beings, did the only thing that I could have done.

Behind me in the house, I hear Miriam and Ben arguing over the TV.

It's way past his bedtime. The kid hates going to sleep. I suppose it's because of the nightmares he's been having lately; he'll wake up screaming and come running into our room and crawl into bed with us. Miriam blames it on the shows he watches, but who knows. He's a perceptive kid, and there's never any telling what gets stuck in that brain of his. As parents do, we coo over him and reassure him that all is well, that the Earth is a safe and benevolent place and there's nothing for him to fear.

That very same morning, by the way, the morning after the terrible night of the comet, my father did something that still never fails to humble and amaze me.

He got up, shaved at the sink, slicked his hair, and knotted his tie. He lined up the pens in his shirt pocket, three colors, red, blue, and black. He repacked his worn-out brown leather briefcase, finished his coffee, kissed his wife on the cheek, and, wearing a ten-year-old pair of spare eyeglasses, headed out the door to his bike. He wobbled on the gravel drive, maybe a bit more than usual that morning, but then caught his balance as he turned down the road to school. Before the first bell rang, he was walking down the hallway to his classroom, swinging his briefcase stiffly at his side. He welcomed us back for the new semester, sniffed, pushed up his glasses, picked up the chalk, and, dependable as the Sun, turned to the board to begin his next lesson.

If I had to put a word to that, I'd call it heroic.

The following weeks weren't all roses, of course. It took many months for my parents to repair their marriage, to sort out all the blame and forgiveness they owed each other. I wasn't privy to these negotiations; they took place mostly behind their bedroom door. But I saw the results. My father, over time, stopped making fun of my mother for her poor grasp of science, while my mother became less apt to complain about his absentmindedness. And neither one of them, from that night on, ever mentioned the Martellos again. They even managed to ignore their house, looking past it as if it weren't there, as if it had vanished from its lot on the other side of the bayou.

A few years later, in a rather satisfying retribution by the gods of fate, Barbara divorced Frank, on the grounds of, so the gossip in town went, Frank's philandering ways. She and Gabriella—dear, sweet, blameless Gabriella—returned to Shreveport, while Frank kept the big house all to himself.

My sister, Megan, having gotten a taste of independence and liking it, continued to live at our grandparents' house until she graduated from high school. That fall she moved to Baton Rouge to start at LSU, where, after a semester or two of not being sure what to study, she settled on child psychology. She practices now in Lafayette, where she lives with her husband and two daughters.

For my part, I grew my hair out, kept my head down, and generally tried to make myself as inconspicuous as possible for the remainder of my high school years. After graduation I followed my sister to LSU, where I majored in English literature. I eventually fell into teaching English overseas, and over the next decade I hopped around from one country to another, from Greece, to Italy, to Austria, to Czechoslovakia. . . .

It was during a visit home, when I went for a health checkup at a clinic in Terrebonne, that I met Miriam. She was just starting out as a new nurse. A pink smock, a cute skirt, a name tag, and a terrifying lack of experience with the syringe: it was love at first jab, as we like to joke to friends.

I stayed, getting hired at LSU to teach freshman composition. With Miriam's encouragement, I also began to work more seriously at the stories I'd started scribbling while I was overseas. She says story writing is a good outlet for my overactive imagination, and she must be right: in the past few years, I've begun to have a little bit of success with children's books. You might've heard of the Star Scout series; that's mine. *Star Scouts on Mars, Star Scouts on Venus*—I'm doing all the planets now.

I like to try out my new chapters on Ben. He's my toughest critic; if he doesn't like something, he'll say it outright: "That's *dumb.* Nobody would *ever* do that." Or else he'll just nod off to sleep while we're reading, and then I know I have more rewriting to do.

Speak of the devil: here he comes now.

"Da-dyyyy!"

The screen door falls shut and Ben sprints ahead of his mom across the yard, yelling wildly and pinwheeling his arms. He bangs so hard into me that I almost topple over. I start to scold him but then check myself and just give a "Hey! Watch it, buster!" He's wearing his bedroom slippers and striped pajamas; he smells of soap and shampoo. I can't help but see my father in his features: his high forehead, his sharp jaw, the wedge-shaped nose. I reach to grab him, but he slips away and starts jumping back and forth over the ditch.

Miriam saunters up and stops beside me. She's still in her hospital scrubs, her hair pulled back into a ponytail.

"What're you doing out here all this time?"

"Thinking."

"About what?"

"Oh . . . everything. The stars."

Making some connection between stars and Terrebonne, Ben asks when we're going to see his Grams and Paps again. He likes mucking around in the bayou behind the house and digging through all the old toys and junk they still keep in rooms and closets. My parents spoil him, I know, but I guess that's what grandparents are for.

Retirement's been good for them. Dad leads a local astronomy club, and he still makes visits to schools and libraries around the parish. He organizes star walks every month for whoever's interested, taking groups of amateurs with telescopes and binoculars out into the fields at night at the edge of town, away from the lights of the city, to see what's up there. You can usually find my mom at his side, carrying a bag of extra star charts and lenses. She's aged well; I believe she looks better at sixty-five than she did at forty. She's settled into herself, you might say. When she's not doting on her grandkids, she likes tending to her garden and playing bourré with her neighborhood friends.

I catch Ben and swing him up off the ground. He giggles and squirms. I help him climb up my back and sit on my shoulders. Miriam reaches up to steady him. "Careful," she says.

"Oof, you're getting heavy." I straighten my glasses and grab Ben's knees again. My side burns; I've twisted a muscle or something during our acrobatics. "You weigh a ton."

"I weigh fifty-eight pounds."

"Soon you'll be carrying me."

"I seriously doubt that."

"How does it feel to be so tall?" Miriam asks him.

"It feels great."

"His head in the stars," I say, and make a few little hops as if I mean to touch his head to the sky.

My father's still remembered in Terrebonne for being the man who brought out the whole town on the night of the comet. Some people will swear up and down that they saw it. They'll tell you how the sirens wailed as the lights went out, and how the comet rose like a second moon above the square, so bright they could read their newspapers by it. . . .

My father doesn't like to talk about it himself, understandably. But I've resolved that one day, when he's old enough, I'll tell Ben all about it. In fact, it occurs to me that what I've been doing when I come down here to the rear of the yard at night is rehearsing the story that I'll eventually tell my son—the true version, the one about how, back before he was born, a comet called Kohoutek came tearing through our lives and very nearly destroyed us.

But not now. Not yet. He's just a kid, for god's sake. Why frighten a boy with all that? Let him enjoy himself while he can, I say.

I reach up and take his hand and trace the constellations with him. We find the North Star, and from there the outlines of Ursa Minor, Capricorn, Hercules. And is that Perseus? Miriam leans in, sliding an arm around my waist; she wants to see them, too.

I imagine the comet, its fire long gone, just a cinder of icy rock shooting through black empty space. Pluto is billions of miles behind it; the great crystal sphere from which it came is still billions of miles ahead. It can never rest; driven by that powerful, mysterious force we call gravity, it'll keep circling again and again around its vast elliptical orbit through the planets.

By the million-year clock of the comet, I know, a human lifetime amounts to next to nothing. In the cosmological scale of things, the whole of human history—the Pyramids, the Great Wall of China, Michelangelo's art, Beethoven's music, trains, cars, planes, computers, rocket ships, world wars, atomic bombs, a man on the Moon— everything grand and terrible we've ever accomplished—barely registers as a *pfft*. When Kohoutek passes this way again, we'll all be long gone. We'll all be stardust.

But for now, stuck here on our tiny blue-and-white planet, it's enough to be human. For now, it's hard to imagine anything much better than this: my wife, my son, and I, standing in the backyard, counting the stars on a mild autumn night, safely tethered to the ground here in our beautiful, our perfect world.

ACKNOWLEDGMENTS

This is a work of fiction. Although most of the scientific and historical details in the story are accurate, I've also taken liberties here and there with the facts. There is a Terrebonne Parish in Louisiana, for instance, but there's no town called Terrebonne. Buckskin Bill's *Storyland* TV show was broadcast out of Baton Rouge, not New Orleans. In 1973, Comet Kohoutek was visible only in the early morning hours before perihelion—not in the evenings, as it happens in this story. . . . And so on.

For cometology background, I drew from, among other sources, Carl Sagan and Ann Druyan's terrific book (Random House, 1985) and the breathlessly sensational *The Comet Kohoutek*, by Joseph F. Goodavage (Pinnacle Books, 1973). Many of the more fantastic descriptions of comets and their apparitions are from the book *Comet Lore*, written by Edwin Emerson and published by the Schilling Press, New York, in 1910 to coincide with the arrival of Halley's Comet that year.

Special thanks to all the good people at Random House who had a hand in this book, especially Jane von Mehren, Kara Cesare, Hannah

Elnan, Caitlin Alexander, Sarah Murphy, Beth Pearson, Marietta Anastassatos, Elizabeth Eno, and Quinne Rogers. Thanks to Amy Ryan, sharp-eyed copy editor. Sincere and limitless thanks to agents Marly Rusoff and Michael Radulescu.

I'm very grateful for the feedback and encouragement I received from readers of early drafts of this book: Joseph DeSalvo, Dana Sachs, Laura Misco, Alan Weiss, Karen McGee, and members of the Tokyo Writers Group. Special thanks to Dr. Martin McHugh at Loyola University, New Orleans, for his astronomical knowledge.

Finally, thank you to the wonderful independent bookstore owners of the South who've been such gracious hosts to me and my previous novel.

ABOUT THE AUTHOR

GEORGE BISHOP is the author of *Letter to My Daughter* and *The Night of the Comet*. He earned an MFA from the University of North Carolina at Wilmington, where he won the Award of Excellence for a collection of stories. He has lived and taught in Slovakia, Turkey, Indonesia, Azerbaijan, India, and Japan. He now lives in New Orleans.

georgebishopjr.com

DATE			